MILLION$
DOLLAR SERIE$

by

New York Times Bestseller
Pepper Winters

Millions (Dollar Series #5)
Copyright © 2017 Pepper Winters
Published by Pepper Winters

All rights reserved. No part of this book may be reproduced or transmitted in any form, including electronic or mechanical, without written permission from the publisher, except in the case of brief quotations embodied in critical articles or reviews.

This is a work of fiction. Names, characters, businesses, places, events, and incidents are either the products of the author's imagination or used in a fictitious manner. Any resemblance to actual persons, living or dead, or actual events is purely coincidental.

This book is licensed for your personal enjoyment only. This book may not be re-sold or given away to other people. If you would like to share this book with another person, please purchase an additional copy for each person you share it with. If you are reading this book and did not purchase it, or it was not purchased for your use only, then you should return it to the seller and purchase your own copy. Libraries are exempt and permitted to share their in-house copies with their members and have full thanks for stocking this book. Thank you for respecting the author's work.

Published: Pepper Winters 2017: **pepperwinters@gmail.com**
Cover Design: by Kellie at Book Cover by Design & Ari @ Cover it! Designs
Editing by: Editing 4 Indies (Jenny Sims)

LIFE WASN'T KIND to anyone.
Some days it *pretended* to be kind, granting gifts and favours, delivering dreams and fancy, but the next, it snatched it all away.
That was reality.
I knew that. Elder knew that.
We both saw the world for its truth, cutting through its many lies. I think that was why I hated him when we first met on the streets of New York. He carried the same toil. The same bitterness. The same heavy shame I did—shame we'd converted into hate and temper.
We'd scrapped over territory and possessions and sometimes, we fought just because we were tired of being hurt by a universe that'd utterly forsaken us.
They said the human race was inherently designed to hate similarities in others. If someone had the same temper as you, instead of recognising that fact, you just hated them. Same legs as you, you'd say they were too short; same nose as you, you'd fixate on how out of proportion it was. Not because you hated that person but because, in some unspoken part of your soul, you hated *yourself*.
Our fatal flaw was to pick on ourselves. To tear ourselves

apart by tearing others apart who remind you of you.
Strange but so fucking true.
Elder reminded me of me, so I despised him.
I reminded him of him, so he abhorred me.
Together, we beat the shit out of each other, and in a way, we beat the shit out of ourselves until one day...that self-loathing we didn't acknowledge just gave up, and we accepted what we hated most about ourselves was also the part we needed the most to survive.

After that epiphany, a friendship-truce was formed—or something akin to friendship anyway. We stopped trying to kill each other. We switched from enemies to grudging acquaintances and slowly to confidants.

Up until tonight, I still saw myself in Elder. I saw my past in his eyes and my heartbreak in his own. But as I'd stood in the shadows and watched him dance with Pimlico at Hawksridge Hall, I finally had to concede that he'd evolved.

He was no longer like me, and I didn't despise anything about him because nothing left of him mirrored my own. He'd started his journey of redemption and acceptance. Finally trading tragedy for true fucking love.

He'd left me behind by finding something he could never buy or steal. I was happy for him but also blisteringly jealous.

Jealous he'd found what I'd lost so many years ago.

Jealous he had a lifetime of fuck-ups and fix-ups to look forward to with the one person who would become his best-friend and partner.

I was out of the job.

I was no longer his mirror, bouncing his mistakes back at him.

I was alone again and quickly drowning beneath everything I'd ignored for far too long.

Grateful for the empty car, I huffed at the whiff of sex and champagne still lingering from dropping Pimlico and Elder off.

Only a few seconds had gone by since they'd climbed out and scaled the gangway, their bodies entwined and hearts sickly besotted, but time had an odd way of making it seem as though I'd been alone forever.

In a way, I had.

I'd been lost for decades, and now that they were disgustingly consumed with the other, I had no one to obliterate the memories gleefully descending.

Tomorrow, I'd get the lowdown from Prest on what exactly had changed. How he said fuck it to a life of misery and threw in everything he had left to the girl he'd rescued. But tonight, I had every intention of being on my own—just the way it should be.

Driving the car down the wharf, I caught another glimpse of Pim and Elder laughing on the deck as they stumbled toward his quarters like lovesick idiots.

I bet a fucking seagull could crap on them and they wouldn't notice.

Fools.

Rolling my eyes, I pressed on the accelerator, speeding down the impressive length of the Phantom to put the car away. The side already yawned wide, and I turned onto the heavy-duty ramp, delicately easing the vehicle into the belly of the vessel.

The familiar switch from land to sea never failed to make my heart beat faster. Unlike Elder—who I swore was part fish—I didn't like the ocean. I didn't like the instability beneath my feet. I preferred the firmness of dirt and rigidity of steel.

But on that fateful night when he'd stolen a winning lottery ticket and I'd somehow convinced him to borrow it—if not outright claim it—he'd invited me to explore a new opportunity: remain homeless by choice, punishing myself with a life of emptiness after having so much, or stand beside him and fight in a war that wasn't my own.

Some men might've said no—especially when he'd mentioned a faction out for his blood and almost certain injury when they found him. But why hold the illusion of a life when really…it was just a big fucking sham?

I had no values left. No honour. No one to fight for. Nowhere to be.

I was alone and figured I might as well be alone with him.

Parking in the designated bay, I turned off the engine and hauled my ass from the car. Pressing a button on the wall, automatic chocks rose from the floor, and wedged around all four wheels to prevent it from slopping around in a storm.

Placing the key in the cabinet with its neatly organised hooks for all sorts of toys on board, I raked both hands through my hair and sighed.

My job as a chauffeur is complete.

Not that Elder ever asked me to do such tasks. I just found memories couldn't find me as easily when I put other's needs above my own and only thought of what I could do for them rather than myself.

A piece of hay fluttered from my hair, reminding me what I got up to while Elder did unspeakable things to Pim.

I didn't know the woman's name. I hadn't seen her face. All I remembered was she wore a mask that looked like a spider's web with morning dew twinkling on silver thread. Her dress kept up the illusion with silver panels and iridescent beads.

It wasn't often I craved companionship, but after a dance or two, she'd offered to give me a tour—even though she didn't know the place any better than I did.

We'd ended up in the stables, fucking like rabbits while a horse watched from the next stall. We didn't undress; we didn't ask to see each other again. We both knew we were using the other for mindless company and parted with a grateful kiss, happy in the knowledge we'd eased some of the mutual pain in each other.

I should climb into the elevator and head to my quarters. I should wash off stable sex and sleep so I was ready to kick Prest's ass in the morning.

However, I wasn't ready to be captive to the ocean just yet.

I wanted land beneath my toes for a little longer. I wanted to be free and not trapped inside when the clawing of my past found me and made me wish I'd died the same night as my future bride.

Stepping toward the open garage door, I pressed the button to close and lock it behind me, then traded yacht for wharf.

Stars glittered above.

Clear nights like these made me crave a cigarette. I'd broken the habit years ago—partly through choice but mostly through lack of funds. I knew it was better to be smoke free, but tonight I craved the tingly taste and sickly rush of nicotine.

With no drink to keep me occupied and no one to distract me, I prowled the wharf, spying a few empty crates piled high as a house against a warehouse.

Perfect.

I could climb on top and be unseen, free to study the Phantom with her pretty lit windows and suffocate beneath my thoughts instead of burying them deep down tight.

Kicking off my dress shoes, I allowed some of my past from street living to ease into my bones as I launched myself up the crates. It only took a few seconds and a few precisely placed jumps to scale the crates and end skyward.

My heart rate didn't change as I reached the top and sat heavily.

The Phantom was indeed pretty from this angle, swooping up like a dark sea goddess ready to decimate any who tried to destroy her. The world settled, the night quietened, my breathing was the only thing disturbing ultimate peace.

And that was where she found me.

As she always did.

The woman I loved and the unplanned pregnancy that killed her. I let the past take me; I allowed the merciless hate for the unborn baby who'd stolen her to drag me deep, and didn't hear the arrival of war.

Down and down I fell, cringing against the last moments

of blood and heartbreak. Wincing against the burn of tears and lamenting all over again at how I could give my very soul to someone, yet remain living when they left this earth with it.

I didn't indulge in my pain often. I hated self-pity and despised self-blame.

But tonight, after watching true love happen for a man I dared call a friend, I was fucking gutted—reminding me all over again of what I'd lost and he'd gained and just how different we truly were now.

No longer the same.

My ears filled with ghost-voices and ethereal-shouts. Of my begs for the doctors to do something. Of my threats when they failed. Of my curses when I was left with nothing.

So obsessed with my agonising memory box of torture, I missed the first gunfire.

And the second.

The *ra-ta-ta-tat* of bullets morphed with the slap of gentle currents and crack of rigging as boats rocked on water.

My fingers grew slippery with past-shed blood. My mouth wide with historical screams. My lungs empty for air, desperate to die to find her and stubborn enough to continue breathing despite the daily agony.

I lost track of time as I embraced the ghost of the woman I missed with every-fucking-thing.

But then another shot.

This one unmasked by tide or yacht.

Boom.

The sound reverberated around the bay, echoing in clock towers and throughout ship masts.

Boom.

Boom.

Boom.

My eyes snapped open.

What the—

A scream.

A shout.

A splash.
Shit, they've found us.
Launching from my spot on the crates, I vaulted down to the wharf and ran. My socked feet were silent as I slithered into the darkness and flew toward the front of the ship. A small boat motor cranked, growling and shredding the night sky with rancid petrol fumes.

French mutterings interspersed with the engine as someone fed it and speed hurtled it forward. I caught a flash of a sparrow painted on the hood and a red and blue bundled figure sprawled in the back.

Pimlico?
Fuck, it can't be...
I'd only sat for a few minutes. They'd been safe. They'd been obliviously, disgustingly in love—
They were ambushed.
Fuck!
The speed boat opened up, skipping faster over black tides. There was nothing I could do. No way I could swim after it and no harpoon I could use to shoot it.

I was helpless as white water sloshed around the wharf as I took off at a dead sprint.

They had Pimlico, but where was Prest?
Tearing back the way I'd come, I gasped for oxygen as I spat profanities at how long this damn yacht was.

Finally reaching the gangway, I snatched the railing and snapped myself into a sharp turn, digging my toes into the rungs, shooting toward the deck.

My skin turned icy with dread.
No noise.
No staff.
No life.
Where the fuck is everyone?
Snagging a gun tucked into one of the many hidey-holes around the deck, I charged toward Prest's room.

Cocking the weapon, I wrapped my finger around the

trigger. Ready.

His doors were wide. Blood smeared the polished deck. Corpses littered his quarters.

Men dressed in black with bright red gloves.

Chinmoku.

If they're dead...where the hell is Prest?

Skidding on the wooden floor, I bolted toward the side where the balustrade stood to attention, and the ladder was thrown to the water below.

I looked down to where the bastards had stolen Pim and found the one man I called a friend.

Far below, barely noticeable in the silver moon shine and occasional wharf light, Elder gasped and coughed, treading water weakly, his face scrunched tight and a hand clamped over his arm.

He went under.

My fingers clutched the barrier as he reappeared, his mouth wide and eyes shut, barely holding on to life.

Too focused on survival, he didn't see me and went under again. And again. His legs useless at keeping him afloat.

Another few minutes, he'd tire and drown. Another few minutes, he'd be dead, and I'd be alone yet again.

Not gonna fucking happen.

Throwing the gun to the deck, I ripped off my jacket and trousers, breaking my shirt buttons in my haste to tear it off. Prest might have minutes, but I would only take seconds.

Naked apart from my boxers, I threw myself off the side.

I didn't think about where the staff were or why dead Chinmoku were bleeding on his bedroom floor. I didn't worry about Pimlico and who'd abducted her. Elder was the linchpin in this floating family and my top priority.

I landed too close, drenching him in yet more water.

He gasped and coughed, sinking beneath the churning waves.

He didn't come back up.

Duck-diving, I connected with cold flesh and hoisted him

to the surface. As his mouth found air, he groaned and inhaled, crying out in pain as I manoeuvred him into a recovery position. Seawater streamed over his face as I wrapped my arm around the front of his chest, making sure his chin was cocked for breath.

Back-stroking, I powered toward the wharf.

He cried out as my legs kicked one of his, his face a mask of torture. "God*dammit*, Selix. Where the fu-fuck were you?" His teeth shattered from shock and cold, his blood spilling like oil.

I wouldn't tell him I'd had a moment of weakness and reminisced. I wouldn't admit that I'd committed treason while he'd been at war. "I'm here now."

"Well, don't worry about me. Go after them—" He wracked with coughs, flinching as more pain found him. "They took her."

I glanced at the black horizon where no sign of the boat or noise of its engine existed. It was as if she'd never been. Even the scent of gasoline had faded to salty nothingness. "They're gone, Prest."

"They can't be fucking gone. They can't have—" He groaned as my legs once again kicked his, tangling in his dead weight as I swam closer to the pier. "They can't have her."

Warm blood flowed over my hand where I'd tucked it under his armpit. I'd seen enough bullet wounds to know he needed to get out of the ocean and fast. He needed to remain calm and collected. He needed to care about himself first then worry about Pim.

"Let's focus on you." Gritting my teeth, I swam harder, very aware of his life rapidly fading. "Then we'll focus on her."

"Christ!" He bowed in my arm-lock. "Shit, it hurts."

"What hurts?" I couldn't see if the bullet in his arm was the worst or least of his problems.

"Fucking everything." He howled at the moon as I crawled the final distance, hoisting him closer, accidentally digging my fingers into a sore spot.

Where the hell is Michaels?

He needed a doctor. Immediately.

I could throw him in the car and screech to the nearest hospital, but what if he didn't make it? His skin was blue. His lips almost black in the night.

Reaching the wharf, I briefly worried how I'd haul his tux-waterlogged ass from the bay. Whatever injuries he had would hurt like a motherfucker.

But my worries were for nothing.

As my fingers lashed around the emergency stair rung and I took the first climb, Elder's eyes rolled in the back of his head, and he turned into a pasty cadaver in my embrace.

My heart stopped as I placed my hand under his nose, checking for breath—fearing nothing and begging for something.

When the softest puff of heat revealed he wasn't dead just merely unconscious, I stopped being so gentle and worked with speed instead.

I hauled his battered body up the stairs. I flopped him onto the wharf like a well caught fish. I landed on my hands and knees beside him, wringing wet and exhausted.

He didn't wake up. But his heart didn't stop pumping more and more blood from his body, slowly pooling beneath him, dripping black into the tide.

My job wasn't finished.

His minutes were almost spent.

Standing, I bent and with a silent apology, somehow managed to manhandle his useless dying form over my shoulder.

I began the long journey toward the gangway, making a deal with Death not to take someone else I cared about.

It took my wife-to-be and unborn child.

It would not take my friend.

Not today, anyway.

ELDER

PAIN.
Considerable, uncomfortable pain.
My eyes flew open as my lips gasped for breath. Last I remembered, I was drowning. Treading water with blood seeping from gunshot wounds and the growl of a speedboat stealing my woman.
Goddammit, Pim.
Launching upright, I cried out as pain turned to filleting agony, shoving me backward onto the bed.
Where the hell am I?
Blinking fuzzy eyes, I reconned my current hellhole. Sheets smelled like me, walls were familiar, furniture known.
My room.
Wait...the last time I'd been here, I'd been fighting for my life while Pim stood captive by Chinmoku. Thanks to that battle, a fair amount of redecoration had happened.
Struggling to sit up enough to look at the carpet, I steeled myself for the crimson splatters of blood and bloated bodies; for smashed furniture and torn curtains.
However, instead of a crime scene, sterile cleanliness stared back. The stringent whiff of bleach and industrial grade cleaners hung in the air, the carpet darker in places where it

remained wet from being washed.
No sign of any struggle or massacre.
Everything righted.
Everything the same.
Did I dream it? Had I smoked a bad batch of weed and believed in a nightmare where Pim was stolen and I was fucking shot by some French asshole who'd singlehandedly destroyed my life?
If I had, why the hell did everything hurt so damn much?
Footsteps came from outside. I glowered at the open door, my muscles locked and ready to defend.
I might be on the Phantom, but everything else was foreign—including my body.
"Ah, you're awake. About time." Selix marched in, a tray in his hands with silverware and something steaming in a bowl. "Michaels said you'd be out for a while, but it's been hours, Prest."
"Wh—" I coughed; my throat burned with salt.
Had I drowned? Was this purgatory where my soul thought it was alive while my body was nibbled by crustaceans at the bottom of the sea? And if I wasn't dead, who had found me? How was I alive?
Where the hell is Pim?
My stupid brain tossed question after question at me, demanding to know every minuscule detail *immediately*.
My heart chugged as stress layered my system. "What happened?" I grimaced as my voice sounded shipwrecked and full of driftwood.
"Chinmoku found you." Selix stepped toward my bed and set the tray on the table. "Then some French fucker arrived, mowed down the Chinmoku, shot you, and took Pim."
So it wasn't a bad joint, after all.
Shit.
"I know all that," I snapped. "I mean, what's happened since? Where were you? Have you found Pim? How long have I been out?" Glancing down at my pain-stabbed body, I pried

up the blanket and inspected.

Holy shit.

Naked, my skin was no longer the blended western-eastern tan I knew but a multitude of bruises, contusions, and trauma. I looked like Pim did when we first met.

My dragon tattoo hid beneath wrapped bandages, twining their way around my ribs, up and over my shoulder and left bicep. My ring finger on my right hand rested in a splint, my left arm nestled in a sling, and a brace wrapped around my ankle with Velcro.

I was a prisoner to medical supplies.

Selix cleared his throat.

My eyes shot to his. I let the sheet flutter over me, pretending my body wasn't in a million pieces.

"Explain," I seethed.

How the hell was I supposed to go after Pim like this?

"I heard them leave. Noticed you overboard. Managed to get to you before you drowned." He rubbed the back of his neck. "I'm sorry, Prest. I'm sorry for not coming sooner and preventing them from taking her."

Whatever he'd been up to while Pim and I had been ambushed wasn't his fault. That was entirely on me for not paying attention. As much as I blamed him for her disappearance, he'd pulled me from the sea. He'd saved one person. Too bad he'd saved the wrong one.

Before I could thank him and curse him in equal measure, Michaels strode through the door with a stethoscope over his neck and black bag in hand. "Selix told me you were alive."

"Alive, yes. But you won't be for much longer if you don't fix me." Waving at my broken body, I growled. "Take this shit off me."

Michaels placed his bag of tricks onto the mattress, nudging my good leg. "Afraid they can't come off yet."

"Well, they have to 'cause we have Chinmoku to hunt and French bastards to slaughter."

Selix crossed his arms. "I'm in the process of tracking

down the men who took Pim. I'm on it, I promise. All you need to do is rest."

"Wrong. All I need to do is get out of this godforsaken bed."

It wasn't that I didn't trust him or appreciate his promise. If Selix said he was doing something to find them, then I had no doubt he was. But it didn't stop my rapidly building rage. I wasn't going to lie here while he did the work. I'd never been good at accepting help. And I definitely wouldn't start now— not when the woman I loved was on the line.

I let Pim down. *I* had to be the one to fix it.

Michaels popped a few pills, grabbing the glass of water on my bedside. "Take these."

"I'm not taking anything until you give me answers."

"Take them and *then* I'll give you answers."

My head pounded as I focused on the painkillers. I couldn't deny my thoughts were scattered thanks to agony. If I could ignore the pain, perhaps I could work better. Faster. Cleaner. We'd find Pim before the end of the day, and I'd have two more kills under my belt when I took the men's hearts for stealing her.

Snatching the tablets, I tossed them into my mouth and swallowed them dry. Glowering at Michaels, I raised my eyebrow for him to keep his side of the bargain.

Nodding, he said, "You were in surgery for a while. I had to enlist an extra pair of hands from a hospital not far from here. That bill is going to sting, by the way. Just letting you know in advance." He cracked a smile, but when I continued to glare, he slipped into bullet-point form of my maladies. "The bullet got you in the shoulder. It tore a few ligaments, which means you might end up with a buggered joint, but I did my best. The stitches in your hairline will come out in a week. Only had to sew seven, even though your thick skull was showing, so count yourself lucky. You over-stretched the tendons in your elbow, so you'll have considerable weakness and pain while you heal, and physiotherapy will be your friend to get full movement back. Two cracked ribs, possibly bruised kidneys, a broken ring finger, and can't forget the fractured ankle."

Glancing at Selix, he quipped, "Did I miss anything?"

Selix shrugged. "Who the hell knows? Sounds more like a grocery list rather than my friend."

I gave him a look, appreciating the nod to our friendship and his wry sarcasm turning this frustrating moment into a more endurable trial.

Michaels shoved his hands into his pockets. "Look, all things considering, you're doing better than you should after being attacked and enjoying a one-on-one altercation with a gun."

I was doing *better* than expected? Christ, I was useless.

A goddamn cripple.

I always hated being stationary and not moving. My brain existed at a faster frequency; I had no choice but to move in time with it. Lying in bed would turn me insane. Not knowing if Pim was okay would turn me into a monster.

We had to chase after her. Surely, Selix had set sail while I lay like a slab of meat for doctors to poke and prod at. He knew me. He would understand.

"You said I've been out for hours." I looked at Selix. "Where are we? What course did you set?"

My ears strained for the comforting hum of propellers. My body searched for the well-known ocean-rock as we sliced through the waves on the heels of our enemies.

But there were no engines.

There was no rock.

We were stagnant just like I was stagnant in this goddamn bed.

My voice lowered to a dark threat. "Someone better tell me where we are and why we aren't moving."

Michaels shot a worried look at Selix. "Shit, I didn't contemplate amnesia. You don't think—"

"Goddammit, Michaels." My temper lashed hot. "I don't have amnesia. I'm not some asshole you have to babysit."

Hoisting myself up against the pillows, I winced as fire and knives worked on different parts of my body. "I remember it all. I understand what happened. I hear the relay of my injuries. I see the bandages and stitches. I get it all, okay? What I don't get is why we're not moving. Why aren't we enroute to find Pim? Why the fuck did you think it was wise to stay in England when Pim is obviously no *longer* in England?"

My brain swam as sickly sweat prickled my body. The painkillers did jack to numb what I'd endured.

Selix placed a hand on my burning shoulder, gently pushing me back against the pillows. "Because there's no point sailing around with no destination. Besides, we don't know if she's not in England. They might've—"

"France, Selix. They were from fucking France and had a speed boat. They've gone across the channel." I fought his pressure, slapping away his touch. "Even if logic didn't give us a destination, there's always a point because moving forward is better than doing nothing."

He scowled. "We'll find her. It's only been a day. Lots of time—"

"Wait, *what?*" I shot upright, uncaring of the searing agony in my bones, ignoring the nausea in my skull. "A *day?* What do you mean a day?" Glaring at the sky, the brilliant sun didn't blind me—the goddamn moon laughed in my face.

The moon I was named after by my romantic mother before her happiness turned to bitter sourness.

It was dark when Pim was taken.

It was dark now.

It's only been a few hours, not twenty-four of the fuckers.

Please, let it only be a few hours.

Michaels rested his hand on my bandaged shoulder, making me hiss with another layer of discomfort. "It's been twenty-seven hours, Prest. The operation took a while then you slept for a crap-load longer than we expected. Thought your concussion had put you in a coma at one point."

A full day?

This just kept getting worse.

I bared my teeth, wishing I could rip someone into pieces. "Fantastic, we've done nothing to save Pim for a full day, and now I have a concussion. Anything else? Because now would be the time to tell me before I lose my goddamn shit."

Michaels said matter-of-factly, "Trust me, a concussion is the least of your worries. Your vitals are fine. You're speaking fine. You slept so long because you haven't been sleeping the past few weeks. Something had to give and something did." He gave me his best doctor don't-mess-with-me-I-know-best stare. "We didn't move from this pier because we didn't know if I was qualified to get you through or if you'd need to be admitted to the hospital. Apologises if we put your life first rather than cast off and bob around the ocean searching for something we have no idea—"

"Pim is not *something*, Michaels." Rage made me ball my hands before the splint on my broken finger and heavily bruised knuckles forced me to rethink such torture. "She's *everything*. If she died while you did your damnedest to keep me alive...well—" I dropped to a whisper. "You better jump overboard before I catch you."

Unperturbed by my threat, he tilted his chin. "You never were good at taking instruction, but believe me when I say you need to take better care of yourself."

I wanted to gut him. "I need to be taking better care of Pimlico."

Selix cut in, physically and verbally blocking our rapidly escalating fight. "And you will. It's not like they're going to get away with this. You're awake now. We'll go hunting."

"It's not about them getting away with this, Selix. It's about how long they've already had her. What if she's been touched? Raped? Hurt? What if all the progress we've made has unravelled all because I couldn't keep her safe?"

Deeper, twistier pain entered my heart.

I'd let her down.

She'd never trust me again. She'd never love me again, and

why the hell should she? I'd failed her and didn't deserve another chance.

Fuck it.

Being this patient? Lying in bed being schooled by a doctor? I was done.

Soldiers at war didn't rest.

I wasn't about to, either.

Slinging the covers off, I didn't care I was butt fucking naked. Hissing between my teeth, I swung my braced ankle and black and blue body to the edge of the mattress. The room spun upside down. I swallowed hard against the metallic rush of old blood and anaesthetic. "Tell Jolfer to set sail. Immediately."

Michaels came forward, holding my bicep, supporting me while trying to push me back into bed. "Don't be an idiot, Prest. You need rest. Your body is in desperate need of healing—"

"And I'm in desperate need of killing someone. It's either that French bastard or you."

When he didn't take his hands off me, I shoved him aside and stood. I ignored the rush of black spots in my vision. I gulped back the crest of sickness and agony. I locked my knees against my unbalanced stumble and embraced the pain—mixing it with rage to make a cocktail that even I feared.

Shoving my nose in his, I snarled, "Choose. Them or you. Because if you get in my way, it's you."

Holding up his hands, Michaels backed off. His face etched with frustration. "Fine. You want to undo all my hard work and screw up your body, be my guest." Throwing a look at Selix, he grabbed his bag and stormed to the door. "When he's enlisted some common sense or passed out, come find me."

He stalked to the door and slammed it with a harsh smack.

Good fucking riddance.

Selix stood there, watching as I plotted my next move.

Pim had been taken by French men. Their accent hadn't

been French Canadian. It wasn't fake or second language. It'd been pure and from birth.

They were frogs born to frog leg country.

Natives to the country only a short sail away from England.

Not bothering to hide my indecency, I limped to my wardrobe, daring Selix to say something. Every footstep killed my ankle, elbow, shoulder, head, ribs—fucking everything—but I wouldn't stop. I wouldn't give in or relax or permit any kindness toward me.

Not until Pim was found and safe once again.

Not until blood ran in her honour.

So help me God.

Pimlico

EVERYTHING WAS WRONG.

The sour fur on my tongue, the dehydration headache behind my eyes, the utter silence of being in a house instead of a yacht—right down to the horror of being imprisoned yet again.

Old habits had instantly kicked into gear the moment I'd awoken a couple of hours ago.

My fingers craved a pen to write to No One. My voice switched from newfound gift to mute preservation. My skin crawled beneath my ballgown, fearing that at any moment, Alrik would walk in and strip me from it. That I'd be made to live life all over again naked and silent and terrified.

In fairness to the space, it was nothing like the stark white mansion I'd been imprisoned in before.

The atmosphere here was elegant and inviting. The bed soft and pillow filled, the bathroom stocked with delicious smelling shampoos and conditioners. It wasn't a jail…more like a hotel suite, dripping in understated wealth and femininity.

But no matter what illusions the soft silver rugs and duck egg blue couches tried to paint, it couldn't ease my panic. The walls kept me against my will. The windows barricaded me from fleeing. This place wasn't my friend, so I didn't treat it as such.

Even though my past drenched me with rules of kneeling and submitting and begging for mercy, I'd investigated and torn apart every inch. I'd marched to the floor-to-ceiling windows, rattled the panes, and searched for a weak spot to shatter and jump from the three-story cage.

When that failed, I ran to the door and jiggled the handle, inserting pins from my tumbled down hair and doing my best to pick the lock.

I hadn't succeeded.

But it didn't matter.

Clutching to hope and ignoring desperation, I'd thrown up rugs for trap doors.

I'd ripped open drawers for weapons.

I'd demolished the bed, looking for anything that could save me.

And nothing.

The suite remained soft and romantic—almost apologetic for keeping me trapped in its refinement.

Stress pounded my heart, reminding me of another time when I'd flown like a wild captured bird in a tiny prison.

Déjà vu of the week's spent at the QMB hotel waiting to be sold made me dry-mouthed and panicky. I'd gone over every nook and cranny of that room, and the only thing I'd found was a chewed-on pencil.

No One had been born from that lucky find. My mind had found a way to save itself even if it couldn't save my body. But in here, paper and pens and make-up and books and everything a normal, cosy bedroom should have existed.

There was nothing to say what my future held other than I'd woken up in a strange dimension where Elder had been shot and I'd been stolen.

Why?

Why was I here?

Where *was* here?

What could I do to *leave* here?

One thing was for sure, I wouldn't sit and write notes to No One like before.

This time, I would fight tooth and fucking claw to get free. I flat out refused to be sold again or inducted into yet another twisted ownership.

I wasn't a belonging or broken toy anymore. The French man who'd kidnapped me—believing he was my rescuer and living in fantasy denial—would curse the day he'd torn my happy new world apart.

He'll pay.

My God, I'll make him pay.

Somewhere deep inside, a furnace cranked hot. My past fears—doing their best to drag me into the darkness from which I'd crawled—morphed into something drastic and fierce.

Consequences no longer mattered.

Terror at fighting back and earning retribution no longer factored.

If I died while refusing to accept this new reality, then so be it.

I was no longer afraid.

Of death.

Of pain.

Of monsters.

All I feared was Elder and if he'd died never knowing my fate.

I'm sorry if I get myself killed while trying to escape, Elder, but if you're dead too...then I guess, I'll see you soon.

The angry heat in my belly climbed up my spine, threatening rage-filled tears.

I didn't let them fall.

I couldn't dwell on Elder's aliveness or death...not yet.

With my arms locked around my waist, I came to a reluctant stop in front of the large windows. I glowered at the view, despising the quaint garden lovingly manicured with hedges and fruit trees. Birds flittered left and right, uncaring that this place was home to a beast who'd broken apart true love.

The crinkle of my ballgown as I hugged myself broke my heart.

The silky satin embellished with its crimson and navy battling-bruising colours hadn't been stripped from me even as I'd lain unconscious. The bodice remained torn and held together thanks to Elder's hastily applied cravat.

Beneath the heavy finery, I was sticky with old sweat and sex, and my bare feet were cold. I wouldn't deny that while ransacking the bathroom, I'd eyed up the shower in longing.

But what was the point in washing when I had nothing to put on afterward? I would never wear the simple clothing hanging in multiple sizes in the wardrobe. I wouldn't accept any form of gifts from this kidnapper.

Alrik had denied me clothes, yet whoever this new asshole was offered me dresses as if I were some kind of Barbie doll.

Not going to happen.

I would remain dirty. I would hope to God I stunk to high heaven if he ever thought of touching me. I would embrace my sex-tangled hair and smudged make-up and residue of Elder's pleasure on my inner thighs because I didn't belong to this new bastard.

I belonged to myself.

I belonged to Elder.

But his name isn't Elder...

The thought came from nowhere, plucked from the mayhem of what'd happened that night. My fingernails dug into my bodice.

Miki.

The Chinmoku had called him Miki.

Elder had been upfront about having another name, just as I did. In fact, the similarities between us were mind boggling when I took a step back and compared notes: we had lost our fathers. We had a mother who wasn't perfect. We lived a life less ordinary than others.

And the most terrifying similarity of all? In some

laughable, strange twist of fate?

I was named Minnie Mouse after my dad's watch present, and Elder...*is called Miki.*

I shook my head in disbelief.

Mickey and Minnie.

Could there be any more outlandish hints that fate had been the driving force bringing us together? That our meeting wasn't just opportune or spontaneous? Life had pushed us together for a purpose. For a reason.

I'd written to him for years as No One. And even before he was No One, we shared the same pairing of names, forever binding us to a beloved Disney couple.

And despite all that written-in-the-stars kind of thing, we've been torn apart!

I laughed out loud, looking at the ceiling. Exasperated, frustrated, mad, sad, confused.

I was every spectrum of emotion but finally one was missing.

Fear.

Every trace had vanished.

Now, I was angry.

So, so *angry*.

I pitied whoever came to touch me because they'd be leaving with no fingers.

The click of a lock whipped my head around just as the door opened and a woman in a cute black and white maid's uniform appeared.

Her eyes shot to the dishevelled bed, searching. When she didn't find me in the torn coverlets, her gaze quickly tracked across the shoved aside furniture and skew-whiff rugs to where I stood in my cascading bruised gown, looking just as rumpled as the rest of the room.

She swallowed, flicking a small smile while questions decorated her pretty face. Round nose, wide eyes, neat and tidy brown hair. She carried a small tray with a plate laden with a thick sandwich and crisps. "Ah, you're awake."

Two scenarios I could choose.

One, I could stay where I was and allow her to call the shots. I could play meek and lull her into thinking I wouldn't fight back. I could be the Pimlico Alrik had created.

Or two.

And I like this one much better.

I could attack now.

I could show her that they'd stolen the wrong girl. That I'd lived this life, and I absolutely *refused* to live it again. I didn't care women were involved in this instance. I didn't care her smile was kind and encouraging. I didn't care that the vibe of this house was welcoming instead of torturous.

I didn't *care*.

All I cared about was Elder and getting back to him. Of finding him hopefully alive and allowing fate to give us what it so obviously wanted.

I was done with this nonsense.

I'm done letting others dictate my life.

Gathering my skirts in clawed fists, I swooped toward her. My bare feet brushed silently, winging me quickly, transforming her smile into a shock of worry.

She back-stepped, crockery clinking on her tray.

Trapping her against the wall by the open door, I snarled, "Let me go. Right now."

She held up the tray as a barrier, shooting a quick glance at me, the exit, then to the sideboard beside her. "Before we work on your demands, can I put this down?"

Her stubborn, unflustered response rattled me a little. Not used to being the aggressor, I struggled to stay curt and rude rather than step out of her personal space and apologise.

I trembled with right and wrong, hoping like hell I hid the battle it took to stand up to her. "I don't care what you do. Just move away from the door and I won't hurt you."

Nodding as if she was used to violent outbursts from ballgowned prisoners, she carefully placed the unwanted food onto the table and held out her palms in pacification. "It's okay.

No one is going—"

"Stop it!" I snapped. Her soft, sweet voice wriggled through my anger, begging me to believe in kindness and not cruelty. She was the worst kind of prison guard as she made me feel like the bad guy for demanding my release.

She couldn't be permitted to brainwash me or to steal my anger when I'd worked so hard to find it.

Everything I did from now on was to get back to Elder. Having someone to fight toward gave me another shot of courage and rage, and I did something I never thought I was capable of.

I grabbed her around the throat.

I snatched her like Alrik had snatched me so many times before and squeezed. My tightening fingers hurt the tendons in my wrist, screaming partly in regret for laying my hand on her and partly in annoyance that I didn't have enough strength to kill her.

Swallowing my remorse and nausea, I hissed, "Keep your lies. Keep your food. No one is going to touch me. Not you. Not the man who stole me. No one." Ignoring the muscle spasm in my forearm from squeezing, I forced myself to be ruthless even when I wanted to let go and sprint to the other side of the room. Prior conditioning and past slavery were so, so hard to overcome.

But I did it.

Because of Elder.

Slightly out of breath, I trembled. "I'm going to walk out of here. Do you hear me?"

Her throat worked beneath my fingers. "I hear you."

"Good."

I didn't know the next stage of my plan. I hadn't thought this through.

I really should have.

At least the door was open and the first stage of my escape was in motion.

"Come." Jerking her away from the wall, I spun her

around and grabbed the neat bun at the base of her skull.

I couldn't continue to strangle her from this position, but I yanked hard on her hair so she knew I would find some other way to maim. "Show me the way out."

Shame coated my insides. Loathing that I'd stepped into Alrik's shoes almost made me let go.

Almost.

I'd redeem myself once I was free. I'd repent for hurting another. But not right now.

"You know...you don't have to do this." The girl stepped forward thanks to my pressure. "It's not what you think. We're not going to hurt—"

I jerked her again, earning a pained squeak. "I'm not listening. I'm not interested in your lies. You're showing me the way out of here, and that's it." I pushed her faster.

"You're not being held against your will, you know. You can just—"

I yanked on her hair again, shutting her up.

I had no intention of letting her finish any sentence because each time she talked, my stomach somersaulted and my fingers begged to unwind from her bun.

"Could've fooled me." I shoved her into the corridor, taking swift notes of space and money and rooms branching off with equally nice boudoirs. "The door was locked. If I'm not being held against my will, why couldn't I leave when I wanted to?"

Why are you asking her questions?

Shut up and focus.

"We do that at the beginning. We never know how mentally broken our guests will be. It's for our safety and theirs."

If she was so worried about her safety, why deliver food on her own? Why not have a guard to defend her and stop me from doing exactly what I was doing?

Ignoring those unhelpful questions, I marched her quicker. "Guests?" I laughed coldly, eyeing up the staircase in the distance. "Funny word for captives, don't you think?"

"You're not our captive. You *were* a captive. Not anymore."

"Wrong. I was in love, and some asshole didn't listen to me."

Her momentum stalled. "Excuse me?"

"You're not excused." Pushing her again, I never took my attention off the midnight blue carpeted staircase. I wanted to leave. My skin crawled with the need. My heart panted for freedom. She was my shield and weapon all in one.

"I think there's been some kind of mistake," my prisoner murmured. "What's your name?"

We reached the landing and I shoved her down the first steps. "My name isn't important."

"Mine's Suzette."

I didn't want to think about her as a girl with a name. I didn't want to know anything about her other than she was keeping me from finding Elder.

What if he'd drowned when he fell overboard? What if the Phantom staff had been murdered by the Chinmoku? What if everything I knew was gone all because some asshole decided to claim me for himself?

The penny-diamond bracelet Elder had given me tinkled on my wrist, fissuring my heart with worry.

I refused to imagine him dead. I kept the picture of him alive and happy in my mind. But as my dress whispered behind me, slithering down steps to a foyer I didn't recognise, I struggled to swallow back heavy washing grief.

"Did you hear me? My name is Suzette and I'm—"

"Good for you. I don't care what your name is." I injected venom into my tone. "If you're trying to make me see you as a person and not a tool to get out of here, it's not going to work."

"No." She shook her head, forcing my hand to move with her. "I'm just trying to figure this out."

"Well, figure it out silently."

God, how long are these stairs?

They meandered around in a circle, imposing and romantic, the perfect backdrop for some epic love scene.

My mind taunted me with images of Elder before he was bloody and shot. He'd been so dashing and handsome in his tux. I wanted to hold that image forever and delete the god-awful splash as he flew overboard with a bullet wedged in his body.

My anger cauldroned into sick rage. I twisted my victim's hair.

This is your fault.

"Ow." She squirmed, trotting down the stairs faster, her hand coming to land over mine in rebuttal. "I'll help you. You don't have to hurt me."

"Give me my freedom and I'll give you yours. I'll even apologise."

I'll apologise every night for years.

Not taking her hand off mine, she said under her breath, "You'll owe me more than that when we get downstairs."

My heart froze. "Why? What's downstairs?"

"My husband."

That word.

God, that word.

Elder...Miki...whatever his name was—I'd given him my heart in every way. If I couldn't have him, then this woman couldn't have her husband. "I don't care."

"You'll care when he shoots you."

"If he's the man who shot the one I love, then good luck to him. I'll haunt him for the rest of his days for killing any hope I had at happiness."

Her shoulders slouched as if affected by the raw pain I couldn't hide. "I don't understand—"

"There's nothing to understand." I wished I'd gagged her. Conversation had the unnerving ability to switch enemy into friend. "I don't want to talk anymore."

Reaching the foyer, I hissed into her ear. "Scream and I'll

hurt you a lot worse. All I want to do is leave."

My threat wasn't empty—I would hurt her. How, I had no idea. But really, she could call my bluff because what leverage did I have to stop her?

"He was there last night, you know. Franco is his name. My husband. He said there was a fight."

So her husband was the henchman of the man who'd grabbed me. The man who'd stood by as I faded from consciousness in the arms of my kidnapper. Her husband had helped Elder by shooting the Chinmoku and then destroyed him by letting his accomplice drug and take me.

My thoughts darkened, no longer regretting hurting her after all the pain I'd endured.

My captive didn't honour my command to stop talking, her voice gentle but cool. "Franco said Q told you who they were. He told me you were under attack, and they saved you. Why are you doing this if you know who Q is and why he took you?"

"Stop it." I shook her again, revelling in her small pained gasp.

"But I need to understand. This doesn't make sense. You should be grateful—"

A strangled laugh fell from my lips. "*Grateful?* I should be *grateful* that they shot the man I love and took me, despite both Elder and I *begging* them to listen. They had it wrong. I didn't need saving. They were too late for that. Elder was the one who saved me months ago. He found me. Fixed me. *Loved* me. And then your asshole husband stood by while his friend shot him."

"But what about the men Franco said were holding you hostage?"

I didn't want to admit that Q and Franco had arrived at the perfect time. In a way, they'd saved Elder from one death only to deliver him to another. If only they hadn't shot him, I would've got on my knees and thanked them a million times over for arriving and shooting the Chinmoku.

When I didn't reply, Suzette slouched. "I'm sorry."

"What?" Her apology threw ice water on the sizzling-flames around my heart.

Her fingers squeezed mine still lodged in her hair. "Truly. I know you have no reason to believe me. But he's never made a mistake before. To be fair…what you're saying has never happened, so…how was he supposed to know?"

I wanted to stay furious, but I couldn't ignore the truth vibrating in her tone.

Unlocking my fingers from around her bun, I dropped my hand. Blood rushed to my fingertips, desperate to erase the feel of holding her against her will.

She turned to face me slowly as if I'd bound away or attack her. "I think you should talk to Tess."

"Tess?" I looked past her to the living room. Mirror images of double doors led to two different rooms. One side of the foyer held a library—dark and brooding with leather and parchment. The other held the welcoming embrace of a comfortable lounge. A dog's chew toy sat on a pretty purple rug. A discarded cardigan draped over the back of the white leather couch. The smells of something sweet like muffins or cakes billowed from the distant kitchen.

What is this place?

It looked like a family lived here, not some rapist or psychopath.

But how could that be?

The front door opened, bringing a gust of chilly air.

Instantly, I grabbed my hostage again, pulling her as a shield in front of me, my arm locking over her chest. "You!" I hissed as the bulkier man of the two from the worst night of my life appeared.

Suzette's so-called husband.

His gaze darted to the woman I held then locked onto me, his arm switching from frozen to whip-fast, unholstering the gun at his waist. "Let her go." Raising the weapon, he aimed at my face. "Right fucking now."

I ignored the urge to duck, fighting every instinct to stay quiet, to turn mute. That handy tool wouldn't save me here. I had a voice. I had every intention of screaming until I was listened to and released.

Staying tucked behind Suzette, I seethed, "Let me go and I'll let her go."

The man inched closer, letting the front door swing closed behind him. He was handsome in a brutish French way. Dark hair and tight lips, he vibrated with loathing. "You're not going anywhere unless you give me back my wife."

Suzette shrugged apologetically, shooting me a look over her shoulder. "Told you he wouldn't be pleased." She made no move to leave me, though. She could easily twist out of my hold and leave me wide open for target practice.

But she didn't.

Instead, she reached behind her and patted my hip with her dainty hand, reassuring me even as the furious man pointed a gun in our direction.

Sighing dramatically, she said in a French accented voice, "I'm fine, *mon amour*. You don't need to worry."

Franco licked his lips like a carnivore. "I don't need to worry, Suzette? She has you in a chokehold."

"Yes, and you snatched her from the man she loves. We're all in the wrong."

Franco rolled his eyes. "How many times have we heard that story? Leave them with their masters long enough and they all fall in love with the cunts."

Suzette shook her head. "This one's different." She threw me a smile. "I believe her. Enough to listen, at least, instead of undermining her own heart. I suggest you do the same."

I sucked in a breath as Suzette patted my forearm wrapped around her chest. "It's okay. Let me go. I'm on your side."

Trust had never come easy for me.

Trust was something I would forever struggle to gift.

This moment was no different.

I didn't drop my arm, but I did loosen it slightly. "I'll only let you go if your husband puts his gun on the side table over there." I arched my chin at the cute table with a porcelain bowl for keys.

Franco snickered coldly. "While you have your hands on my wife, I'm not putting my gun anywhere."

"Then I guess we're at a stalemate." The door behind him mocked me. Freedom existed just beyond it. If I could somehow teleport and appear on the other side, all my problems would be over.

I could run.

Far, far away.

I could find the ocean and swim, swim, swim toward the Phantom...wherever it may be.

Dog claws scrabbled on tiles, followed by a bark.

I didn't mean to look—I should've kept my full attention on Franco in case he made a move, but a fat sausage-shaped bullet charged from the lounge with the half-chewed toy from the rug in its mouth, barrelling into Suzette's legs.

"*Umph!*" She stumbled back. "Darn you, Courage!"

I switched from keeping her prisoner to helping her balance.

The crazy dog didn't pause, galloping up the staircase, its tail wagging and round belly bouncing on every step.

What on earth is going on here?

Husbands and wives.

Cardigans and pets.

"Courage! Don't you dare run away from me, you little brat!" A pretty Australian voice yelled, followed by running footsteps. "Why can't you be more like your brothers and sisters?"

Another woman appeared, slamming to a stop as she found our standoff in the foyer.

Instantly, the love and happiness glowing on her face transformed to chilly assessment. Her eyes hardened, flitting quickly to Franco and Suzette. Instead of asking if her friend was okay or demanding the man with the gun execute me, she crossed her arms and slouched against the door frame. A viper coiled to strike but ready to sniff its prey first. "So…what's going on?"

Suzette shrugged. "Seems there's been some kind of mistake."

Franco snarled. "This bitch won't let her go."

I snapped, "I just want to leave."

All three conversations layered in a messy cacophony with no clear message.

"Interesting." The blonde woman raised an eyebrow. "Let's focus on what Suzette just said seeing as I like her the most right now." She smiled quickly at the maid in my hold, revealing years of history and trust and friendship far beyond anything I'd ever experienced. "You're up. Tell me…what sort of mistake?"

Suzette laughed, instantly at ease and comfortable enough to turn tension into mirth. "A Q mistake, of course. What else?"

"Ah." Blondie nodded, biting her lip to stay stern. "Can't say he's a saint but what's he done this time?" Locking eyes with me, she added, "Care to tell me…whoever you are?"

When I didn't take the hint and give her my name, she tried a less subtle approach, her humour evaporating. "Let's get something straight. My name is Tess, and that is my very best friend you've got."

She pushed off from the door frame, pointing at Franco who hadn't lowered his gun. "And that's her husband who is eerily similar to my husband and won't hesitate to hurt you if you hurt her."

Padding barefoot, she came closer, circling around me and Suzette as if we were a museum exhibit.

Her jeans fit snug, showing long legs and curvy hips. Her basic grey blouse billowed over full breasts with the hint of lacy bra underneath. She was one of those lucky women who could wear simple clothing but look effortlessly expensive.

"We're not in the habit of hurting our guests and in return

expect the same courtesy. However, if you don't let my friend go…we're going to have a serious problem."

My heart galloped, smoking with indecisions.

I couldn't let Suzette go because I couldn't be left vulnerable. I couldn't keep up my threat to hurt her because she'd proven to be sane amongst all this crazy, and perhaps, just perhaps, this new captivity was nothing like my last.

All I could do was remain in the current status quo and hope no one shot me. "I just want to go home."

I sounded pitiful.

Heartbroken.

Riddled with enough pain to lower Franco's gun and send a flicker of concern over Tess's face.

Suzette leapt to my defence yet again. "From what I can gather, she was a slave but then it got complicated."

"Complicated is normally the case when dealing with slaves." Tess pursed her lips. "You know that as well as I do, Suzette."

Clasping her hands together, Tess stared at me as if I had it all wrong. As if I didn't know my own brain and heart. As if she pitied the screwed-up existence I'd bought as real. "Look, let's try this again. We won't hurt you, but seeing as this is our home, we're not comfortable with our guests manhandling loved ones. Let Suzette go and I give you my word Franco won't shoot and I won't retaliate. All I ask is you come with me and talk."

"Go with you where?" My arm shook.

The tricks my mother had taught me to read body language fritzed and misfired. I tried to uncover everyone's true agenda, but there were too many people at once.

Franco was the easiest to read: cold, aloof, mercenary, but undoubtedly in love with the woman I held. Intelligent and not afraid of dirty work judging by how comfortably he held the gun and the way he helped shoot the Chinmoku last night.

Suzette: slender, shorter than me, came across sweet and courteous but a steel rod ran through her spine, hinting at a ferocious temper.

Tess: sharp-witted, courageous, steadfast. She looked at me with displeasure but beneath that lurked a hint of kinship as if she understood my actions more than she should.

"Nowhere special. Just to the kitchen. We'll have some tea or coffee…maybe a freshly baked blueberry muffin or two. We'll keep the weapons and threats far away and just talk." Tess pointed into the room where she'd come from, completely forgetting the dog she'd been chasing. "I think talking is rather important, don't you?"

"I just want to go back to Elder. If he's even alive."

"Elder?"

"The man I love."

"The man you *think* you love." Her face fell with sympathy. "You're not the first to try to return to her master. A few attempted when they first arrived. Depending on how long you've been his property, the mind distorts what's right and wrong. What's real."

I glowered, jerking Suzette closer. "Don't belittle me and say I don't know my own heart."

Tess held up her hands. "I'm not belittling you. I'm telling you what I've experienced. However, if you want to tell me your side of the story, then I'll gladly listen." Her eyes narrowed. "But first, you must let my friend go and agree not to hurt anyone."

I snorted at the irony. The way I was holding Suzette was nothing. I was embracing her compared to the bone-breaking pain I'd been given.

Suzette whispered under her breath, "She'll listen, you know. If it's truly a mistake, she'll fix it. She's married to Q and—"

Oh, hell no.

Shoving Suzette away, I balled my hands, glaring at Tess. "You're *married* to the bastard who stole me? The idiot who shot the man who rescued me? The asshole who left him to die?"

I didn't care I was wide open for a bullet.

I couldn't believe this woman.

I couldn't believe she had the *audacity* to judge me as if I'd given my heart to a lost cause only to give hers to a man who never listened and ripped apart lovers.

The hypocrite!

Tess stiffened, looking me up and down. Finally, she glanced at Franco and Suzette. "I think you guys had better go."

Franco never lowered his gun. "I'm not leaving you with her. If Q was here, he'd—"

Tess spun to face him. "He's not here, and I'm fully capable of looking after myself, Franco. Thank you for your concern but you and Suzette spend the afternoon somewhere else."

Dismissing them and zeroing her entire attention on me, she backed into the lounge and beckoned me to join her. "Come on. Let's talk."

ELDER

AN HOUR INTO the cruise from Southampton to Calais and my temper had burned through most of the painkillers Michaels had given me.

The only saving grace of being enroute to France was the waking water beneath the hull. The stagnancy of the harbour had gone; my fast-paced mind happier with the quick speed and hum of engines. They pacified me enough to wince my way through a shower and dress in something that wasn't bullet-torn or blood stained.

It'd taken five times as long to do something so simple, but I'd obnoxiously refused help, telling Selix to piss off and somehow managing to unwrap the many bandages and hiss my way into the shower. Balancing on one leg with an elbow and shoulder unable to function was a lot harder than I thought.

I probably shouldn't submerge fresh wounds and stitches and definitely shouldn't remove slings and splints, but I had to get clean.

Not once.

Not twice.

But three times.

I had to wash away the shit I'd done so I could focus with a fresh mind to bring Pim home.

By the time I'd wrangled my way back into the brace and bandages and fought one-armed into a dark grey shirt and fumbled with the buttons, my forehead shone with agony-sweat. My elbow bellowed from contorting and being used against its will while my bones ached, deciding the effort to be human and wear clothing wasn't enough to justify the nausea and fever decorating my skin.

But then I had to do it all over again, hoisting on a pair of trousers to complete my wardrobe and prevent giving people an eyeful of my crotch. The bottom half gave double the trouble—pulling on linen slacks instead of my first attempted jeans after being too tight to maneuverer around my fractured ankle. I used every curse word imaginable before the zipper was up and the dreaded things secured.

Dressed but out of breath, I scowled at the array of walking sticks and crutches Michaels had left by my bed. The brace on my ankle was as far as I was prepared to go.

I refused to hop around like a broken rabbit.

Selix had given me a quick rundown of what'd happened.

Obviously, I was aware how idiotic I'd been not to notice how silent the Phantom was or the missing staff. But the rest, I wasn't savvy on.

Two deck hands had been killed when the Chinmoku first climbed on board. Their bodies were found by the emergency siren in the back of the yacht. Luckily, they'd had enough time to pull the cord and alert everyone to evacuate into the safe room.

Everyone, including Jolfer and high-ranking crew officials, managed to get in before they'd sealed the space and settled in to wait out the Chinmoku.

Unfortunately, in their rush to hide, cell phones had been left behind, but even those who had them weren't able to warn us due to the thick armoured plating blocking mobile signals.

Another staff member, a female who worked in housekeeping, had been found in a corridor with her throat slashed, her hands crisscrossed from a blade as she'd defended her life.

We'd already dealt with the bodies, called their families, and arranged a substantial grievance package and flights home for their deceased. It wouldn't take away the loss but at least the ones left behind needn't worry about financials.

Death was such a major event, yet the cleaning up of blood and signing of paperwork felt inconsequential. The ending of a human existence, and it only took a few hours.

The Chinmoku had taken three more lives of people under my care.

I swore on my godforsaken soul that that was the last of it. *No more.*

The moment I found Pim and killed the two men who had no business messing in my world, I'd hunt down the Chinmoku and *fight*.

I was done waiting for them to come to me. I didn't care if the battle happened on their turf or mine. All that mattered was it happened and I *won*.

Rage glossed my vision as I looked at the bronze genie bottle I'd bought Pim in Morocco. It sat on my desk as if she'd placed it there when I wasn't looking, ready to grant me any wish I desired.

My heart folded in on itself in gruesome origami.

I had a wish I desired. No, I had more than one. I had multiple: repair my body so I wasn't so useless, track down the men who'd taken Pim and slaughter them, kill every last Chinmoku so I could keep Pim safe, then work a miracle and earn her trust all over again.

All of them centred around the woman I'd fallen in love with.

A common theme for *her*.

Funny that I didn't think of forgiveness from my family, only forgiveness for my latest transgressions. Pim had successfully filled every emptiness and longing inside me until all I needed was her.

And now, I no longer had her and felt ten times fucking

worse than I ever had before.

Loneliness and wretchedness were tormenting sons of bitches.

Glancing at my watch, I counted the minutes to go before yet another battle. France was only thirty minutes away, but when we got there...what then? How did I go about hunting down two French men in a city full of Frenchies?

My mind spiralled, latching onto every method I could use to hunt: stalking the streets, marching into police stations with their descriptions, doing a similar web search on them that they'd done on the QMB, putting out a ransom for any mercenary who brought me their heads.

So many scenarios and I doubted any of them would yield results in time.

What are they doing to her?
Is she alive?
Is she cursing me? Crying for me? Begging for help?

My heart double pounded and my head swam from temper and agony. Sweat trickled down my back from the sick concoction. I had every intention of teaching those bastards a lesson—broken or whole.

One thing was for sure, I wouldn't hold back next time.

I wouldn't struggle to forget decency before embracing the animal inside. The moment I set eyes on the man who'd shot me...he'd be in pieces.

Needing to distract myself, I half-stalked, half-hobbled to the cupboard where my cello lived.

Up close, I noticed what distance had hidden.

Christ, no...

My hobbles turned to staggering hops.

My fingers reached out, tracing the pockmarks of bullets, running over splinters missing in the wood.

Goddammit, they didn't—

I wrenched open the cupboard and howled.

My cello.

The one remaining link to my father. The one thing

reminding me that I'd been worthy of love once upon a time and the only thing with the power to keep me in check when my tendencies overpowered me, lay victimised and shot.

My father had borrowed money from the Chinmoku to buy me this beaten-up, second-hand cello. He'd put his own life on the line to do something nice, and I'd repaid him by selling my life into their debt.

My cello was more than just an instrument; it was every mistake I'd caused and every happiness I'd enjoyed.

And now, it's ruined.

Unstrapping the large stringed device from its protective harness, I clutched the weight and dragged it into the light. The smooth spruce top and well-stroked maple sides and neck were shattered where bullets had pierced it. The fingerboard flopped sideways, snapped with its strings dangling like ghastly garrottes.

The scratches from its previous owners and patina stains from my fingers playing it over the years weren't enough to hold it together.

Grief wrapped cold and savage around my chest.

How could an innate object butcher me so completely?

My hands turned to claws where I held it.

First, Pim had been stolen—the one person I loved above all others. Now, my cello had been murdered—never to play again.

Its music silenced. My sanity destroyed.

Christ, I would make them pay.

Over and over.

I won't stop until they feel a tenth of the pain I do.

Running my fingers through the holes and splinters of my beloved belonging, my teeth wedged together and another level of pain filled me. An emotional pain. A soul-deep agony.

I couldn't bring my father back to life and I couldn't fix my cello.

It was as dead as my family and loneliness slammed into me with a vicious, vicious fist.

I doubled over, grabbing the fingerboard and throttling it. How dare it be in the crossfires? How dare it cease to play my melodies?

My rage overflowed, and I couldn't stop it anymore.

I didn't have the men responsible for this mess.

I couldn't kill them…yet.

I didn't have Pim to take care of.

I didn't have a way to reincarnate the dead.

I only had my wounds, my agony, my temper, and my bullet-broken cello.

Holding the spoils of war, I no longer saw my cherished instrument that'd saved me from so much emotional shit. I only saw everything I hated and everyone I would destroy.

Buggered shoulder be damned. Ruined elbow be fucked. Broken finger and fractured ankle be screwed. I swung the cello up over my head and smashed it against the ground.

Ricocheting wood and pegs pinged and cracked. Fingerboard pieces flew and end pins harpooned into the floor.

My body begged to rest.

My ankle couldn't hold my weight. My ribs screamed. My head throbbed.

But I didn't stop.

I destroyed my cello until it was nothing but dust.

I gave it the memorial and burial of a lifetime.

And I promised I'd do the same to the bastards who took Pim.

Pimlico

FOR ALL MY out of character rage and holding Suzette hostage, I struggled to harness fake bravery the moment the standoff was over.

My voice and confidence were still so new that using them drained me to the point of utter exhaustion. Being so inexperienced at barking commands and not cowering under retorts meant I sat opposite Tess with my heart impersonating a cheetah, beating as fast as it could, hoping against hope that she didn't see how everything I did was an act—a role I desperately wanted to play but had yet to learn the script.

Tess's head cocked, her gaze sharp and unforgiving. Nerves catapulted down my spine as she sniffed, perhaps seeing more than I wanted her to or correctly assuming things I couldn't hide.

Anxious shakes found me.

Nervous flutters filled me.

A suddenly dry throat stole the rest of my debate.

Tearing my eyes from her, I glanced around the library where we sat.

She'd changed her mind against escorting me into the lounge the moment I'd nodded and went to follow. She'd glanced at the general untidiness of the living room and quickly strode across the foyer into the oppressive but impressive library.

Red leather-bound editions, midnight blue novels, and more recent colourful paperbacks slept on shelves towering around us. It might've been a shadowing, looming place if the artfully placed lamps didn't turn it into a full room embrace.

Interspersed with ancient, expensive classics sprawled the bright garish illustrations of children books.

I inhaled sharply as yet more baby stuff appeared now I'd noticed.

A tiny bib sat on a closed laptop on the desk by the window. A rattle lay forgotten on the sheepskin rug by the fireplace. A pacifier lolled on a blue blanket on the arm of the chair Tess sat in.

The anxiety in my stomach hardened into yet another reminder that my life would never have such things cluttering it. If I ever had a library as nice as this, it wouldn't be decorated with baby paraphernalia.

Tess caught me staring at the pacifier. Picking it up, she placed it smoothly into her jeans pocket as if she didn't want me looking. "So..." Clearing her throat, she relaxed into her chair, the back soaring up like wings behind her. "Let's start at the beginning, shall we? What's your name?"

For someone who'd grown used to talking to strangers and friends—for someone who'd been held in police captivity and had no choice but to say her true name—I still wasn't comfortable handing out such personal information.

It wasn't right.

Society had taught us a name was the first thing given to a stranger. That it was unimportant.

Can't people see it's the total opposite?

A name was the most personal thing anyone could give. It was their title, their identity, the one word that could summon or dismiss them.

Tasmin was alive and breathing inside me now. I could no longer deny her existence or the knowledge that one day...I would claim that name for myself.

But if I wasn't ready, if I wasn't worthy...what made anyone else so?

Letting heavy silence scatter into the carpet by our feet, Tess didn't ask again or prompt me to reply. She didn't seem to mind the tautness existing between us, and I'd lived with such angst-ridden silence for too long to cower beneath it.

Our eyes locked.

Blue to green.

And something strange happened.

I *recognised* her.

Not from a magazine article like I'd recognised Nila Weaver but a soul-deep recognition.

A nudge inside that said...*you share something with this woman. You have more in common than you think.*

Needing validation on such a wild theory, I murmured, "Before I tell you who I am...can you tell me who you are?"

The steel in my tone softened to a more malleable fabric. Something that wouldn't break but wouldn't stay in one unyielding entity either.

Tess dropped her gaze to my ballgown, licking her bottom lip. The dynamics between her everyday casual wear and my fancy evening garb didn't go unnoticed. We were opposites even if something linked us that we couldn't explain.

Ghosts shadowed her gaze, followed by a quick smirk. "All right."

When she didn't start straight away, I held my breath, wondering if she'd changed her mind.

But then she said softly, "For some reason, I don't think you're asking who I am now...more so...who I was before. Am I right?"

I didn't fully understand but nodded. "Why do I get the feeling you know what I've lived through?"

She smiled gently. "Because my husband has been saving slaves all his life and I've embraced his calling as my own. We've both seen things that severely lowers our opinion of the human race—"

I shook my head. "It's more than that."

She paused, studying me. "You're right."

We stared, doing our best to read the other. Her body language gave nothing away, revealing nothing more than a woman who was used to wealth and love and confident in her position in life. But then something damaged flickered in her gaze as if she permitted the past to shadow for a split second.

That was the part of her I recognised.

A question stained my tongue, begging to be asked, but wasn't something anyone could slip into normal conversation.

Were you sold too?

I lowered my gaze, stroking the bruised pretty colours of my gown. My penny bracelet glittered against the maroon and midnight, bright in its affection. Elder's kindness and love existed in every diamond-coin.

Elder...please be alive.

"I've never done this before, but I'm going to ignore my usual speech on how I'm the mistress of this house and forgo the necessary introduction about where you can go, what you can expect, and other housekeeping requirements."

My eyes shot up.

"You already know I'm married to a man I hold in the highest regard and obey with utmost loyalty. I say obey, not because of archaic marriage vows, but because he is my master. My *chosen* master."

I gasped.

The language she chose hinted at her past. Phrases such as master and obey I knew well. For the first time since leaving Alrik's, I found some resemblance of familiarity even if it was twisted and wrong to find comfort in such things.

Living with Elder, the emphasis had been on freedom and personal choice.

Here, with Tess, she spoke of love in rules and affection in laws. It upset me to almost miss those boundaries—to know how big my world was and the consequences of trying to stretch those borders. Those guidelines were more acceptable than being told I could do anything and be anyone with no repercussions.

Sometimes (and I would never tell Elder this) but sometimes, the world he offered and choices he gave and experiences he presented were too big, too much, too soon.

Tess gave me something I hadn't known I needed to hear—that it was okay to love the way you *wanted* to love.

She sat forward, pinning me with her intense stare. "Q is my master, but that doesn't mean I obey him in all things. In fact, I'd say I hold all the power because I know how much he loves me." She smiled ruthlessly. "Knowing I could break him is why I can give him every part of myself. And that is what was missing in your relationship with the man who owned you. He might've told you he loved you. You might've believed *you* loved *him*. But believe me when I say that wasn't true."

I didn't know how to reply.

She had it all wrong. I understood the power she mentioned because I'd felt it when Elder confessed he loved me. The brittle desperation in his touch as he held me. The clawing hunger as he entered me. He'd given me everything, and I'd taken it without thought.

The same had happened to me.

And there was nothing fake or wrong about our connection.

If he was dead...then that would be the moment I truly broke. Not from rape or punishment but from trading hearts with him then destined to live heartless and empty without him.

The leather of Tess's chair creaked as she said, "Before I was Tess Mercer, I was Tess Snow—unwanted by her elderly parents, throwing herself on a boy who could never fulfil her, and begging for answers about who she truly was. Then...I was kidnapped."

I sucked in a breath as yet another déjà vu moment knocked on my mind. Somehow, even though our beginning stories were different, we were so similar.

I'd found a kindred ally in this girl.

Pity she still believed I was delusional when she could potentially be a friend. If only she listened instead of being so blind, I could find another avenue of healing.

"I was kidnapped in Mexico." Her voice turned harsh with hate. "I was branded, repurposed, and sold."

Tears warmed my eyes, knowing she'd suffered the same fate.

She knew what it was like to be washed and dressed by men who only cared about your health because it dictated how much they could get for your body.

It didn't matter frustration steadily grew at her incorrect assumptions about Elder and me; I grieved for her just like I grieved for me. "I'm so sorry."

Tess didn't acknowledge my commiseration. Instead, she sat taller with a pride glinting in her gaze. "I was sold, and for a few months I was tormented by the man who took me."

I shook my head. I didn't want to hear anymore. To listen to the mirror image of my tale of rapes and silent screams. Of starvation and broken bones. "You don't have to say anymore. I understand."

I dared glance up.

Her gaze softened to melted butter with a knife of pain—not for herself but for me. "You do understand, and that makes me so sad. That's why it kills me to hear you say you love the bastard who did such things to you." Tess slouched. "How long were you…"

I was glad she didn't finish that sentence. That she didn't ask how long I'd put up with having someone dominate and control my every twitch and thought. "Two years. But the man who kept me isn't the man I'm in love—"

"Yet you manhandled Suzette with a spirit that isn't broken." She laughed under her breath, disregarding my need to clarify. "I'm glad Q didn't find you before he met me…who knows what might've happened."

I frowned, side-tracked. "What do you mean?"

"I mean, I was like you. I didn't let them break me." She shook her head, snorting depreciatively. "However, unlike you, I wasn't in slavery for two years. I'm the one who must say sorry. You're far stronger than I am, even if you do believe you're in love—"

"You keep misunderstanding me. I *am* in love with Elder, and he's in love with me, but he's not the man who bought me."

She pursed her lips. "He really did a number on you, didn't he? Just because he might've changed and grown to treat you fondly throughout your imprisonment, doesn't mean he isn't still the same man who bought you for pleasure."

Ugh, I can't handle this woman.

Crossing my arms, I fought the urge to cuff her around the head and demand she actually *listen* instead of regurgitating pamphlet information on a rescued slave's mental health.

"You don't understand what I'm saying."

Instead of matching my frustration with her own, she gave me a sympathetic smile. "Look, I'll be the first to admit I enjoyed some parts of those few months. The circumstances my master put me in...well, some were wanted while others were not."

"*Excuse* me?" What sort of hypocrisy had I been dragged into? "So you can say you actually *enjoyed* being tortured, yet I can't say I'm in love with the man who—"

Tess reached out and took my balled hands. "I'm sorry. Forgive me. That was super insensitive. I'm only trying to show you how nothing you tell me will be judged. I understand if you're in love with him. I get that. Truly, I do. I also understand two years is a very long time, and you're bound to have found some slivers of acceptability—enough so that your mind might warp what was normal behaviour and what wasn't."

She squeezed my fingers. "You're not alone. Not by a long shot. That's all I'm trying to say."

"I know I'm not alone because Elder made sure I wasn't.

He was the first to show me how love should be."

She nodded quickly, accepting what I said but still believing Elder was Alrik and not two separate people. How much longer would I have to repeat myself? Elder didn't deserve to be thought of as a rapist. He wasn't. He was my guardian angel. My genie. My best-friend.

Tess sighed heavily, almost as if she didn't want to admit something. "Look, there's something about you I find familiar, and I think it's because I see myself in you. Because of that, I need you to hear me when I say I'm here for you—we all are. But returning to your normal life—going back to family and friends—will be so much harder if you keep believing you're in love with your past owner. I understand because I was sold to a man most would call a monster. I stood up to him like you stood up to me today. I told him I would never call him master. I spat at him. Ran away from him. Never, ever bowed to him."

My heart hammered for the beatings she must've received. The horror she must've endured. "How-how are you still alive? How did you escape?"

"I didn't."

Were all conversations with this woman going to be a riddle? "Who saved you then?"

She must've had a man like Elder. Someone who loved her so much they tracked her down and gave her a new life.

"He did."

"Who?"

"My husband."

"Ah." I nodded as if I understood completely when I had no clue at all. But then I remembered who her husband was and what he'd dedicated his life to: hunting slaves and saving them. A vigilante with no moral compass. "Q saved you from your old master?"

So she does understand.

Our tales copied each other.

"Not in so many ways."

My brain hurt. "In what ways, then?"

"He saved me from himself. He saved me from myself." She sighed, finally revealing her sordid secret. "Q was the man I was sold to. He literally is my master first and husband second."

My thoughts screeched to a halt. *"What?"*

She had the *nerve* to school me on my incorrect love choices, yet she'd fallen for the man she was sold to! At least, I'd fallen for the man who'd saved me from such a fate. She looked at me as if I was tangled and twisted when the only person who needed help was her!

"So you see, I totally get it when you say you've fallen for your master." Tess rushed, noticing my gobsmacked look. "I did the same thing. Only, after those first few months, Q never laid a hand on me that I didn't want."

Her gaze dropped to my chest where fading bruises might always remain and to my arms where bumps from broken bones ruined slim line limbs. "I see how badly you were hurt, and I honestly want to slaughter the man who did that to you. To hear you say you love him? To have you sit here, safe and far away from him, and still do everything you can to return to his abuse? It's more than I can stand. I can condone falling in love because I committed the same sin, but what I can't condone is allowing you to believe the way he treated you is normal. It's not. No matter what he tells you."

The house switched from welcoming to mausoleum.

Scenarios and theories span out of control. Maybe I had it all wrong. Maybe I wasn't the recovering slave with issues but *she* was. Perhaps, she was held here against her will and conditioned so completely, she not only bowed to her master's wishes but went along with his crazy ideas about saving women, only to secretly condemn them instead?

What if this was an elaborate sham to lull women into thinking they were saved only to start the same cycle of mental and physical abuse all over again?

All of this was some disgusting mind game.

A trap.

I have to leave.
Right now.
I shot upright, fear twining through my limbs. "Let me go. I want to go. Please, please let me go."

Tess stood too, eyeing my gown. "Where would you go dressed like that?"

"Back to him. Back to the man who saved me."

"I just told you. What you feel for him isn't love, no matter how he spun it." Her eyes flashed. "Q saved you. My husband saved you. You're safe here. With us."

"No, I'm not. You're sick. You tell me I'm wrong for falling in love with my rescuer, yet you fell in love with your owner. Which one of us is wrong in this scenario?"

I'd been wrong when I thought she could be a friend—someone who traded the same existence I had. The woman before me had become corrupted by whatever her owner had done long ago. And she still believed in his lies.

Dragging hands through my hair, I threw my own tale in the face of the strange one she'd told me. "I've listened to you. Now, you listen to me. You have it all wrong. Like you, I was kidnapped and sold. Like you, I fought against my master and managed to keep a part of myself from his evil. I lived with him for two years, and they were the worst two years of my life. I have mementoes from that time. I have scars and nightmares. But that was over. Your husband didn't save me. He didn't infiltrate that white devil mansion or take on the bastard who raped me. He didn't help me shoot Alrik or carry me from that place with my tongue almost cut in two. He didn't spend months making me come alive again, teaching me kindness instead of cruelty and love instead of hate. Your husband didn't kill for me. He didn't sail away with me. He didn't fall in *love* with me."

My dress whispered on the carpet, cascading over the rattle on the sheepskin rug as I stalked toward her. "Your husband did none of those things, but I'll tell you who did. Elder Prest. The man I keep telling you about. The man you believe is my owner. Pay attention when I tell you Elder was *not* my owner. He was my saviour, and you stole him from me!"

I shook with the need for her to understand, to see, to believe, to finally get how stupid she'd been. "Elder was that man. He did those things. He rescued me months ago and has been bringing me back to life ever since. You say I'm not broken. That I'm like you. But I'm not. I'm nothing like you. I *was* broken. I was all kinds of broken. Before Elder, all I wanted to do was die. I was days away from making that wish come true, so don't say I'm like you. Don't say they didn't break me because they did. And only Elder had the power to bring me back."

I couldn't stop. I couldn't prevent my snarl and snap. "You and your husband ruined the only good thing in my life. You stole me from the man who gave my life back. You destroyed everything. Don't you see? Your husband shot him. *He. Shot. Him.* And I don't know if he's alive or dead or even where he is because you keep treating me as if I'm a child who doesn't know her own thoughts."

Tears trickled down my face, unable to stay bottled up.

The fissure of missing Elder echoed like an arctic gale. It hurt more than anything, and I wanted to pass that pain onto Tess who glowed with adoration whenever she mentioned the hated man named Q.

She could never be my friend because she'd married my nemesis.

"I'm done with this, with you, with that bastard you call your master. I'm done, do you hear me!" Stalking to the library double doors, I clutched my skirts and bowled through them tossing a livid growl over my shoulder. "Now you know the truth, I'm leaving. You can't stop me. Don't you *dare* try to stop me." My voice wobbled but from anger instead of tears. "I'll kill you if you do."

Tess darted from the library as I beelined for the front door. "Wait—"

"Don't!" I fumbled with the lock. "Just don't. If you truly

are in the business of saving slaves, then stay back and let me go."

The lock sprung open; I wrenched the door wide. Dusk had fallen, casting everything in a sleepy haze.

I ran.

Tess didn't try to grab me or shout, but she did chase after me, flying down the sweeping grand entrance, her feet bare like mine, equal slaps on marble.

I daren't turn around or yell at her to stay away. I was out of breath, heart wild, mind manic; all I wanted to do was *run*. I didn't care where at this point only that I had to get away from her.

Immediately.

A water fountain splashed merrily in the middle of the driveway, roosting birds filled the sky with chirps and twitters.

I hated the beauty of this place because it had come from the happiness of others.

"Wait, please!" Tess called, running after me but not trying to overtake. If her goal was to outrun me until I faltered, then she'd be running for a while.

I had enough adrenaline to power ten marathons.

Dashing past the fountain, I winced as asphalt switched to gravel. Hop-running, I darted for the grass verge just as a black car rounded the corner and coasted to a stop in front of me.

No!

Footsteps crunched behind me as the car's back door opened and out stepped Q Mercer—my enemy.

His black suit matched his black aura, his jade eyes aloof and unreadable. I hated that he was handsome. I hated that he had the woman he loved. I hated everything he'd done to me.

But most of all, I hated what he held tucked close to his chest, protecting it with his body.

It wasn't a gun or syringe in which to destroy my life.

It was something I wanted more than anything, and something I would never have.

A fat, squirmy baby in a green two-piece.

The strange image of a monster holding an infant slammed me into a brick wall, but it didn't stop Tess running behind me.

Air rustled as she charged past, ran directly up to her husband, and instead of kissing him hello, or telling him to subdue me, or even reaching for the baby cooing happily at her arrival, she braced her legs, raised her hand, and slapped her damn husband on the cheek.

ELDER

DOCKING IN CALAIS didn't settle me.
It made me worse.
We'd arrived at our destination, but I had no satisfaction, no men to slaughter, no place to invade.
I still didn't have a clue where they might've taken Pim.
"What do we do now?" Selix asked as he entered my quarters and crashed to a halt when he noticed the desecration of my cello.
The pieces of my beloved instrument decorated every inch of the carpet. Tiny splinters and string smithereens. That was all that was left.
That's all that will be left of the bastards who took Pim when I get my hands on them.
"We start hunting," I growled, not looking up from my laptop where I'd typed some computer code to do an impossible but hopefully fruitful search.
I triggered Pim's true name again. I input physical descriptions of the men into the dark web where criminals proudly bragged about extorts and laundering. The dark web was where their resume and accomplishments hid, impressing or threatening other outlaws they wished to do business with.
I'd already looked up Sullivan Sinclair from Hawk's

masquerade and found he had a simple file. Men like him scared me the most—the ones who didn't have the need to discuss their accomplishments because they either had too many to list or they were too dark to mention.

All he'd been willing to share was a PO Box with the cryptic tagline: *provider of leisure and pleasure. In my world…new rules apply.*

That was it. No photos of his services or inflated ego trips. Not even a business name. He was almost boring in the colourful underworld with no way to tell if he was lethal or law-abiding.

Unfortunately, even in my manic trawling for the men who'd shot me, I'd come up empty. Pim's name didn't herald any alerts. My digital composite of what I thought they looked like sank into internet obscurity. My options were running painfully thin.

"Should I get the car organised? Do you have any idea where they might've taken her?"

My head whipped up, my gaze narrowing on Selix. "No."

"Want me to drive around anyway? See if we can find clues the old-fashioned way."

"No."

"What do you want to do then?"

My fingers—minus my broken one—flew over the keyboard, searching…always searching. "I want to fucking kill them."

"Okay…" Moving to take a seat in front of my desk, he picked up a sliver of wood from my cello. Using it to clean beneath his fingernails, he muttered, "We're in France but at a stalemate. Who's to say they even have Pim here?"

"They have to."

"Why?" He cocked his head. "They could live anywhere in Europe. Hell, they could be in China for all we know."

"They're from here, and they're tied to their country. I believe they live here, and until something hints otherwise, I'm not leaving."

Here I'm close to Pim.
Even if I can't get to her.

"What info have you got so far?" Placing the cello shard on my desk, he watched me expectantly.

Stilling my fingers on the laptop, I reeled off, "They have to have money, judging by the getaway boat you described. They have to be involved in criminal activity to know how to hack into a police file. They have to be French because of their accents—they were thick, not watered down with different dialects or time overseas. They have to be trustworthy for someone to sell them the automatic guns they were using. They have to be—"

Selix held up his hand. "Okay, I sense your OCD coming out to play here, Prest. How about you tone it down some? Give me something to do instead of taking it all on yourself?" Pointing at my multitude of injuries and bandages, he added, "I know you're fully capable of ripping the entrails from these motherfuckers but let me help." He hung his head. "Let me ease some of the guilt for not helping in time last night."

I wanted to bellow that he could help by leaving me alone; that a part of me blamed him for not coming sooner while another part was glad because if he hadn't been on the dock, he might've been shot too, and we both would've drowned.

My thoughts were a tangled fucking mess; I'd be the first to admit I was close to losing it. I couldn't afford to lose my cool and yell because if I let go, everything would come pouring out. I'd blame him and me and even Pim.

I'd give in to the itch inside my brain to find a logical explanation for how and why this had happened. I was so fucking close to going crazy that I clutched to rationality with bloodied fingernails.

Focus on Pim and only Pim.

Once she was safe, then I could work through the rest of my shit.

"Just...let me do this, all right, Selix?" I looked up, sighing with pain and exhaustion. With every keyboard peck, my elbow and shoulder screamed. With every shift, my ankle and ribs cried.

I hated how weak I was.

I hated everyone because of it.

Holding eye contact, he gnawed on his bottom lip before nodding slowly. Glancing away, he shifted in his chair and pulled out my weed tin from of his pocket.

With a wry smile, he smoothed out a paper, spread a generous amount of dried skunk, then licked the seam and rolled. Holding out the fat joint, he grabbed the lighter from my desk. "Do it your way, Prest. I'll be there to help exterminate when you find them."

It wasn't often I was speechless, but I had nothing as I took the joint, pressed it between my lips, and lit the end. The spicy smoke gushed into my lungs as I inhaled deep.

If my go-to saviour could keep my mind on one thought and my pain far away, then I might have a chance at finding Pim sooner rather than later.

Because one thing was for sure, I wasn't leaving the Phantom until I had a name and address.

And once I did...well, war was coming, and I didn't care who would be making my enemies' funeral arrangements.

Pimlico

I FLINCHED FOR the fiftieth time since grudgingly accepting Tess's request for a few more minutes of my time.

Ha! It was more like an abduction than a request.

The second she'd slapped her husband, she'd yanked the baby from his embrace, hoisted him onto her hip, then turned and stalked toward me.

With the child squirming in one arm, she'd muttered something about needing another ten minutes to explain, then grabbed my wrist, and dragged me quick-sharp back into the house.

What I should've done was keep running.

What I should've done was given her the finger and refused.

That was what Tasmin would've done.

But Pim became my guiding force, slapping a gag over my lips and bowing my head in acquiescence.

I'd returned to the French chateau, but nothing could calm my over-sensitive reactions—not sitting on one of the comfy couches in the lounge. Not the French bull dog mix that'd passed out on the rug by my feet. Not the unwavering stare of the baby boy in his green two-piece.

I wish I'd kept running.

Nothing Tess could say could heal the bone-deep anger inside me.

I couldn't look at her husband without my hands curling and fingernails imbedding themselves into my palms.

I'd never been a violent person. But sitting in that cosy lounge with true love tainting the air and a baby chirping happily in its mother's arms, I was a hurricane of loathing ready to unspool.

Just as I couldn't look at the father, I could barely look at the son.

The baby had such an intense stare it stripped me to my marrow. That shouldn't be possible nor could it be allowed.

"Right then," Tess snipped, glaring at her husband who still lurked in the foyer as if closing the front door was a mammoth task. She flashed me a worried smile. "Let's get this mess sorted, shall we?" Bending down, she plopped the baby on the floor with a mismatch of toys, then crossed her arms and tapped her foot until the man I hated prowled into the room.

And he did prowl.

He moved like a predator—like something ready to tear into its prey with sharp teeth and lethal claws.

In another world, I would've found him handsome with his dark hair and widow's peak, his calculating eyes and iciness that only true killers carried.

But now, I merely despised him.

His eyes narrowed as he rubbed his red cheek bright with her palm print. "Care to tell me why you slapped me, *esclave?*"

My ears twitched at the word. What did that mean and why did Tess shiver when he said it?

As quickly as she'd shivered, she turned into a statue, pointing a finger in his face. "You stupid man."

His face turned black. *"Pardon moi?"*

"You heard me. You're a moron. An idiot."

"I suggest you stop calling me names, Tess. Otherwise, I'll give you plenty of others to scream." He didn't look my way.

He didn't apologise for the heavy sexual undertones. He didn't care in the slightest that I watched in my red and blue ballgown on their couch.

Before my father died, my parents had had their fair share of domestics.

But this...this was on a different level, and it wasn't the words they used but the fierce passion in which they wielded them. I'd often heard my mother say only the finest line existed between love and hate.

And these two...they'd blurred that line into something passionately crucifying.

"I can't believe you, Q. How many times did I say to check all the facts? To not let what happened to me dictate your choices and overrule common sense?"

"Don't you dare lecture me, woman. Especially on something you have no fucking right to—"

"Watch your language." She threw a quick look at her child who slobbered on a cream teddy bear.

"Watch what *you* accuse me of." Her husband stalked closer, his head lowered, watching her from shadowed eyes. "You know I don't do well with slurs, Tess."

"It's not a slur if it's true! You screwed up. Just like I said you would if you didn't stop to listen!"

"Oh, I listen," Q seethed. "And I'm listening well to this conversation. You have no right to scream—"

"No one is screaming."

He chuckled as black as hell. "You will be."

My mouth fell open.

It was as if I didn't exist.

Who were these people who blatantly flaunted whatever kink they were into with no regard to my opinions?

Then again, I was a stranger. Why did my opinions matter?

I was no one to them and was being treated as such.

I cleared my throat, hoping to remind them that I might not use my voice currently, but I most certainly used my ears.

Tess spun to look at me, her hand flying wildly—gesturing

as if I'd saved her from a tangent and reminded her of the point. "Her! I'm talking about her."

Q directed blistering eyes on me. "What about her? She's safe. Why didn't you dress her in something her old master hasn't destroyed?" His gaze dropped to my torn bodice and the flash of skin beneath. "For God's sake, woman. Have you forgotten the protocol when a new guest arrives?"

I wanted to stab him. I wanted to shoot him. *Let me drug and kill him and see how he likes it.*

Tess snorted. "Bah! Nothing about this is following *protocol*, Q. And it's all your fault."

"*My* fault?" He stiffened like a scorpion about to strike.

"Yes, yours!" Tess was unfazed by the sheer power rolling off him. "Tell me what happened last night."

His eyebrow rose. He shot me a quick glance. "Nothing you need concern yourself with."

"*Everything* I need to concern myself with because it turns out you shot someone."

He laughed again. "Come now, *esclave*, that can't be what this is about. I shoot all the cunts who possess—"

"And I thank you for that. The slaves thank you for that. The world thanks you. Shit, even the police thank you."

"So what's the problem, *mon amour?*"

Tess's gaze immediately lost its blue spitfire, warming at the mention of being his love. "The problem is, *maître*, you shot an innocent man."

"What are you talking about?" He crossed his arms.

"I'm saying you didn't listen. Didn't see. Didn't believe what she was telling you." Her shoulders slouched as the crackle of their argument faded. "Tell me what happened last night with..." Sighing, she looked at me. "I'm sorry. I never did get your name."

Tess might've frustrated me in the library, but she'd proven to be on my side. She'd gone to battle against her own family for me. She deserved at least something to call me by even if it wasn't my true address. In reality, my slave name was my real identity anyway. "Pimlico."

"Right, of course. Pimlico." She repeated it as if she'd known all along and embraced me as a soul sister.

Returning her attention to her husband, she asked, "Did Pimlico tell you she loved the man you shot last night?"

Q froze. "What?"

"Answer the question, yes or no."

He scowled. "You know how many have professed the same thing, Tess. If they've been captive for long enough, tormented long enough, they all snap in the end. It's human nature to fold and fit into the current existence if constant fighting and refusal haven't worked."

Tess paced in front of him, reminding me how Elder couldn't stand still when venting his temper. Q, on the other hand, remained deathly calculating and unmovable.

"And what did the man say? Before you shot him?" Tess threw me an apologetic glance as if she could atone for her lover hurting mine.

Q replied carefully, "He said she was his and not to touch her."

"That's a lie," I hissed.

Both of them locked eyes on me before I could slap a hand over my mouth. I hadn't meant to intervene, but I couldn't let the truth stay untold.

Silence fell, begging me to fill it. I swallowed and spoke loud and clear with my chin held high and my heart singing with loyalty. "He said he loved me, too. That you were making a huge mistake."

"Huge *fucking* mistake, I believe were his words of choice," Q muttered. "But once again, it's nothing I haven't heard before. They all say that when I come to take away their property."

"I wasn't his property." I bristled. "I *meant* something to him."

"And you think property means nothing to men like him?" Q looked at me as if I knew nothing of the world and needed teaching, fast. "That he didn't value you or even love you in some twisted way? Of course, he did. You were worth everything to him because with you he could be free. He could embrace the creature he truly was and no longer hide. He could hurt you behind closed doors—take you however he damn well wanted—and no one would know. He could be the monster he forever denied himself." His voice cracked as if he spoke from aching experience.

Shaking his head, he spat, "Enough. I don't have the patience for this." Glowering at his wife, he added, "You were the one who wanted to be in charge of rehabilitation, Tess. You agreed that you'd help heal their minds while I saved their bodies. Don't drag me into one of your therapy sessions—"

Tess screeched under her breath as if she couldn't stand his obtuseness. I honestly didn't know how she had the patience to deal with him—let alone marry him. "You don't get it. Normally, you're right. Normally, you would've done the right thing. But this time...instead of listening, *truly* listening...you painted everyone with the same brush. You only saw an abused slave professing her love for a man who repeated her sentiments—same as before but not the same, Q. This time, it wasn't a lie. This time it was real and instead of seeing that...you destroyed it."

Slowly, the black disapproval on Q's face faded. He gave me a look bordering aloof uncaring and desperate apology.

Tess continued, "You fucked up, my love. And we need to fix it. If it's even possible."

His gaze snapped to hers. His lips parted, and a stream of French erupted.

My ears throbbed with the bruised romance falling from his mouth, threading with argument, demanding more proof perhaps, giving himself more time before fully accepting his crimes.

My heart searched for a translator, clutching at phrases I could never spell let alone remember to look up later. Whatever they spoke about, their feet guided them closer until their hands reached for each other and their matching tension evaporated as if touching reminded them they were on the same side. That they were together, regardless if Elder and I were.

They still have each other.

And that butchered me to be so alone and lost and absolutely terrified that Elder hadn't survived what this man had done to him.

Angry, hot tears glassed my vision as I struggled not to cry. Tess might forgive him, but I never could. My body wracked with silent sobs and I did everything I could to stay stoic on their couch, but as their voices switched to decibels full of love and forgiveness, my lip wobbled, and I gave up the fight.

Covering my face with my hands, I sank teeth into my traitorous lip and gagged on salty tears.

I will not cry.

I will not cry.

My eyes somehow managed to obey, but my body continued to sob. My shoulders quaking silently. My screamed despair once again mute.

Blind to the two people putting on a performance before me, my ears twitched as Tess switched French for English, "The day you met me, you didn't let prior interactions twist who I truly was. You saw me that day, *maître*. Now, I'm asking you to see Pimlico and her situation without the mess of the past few decades."

I glanced up as Tess looked at her baby on the carpet then linked her arm through Q's to guide him closer to me. The dog raised its head, wagging its tail before snuggling back into slumber.

No one spoke.

No one breathed.

We only stared and studied and tried to see past first impressions of me being the victim and him being the instrument of my heartbreak.

Q looked, truly looked. The stripping back of who I was hurt as he took in my dress, my hair, my face, my penny bracelet tinkling quietly on my wrist whenever I moved.

Finally, he sighed. "I believe my wife. I didn't study you last night, but now...it's obvious."

Before I could ask what was obvious, he waved his hand. "Your wounds are old; your scars are healed. You look like a girl who's been rescued months ago." His gaze fell on my penny bracelet. "Slaves are permitted gifts, but it's normally something the master gains equal pleasure from. That bracelet...it's from him, isn't it?"

My stomach hollowed out as I cupped the diamond inlaid circlet, my mind full of Elder and the Phantom and every moment I'd fallen in love with him.

I didn't know what to say so stayed silent, but gave a single nod—an acceptance of his white flag, an acknowledgement that my hate might never go away but I was strong enough to be civil.

"Somehow, I doubt he only thought of your worth in pennies." He pinched the bridge of his nose as if a headache suddenly skewered him. "He probably called you his Dollar Duchess or something just as sickening. He probably showered you with gifts because he was so in love with you. *Fuck...*" Looking at the ceiling, he muttered, "*Je suis désolé*. It seems I've made a terrible mistake."

My ears rang, disbelieving that this man who'd destroyed my life yesterday apologised so heartfelt today.

But it doesn't matter.

He could be as regretful as anyone, but it wouldn't bring Elder back. It wouldn't reincarnate the dead if his shot had been true and Elder's life stolen.

Tess gave me a look as if begging me to absolve him. As if this man would care what I thought.

But I couldn't.

Not yet.

And never if Elder was dead.

If he was alive and we were reunited, then maybe, possibly, hopefully in the future I could let go of my loathing.

But not right now.

Dipping my chin, I wrapped my arms around my waist, flinching as my pennies tinkled, and Q winced as if I'd physically slapped him.

Wrenching from Tess's hold, he reached into his back pocket and held out a glossy black cell phone. "Call him. I know where I shot him. I didn't hit his heart. It wouldn't have been my bullet to kill him—" He bent closer, urging me to take his phone. "Please, call him. Let me fix this."

I sat frozen.

It wouldn't have been my bullet to kill him.

That might've been true, but he hadn't finished that sentence. He hadn't added who else would've killed Elder. If he hadn't arrived when he did, the Chinmoku would've killed Elder without a doubt.

Q had been the Grim Reaper's servant who'd arrived to kill what was mine but somehow saved his life instead.

He could've held that over me. He could've reminded me that I'd been in the clutches of yet more peril and Elder slowly dying.

But he didn't.

He stood there accepting full responsibly when really...the blame wasn't entirely on his shoulders. If anything, he deserved my thanks.

I choked on the idea of an apology. I wasn't in the right place to do such a thing but, perhaps, I could stop cursing him so much.

"*S'il vous plaît.*" He dropped the phone onto my skirts. "Call him."

The oddest sensation of ludicrous laughter bubbled in my chest. How awfully coincidental—how similar to the first night with Elder when he'd offered his cell phone to call my mother and her line had been discontinued.

Now, I had the means to call Elder and didn't know his

number.

Fate's cruel joke.

Q pursed his lips. "You don't know how to contact him...do you?"

I shook my head, the bubbles of crazed laugher fading inside. "Not by phone. No."

"How then?"

I looked up. "His yacht."

"The Phantom?"

"Yes." Glancing at Tess, her child, then back to Q, I added, "Find out where the Phantom is. Send a radio call. His captain, Jolfer, will answer. I know he will."

My thoughts left the couch, galloping into scenarios.

Of Jolfer saying Elder was dead.

Of Jolfer saying I no longer had a home.

Of Jolfer saying...*he's alive.*

Of Jolfer saying Elder had figured out who Q Mercer was and was coming for me.

The laugher bubbles returned full force. I let a few escape as I glanced at Q with almost pity.

He scowled, tilting his head. "What is it?"

"If what you say is true and Elder is alive—and I very much hope he is—I suspect you'll find he's closer than you think."

Q frowned. "He is close. He's in England."

"Wrong." I let the hope in my heart blossom, giddy with the anticipation of seeing Elder and apprehension at what he would do when he found me.

This happy family. This man who pumped lead into my lover. True love was a fiendish defender and didn't take attempted murder lightly.

Where would I stand?

Defending them for Q's strange role in saving my virtue or standing by and permitting Elder to beat him bloody?

I didn't know yet.

I wouldn't know until I heard the blessed words...*he's alive.*

For now, all I could do was deliver a warning. A hint that Elder held karma highly, and it wouldn't matter that Q had helped defeat the Chinmoku.

He'd taken me.

That was punishable by agony.

Holding Q's green eyes, I murmured, "If he's breathing, I'd bet you my life he's already in France."

ELDER

FUCK.
How much longer would it take to find those bastards? With every ticking minute, I couldn't ignore images of Pim being tortured, Pim being sold, Pim being raped.

I trembled with a mix of fever, agony, and out of control rage at letting her down.

As minutes turned to hours, more and more pain layered, more and more guilt suffocated.

Goddammit, I can't just sit here anymore.

I was doing everything I could—enlisting every hack, contacting every narc, but sitting still felt as if I didn't care. As if knowing she was out there with strangers wasn't the most urgent, heart-shattering problem I'd ever had to solve in my life.

Hoisting my broken ass from my chair, I slammed my laptop closed.

Fuck it.

I couldn't stay here anymore. I had to be out there—storming the streets and physically hunting. *Anything* to keep my mind from spinning into deep, dark places.

Hobbling from my work-station, I flinched as my cell phone rang, chirping across my desk. The sounds of Calais couldn't drown out the piercing ring as I snatched it and fumbled to answer.

The screen showed it was a patched intercom call from the bridge.

Not what I wanted.

I wanted a tip from a blocked number from a snitch on Calais streets. I wanted a criminal spilling an address for his reward.

My temper frayed, but I pressed the phone against my ear. "What is it, Jolfer? Be quick."

If it had anything to do with docking issues or pier fees, I wasn't fucking interested. I wasn't moving from this wharf until I had Pim. End of story.

"Just received an interesting radio communication."

"Interesting how?" My heart rate spiked at a thousand miles a second.

"A man named Mercer. Said he made a mistake and has something of yours. Gave an address."

The world stood still.

I stopped breathing.

I stopped hurting.

"Hold on."

Hopping back to my laptop, I wrenched open the lid and waited for the web browser to pop up. One-handedly, I typed in the name Mercer and pressed enter.

Immediately, images of the same bastard who'd mowed down the Chinmoku, myself, and my cello, stared arrogantly back.

My eyes skimmed contradicting articles. Some claimed he was France's golden boy with more charities and good will to his name than the goddamn Queen. Others called him a ruthless psychopath. An abuser of slaves. The lowest form of scum.

A two-faced bastard.

Same as all the rest.

"The address?"

Jolfer cleared his throat. "A chateau in Blois."

"How far away?"

"According to my calculations, four to five hours by car."

Way too long.

"And by air?"

"About an hour and a half, give or take."

Still too long. But my only option.

"Tell Martin to prep the helicopter."

"Right-o."

I hung up.

I didn't know what sick game this bastard was playing or what fire-power would welcome me. I didn't know how I'd overcome my injuries to deliver the vengeance he was owed, or what I'd do once I'd delivered it.

But I didn't care.

I had an address.

Pimlico was at that address.

And I was taking war right to their doorstep.

Pimlico

I COULDN'T STAY still.

The short conversation Q had had with Jolfer wasn't nearly enough. He'd said his name, that a mistake had been made, and reeled off an address, then almost hung up before I swooped from the couch and tugged his suit sleeve.

He'd looked at my fear and barked into the phone. "Is he alive?"

Jolfer's voice had reached my ears the same time as Q's. "Yes."

Yes!

A single word that packed such a punch.

I toppled backward onto soft cushions, my skirts billowing around me.

Yes, he's alive.
Yes, he's coming.
Yes, I'm not alone.

Nothing else mattered after that.

After Q hung up, Tess somehow encouraged me off the couch and guided me upstairs.

But my mind stayed stuck on *yes, yes, yes.*

He's alive!

I wished Q hadn't hung up so fast. I wished he'd asked

where the Phantom was, what sort of condition Elder was in, if the crew were unhurt from the Chinmoku's attack, and why Selix hadn't been there fighting beside us.

So many questions, but for now, all I knew was he was alive. He knew where I was.

I'll see him soon.

Once again, that was both an incredible and terrifying thought.

Tess escorted me, her gentle murmurings about having to feed her son and how I should shower and dress in preparation for Elder's arrival flitting around my head.

Climbing the stairs, she'd given me a quick history lesson (that wasn't fully listened to) as if determined to put me at ease in this strange place. She repeated that Q saved women and brought them here to heal until they were happy to return to their families. How my bedroom and many others like it were stocked with everything a normal girl would recognise after being denied for so long—cosmetics, clothes, entertainment, safety. She hinted at the long, arduous journey of reminding them how to exist as *someone* instead of *something*.

I wanted to care enough to ask questions and be grateful for their kindness but knowing Elder was alive was infinitely better than thinking he was dead and that took precedence.

However, as Tess chatted my bleakness from before slowly crept over my happiness, shadowing it in doubt.

Was Elder alive?

Could Jolfer have lied?

It didn't matter Q believed he hadn't aimed correctly and missed Elder's heart. I'd heard the shot, I'd seen a spray of blood, I'd watched him tumble overboard. Until I physically kissed him, touched him, heard his gorgeous voice, my heart stubbornly ignored truth's sweet promise.

Probably because if anything happened, or if by some horror Elder died on his journey to claim me, then I didn't want to shatter into a million pieces after floating in false happiness.

Nudging me toward the bathroom, Tess headed for the wardrobe full of clothing in multiple sizes that I'd discounted the moment I'd awoken. "I know they're not high fashion or all that pretty, but at least you'll be clean and warm." Selecting a pair of jeans and a soft grey jumper, along with a white t-shirt for underneath and black cotton knickers, she held them up, roughly judging my size. "These will do, I think."

Disappearing into the bathroom to deposit the items, she smiled on her way back out. "Shower then come downstairs and we'll eat." Moving toward the exit, she pushed the door wide, blatantly showing that I wasn't a prisoner, despite my earlier conclusions. "See? No locks. No gimmicks. I know after the life you've led, it's hard to trust, but this isn't a ploy or some sick act to get you to relax. I hope you understand that."

Giving me a quick wave, she vanished down the corridor, leaving me with a silence that didn't know if it should throb with despair or shimmer with happiness.

* * * * *

By the time I'd showered, dressed, and padded downstairs, my heart smoked from beating so hard.

With every minute that ticked past, I wondered if this was the minute Elder would arrive.

Or this one.

Or the next one.

How far away is he?

How much longer until all hell broke loose in this gorgeous family chateau?

Jolfer had given Q no word of travel time or arrival expectation. He hadn't mentioned if they'd be travelling tonight or a week from now.

If Elder was badly injured, they might stay away for his safety before attending to mine—especially if he was unconscious to make the call to come for me.

God, I'm exhausted.

I couldn't rest because I didn't know what the future would unravel. I couldn't make friends because I didn't know if they should still be my enemies. Anarchy could happen or a truce could form.

Already, my insides clenched at the thought of more bloodshed. Good intentions had led to bad screw-ups. Was it right that pain must be the price, or could I somehow reason with Elder?

And if I *could* reason with him...did I have the right to take away the ending he would need to assure himself I was safe?

Ah, be quiet, Pim. You're driving yourself mad.

Rubbing my temples, I crossed the foyer and entered the warm lounge where floor lamps glowed and a fire roared. Immediately, I searched the corners of the room for Q.

Did I owe him enough to warn him that Elder had a helicopter? Did I give him a heads-up that my lover had a temper and share the grisly story of what'd happened to the last men who hurt me—that they were now bloated and decomposing corpses in a house somewhere in Crete?

As much as I hated Q for shooting Elder, I didn't want this family to suffer. Q didn't deserve to die for his mistake, and his wife and son definitely didn't deserve to be punished.

Running my fingers along the hem of my newly acquired grey jumper, I made a promise to intercept Elder when he arrived. I'd tell him as quickly as I could that it wasn't what he thought and to listen to me.

I'd do my best to end this nightmare peacefully.

Then again, perhaps Elder was in a hospital somewhere and all my worry was for nothing. Selix or Jolfer might be the ones to take me home, and they would be more open to discussion.

Home...

Terrifying to think if Elder had died, the Phantom was no longer my home. I would've lost everything I'd come to love all in one night.

My morbid thoughts tormented me as I stole into the kitchen and unwillingly gate-crashed dinnertime with Tess's son.

Q wasn't around, but Tess sat on a barstool in front of the high chair holding her baby, pulling strange faces and making airplane noises while swooping a spoon with mashed orange goo into the boy's mouth.

He gurgled as his toothless gums chomped on the spoon, most of it hitting his bib and only some providing nourishment for the uncoordinated child.

I gasped as a fissuring hunger ripped through me. Hunger, not for food, but for the mess sitting in the high chair and looking at his mother with utmost adoration. What would it feel like to be the moon and stars and everything in between to a creature you created?

I can't be here.

I can't watch this.

Backing up, I tripped over a damn dog toy. I hissed between my teeth as pain ripped through my ankle.

Tess looked up. "Ah, did you have a good shower? You look nice. Not as grand as your ballgown but the grey suits you. Brings out the hazel in your eyes."

Scooping up more orange mash, she wiped the excess off the spoon onto the glass bowl she held. "Don't run away. You're welcome to join us if you want."

Words? Had I once spoken words?

I was mute through and through, terrified of the opportunity to spend time with her infant. I didn't know if I wanted to bolt away or snatch him.

She grinned, following my eyes as they locked onto the messy baby. "Abelino."

The strange word wriggled through my emotional tangle. "Excuse me?"

She cupped her child's cheek, smearing away stray orange. "His name is Abelino. Lino for short."

"Oh."

"It's French. Long story." She layered more dinner onto the spoon and managed to get it into her son's mouth without too much of it smearing his face. "Do you—" She flinched.

"Sorry, extremely insensitive question." Flashing me a pained look, she murmured, "I've long since learned not to ask women who stay with us if they have children."

Lino babbled something, his tiny hands opening and closing as Tess guided more food his way.

Staring at him but talking to me, she said, "Sometimes, I think having Lino around does more harm than good when they're healing."

The thought of running away faded, thanks to Tess's humanity and the uncertainty in her voice.

Moving closer, I dared ask something I already knew had no good answer. "Why?"

She flashed me a glance. "Well, if they're old enough to have children before they were stolen, then they've missed out on potentially years of their upbringing. To their family, they were dead only to come back broken and possibly never able to be the mum they remembered." She shrugged helplessly. "And if they didn't have children before their abduction but do *now*.... Well, that means those infants were born of pain and torture to men who made their lives living hell."

Swiping a tissue over Lino's little lips, she sighed heavily. "Life is never easy."

Silence fell for a time, our thoughts on the complications of lust and betrayal.

Finally, I said, "But love...that is easy." I twirled the spare fork in front of me on the kitchen bench. "Or at least...giving it is easy. Earning it can sometimes be incredibly hard."

She nodded. "You're right."

I wanted to ask more of how she'd not only been sold to Q but fallen in love and married him, but a loud hum rapidly built to a buzzing crescendo outside.

What on earth...

"Uh-oh." Tess checked Lino was tightly strapped into his booster seat then gave me a sharp look. "This man of yours...he doesn't happen to have a helicopter, does he?"

My heart coughed as my head whipped to face the large

glass doors leading to the garden.

Night had fallen, and our reflection bounced back rather than manicured lawns and trimmed bushes.

A flash of light appeared, spotlighting the paddock in the distance.

The buzzing grew louder.

Oh, my God.

He's here.

Tess wrapped arms around herself. "I'm assuming by your silence that's the man you call Elder?" She marched to the patio doors. "Crap, I don't know where Q is."

Looking at me over her shoulder, she scowled. "You'd better tell me...how bad is this going to be?"

Drifting forward, I slotted myself beside her, mimicking her stance and hugging myself.

How bad is this going to be?

I swallowed hard. "I honestly don't know."

"Oh, I do." Tess rolled her eyes. "They're men. They're morons when it comes to defending honour and all that bullshit." She huffed. "I wish Q wasn't lurking around somewhere. If we could keep them apart, this would all go a lot smoother."

I agreed with her even as my heart blew iridescent bubbles, filling my ribcage with happiness. I struggled to stay rational. Last time I'd seen Elder, he'd limped and looked worse for wear—and that was thanks to the Chinmoku before Q ever shot him.

I'm asking for a miracle if I expect him to be here, let alone walk without assistance.

Selix had probably banned him from coming.

Even as the thought appeared, my common sense discarded it. If Elder was awake, no one could tell him what to do—and therein lay the problem.

Slowly, the helicopter descended from sky to grass, its rotors diminishing in speed once on the ground. Almost immediately, the side fuselage slid open and Selix hopped out.

I needed to know the story of where he'd been while the Chinmoku attacked, but for now, my mind was on a single thread.

Elder...did he come, too?

My fingers pressed against the glass, doing my best to see past my reflection and the brightly lit lounge to focus on whether the helicopter had brought any other visitors.

No one.

No flicker of legs or flash of hands.

My heart plummeted.

And then...he appeared.

A small grateful moan escaped.

Where Selix had leapt out, Elder gingerly climbed. Where Selix darted around, Elder painfully stalked.

He was naturally graceful from his martial arts and exotic breeding, but tonight, he reminded me of the tin man from *The Wizard of Oz* badly in need of oil and rest.

I winced as he stumbled then doggedly continued across the lawn toward us.

I couldn't stand here and not run to him. I couldn't watch him hurt and not offer aid.

Fumbling with the door handle, I flicked the lock and practically fell out of the house.

"Wait!" Tess called. "We need to think this through!"

She was right. We *did* need to think this through. But I'd done far too much thinking and knew where my loyalties lay.

With him.

Tripping once in haste, I found my legs and bolted across the patio.

The pretty flower beds and bird tables were nothing as I traded tiles for grass and added every inch of speed I could muster.

Elder's head snapped up as I galloped toward him. His limp turned quicker, one hand fisted by his side while his other stayed strapped to his chest. Something bulky wrapped around his ankle, preventing speed. More bandages and splints only made me run faster.

My lungs gasped and my legs burned, and when I was in touching distance, I slammed to a stop, breathing hard, eyes wide, lips parted.

I wanted to throw myself at him and delete the horrible distance. I wanted to kiss every inch of his bruised, beautiful face and finally convince my pessimism that he was alive and not a ghost.

But I swayed on the spot, unable to grab him for fear of adding yet more pain.

Up close, the lines around his gorgeous black eyes and furrows on his brow hinted at how much this excursion taxed him. A faint sheen of fever pinked his face, saying he wasn't as invincible as he seemed.

His eyebrow rose, studying me with parted lips; his black hair tussled and wind swept from the still roaring helicopter blades.

Every emotion and reaction and spark and connection fizzed in the air between us—tangible, visible, almost alive with delicious taste.

For an endless second, we didn't speak. We just reacquainted that his soul was mine and mine was his and not even death could part us.

Slowly, his head tipped down, lowering his brow, shadowing his eyes. His uninjured arm came up as he stepped across the final space. "Pim…"

And whatever spell I'd been in popped, collapsing me into his one-armed embrace.

Pressing my nose into his unique incense smell, I forced my shakes to subside.

His arm twitched possessively, jerking me harder. His neck bent, and his face burrowed into my freshly washed hair.

I gripped his waist, raising my head, needing more to this hello.

Understanding, his chin raised, just enough to guide his lips to my jaw, to my cheek, to my lips. His warm mouth claimed mine, and I melted.

Our tongues danced instantly, kissing deep and uncaring about location or circumstance.

We might not care, but unfortunately, it didn't mean other people didn't.

Selix didn't permit even a few seconds of kissing before breaking us apart with a stern reprimand. "Prest. Unfinished business, remember?" He gave me an apologetic smile. "I'm glad you're alive, Pim, but we have other things to take care of before—"

"Oh, don't worry, Selix. I remember." Elder's body twitched from loving to brutal. He pulled away, capturing my hand instead of my body. "Where is he, Pim?" He squeezed my fingers hard. "Where is the bastard?"

I blinked. I knew who he meant. I understood the blackness in his gaze. I foresaw what would happen the moment he and Q came face to face. And as much as I wanted him to teach Q a lesson, so next time he might listen if a girl spoke the truth, I didn't want more violence or Tess getting hurt.

And she would be hurt.

No one would enjoy their husband being mauled by another. No matter how justified.

"El...don't. Let's just go home—"

"*What?*" The blackness on his face deepened, his temper slashing. "What did you just say? Go *home*? After he almost ruined *everything*?" He laughed low and cruel. "Not going to happen. He has to pay, little mouse. No negotiations."

I fought the need to submit to his rage. To step aside and let him march into Mercer's home and teach him a lesson—if he even could with his injuries. But instead, I fought my programming and stood my ground. "He made a mistake. He apologised. I accepted that apology for both of us. You're hurt and need to rest. Picking a fight is stupid."

His nostrils flared, rage overflowing from me belittlingly his need to balance out honour.

Saying it was stupid probably wasn't the best thing.

Laying my hand on his good arm, I tried again. "Please, El, I don't want you hurt more than you already are." I threw a fleeting look at Tess standing silhouetted in the window with Lino on her hip. I owed it to them to make Elder see reason.

His voice whispered deathly calm. "I can't decide if you want me to go home like a defeated asshole for *my* safety or for *his*. You should know, Pim, a few broken bones and whatever other shit the Chinmoku did to me won't stop me in the slightest once I find the fucker."

Ugh, I sucked at this. "I'm not calling you weak, Elder. I'm not saying you can't kick his ass. It's because I believe you *can*—even battered like you are—that I'm asking you to be reasonable." I waved my hand at the mother and child behind me. "He has a family. He made a mistake and apologised. We need to let it go…for everyone involved."

"Oh, I'll let it go." He chuckled. "Once he knows he never had the right to take you."

"But he thought—"

"I don't care what he thought, Pim. It's what he *did* that counts."

"And what he did was justified in his mind. He saves slaves—"

Elder turned positively monstrous. "Saves slaves? So he thought I was keeping you against your will? That I'd somehow forced you to fall in love with me? That what I feel for you must be a sick joke? That I'm fucking *Alrik*?"

He laughed at the stars. "That goddamn cocksucker."

Cracking his neck, he tore at the sling over his arm and threw it to the ground. Shaking out his limb and ignoring whatever injury needed the contraption to heal, he barged past me. "I'll show him—"

I stumbled as his shoulder clipped me. Before, he'd revealed the level of discomfort he was in. Now…there was no limp. No hint of weakness just *war*.

"No, wait—"

A rumbling growl escaped Elder as I spun to go after him.

I slammed to a halt, locking eyes with what he'd fixated on, sinking fast beneath the knowledge that I'd failed and no words could stop what was about to happen.

Oh, no.

Standing brazen and unfazed, framed by the wide open front door was Q Mercer.

Tess flew from the lounge and spoke frantically, trying to slap sense into her husband just like I'd failed with Elder.

Q merely ignored her with his hands in his pockets and waited. His posture lethal just like Elder's. His temper unfurled and ready to defend his territory and woman, no matter the cost.

Elder stalked, cursing under his breath, sounding more and more dragon as he approached.

I chased after him, but Selix grabbed my bicep, incinerating me with a look that froze me to the spot. "You are not to interfere. You can't. He needs to do this."

"He doesn't need to do anything." Ripping my gaze from his, I called after Elder. "Elder, please! *Please*, don't do this."

But he didn't turn around.

He didn't stop.

With ears deaf and mind on retribution, he prowled toward his enemy.

ELDER

I'D KILL HIM.

I didn't care I had injuries slowing me down and there was no logical, realistic way I could fight, let alone win.

I didn't care Pimlico had taken his side over mine even though it fucking cleaved me in two.

I didn't care I might pass out from fever and agony halfway through the battle and lose.

I had to do this to avenge Pim, to prove to myself I hadn't let her down, and balance whatever scales I'd ruined with my fuck-ups.

Q Mercer was a dead man.

That was all there was to it.

If I died in the process of delivering that sentence...*so be it*.

The ankle boot around my leg hindered my prowl, but as I sank deeper into war lust, I no longer felt the bone throb beneath. That was the thing about fighting—it was a drug. As consuming as marijuana; as cloying and addictive as any contraband.

I no longer thought about what was possible but only what I needed to do.

Kill him.

Knowing I was on the cusp of violence deleted everything unnecessary out of comprehension. I had two fists (minus a broken finger). I had two arms (minus a bullet tear in my shoulder). I had two legs—

Fuck it, this asshole doesn't stand a chance even with my handicaps.

And he was an asshole.

Instead of coming to meet me—entering this duel and taking his punishment like a goddamn man, he remained steadfast in the doorway, gatekeeper to his home and anyone stupid enough to care for him.

A woman flittered around him with something bulky bouncing on her hip, only for a petite girl in a maid's uniform to yank her deeper into the house.

Left alone, Mercer didn't move; he merely watched me waste precious energy traversing his lawn.

Bastard.

I could shout profanities at him. I could murder him with words. But he knew what he'd done.

He'd pulled the trigger. I'd ended up in pieces. It was his turn to know what that felt like.

With only a few metres separating us, the bastard had the gall to say, "You're hurt, Mr. Prest. I suggest you stop before you begin. I'm not opposed to hurting you some more if you try to enter my home with violence."

I didn't reply.

Pity for him I wasn't afraid and I'd stopped doubting my odds at winning in my current state. I had fury on my side, and it was a vicious instructor when it came to survival.

He could be a great fighter for all I knew. He could have mastered martial arts like I had. But unlike me, he'd been taught with rules and parameters in place. When I'd learned to fight, the Chinmoku had taken the rule book and shredded it with a machete.

I could beat him with a fractured ankle and busted elbow and any other malady without even breaking a sweat.

Three metres remaining.

Two metres.

One.

My hands locked into fists, my distended finger bellowing at being forced to curl. After this, I'd need another splint after throwing the last one on the helicopter floor, but for now...it had a job to do just like the rest of my body.

I swung before I'd even climbed the top step.

His eyes flared as he staggered backward, my blow striking his cheekbone.

If he'd expected some sort of conversation or ceremony before I began, he knew now I had no such intention.

The crunch of his face ricocheted up my arm as I stomped into his home, inhaling lemon and leather and baking.

"You fucking took what wasn't yours to take." I breathed hard, already drunk on what I would do, how I would parry, what death I would deliver. "You shot my cello. You tampered with my world. Prepare to die."

A woman's shout echoed through the house followed by the screech of something animal-like.

Mercer removed his hands from his pockets, and spat a mouthful of blood onto the white tiles. "Don't look so smug, Prest." His eyes narrowed. "I gave you that one. I'm apologetic enough to allow you to draw blood. But heed my warning when I say it won't happen again."

"Good." I swung, missing him by a hair's breadth as he ducked. *Fucker is fast.* "I don't listen to warnings. Never have."

Mercer ducked to the side, avoiding another volley.

With his hands free from his pockets, he raised them like a boxer. If he'd had training, it wasn't professional. He looked as if he favoured knives and shanking his enemies rather than the old-fashioned way of blows.

He returned my punch, wielding it with a precision I hadn't expected.

I arched backward, narrowly missing being pummelled in the nose.

His face lost its French arrogance, reforming into a mask of cold-hearted evil.

We didn't speak again as we circled each other.

I catalogued him with more respect, seeking his weaknesses and finding none. He studied me as a slaughterer would study the pig it was about to skin.

No soul left in his eyes. No compassion.

Just sheer-minded aggression.

I actually relaxed.

Men like him I knew. I spoke their language. It meant he was a worthy opponent. And when I handed his ass to him, it would be worth the new aches and bruises I'd undoubtedly be covered with.

Our assessment of each other happened in a split second—one breath and we knew all we needed about the other. As much as I didn't want to admit, we were cut from the same cloth. Both outsiders to a world where love and friendship were the norms.

Somehow, I believed he'd missed out on that elusive feeling for most of his life—same as me. He'd been lonely—same as me. He'd channelled such flaws into unsatisfactory attributes—same as me.

But that was where our similarities ended.

He'd taken what wasn't his to take.

That was treason and deserved consequence.

Forgetting the pain coursing through my blood, I inhaled deeply and let go.

I sank.

I embraced.

I round-housed him with my fractured ankle and swallowed the groan of agony.

He flew backward, landing on one knee, gasping as his lungs collapsed.

I advanced, ready to make short work of this. I wanted him to die so I could earn forgiveness for my crimes.

However, he soared up, sucker-punching me in the ribs.

I fought my body's natural response to curl around the injury. Absorbing the fresh pain, I struck him again.

Die. Just die.

Time blurred as we danced in his foyer. He met me blow for blow—some landing, some not. His punches power-delivered and sharp-fast, but he still wasn't as quick as I was.

We circled and snarled. We kicked and punched.

He struck with hard fists, breaking the thin skin on my forehead and sending a river of blood into my eyes. But it didn't stop me from advancing—always advancing.

I was right when I thought him a worthy opponent. I was the better fighter. But he had a talent I hadn't pre-empted—a talent that meant he not only stayed alive but also became more adapt at kicking my ass the longer we warred.

He watched and learned.

When I threw a crane kick followed by a sequence of Kung Fu chops designed to eliminate the enemy's ability to breathe, he threw the same combination back at me—slightly sloppy and with untrained power—but enough to stop me from gaining ground.

Our breathing mixed with grunts and groans as we gave up our stance as men and returned to our natural state as beasts.

I threw a mismatch of uppercuts. He kicked at my knee caps.

Somewhere in our fight, the sound of women's pleas rang. Men's shouts tried to interrupt the roar in my head of win, win, *win*. But Mercer didn't look away, and neither did I.

Punch.

Kick.

Fight.

Die, motherfucker, die.

All I knew was bone-crippling pain and a swimming mind. My ingrained skills at battling were the only thing marshalling my trembling limbs into action.

Every punch, a sickness bubbled in my veins.

Every kick, a weakness crept along my skin.

I wasn't losing to him. I was losing to the fever and prior wounds steadily stripping me of power and stamina. I just hoped he couldn't see how close I was to losing my grip on this reality.

My vision danced with spots and not from his punches.

My ears popped and affected my balance and not from his uppercuts.

It was my own goddamn body slowly condemning me.

Every injury, every gunshot and stitch and scab leeched me of my normal endurance.

Perhaps Selix was right, and I didn't stand a hope of success. But I had to try for Pim. I had to prove to her—even if it was subconsciously—that I was still man enough to take care of her. Still feral and dangerous enough to keep the monsters of her past at bay.

And I'm fucking failing.

I struck harder, quicker, crueller.

Mercer gasped for breath, a mixture of blood and spit marring his chin.

Unprepared for yet another level of chaos, he lost ground quickly.

Tasting victory, I added yet another layer of crazy, throwing everything I had left, begging the fever in my blood to leave me alone and for my broken body to behave just a little fucking longer.

But for every step Mercer lost, he gained an inch. His focus switched from defending himself to studying my slovenly swings, then doing his best to deliver it back to me.

His dark hair shone under the foyer lights as I backed him closer to a corner, straining for the finish line where I was the victor, he was dead, and Pim was safe once again.

He was good. Better than good.

But I was better still.

But I was also faking it.

My vision only showed shadows now not full detail. My ears no longer worked. My hands numb. My body a dead weight with injury. I'd been unconscious enough in my life to recognise the warning signs: the chugging breathing but still dying for oxygen. The rapid blinking but still stupidly blind.

I swung another fist, missing even though I was sure on trajectory. It gave Mercer enough time to get one over me, connecting squarely with my temple.

I groaned, slipping closer to the empty cavern inside, greedily pulling me from all angles.

He struck again.

I managed to block and deliver my own temple dusting blow.

Then something wriggled out the corner of my eye, distracting Q just enough for me to land a square pummel to his cheekbone.

He fell to his knees, shaking his head. Blood ran from his nose and corner of his mouth.

I stumbled on the spot, half-awake but mostly dead. Had I won? Did I want to kill him, or was this enough? Would I be satisfied having him kneel, or did I need him in a coffin?

Before I could decide, he spat a wad of blood onto the floor and something triggered in him.

He charged up, growling like a deranged animal, ramming his shoulder into my ribcage and hurling me backward.

I slammed to the ground, utterly robbed of air as my cracked ribs threatened to puncture my lungs.

Sensing my weakness, Mercer straddled me, pressing his knees onto my biceps and pulling out a sharp knife from his waistband.

He had a knife this entire time?

Poor form, fucking cheater.

"Enough." Pressing the sharp blade against my throat, he hissed, "I said *enough*."

Our eyes tangled.

Wolf to wolf.

Dragon to dragon.

I would decide when enough was enough, and this wasn't it.

With a colossal burst of strength and the final dregs of my

energy, I shoved him off me and slammed him onto his back.

Grabbing his neck, I snarled, "You didn't listen. You didn't see how much I fucking love her." Squeezing hard, I begged him to die. "You fucking shot me and took her from me, and now you'll pay the goddamn price."

His neck strained beneath my fingers, but he restrained himself from scrabbling at my arms. He stared steadfast while I strangled, understanding that this wasn't about what he'd done, but what *I'd* failed to do.

I hadn't protected Pimlico.

I'd deserved to be shot that night.

If it wasn't for him, the Chinmoku would've killed me and taken Pim. And that truth fucked me up because as much as I wanted to kill this bastard, I also owed him a debt of gratitude.

Men were dogs, and the ones involved with trafficking women ought to be put down with a bullet.

But not me.

And surprisingly, not him.

Beneath his ice-cold temper, there was humanity inside him.

If I needed any other proof, I got it when he glanced to his left, dragging my woozy attention to the audience we'd attracted.

Selix held a gun on a tallish French guy who had a gun trained on me. A standoff while we wrestled on the floor.

Neither Mercer nor myself cared about the men we called our friends. It was the women we called our soulmates who mattered.

Pim stood beside a woman slightly taller than her, their faces white and lips bitten. They hadn't intervened, but their matching terror spoke of panic barely kept in check.

The blonde couldn't tear her eyes off Mercer, her hands clutching at the baby crying on her hip.

Shit.

A baby.

Mercer is a goddamn father.

My fingers loosened around his throat, and my mind flickered, unable to fight the tug of blackness.

Feeling my pressure fall from around his larynx, Mercer shoved me off him and stood.

I followed even though it took everything I had left.

Every last shred of energy to stand, face my enemy, and swing one last time.

I swung.

I missed.

I lost consciousness and fell face first into oblivion.

* * * * *

The thick cesspool of fever broke just enough for me to crack open my eyes.

My heart galloped, searching for more energy to finish this fight. But I didn't wake on hard marble. And no bloody Frenchman waited to kick my ass.

The softest mattress cushioned me, and a gentle hand cupped my cheek.

Voices reached my ears before my vision cleared.

"I don't know. Should we call Michaels?" Pim's touch shook on my skin. "I knew he shouldn't have done this. Look at him." A catch in her voice hinted at a mix of rage and tears.

Goddammit, the fight couldn't be over. I couldn't be the pussy who passed out. I couldn't be the stupid little invalid comaed in bed.

Slowly, I shifted on the pillows, moving away from Pim's stroke.

Christ, that hurts.

She gasped as I groaned under my breath, throbbing with untold agony.

The bed rocked as she threw her arms around me. "Oh, thank goodness, you're okay."

Okay?

Of all the different layers of okay, I was at the very bottom of the spectrum.

Fuck, *everything* hurt.

I didn't hurt this much when I'd almost drowned in the harbour with an open bullet wound attracting sharks. I could barely think without succumbing to the numbing welcome of sleep.

What the hell is going on?

I didn't even have the energy to hug her back or inhale her gorgeous scent. Every heartbeat pumped blood into swollen extremities and pain-heated joints. Every wound was on fire. Every atom ablaze.

I wanted to snap my fingers and be well again. I wanted a joint. I wanted Pim alone so I could tame my scrambled sick-infested thoughts.

"Gave us a bit of a fright, Prest."

My eyes coasted upward. I jolted to find Pim wasn't the only nurse waiting for my ass to wake up.

Selix gave me a curt nod, his finger still latched around the trigger of his gun even though the muzzle pointed at the floor. "Glad you're awake. We have a bit of a problem."

Problem?

I wanted to demand he elaborate, but the metallic corrosion of blood on my tongue and pounding jaw meant I only managed an angry grunt.

He cocked his chin at Mercer standing at the foot of my bed with his wife and child. The other Frenchie, with his gun still trained on me, wouldn't lower it even when Mercer glowered at him in silent reprimand.

The blonde cuddled up to Mercer.

Never tearing his eyes off me, he kissed her hard, smearing his own blood over her mouth in some sinister declaration of love.

The contents of my stomach roiled from the hypocrisy of his kiss and the arrogant way he stared. He thought he'd won.

The bastard.

He hadn't.

Not by a long shot.

Round two, asshole.

At least, his face hinted at some damage with contusions and cuts.

Doing everything I could to mask how close I was to passing out again, I hoisted myself up to my elbows. The gunshot wound in my shoulder promised to rip me to shreds if I attempted to swing my fists again. "Th-this—" I coughed, wishing I could eradicate the fever-sweat drenching my forehead and dripping into my eyes. "This isn't over, Mercer."

His bodyguard twitched, his gun glinting blackly from the chandelier above. "We've all decided otherwise while you've been taking a nap in la-la land."

Mercer's wife smiled as sharp as her husband, handing over her son. Mercer opened his arm gingerly—almost as if he hurt as much as I did—accepting the squirming, fussy child who thankfully had stopped crying but had blotchy tomato red cheeks.

"It's done, Mr. Prest," his wife said. "It's over."

"It's not over until I say—"

Pim slotted herself beside me. "El, please, you can't fight anymore."

"Don't undermine me, woman." I shot her a harsh glower. "Especially in front of my enemies."

"Are you so sure I'm your enemy, Prest?" Mercer asked, bouncing his son as if the fact he was still covered in blood and bruises didn't matter when holding fresh innocence.

I refused to answer that.

He was my enemy, but he was also my saviour from the Chinmoku. Not killing him would be my way of showing thanks if he apologised for shooting me in the goddamn shoulder.

I flicked a look at the raised gun in my face. "Funny you say this is over when you still have your goon training a gun on me."

Mercer narrowed his eyes at his friend, reeling off snipped instructions in French.

The men argued for a few seconds before the henchman

lowered his weapon. He didn't holster it, though, nor did he put the safety on.

Selix gave him a look, keeping his own gun at the ready. A truce but not quite.

"It's finished. Whatever this was, it's over." Mercer stared pointedly. "You've proven I was wrong, and I've accepted that you had a right to attack me in my own home. But you also have to accept that I might have tried to kill you, but by doing so, I just so happened to save your life."

My eyes trailed to the baby boy in Mercer's arms. He seemed fascinated by the streak of crimson across his dad's cheek. Chubby fingers wiggled in the air to reach.

Mercer looked down and smirked as if he knew exactly why his offspring was fascinated with gore.

The seemingly normal domestic moment crippled me. It damn well took away all my power and arguments and memory of why I wanted to slaughter this man.

My fever crested hotter, sicker, sucking me back into a haze.

"I think you should go," the henchman growled. "You've enjoyed our hospitality long enough."

"He's knocking on death's door, Franco. We can't just throw him out." Mercer clucked his tongue. "Where's your European welcome?"

"In the gutter the moment he punched you."

The conversation twisted and turned until I no longer understood any of it. A spiral began in my head, a hypnotic circle—one I had to chase, growing dizzier and lighter the longer I tried to reach the spinning centre.

"Elder..." Pim's sweet voice sank into my ears, joining me on the downward spin. "Do you want to go home?"

Home...

Yes. Hell, yes.

Where painkillers and weed waited. Where Pim could be naked and I could be strong again.

I liked that idea a lot. It granted enough energy to believe I could walk out of there unassisted—enough lunacy to threaten Frenchmen with guns.

Slurring my words, I said, "Come shnear us again and zhI'll gut you."

Mercer nodded, cradling his child. "I have no reason to come after you now I know the truth."

"The truth I told you on the Phantom. The one you ignored and shot him anyway," Pim snipped, linking her fingers with mine despite the slippery blood coating me.

"Respectfully, if you've been speaking to my wife, you'll know why I couldn't trust what you were saying," Mercer replied in his thick accent.

Pim frowned. "I understand, but perhaps next time…you'll listen harder."

"Yes, Q. Listen." Mercer's wife piped up, siding with Pim. The two women smiled at each other as if they were on the same team and not on opposite ends of this war.

Mercer glanced as his wife, doing the same as me and trying to understand how our significant others had bonded while we'd done our best to exterminate each other.

And then, nothing else mattered as my heart gave in to the gush of fever, and my mind reached the centre of the swirling circle, and the spinning, spinning, spinning turned into a deep, endless black hole.

I was nothing but agony and fever, holes and hurting.

I tripped into unconscious and failed my woman for the second time.

Gone.
Nothing.
No One.

Pimlico

SIX HOURS.

Tess convinced me to give Elder six hours of uninterrupted rest.

No washing blood from his skin.

No stripping his body of clothes.

No food or water.

Just *rest*.

She promised me sleep would do what nothing else could. That Elder was so close to depleting everything he had left, nothing else mattered to his system but remaining unconscious long enough to stitch together the pieces he'd shredded.

She'd used case studies of women who'd come into her care from Q's vigilante hunts to convince me. Mentioning how some of them would sleep for weeks until they were mentally and physically ready to embark on the rest of their healing.

I knew from living with Alrik that sleeping had been the only thing he couldn't take from me. Sure, he could deprive me and torture me, keeping me awake for days, but when I finally slipped into slumber...well, Tess was right.

There, I healed just enough to face the next day. My bruises faded just enough to climb out of bed. My soul bandaged enough not to use the curtain cord to hang myself.

Elder would rest safe and unmolested.

And I would be there for him to tend and take care of the instant he awoke.

Reluctantly, I'd followed the crowd from my borrowed room and looked one final time at Elder, bundled beneath the bed covers and passed out cold.

Our footsteps had been hushed as we descended the stairs to find staff members wiping away globs of blood smeared on the foyer's floor.

A vase had shattered from someone barrelling into the side table. A framed picture had fallen from the wall and glass sprinkled like crystal dust everywhere.

In a daze, I'd accepted food—what, I couldn't remember. In a fugue, I'd counted the clock above the fireplace.

With my heart turning worrywart and nursemaid, it'd winged upstairs to never leave Elder's side even as I'd sat in the lounge and listened to the hushed French tones of Tess and Q's conversation.

No doubt they discussed Elder's condition, my circumstance, and how to get everyone home safely. There was no mention of kicking us out until Elder was able. Their hospitality after so much ill will made tears prick and nerves form.

Part of me wanted to go home—to return to the Phantom where Michaels could fix Elder and we could continue running from the Chinmoku. But the other part wanted to stay here where ancient castle walls were ten times thicker than any yacht and Elder could heal in the heart of it.

If he was here, the Chinmoku couldn't find him.

If he was here, he could get better before he had to fight again.

If the Chinmoku find him before he's healed...they'll kill him.

I choked on a worried gasp, my eyes soaring to the clock again.

Five hours.

Elder had rested for five hours. Could a miracle have

happened and broken bones and bullet holes no longer exist?

Dawn wasn't far off, and we'd overstayed our welcome already. Elder must be capable of surviving because I couldn't permit anything less.

Q had left the lounge an hour or so ago, and Tess appeared from the kitchen to join me on the couch.

Her voice remained hushed as if she was aware of the witching hour and all the nasties that lived within it. "*Maître* and I have come to an agreement. You and Elder are to stay here until he's healed. Don't think for a moment that just because day breaks you have to leave. Mrs Sucre loves any excuse to cook a feast, and her talent in the kitchen is bound to pile some healthy weight onto both of you."

The men might've called a truce (for now), but I didn't think that truce covered sharing food.

"Suzette, I'm sure, would love to talk to you more—now you're not using her as a hostage." Tess laughed. "And I, for one, would be happy to have someone I can talk to and not have to heal. It's a very rewarding life we lead, but sometimes…it would be nice not to have to worry about what I say in case it's incredibly painful for our guests."

I tore my eyes from the fire's flames to look at hers. The invitation to be her friend blew me away.

She smiled. "Of course, if that all sounds too much, then you can have food in your room and leave the moment Elder wakes."

I didn't know how to say how honoured I was. That the thought of talking—*truly talking*—was a dream come true, especially for a psychologist's daughter who'd been taught to verbalize her demons in order to tame them.

But all I focused on was Elder.

All I could think about was Elder.

He was where my thoughts and heart lay. He was my first and only priority. "You're very generous, and I'd love to say he'd accept your offer, but he won't want to stay."

She shrugged. "Is it really his choice when he can barely

speak, let alone move?"

"He'll be rude about it. He'll say something like '*I won't sleep in my enemy's house. Hell no.*' or something along those lines."

Tess nudged my shoulder with hers, laughing under her breath. "You sound like you know him well."

I cracked a smile. "I know enough to understand when he feels backed into a corner he snaps. He doesn't mean to be cruel or ungrateful; he's just so used to relying on himself. He refuses love and care from others as he can't bear to be hurt again."

"I know that feeling." She rested her head on the couch. "He won't change his mind on that matter. He won't be able to after a life of conditioning."

"So you're saying he'll forever need to be alone?" My heart squeezed. "That eventually, he'll push me away, too?"

She closed her eyes, shaking her head a little. "I said he wouldn't change *his* mind. It will always be there...that little survivalist telling him it's safer to be alone. But he won't be able to stop another changing it *for* him." She chuckled. "You've already done that. He fell in love with you. He's relying on you whether he wants to or not."

I fell silent, absorbing that revelation.

Tess murmured sleepily, "If you make this about you, he'll stay because he'll do anything you ask of him."

"I think you're over estimating his love—"

Her eyes snapped open. "I'm not. Believe me. And you know that's true. He almost died fighting for your honour. If you make it sound like staying here benefits you, he won't argue."

Patting my hand, she hauled herself to her feet. "I'm going to bed. I suggest you check on him, if only for your peace of mind. When six hours has passed, feel free to wake him and offer food and water. Perhaps a sponge bath would do him good as well."

With a soft laugh, she left me alone, and I returned to counting the clock.

* * * * *

The scent of unwashed male and coppery blood met my nose the moment I cracked open the door.

I swallowed hard, allowing my eyes to adjust to the darkness as I stepped into the room.

Dawn pinked the sky and the gardens dazzled with newness but shadows held supremacy in here, holding court and casting long fingers over Elder, cloaking his injuries.

He didn't stir as I turned and closed the door, holding my breath as I twisted the lock, and the soft click of it engaging echoed in the silent space.

Funny how only a few hours ago this door had been locked from the outside with enemies all around me. Now, I barricaded it from the inside with almost-friends keeping us safe.

I shivered from a sudden fear that he wouldn't want me here. That he wouldn't want me to see him like this even though it opened my heart to yet another level of love. Ever since he'd rescued me, I'd seen him as some immortal being who could slay anything and conquer anyone.

To see him this...*human* made me tumble all the way down from puppy love to bone-deep forever love. He was stuck with me in sickness and in health—regardless if he wanted me or not.

Breathing quietly, I made my way toward him, coming to a stop by the side of the bed.

In the silver-pink light, everything was pure and multi-dimensional. His ebony hair scattered on the white pillow, his cheeks hollow from pain and skin pinched from fever. New bruises mottled his cheekbones while one eyebrow swelled and his jaw had turned a sickly shade of green.

Beneath his blood stained clothes, his stomach rose and fell with breath, but concave with loss of food and energy. Even his hands weren't safe from punishment with a finger bent abnormally and grazes on his knuckles.

And that was just the parts of him I could see.

What does he look like beneath his clothes?

Even with my morbid curiosity, I didn't want to wake him—revelling in the opportunity to study him.

But either his instincts were too finely tuned or he'd been faking sleep as his eyes snapped open, unfocused but severe, ready for more war.

He groaned loudly as he tried to throw himself upright, only for every part of his body to scream a loud, unequivocal *no*.

Falling against the mattress, he grunted with agony, panting hard.

Grabbing his hand, doing my best not to squeeze parts I shouldn't squeeze, I rushed, "It's me. Just me." My heart grew to the size of a forest, full of new leaves and old, a change of season from needing to be the one protected to the one doing the protecting. "I'm here. No one else. Just us."

His breathing continued fast and ragged, but his eyes warmed and a gentle smile twitched his lips. "I thought you'd left me here to rot."

I shook my head. "No, I was told not to disturb you. That you needed rest."

"How long was I out? Ten minutes? Fifteen?"

My eyes widened, studying him for a prank. Did he honestly believe it'd only been that long? Glancing over my shoulder at the rapidly pinking sky, I said, "It's almost a new day, El. You've slept six hours."

"What?" He launched himself up, unsuccessful and crying out with a few growled curse words as the bed once again claimed him. "Goddammit, why didn't Selix get me out of here? I don't want to sleep in my enemy's house. No fucking way."

I laughed. I couldn't help it. It was almost word perfect to the prediction I'd given Tess. "I thought you might say that."

"And what did you think my reaction would be when I woke up to find I'd wasted almost an entire evening here?"

"I thought you'd be angry and suspicious and not able to

relax."

He huffed. "If you can guess my moods and pre-empt my needs, then why the hell are we still here and not on the Phantom?"

Tess's advice swam in my head. *"If you make it sound like staying here benefits you...he won't argue."* Wasn't that emotional manipulation? Wasn't that unethical between two people who supposedly trusted each other?

I'd been lied to and controlled for too long to do it with Elder. The truth was the only way.

Straightening my back, I whispered in the dark silence, "I accepted their offer of staying for a little while."

His face turned red with unchecked frustration. "You did what? Why? We don't need them, Pimlico. That asshole shot me. I don't want to spend any more time than necess—"

"You need rest, Elder." Not letting his temper affect me, I remained calm and quiet. "You're hurt. I can't imagine Michaels advised a punch up so soon after being shot and beaten. You aren't capable of going anywhere without it being detrimental to your health. Your finger needs attending to. Your ankle. Your arm. Not to mention all the other parts of you I can't see beneath the covers."

I tugged at the sheet around his chest. "What other injuries are you hiding? Can't you admit for once that putting your health first is the best thing for everyone?"

He clutched the sheet, holding it tight and refusing to let me see. His eyes blazed, burying me beneath tension and guilt. "I want to be back on the Phantom, Pim. You know how I feel about being on land."

I sighed. "I know. I get that. But would one night truly hurt?"

"One night? We've *already* endured one night." He glowered. "That's enough." Tearing his gaze from mine, he looked at the door. "Go find Selix and tell him it's time to leave."

Leave?

God, I suck at this.

He couldn't leave. He could barely sit up. I couldn't let whatever fever stalked him and whatever wounds drained him to make him worse.

I'd tried the truth, and it hadn't worked with this pig-headed specimen of a man.

It was time to try a little white lie...*for his benefit.*

Twirling my fingers into the sheet, I allowed some of my shame and guilt to show. "Did you know Tess was sold to Q...before they were married?" I didn't wait for Elder to answer—it was purely a rhetorical question, leading into my attempt at misdirection and trickery. "Her past is fascinating, and having another woman who knows what it's like to be captured and sold..." I looked up beneath brown bangs. "I'm not ready to go yet. I have things I need to ask her."

He froze, searching my face. "What things?"

I inhaled, doing my best to think on my feet. Luckily, I didn't have to lie on this point. "Like talking through the parts of what happened to me with another woman."

"Why can't you talk about it with me?" His forehead furrowed, hurt glistening in his eyes.

Grabbing his hand again, I smiled. "I can, and I have. You know more about me than you probably should, and I wish I could stop bringing *him* up. Especially because what he did to me has no control or place in our future."

"Then...let's go home." His hand turned in mine, twisting to capture my wrist, his fingers searching for my pulse as if reaffirming to himself I was alive, he was alive, therefore we should be anywhere but here.

"We will. Just...one more day." I threw everything I could into my implore. "The moment I'm away from Tess, who knows if I'll ever find someone who has such similar trials in her past. You rescued my body and soul, El, and I'm almost whole thanks to you, but I think she might be the final piece I need to fix my mind."

He slouched into the pillows, half of his face in shadow

with disagreement and the other in dawn with understanding. The two battled for domination, one choice meaning he gave me what I wanted at the expense of what he preferred, and the other making me leave after I'd explicitly asked—for the first time in my life—for his agreement. A simple request to stay another night so we both might heal a little more.

Before we're at the mercy of the Chinmoku again.

Endless seconds ticked past while he bit his bottom lip, deliberating. The harsh lines around his eyes spoke of unwillingness to give in, but his silence hinted that he didn't want to bark commands or order me to obey.

Finally, his face melted into glowing affection, ripping the air right from my lungs with how beautiful he was. "You are your own person, Pim. If you want to stay, then I won't stop you. If anything, it will be my honour to stand beside you." With gravel and caramel, he added gently, "In fact, you've just given me something I didn't think would happen for a very long time...if at all."

Cupping my cheek, he brought me closer until his lips brushed mine. "After two years of distrusting, you're finally learning that not all humans are evil. In a way, I'm jealous. I'll no longer have your undivided attention; I won't be the only one you want to be close to—"

"It's not about that. I didn't mean to make it seem like I—"

"I know, and you didn't. You didn't let me finish." Smiling, he kissed me bittersweet. "What I was about to say was, I'm so damn proud of you. Of how strong you are. How fearless. I think I just fell even more in love with you, and I honestly thought I'd fallen all the way. I love you, Pim. So fucking much."

I gasped.

My heart scurried, hating itself for lying when Elder just gave me something so unbearably precious. His praise wasn't justified even if I did want to talk to Tess. His honour and pride misplaced even if I did see humans as individuals now rather than as one mass of devil-incarnate.

If I had the choice of returning to the Phantom with him with no injuries and never see Tess again, I would *leap* at the chance. But his circumstances meant I got a chance to seek female companionship, and after that initial craving in Monte Carlo—thanks to the fresh-faced, sweetheart Simone—I wanted to know what it felt like to tell a girl secrets and have them *get* it.

I was selfish.

Really, I should find the courage to discuss the awful, awful things my body had endured with Elder.

But does he truly want to know?

In his eyes, I'd been a broken, weak little thing, but now I was strong and unbruised.

If I told him what remained festering in my heart, I might tarnish his pride and turn it into something that could push him away from me. It could stop him from sleeping with me or prevent him from believing I could handle his desires.

No. I can't risk ruining what we have.

I didn't know the answers to what I should and shouldn't do. I didn't know how to reconcile lying when really my lie was wrapped up with truth.

Guilt ate me alive as Elder caressed my cheek then twined his fingers into my hair. "You've gone quiet on me, little mouse."

I closed my eyes, falling into him, kissing him. "I love you, too. So much."

Chuckling beneath my lips, he groaned. "I love hearing you say that. Say it again."

Another kiss. "I love you, Elder Prest." And another.

His groan turned to a growl. "Okay, we'll stay. One more night. Now kiss me again and make me forget where I am."

ELDER

KISSING PIMLICO MADE energy drench my bruised and bellowing limbs.

Her touch made me think I could easily climb from this godforsaken bed and carry her out of here. Her taste made me believe I was cured. Her mews and moans made sex infinitely more appealing than returning to the Phantom so fast.

Why leave yet?

We had a bed and privacy.

I intend to put it to use.

The longer we kissed, the more I sank into the pillows and yanked her closer.

I needed her. I wanted her. My pain vanished under the weight of it.

Placing her on top of me, I hissed between my teeth as blades of agony knocked on my skull—hinting that the pain might not have vanished, after all.

Her hands pressed against my chest, bruising cracked ribs, arguing against my insistence at having her close.

Her mouth danced with mine but with hesitation.

I breathed harder, arching my hips into hers to show her exactly what I wanted and to stop denying me.

But then, the spinning returned. That damn fucking

spinning that sent me under last time. The hypnotic black and white spiral, stealing gravity and my innards and hurling them around and around in a washing machine of sickness.

Kisses turned from miraculous healing to energy draining. Fighting her switched from adventurous to exhausting.

Spinning, spinning, spinning.

One moment, I was kissing her.

The next...I was not.

Pimlico

HAVING ELDER PASS out mid-kiss affected not just my worry but also my ego—some superficial part of me that believed my presence was enough to cure him was slapped back to reality and given a stern talking-to.

A kiss would not heal him.
Only a doctor could.
Tess had been right.

Rest had done him a world of good. But now, his injuries needed tending to and food needed to be consumed. And the only way to do that was to enlist the experts.

Leaving Elder unconscious once again, I waited until dawn switched to acceptable morning politeness and padded downstairs to the kitchen.

There, I found Q dressed in a striking blue suit with graphite shirt and maroon tie, laughing with a plump lady who I assumed was the cook.

Their French quips and inside jokes stopped the moment I intruded. His face lost the ease of conversing with family and slipped into a polite mask of helpfulness. "*Bonjour*, Pimlico. *Comment allez-vous?*"

I knew enough basic one-liners to understand he'd asked how I was.

I nodded with a mirroring smile. "I'm fine." I would've much rather bumped into Tess to tell her what I needed rather than her husband, but beggars couldn't be choosers.

Taking a deep breath, I asked, "Do you mind calling a doctor? Or radioing the Phantom and asking Dr. Michaels to come? Elder is unconscious again, and I think he needs better care than what I can provide."

Immediately, he put down his coffee and reached into his blazer breast pocket for his cell phone. "Of course. I'll call my personal physician immediately." Kissing the cook on her two flour-dusted round cheeks, he murmured something in French then passed me while pressing digits on his phone. "He'll be here in thirty minutes. Wait upstairs. I'll send him to you."

He didn't even wait for my thanks.

A whirlwind of efficiency, he was out the door and onto whatever vigilante endeavours or business dealings he favoured.

* * * * *

The day passed in yet another blur. Q's doctor arrived and briskly stripped Elder down.

He assessed his bruises, bumps, and breaks, reset his bent finger, checked the strappings on his chest, noted his fever, then turned his attention to the stitches in Elder's gunshot wound.

I kept a hand clamped over my lips as the doctor washed out the wound and re-stitched two areas that'd come undone.

I could handle my own broken bones and gushing blood. But seeing Elder's…it hurt because I didn't want him to be in pain. I wanted to take it away, and I couldn't.

All I could do was hope and wait and beg him to be okay.

Once tended and tutted over, the doctor cleaned Elder's injuries with antibacterial gel and secured yet another bandage over his stitches to keep the skin supple enough to knit together without forming too proud a scar.

I hated that Elder didn't wake up while the doctor fussed and fixed. His eyelids didn't twitch, his body didn't jolt even when an IV needle was inserted into the back of his hand to deliver a drip full of antibiotics and glucose.

According to the doctor, Elder's zombieness was fairly common for someone who'd depleted themselves to the level he had.

Six hours of sleep for a healthy person meant they'd be ready for a brand-new day.

Six hours of sleep for a sick person meant nothing. His resting would be entirely reliant on how quickly he healed and how fast his body fought his fever.

The doctor's final task was checking Elder hadn't torn the tendon off his ankle bone and re-securing the leg brace.

Before he left, he reeled off warnings and caveats, telling me with harsh command that although Elder wouldn't die and most likely wouldn't suffer long-term ill effects, it was his medical recommendation that he go straight to a hospital when he woke and arrange X-rays on his ankle and a cat scan for his shoulder to pick up any areas that might cause future damage.

I nodded and agreed, shooing the doctor out, knowing exactly what Elder would say to those suggestions.

No fucking way...or something to that end.

I smiled, loving the sensation of knowing Elder enough to hopefully predict what he might do. If I could predict, I could challenge. And if I could challenge, I might even win a few arguments.

Today, though, I'd won the war on getting him to stay and was in charge of paying the invoice the doctor had assured would be sent by the end of the week.

I had responsibility.

People looked at me and listened to my instruction and believed I was normal enough to do things like pay bills and look after loved ones. That I had possessions like bank accounts and credit cards. That I hadn't been a prisoner for two years and my entire future hinged on the man passed out with blood staining the sheets beneath him.

I was his guardian angel now, and I wouldn't rest until he was healed.

* * * * *

I lost track of time.

I didn't care if it was morning or evening, day or night.

Suzette brought food in at random intervals, I helped a groggy Elder somehow crawl from the bed to the bathroom before passing out again, and Tess popped by to see how the invalid was doing.

We chatted a little, but the exhaustion that clutched Elder finally found me, and I dozed beside him with my knees pressed against his thigh and my arm thrown lightly over his chest.

I probably shouldn't touch him in case I hurt him, but I *needed* to touch him. I needed to sleep with his heat and bulk in my arms; otherwise, nightmares of him being shot and falling overboard tortured me on repeat.

Again and again, I heard the boom and splash. Smelled the sulphur and salt.

I clutched Elder harder.

* * * * *

Sometime later—who knew exactly *how* much later—while the sky inked black and the house hushed quiet, Elder finally mumbled something and flinched.

I shot upright, blinking away sleep, begging him to open his eyes. He'd woken a few times before—sometimes for a bathroom break and others while still in a dream—but each time, he'd not quite returned to me.

This time seemed different. His natural awareness and readiness to fight filled his body before his eyes cracked open.

Slowly this time, no longer unfocused and dazed but suspicious and lethal. His dark eyelashes feathered in the gloom.

I didn't speak while he glanced around, studying, assessing. The tautness in his shoulders said he remembered our last conversation and most likely our kiss.

Does he remember passing out?

"Fuck..." he groaned, squeezing his eyes and shaking his

head. "Did I really faint while kissing you?"

I laughed softly, glad to hear strength in his voice even if it was soft with sleep and rough with injury. "You did."

"I'm an ass."

"You're sick."

"I'm not sick." Raising his hand off the sheets, he squinted dangerously at the needle piercing his skin. "Who the hell put that in?"

I wished I could tell him Michaels did—at least he knew him and had some element of trust. I didn't even know Q's doctor's name. "The Mercer family doctor came. When you passed out mid-kiss, I thought it best to get a professional."

Grumbling under his breath, he dropped his hand. "I bet that bastard had a great time gloating about putting me in the infirmary."

"It wasn't like that, and you know it."

He sighed. "I'm assuming I haven't been out for ten minutes, either?" Glancing at the sky, he glowered at the fresh moon slightly thicker in crescent than the day before. "Shit."

"A little longer than that, I'm afraid." Swinging my legs off the bed and standing, I stretched out the kinks from sleeping stiff beside a healing patient. "I sort of lost track of time." Looking back at him, I did my best to hide my wince.

He looks awful.

Somewhere along the way of battling and now, Elder had lost the strict rigidity he always carried in his spine. He'd given in to the bed's embrace, collapsing into pillows, looking tamed and not at all happy about it.

With the sheet tossed to the side, the ankle brace clung to his limb like a growth—a manifestation of his pain.

In a way, he looked utterly exhausted and in another, he looked almost relieved to finally admit he needed someone to care for him...just for a little before he was back to his overly-generous, terribly-stubborn self.

Despite the dirt and blood still lingering on his skin, he warmed my heart and filled my thoughts with pastimes unsuited for patients and nursemaids.

"Why did you get up? Where are you going?" He yawned, white teeth flashing in the dark.

I had thought to head to the kitchen and retrieve dinner for him, but I didn't want to leave.

I needed to be around him while he was awake, just in case he passed out again.

I have a much better idea.

"Don't move," I whispered.

His eyebrow rose. "I don't think you need to fear on that account."

Smiling, I left the bed and padded to the bathroom. There, I found a dish holding face towels and cute soaps shaped like feathers.

Tossing them out, I filled up the dish with warm water, stole two towels and some soap, then headed back to Elder.

His forehead scrunched while his eyes squeezed shut as if every breath hurt.

The moment he heard me, however, the truth of his discomfort vanished and his face smoothed out with a love-filled smile. "You came back."

"Of course, I did." Carrying my stash, I did my best not to spill warm water as I placed it on the bedside table. "I wouldn't leave you." I filled my voice with sincerity. "Ever."

His gaze widened, drenched with tiredness and healing but dark with hunger and lust. "Even if you hadn't just given me your word to never leave me, I would never be capable of letting you go, Tasmin." He swallowed as his voice thickened. "You're stuck with me. For however long my stupid heart keeps me alive."

There he went again, using my real name in a suddenly passionate fragment.

"Your heart isn't stupid." Goosebumps scattered over my arms as I dropped my eyes. "It's perfect."

"You're right. It isn't stupid." He reached for me, linking his fingers with mine. "It chose you." His heat soaked into mine. "Come to bed."

His touch somehow deleted everything, making me crave. I stumbled closer as he dragged me toward him.

Scooting down the bed, doing his best to hide his flinch and jolt from battered bones, he tugged until I kneeled on the bed beside him.

Gazing down, I tucked glossy strands of black away from his forehead, checking partly for his fever and partly for strength. The way he watched me hinted he could pin me to the bed and be inside me in moments. But the reality was his breathing remained laboured; his skin filthy from his fight.

If he was in agony, then he needed to rest, despite our rapidly building chemistry.

I shook away the lust waking up in my veins, then tugged at the sheet covering his chest. "May I?"

He smirked. "You know you don't need to ask."

Bracing myself, I pulled the covers down his black and blue body, revealing a patchwork quilt of defeat, victory, and scars.

Oh, El.

My fingers moved on their own accord, stroking along his collarbone and a large scratch living there.

He arched into my touch, a groan tumbling from his lips. "As much as I like you focusing on that part of my body, other parts need tending to more."

"Like every other bruise and bump, you mean?"

He chuckled under his breath. "I mean what's between my legs."

"I'm sure that's the only thing at present that *isn't* hurt."

"Ha!" He shivered as I drifted my fingers down his chest. "It's the one place that's hurting the most." His gaze narrowed with heat. "Whatever you're doing is driving me insane, Pim. Lie down or get away from me. I can't have you sitting over me like that and not want to fuck you."

I sucked in a breath, tearing my eyes from his to focus on the bowl full of water. "Well, you can't. Not yet. Not until you're better."

"I *am* better."

I leaned forward and dipped a towel into the wet warmth. "*I'll* say when you're better." Wringing out the excess, I moved to his hips, taking the covers with me.

"What the hell are you doing?" His nipples peaked from either cold or desire as a few droplets landed on his belly from my cloth.

I did my best not to focus on the blood-stained bandages and the stitches holding him together. "Looking after you the way you looked after me."

His eyes burned as I continued to push away the coverlets to the bottom of the bed. He winced as I brushed against his ankle encased in its boot.

"Sorry." I climbed back up, settling so close my thigh kissed his hipbone. "I'll try to be as gentle as I can."

Bandages around his chest and over his shoulder blocked me from staring at his nakedness, but it didn't stop the tail of his dragon and the tip of its snout peeking from the sides.

Tears sprang to my eyes to see him so decorated in pain. I pressed a kiss to his bandaged shoulder. "I hate seeing you like this."

He swallowed a black chuckle. "Imagine what it was like for me when we first met and you were worse than this." His good hand captured my chin, his thumb shaking a little as he ran it over my cheek. "It gutted me every time you were naked. Seeing how beautiful you were beneath all those marks and punishments. I wanted to fucking kill him all over again for what he'd done to you." His voice wavered with loathing. "How skinny you were. How beaten. He'd tried so hard to break you but never could."

I had no reply because now I understood yet another layer of what he'd embraced by saving me. He'd come from a world where he didn't need reminders that pain and suffering existed to living with a very clear example.

He'd fallen for a woman who preferred nakedness to

clothing, providing the constant reminder of what'd happened to her outside his control.

God, I was so selfish.

Leaning forward, I brushed my lips over his, my hands falling to his boxer-briefs. "I'm sorry, El. For making you see me that way when it was so hard for you."

"What the hell are you apologising for?" His nostrils flared. "Seeing you that way made me grow the fuck up and remember I had a heart, after all. You helped me remember how to care for another without fear."

My fingers inched around the elastic holding his underwear in place—the only thing the doctor had left on after his examination.

Elder stopped breathing as I gently tugged them down. As my hands undressed him, I leaned closer and pressed my lips once again to his.

His mouth parted, willingly letting me orchestrate this connection, content to follow my direction even though energy hummed and burned hotter and hotter with every heartbeat.

My attentions could be taken as sexual, but they came from a nurturing place deep inside.

I *needed* to take care of this man.

I needed it more than I could stand.

Breaking the kiss, I shimmied down his body, intending to pull his underwear off.

His stomach clenched, eyes hot and wild.

"Let me..." I implored, tugging a little for his cooperation.

Slowly, he raised his hips just enough for me remove his boxers.

His decency went from covered to revealed, his cock swiftly thickening as I paid attention to his broken body. Ignoring the lust building in every avenue, pathway, and neuron, I tossed his boxers to the floor.

Breath vanished from my lungs as I fully took him in. Even wounded, Elder was a magnificent man.

Time ticked onward as we both stared. He bit his bottom

lip as he devoured every inch of my t-shirt and jean clad body. "Something isn't fair in this scenario. You should be naked, too."

I dropped my gaze. "If I was naked, my idea of taking care of you wouldn't work."

"You could take care of me in other ways." The invitation should've been light-hearted, but it came out heavy and heated and just as hard as the cock between his legs.

It took every willpower, but I clutched my wash-cloth and shook my head. Scrambling off the bed, needing some distance, I dipped the towel into the warm water again.

Elder never looked away as I soaked it, lathered some soap until sweet honeysuckle surrounded us, then wrung out the excess.

I'd repeated what I'd done because I couldn't get my body under control to trust myself around him. My insides echoed to be filled. My mouth watered to be kissed. My skin bruised to be touched.

But this wasn't about him taking me tonight. This was about me thanking him for everything he'd given me.

I need to remember that and get on with it.

Taking another deep breath, I climbed onto the bed and poised on my knees. I couldn't magic away his injuries, but I could tend to him. I could make sure he was clean from his battle and relaxed from his fight. I could lavish him with affection and appreciation for everything he was and had become.

And then, I would let him sleep.

"I want to wash you. Do you give me permission?"

His face etched with torture. "You want to *wash* me?"

I nodded.

Would he see this for what it was or think I enjoyed him in this position of weakness? Had I honoured or emasculated him?

I opened my mouth to give some sort of explanation, but he strangled. "You want to touch me. Everywhere?"

I nodded again. "If you'll let me."

"*Fuck,*" he cursed at the ceiling. "Of course, I want you to. I'd let you do anything you wanted, Pim. But that...goddammit, knowing you want to serve me that way?" His eyes glittered raven. "It makes me want to bow to you and corrupt you in equal measure."

"You can do both...when you're better."

"Christ, you can't—"

Before he could finish, I pressed the warm cloth to his cheek. "I love you. Let me show you how much."

He froze, every muscle locking as the bed vibrated with every restriction he placed on himself. The only thing that moved were his eyes, dancing over my face, fevered and desiring as I washed his jawline, erasing the blood splatters and sweat.

He didn't moan or flinch as I worked my way down his throat, swirling softly, leaving a wake of clean skin, but he did suck in a breath as I meticulously bathed around his bandages, licking my lips at the ridges of his muscles, enjoying myself far too much.

My heart swelled with love and power but also sank with guilt for enjoying the role reversal. It brought tears to my eyes to express my affection this way but shame for revelling in his every hiss and groan.

I grew wet and heavy, my legs squeezing together the longer I cleaned his body.

Was this how Elder felt when he tended to me? Drunk on protecting and curing me? A strange aphrodisiac as I slowly grew stronger, knowing in some way—he was the reason I was better?

If he felt a tenth of what I did as I ran the washcloth down his arm and wrapped around each finger, then he must've been constantly turned on.

My skin was on fire. My nipples hard as stone.

I shivered as I dunked the cloth and applied more soap, wringing it out before returning to his body.

His breathing ratcheted as I repeated the attention with his other arm then around his belly and parts of his chest not bandaged.

Once the top part of him was clean, I repeated the process with a rinsed cloth, ensuring I removed every trace of soap and grime.

With a clean towel, I prepared to focus on the other parts of his body, that until now, I'd done my best to avoid.

Elder stiffened, knowing that things were about to get a lot more...*personal*.

Prickling with electricity and wetter than I'd ever been, I slowly moved down his chest to his legs. My heart raced as I trailed the tip of the towel over his erection.

His back bowed off the bed. My core clenched. We both groaned in unison.

Too much...

His chest rose and fell as his cock bounced, begging for touch.

Too tempting...

He was hurt, and I wouldn't be able to control myself.

Focus on something else.

Gritting my teeth, I shuffled farther down, avoiding the tops of his thighs and groin.

For now.

He huffed impatiently but didn't command I return. He glared into my eyes as I repositioned myself by his feet. Never looking away, I draped the towel over his toes and massaged his sole.

His gaze rolled back, and his breath came short and laboured.

"You're killing me, little mouse." Harsh and guttural, begging for everything I was denying us. Yet he didn't try to stop me. He didn't grab me and wrap my hand around his length.

He balled his hands—or the best he could with a broken finger—and gave himself to me, enduring this specific brand of torture I'd stupidly designed for us.

What the hell am I doing?

All it would take was a few short seconds to shed my clothing and climb on top of him. I could heal him in other ways. I could grant an orgasm, and he could fade back into sleep.

But even as I imagined riding him until we both dripped in sweat, I continued to massage his legs and feet.

Elder wasn't simple in bed.

Once wouldn't be enough for him.

Twice, neither.

He would have to have me three times to put the compulsion aside, and I doubted he had enough energy to complete one round, let alone multiple.

This is about him...not you, remember?

With my teeth tightly locked, I carefully undid the Velcro from around his ankle and unwrapped his leg.

He stayed locked tight, barely breathing as I set aside the brace and washed his inflamed joint.

Swollen tissue and heat painted bright red around the bone and halfway up his leg.

He jolted with the gentlest pressure, enduring new pain. He didn't relax until I'd re-wrapped and fastened and switched to washing his other leg.

The reminder he wasn't whole—that he most likely should be in a hospital and not in some stranger's French chateau—helped me focus. I didn't turn my nursemaid routine into sex-maid escapades. I ignored what was between his thighs and climbed off the bed to replace the water for new.

Elder's gaze seared me with every step across the room, and I prickled with loneliness the moment I entered the bathroom.

I was empty away from him. I wasn't used to the heavy breathlessness I endured. Was this what it felt like to crave sex? To be so mindless with my body's insistence to be fucked that no amount of rationality or distance could stop the quakes in my womb?

All I could picture was feral kisses and aggressive thrusting.

God...

My hands shook as I tipped the pink-grey waste down the drain. I fumbled to turn on the tap.

While the water ran, I looked at myself in the mirror, noticing the high points of red on my cheeks and the crazed lust in my eyes. My hair curled around my face as if Elder had already had his fingers digging into my scalp while fucking me.

For the first time in my life, I toyed with the idea of touching myself. Of somehow finding relief from the pressure-cooker passion inside, so I didn't pounce on Elder the moment I returned.

Squeezing my eyes, I scolded myself with every reason I couldn't have him.

He's sick. He's recovering. He's black and blue and probably still has a fever. Your job is to help him heal. Then and only then can you ask him to take you.

The pep talk didn't work, and I padded back to his bedside with blood boiling and mind on fire.

I dared look at his face. He seemed to be in the same brimstone, hellish place I was. Halfway through a sponge bath, he ought to look relaxed, spread out on the mattress.

He was the exact opposite of relaxed.

Every cord of muscle and sinew etched beneath scratched and bruised skin. Every ridge and hollow of his stomach tightened, ready to give me exactly what I wanted.

He didn't say a word—he didn't have to. The way he glared at me stripped me bare and commanded I straddle him.

But some sadistic part of me still had the power to say no, and with a ragged gasp, I tore my gaze away.

I made the smart decision to stay standing by his bedside and not sit.

The distance helped.

I would stay professional and look after him the way he

deserved.

Dunking a fresh towel and lathering it with soap, I studiously focused on washing his legs. Calves and knees. Shins and thighbones.

Not once did I go higher.

Not once did I *look* higher.

His breathing turned harsher with every stroke. His hand lashed out once I'd rinsed him, latching tight around my wrist. "We both know there's only one place you haven't washed yet."

I froze.

He guided my hand past mid-thigh to upper thigh. "If you won't do it...I will." His fingers branded my wrist, hotter, fiercer, filled with every frustration I felt. "I'm dirty, Pim. So filthy you'd better spend extra attention with that towel of yours."

I swallowed a moan as he guided me. "I shouldn't..."

"Yes. You should." He licked his lips. "Please..."

His plea unlocked my self-control, and I yanked at his hold. "Let me go."

His eyes flared as if to argue, then glazed over as I slid the final way on my own.

His head fell back, understanding exactly what sort of demoness he'd unleashed and all too happy to play the victim.

My whisper tasted sweet as sin and sugar. "I'll make sure you're extra clean."

"Holy shit." He writhed on the bed, sweat gleaming on his freshly washed brow. "Who are you, Tasmin Blythe?"

I didn't know the answer to that question. Maybe I'd never know. But tonight, I was his just as much as he was mine.

"Be quiet and let me wash you." I slid my towel between his legs and grazed the tight twin balls beneath his erection.

"*Jesus*—" He let out a strangled grunt, clutching the bed with his good hand.

My nipples tingled and belly flopped and breath choked and heart heated as I slowly, carefully, *maddeningly*, ran the washcloth over him. I cupped his balls, rolling them gently, cleaning and seducing at the same time.

His head tossed to the side. His neck strained, jaw wide, teeth sharp as he bit into the pillow. His entire body twitched as I slid upward, wrapping my fingers around his hardness.

I'd never been so consumed by something before. All I wanted to do for the rest of my life was *this*—destroy him to this quivering, pillow-biting animal and have my hands on the one part of him no one else ever would again.

Clutching his entire length, I pumped him through the towel. My fingers slid up and over his crest, washing away the past, cleansing him until he was completely, utterly mine.

I'd never owned something...*someone* before.

But here, now...I *owned* Elder.

I couldn't just give that power back.

I could *never* give that back.

Shaking, I somehow managed to swirl the towel in fresh water and wipe away the soap before the possession in my blood forced me to do something I couldn't possibly deny.

Leaning over him, I fisted his erection and inserted his heat into my mouth.

I wasn't prepared for my reaction or his.

His hands sank into my hair as his hips thrust up, forcing himself deeper onto my tongue. His groan rattled windowpanes and shattered the glass frosting around my heart.

My legs buckled until I half-kneeled, half-hung in his hold, sucking greedily, not caring how I sounded or seemed.

We both lost our last shreds of dignity.

I could pleasure.

I could *be* pleasured.

Everything to do with my body and Elder was right and perfect and *pure*.

His cock rippled in my mouth as I sank deeper, widening my jaw.

His fingers tore at my hair, ungentle and brutal but somehow utterly worshipping. "God. Fuck. Holy—" Sentences no longer fell from his mouth, just punctuation in the form of crude cursing.

The first droplet of salt teased my tongue, hinting that Elder wasn't equipped with his usual stamina.

I loved it.

Loved that he was so undone that it would only take him seconds to come. That I had the control to make him do something he probably wouldn't want to do.

Not yet anyway.

Not until he'd had his fill of my mouth.

I bit him gently as I slid as deep as I could go. Humming, I switched every trick I'd been taught and turned every disgusting skill I knew into something I was proud of.

I wasn't a virgin.

I wasn't pure.

But he knew that and accepted me anyway. He'd tried to rent me for pennies and buy my thoughts for millions and now he'd get my everything for free.

I whispered around his length. "You're clean now. Every inch."

His body jerked off the bed, his large hands splaying over my head. "Christ, stop."

I didn't.

He teetered on the edge. "Pim!"

I sucked harder.

"Stop!" Pushing me away, he hissed as his cock bounced and the smallest drop appeared on his crown; his face turned ugly with denied release. A few seconds while he glowered at the ceiling and chanted, *"Not yet, not yet, not yet,"* before he blinked and gave me a rueful, devilish smile.

Not one hint of injury.

Not one note of pain.

Only lust—the strongest drug of all.

"I'm in so much trouble with you."

The smile on my lips wasn't from me but from sex itself. I owned it. I matched him dirty for dirty. I was finally whole enough to admit it. "I don't know what you're talking about."

He laughed, torture and addiction equal tones. "You know *exactly* what I'm talking about." He grabbed my hand. "You're a temptress who's going to give me a goddamn heart attack if she doesn't get naked and sit on my cock right now."

My entire body flushed. "I can't."

"You can." He tugged me forward. "I'll even show you how." His attention fell to my rapidly breathing chest. "Undress, Pim. Let me see you."

"I shouldn't."

"Why not?"

"Because you need to rest."

"I *am* resting. You've got me on my back, woman. I can barely see straight from wanting you. I'm utterly paralysed unless you fuck me."

"Paralysed?"

"Completely."

"That's my fault." My cheeks pinked. "I shouldn't have sucked you."

His face darkened, buying into my blush, the predator revealing itself. "If you knew you shouldn't, then why did you?"

"I couldn't help it."

His throat worked as he swallowed. "*Why* couldn't you help it?"

His questions sent yet more liquid heat pooling. "I needed you in my mouth."

He groaned loud. "And I need you on my cock."

"We shouldn't have sex."

"Who said anything about sex?" He visibly trembled. "This isn't sex, Pim."

"It *is* sex." I stumbled as he yanked me harder against the bed. "It's—"

"It's so much more than just sex." His tongue wet his bottom lip, sending another coil of desire. "It's the only thing keeping me alive right now."

Every second we discussed reasons for yes and no, my

mind blacked out every argument. We needed this. But I also needed him to be healthy.

And this...it wouldn't be healthy.

"We can't." Standing firm, I tilted my chin. "Not until you're stronger."

His eyes blackened. *"Stronger?"*

"Better."

"I *am* better." He never looked away as he grabbed the IV needle and yanked it from his hand. "See? All better."

Throwing the medicine off the bed, his voice slipped to dangerous seduction. "Now strip, Pimlico, and get into bed. I won't ask again."

ELDER

IF SHE WANTED a fight, I'd give her a fight.

Even broken and living in eternal damnation, I would happily leap off the bed and chase her if she so much as looked at the door.

Compared to the agony she'd injected into my cock, my body could shut the fuck up. Sex wasn't just a pastime to indulge in anymore; it was my cure.

Literally, figuratively—every way I needed.

"Naked. Now, Pim."

Nibbling on her lower lip, she slowly nodded.

Despite my urgent desire, my show of strength and belief at being able to pounce on her was as fictional as my ability to fly.

Only, she doesn't need to know that.

As far as Pim was concerned, I was one hundred percent better and in total control of my faculties.

Inhaling like wary prey, she grabbed the hem of her top and pulled it over her head. Bare breasts beckoned: perfectly rounded flesh with pert pink nipples.

The agony in my cock grew to mind-seizing discomfort.

It hadn't escaped my notice that she was no longer in her Bruised by Beauty gown. It lay discarded and torn over a chair—almost a voyeur to us now.

I hated to think of her showering in this place, eating in this place, talking to the people living in this place while I'd slept like a fool.

What conversations and experiences had she enjoyed without me? Had she talked about me? How long exactly had we been here?

My questions vanished as Pim's fingers drifted to her waistband and undid the button before slipping the zipper down. She didn't mean to be a seductive minx, but fuck, everything about her was seductive.

I couldn't look away as she inched the denim down her legs.

Once again, no underwear.

My breath caught as I feasted on how drop-dead gorgeous she was. How her hips had filled out and formed curves instead of edges. How her body had strengthened and showed muscle instead of bones.

"Christ, you're beautiful." I patted the mattress. "Get into bed."

Climbing up, she lay down smoothly beside me. She moved like water while I jerked like machinery. She was healed, and I was wounded. The stark contrast to how it was when we first met scrambled my thoughts.

Rolling onto her side, she pressed her hand against my bandaged chest. "I can't stop comparing this to when we first met."

A smile tugged my lips. "Me, too. It was hard for me to be gentle with you while, at the same time, I wanted to do anything to protect you." I reached out and traced a fingertip over her shoulder. "Even if it meant protecting you from myself."

"I feared you at the beginning but not because of what you would do to me." She shivered as I ran my touch down her arm.

"Why were you afraid?"

She blushed. "I feared what you made me feel. I was weak to want to end my life, but I could forgive myself for it as long as I felt nothing. But then you went and made me feel *everything.*"

Gritting my teeth against agony, I shifted as much as I could onto my side. With painful limbs and useless fingers, I clamped my hand on her hipbone and pulled her into me.

Our skin connected.

Our lust ignited.

We shuddered as lust trampled over our desire for talking. "I want to feel you, Pim." My hand cupped her breast. Soft, beautiful...*mine*. "I want to—" I couldn't finish, crashing my lips against hers.

She liquefied in my arms as her mouth opened.

No hesitation.

No refusal.

She kissed me back as hard as I kissed her. Sharing body heat, sharing electricity, sharing all the things we knew and felt.

It was the best kind of fantasy.

Was I dreaming? Was I awake? Having Pim in my arms, thrusting against her soft belly and dipping my tongue into her sweet mouth *felt* real, but was it?

Does it matter?

All that mattered was it felt so goddamn good.

With my heart pounding and my injuries flaring hot, I pressed Pim as tight as I could against me.

Nothing between us.

Nothing stopping us.

Her lips moved beneath mine, matching me lick for lick.

Our bodies listened to the same song, hardening me, softening her, preparing us for something primal and true.

I groaned under my breath as my need grew. I'd never been so sensitive in my life.

Our noses brushed as we kissed faster, deeper, diving into the cyclone we'd created. Our legs tangled, and I didn't care about the pain in my ankle or shoulder or any other piece of me.

All I cared about was *her*.

She'd worshipped me by washing me. She'd understood my need to wipe away the grime without me admitting the level of exhaustion I battled. I hadn't had to confess or ask for help and reveal my worst nightmare of looking weak.

She's perfect.

Clutching her harder, our teeth clacked together.

She smelled different. She smelled of this place. It tore me apart to think of her on her own, defending me when I should've been fulfilling that role.

Did he talk to her?

Did the asshole who shot me dare speak to my woman?

Jealousy mixed with desire, robbing me of peace. I shifted, wedging my leg between hers. "I missed you."

Her eyes snapped closed. "I've always been here."

"I need you to remember me."

"I never forgot you." She groaned as I rocked higher, rubbing against her clit.

"I shouldn't do this." I kissed her fast, deep. "I should stop."

"Yes...you should." Her breathlessness didn't match the grasping demand of her fingers. "You're not well enough."

"Don't tell me what I already know." Removing my thigh, I lowered my hand between her legs.

I found her instantly.

Drenched and scorching, she clamped her legs instinctively around my wrist as I plunged a finger inside her. "Nothing can stop me from having you, though."

"*God*, El." Her head fell back as I drove upward, filling her body and thoughts of me.

I knew what arguments she wanted to deliver. I argued the same thing even as I ignored common-sense. I shouldn't undertake anything that would drain me of what little energy I had left. Everything pounded. Everything hurt.

One moment I was hot, the next I was cold.

I was lightheaded and heavy with pain.

If I was smarter, I would swallow more painkillers and rest. This was a terrible, terrible idea, yet I couldn't stop.

Arching my hand, I relished in her moan. "Could a sick man make you feel like this?" I inserted a second finger, stretching her, touching her deep. "Could a broken man get so fucking hard for you?" I thrust against her leg while feathering my fingers inside her.

She convulsed, lips wide, eyes tight.

"Answer me, Pim." I rolled my thumb on her clit, attacking her with sensation.

She moaned, her forehead crashing against my shoulder as her body squeezed around my invasion. "No, he couldn't."

"So I'm capable of fucking you?" I grabbed her chin with my free hand, holding her prone for a depraved kiss while my fingers worked deep.

"Yes!" she cried beneath my lips. "God, yes."

"Good answer."

I wished I could take her once—just once to ease the frustration at having her stolen from me.

But one wasn't a pretty number.

It was single and straight and ugly.

Three was a much prettier sum with its curves and hollows.

Sex for me wasn't a normal endeavour just like most things in my life—constantly hounded by that cruel number three. I wished I had another trick to tame my crazy brain.

But I didn't.

And tonight was even worse because I was exhausted and didn't have self-control. Pim wasn't entirely safe around me just like I wasn't entirely safe around her.

But none of that mattered anymore.

"I need you." The gruffness of my voice rasped across the softness of her skin.

Her breath hitched, eyes heated. "You have me."

"I want you in every possible way."

"Name it. I'll do it."

Positions and filthy commands dripped off the tip of my tongue, but for once, I stayed within my limitations.

I would fuck her.

But I would make her do all the work.

"Get on top of me." Withdrawing my fingers, I rolled gingerly onto my back. My shoulder screamed, pain tugging at torn ligaments. With an agonised snarl, I placed my arm over my belly, discomfort from my elbow joining in the screaming.

It almost overshadowed the thick demand in my cock. *Almost.*

Christ, how the hell did I beat up Mercer with this body?

Had I dreamed that, too?

Pim winced on my behalf as I shifted, doing my best to find relief from the drumming, cymbal-smashing pain in my ankle—deciding to join in the symphony from my elbow and shoulder.

Whatever adrenaline I'd been swimming in rapidly faded. Her hand fluttered on my chest. "Perhaps we should—"

"Don't." Grabbing her wrist, I pulled her until she sprawled over me. The slipperiness of her body on mine made the pain fade a little.

If I could stay focused on her, I could do this.

"I need to be inside you."

With worry and obedience, she placed her hands on the mattress and pushed up. Spreading her legs, the flash of her wet pussy drove me insane as she did what she'd done on the floor of Hawksridge and prepared to ride me.

Unlike that time—when I'd grabbed myself and lined up to spear inside her—she clutched my length and jutted me upright. She remembered my lesson when I was bound and helpless in the hotel in Monte Carlo.

She knew how to take me, and I gave up all control.

I trembled as she angled over me then slowly, teasingly lowered.

We stopped breathing; both watching the delicious sight

of her body enveloping mine.

Christ...

I'd wanted to take her, but she undoubtedly took me.

In *every* fucking way.

My back arched as finally a better sensation overrode my agony. I focused on the heat of her body, the snugness of being inside her, and the righteousness of being home where I belonged.

She moaned as she slid the final distance, locking herself around me like a key in a lock. My fingers dug into her hips, pressing her down, ensuring no space, no distance, nothing left between us.

We joined as tight as we could. Her clit on my belly. My balls against her ass. Our breathing just as wild as if we'd been fucking for hours and not just connected.

Pinning me in place with sex-feverish eyes, Pim folded over me and placed her hands on the pillow beneath my head. Her breasts hung heavily, taunting me to devour.

She rocked once.

My head sloshed. My brain begged. My body bellowed.

It was the worst, best, most confusing cocktail I'd ever experienced.

Pain and pleasure. Sickness and sex. I couldn't tell if I hated or loved it. One thing I knew...I could become utterly addicted to the rush.

I grew harder, clamping my legs together, fighting off the sudden spine-tingling ripple of an orgasm.

Her face strained with concentration as if determined to finish me quickly to avoid any unnecessary drain. Her own orgasm etched into her skin, revealing how much she wanted this, despite her worry.

Knowing she was as close as I was whispered for me to let go. To give in now. To come immediately. I was greedy to release. Already my fractured mind wanted to finish so it could start all over again. It wasn't satisfied. It wanted to claim that beautiful number three—to devour Pim until she was nothing but a ragdoll in my arms, then be worthy enough to fall asleep.

Sleep...

My vision wavered as a wash of weakness found me. Even heavy lust couldn't protect me from the demanding wooziness.

No.

I wouldn't be inside this woman and pass out.

I couldn't be that selfish.

My good hand dug harder into her hipbone, pulling her forward then pushing her back in a time-old rhythm.

She obeyed, fucking me deep and slow. The obstruction of her body hit the tip of my cock. I stared at her flat belly, awed that I was so far inside her. I wanted to press against her middle and feel myself thrusting. I wanted to flip her over and drive vicious and unforgiving.

I wanted so much, but for now...all I could do was lie back and belong to her.

She moved again, no longer seeking my guidance on speed. Her hips undulated to her own pace. She looked so fucking sexy, I fought another wave of release.

Her eyes flared as she swelled around me, mirroring my battle not to come.

Our gaze locked and we smiled, recognising the brittle rope we walked, desperate for it to snap but terrified of the fall.

A touch of savagery filled her, freezing me at how goddamn gorgeous she was. How multi-layered and unconquerable. How capable. How complex. How kind. But most of all, I loved *this*—this moment where it was just us. No more pretending. No more history or hardship or horrors. No masks.

We *saw* each other.

She was a hellcat, and I was the devil, and together we played in Hell.

Her skin slicked with sweat; my heartbeat a revving engine in my ears.

There was nothing else but us.

Digging my fingernails into her flesh, I increased her

rhythm, commanding her to fuck a little faster, rock a little harder, push a little deeper.

She licked her lips, her fingers clutching the pillow as she obeyed. "Okay…" she breathed, giving herself over. "Okay…" Her eyes fluttered as her body pulsed around me.

Fuck, the added heat.

The extra thrill.

The razor-sharp whip of no longer being in control.

I can't…

Denied pleasure shot down my spine, knocked on my bones, and bubbled in my wounds. My belly tightened as tingles and tangles snarled and snapped, wrapping around my balls and jettisoning into my cock.

"Pim!" My strangled warning was the only thing I could give.

My world blacked out.

I lost sight, touch, sound as everything zeroed in on the electric waves of release.

Over and over, I spurted into my woman, clamping my hands on her so she had no escape—no choice but to accept every drop.

Instead of slowing down, instead of giving me a chance to apologise and return the bone-crumpling orgasm, she growled a kitten growl and reached behind her and clutched my balls.

"Holy *Christ*—" My mouth tore wide as my release turned cruel with ferocity. There was no land, no finish line, no end. Just a knife called Orgasm, slashing at my insides, making me bleed pure pleasure.

She treated me as her conquest. She knew me too well—sending me into a brutal tailspin.

My feet dug into the mattress as I climbed further into her, snarling at the ceiling and the agonising ecstasy she gave.

Maybe she secretly hated me and this was how she'd devised my murder. Or maybe she fucking loved me and wanted to give me the best goddamn release I'd ever had.

Either way, I came and came and *came*.

And when I had nothing left, I flopped onto the bed—a drenched, gasping buffoon who no longer had a clue who he was.

I was her slave for life. I was nothing if I didn't have her.

For a few wonderful moments, I was numb and beyond content. My heart calmed, my mind quieted, and I basked in the aftermath of being so fucking in love with this girl.

I cupped her cheek, guiding her down to kiss her.

Our lips touched gently, our tongues soft and sweet. She sighed into me, draping herself like a hot blanket. I cuddled her close, tasting her, thanking her.

But then the familiar curse rapped on my thoughts. A whisper, a command—an unignorable shout for *more*.

My fingers looped around the back of her neck, kissing her harder, doing my best to stay in this sweet, simple moment. I fumbled beneath her, desperate for something to grab so I didn't drown beneath the rapidly building shout.

More.

More.

Wrung dry and mostly dead, I wanted to slip into exhaustion. I wished I was normal where the addiction to reach that pretty, perfect number wasn't strong enough to override the anaesthesia licking through my blood from the best orgasm I'd ever had.

But I wasn't strong enough.

I was undone in the worst possible way.

At my weakest.

At my most susceptible to addiction.

And Pim wasn't aware of the mind space she'd shoved me into. If she knew, perhaps she would've climbed off me and stayed away. She would've saved my life by stopping me from destroying myself.

But she didn't climb off me. She didn't stop. She fucking ruined me by sitting up and using the same fingers that'd grabbed my balls to circle her clit and shed any remainders of her past.

She used me.

She took me.

She fucked me while touching herself just like I'd fantasied all these months.

All I could do was watch and crave and give in to the rapidly building electricity crackling down my spine.

And when she came.

Fuck me.

She *annihilated* me.

I had no anchor. I was in a sea of sickness. Drowning beneath fever and pain. The strange ingredients of injuries and sex once again threw me overboard. All I could see through the blackness was her.

I couldn't fight it.

I'd *never* been able to fight it.

With her lips wide and eyes glazed, Pim found her perfect ending, and with a scream that tore my heart from my chest, she gave in. Digging her nails into my brutalised body, granting another layer of pain, she rode me hard and rough—completely uncaring as she chased her own pleasure.

I begged for change.

I wished I could watch her come and be finished with this.

I wanted to rest.

I *needed* to rest before I passed out cold again.

But my body launched itself after her like a killer after its chosen, filling my blood with lava, bubbling with the ability to come again. The pounding agony and painful wisps in my brain didn't stand a chance.

"Fuck!" I jolted with every fever-tinted wave, mixing agony with blissful, heaven with hell.

I hated it.

I loved it.

I would die if I had any more if it.

But my body was determined to kill me, ratcheting the intensity with every ripple of release.

I clamped my eyes closed as I lost track of east and west,

up and down.

On and on, I came.

And when I finally jerked and groaned, drained within breaths of passing out, Pim made to move off me.

Oh, hell no.

The cycle wasn't complete. She couldn't be permitted to leave.

In reality, I should help her. I should throw her as far away from me as possible. But I wasn't myself. I was nothing but addiction and two was nearly as ugly as one.

It wasn't three.

"Where the hell do you think you're going?" I locked my hands on her hips. "We're not done."

"You're fading between sleep and awake, El. I think we should stop."

"We can't." Already the compulsion was back, riding my body, keeping me painfully hard.

Blackness erased the room for a second. I blinked, bringing everything that mattered back into the light.

I need to sit up.

I had to keep my brain alive just for a little longer—after that…*who cares.*

Digging my heels into the bed, I braced against excruciating pain. "Move with me. Don't let me slip out."

"What are you—"

"Just do it."

With her lips pressed together, she nodded and took her weight, hovering over me on her knees with my cock still firmly impaled inside her.

I wedged my fists into the mattress and hoisted upward.

Holy shit.

I blacked out for another second, shaking my head to rid the cloying stars. It took every bit of remaining energy, but I managed to haul myself up the bed and lean haphazardly against the bedhead.

Pim slipped down my length the moment I stopped.

I panted as if I'd swam the Pacific Ocean. Sweat ran down my face. My heart double beat with warning, but I ignored all of it.

All I could do was obey the conniving, destroying chant to finish this.

Unable to catch my breath, I cupped her chin. "You're so beautiful after you've just come."

Bringing her mouth to mine, I kissed her. I grew harder, my body already in the process of preparing itself for the final call.

She kissed me back, her pussy clutching in gentle rhythm as if encouraging me to take her one last time.

Kissing my way to her ear, I whispered, "You're beautiful, but right now, I need you to turn around."

She froze. "What?"

"You heard me." I spun my finger in the air. "Spin on my cock. Face away."

"Why?"

For a moment, I worried she had bad memories associated with this position. But I couldn't have her facing me, watching me, seeing how far I was about to fall.

I barely clung to lucidity. Another orgasm was bound to knock me straight into unconsciousness.

I knew the risks, yet I had no choice.

I didn't need to fuck her while staring at her judgement.

Gritting my teeth against those damn swirling stars, I snapped, "It doesn't matter why. I told you to turn." I pushed her shoulder. "So turn."

Her eyes dove into mine, seeing past my false strength and reading my ragged truth.

"Whatever you need, El." Her voice switched to a soothing murmur, "But afterward, you're resting. We shouldn't have done this, and you're not touching me again until you're able to walk out of here."

Conversation was a waste of time.

Nothing else was as important as a perfect trio of orgasms.

I nodded sharply. "Deal." Anything to get her to obey so I could come one last time. Shit, I'd make a deal with anyone about anything if it promised a third release. If it meant perfect symmetry.

"Show me how you want me." Raising her leg, she waited for me to adjust her on my lap, spinning her while staying on my cock. I helped, keeping my touch as gentle as I could when really, I wanted to rush her into the right position as fast as possible.

We never disengaged; I shuddered against the delicious sensation of her body corkscrewing around mine.

I hardened even more, throbbing with unbearable need.

I'd lost touch with who I was and everything that mattered.

I was nothing more than a victim to exhaustion, loopy with pain and woozy with fever.

My temper frayed. My patience buried beneath selfishness.

I didn't even have enough kindness to thank her as she settled back onto my cock with her back arched and shoulder blades stark like wings.

Reaching forward, I stopped being human and gave myself over to the addictive creature inside. My fingers turned to claws as I dragged them down her back to the swell of her ass. The spear of my cock vanished into her body, glistening from angry desire.

I was angry.

Fucking furious.

Livid at myself for what I was.

I thrust, driving her forward. She moaned, her head lolling, hair falling over her shoulder, giving me a perfect view of the beads of her spine and scars that would forever remind me of where she'd come from.

I was no better than him.

I thrust.

No better than an animal.

I thrust.

She would hate me.
I thrust.
She would curse me.
I thrust.
She would pity me for being this screwed up.
I thrust and thrust and *thrust*.

As Pim bounced on my cock, the pain in my ankle marched to a war beat, the pounding in my shoulder intensified, and my elbow, ribs, bones, and finger all added a chorus to the worst song I'd ever heard.

Pain.

Just crippling, horrible *pain*.

My body's last attempt to prevent me from draining myself past survivable.

But I couldn't stop.

I could only gasp for air and throw myself into the agony because pleasure lurked there, too. Pleasure wrapped around the perfect beauty of three.

And something happened.

A buzzing.

A purring.

First in my head, then in my ears, my fingers, my toes, my legs, my torso.

Everywhere.

A thick vibration distorting my pain to new wavelengths. My adrenaline switched to endorphins, my anger evolved to relief.

The humming grew louder, living behind my eyes, dancing in my veins, taking every chemical in my bloodstream and turning it into a toxic cocktail I couldn't avoid drinking.

My eyes lost their ability to focus.

My mind lost its ability to think.

I became lost to nothing.

Nothing but Pim and what she was doing to me.

My head fell back against the headboard as I floated—up, up away, away, leaving pain behind until only one thing remained.

Pim and how incredible she made me feel.

I was serene.

I was happy.

I no longer had to fight…anything.

And on the heels of such potent serenity came thick, thick need. Lust amplified as pain de-magnified. My gunshot shoulder and distended elbow no longer had government as I wrapped my arms around Pim and tugged her back to lie against my chest.

She moaned as I bit her neck, her head thrown back, her hair sticking to my bandages, her skull pressing against my stitches.

Yet I felt none of it.

My eyes were utterly useless now—just blackness and buzzing. I closed them as syrup filled my head with yet more dopamine and chemicals.

I'd never endured anything like this. Never swam in arousal so inviting, so intoxicating.

I had no power whatsoever.

I forgot who I was.

I forgot sentences and speech.

I forgot where we were and why any of that shit mattered.

I became one purpose.

One nucleus.

Come.

The moment I thought it, I was done for.

Come.

I sparked and fizzed like a live wire. Thick, thick heat. Delicious, delicious wetness.

The electricity increased until it spat and crackled, dangerous and demonic in my veins. I shivered and gasped as the pain I'd escaped from shot into all areas and became one blazing phenomenon.

Red.

Hot.

Blistering.
Too much.
Too intense.
Too *perfect*.
It was addicting.
Better than any joint.
Deeper than any drug.
I was mad with it.
Obsessed with it.
And fuck, I'm coming.
And unlike all the times before, I *smelled* colours, I *felt* sight, I *heard* sensation.

I was in a wormhole of space where stars and asteroids pummelled me to pieces.

I spun and swam and shouted in the vast void of nothing.

And then, it was over.

Murmurs and words drifted over me like droplets, sending my mind reeling with pictures of oceans and wetness. I wanted to swim. I wanted to cool down. I wanted to stretch and give in to the calm serenity.

But then something was tugging me, reclining me, rolling me onto my side and wedging itself into my embrace.

I opened my eyes, but the wonky world of nothing came back. I tried to speak but the incomprehensive world of language avoided me.

I buried my face into the strands of silk in front of me. I cupped the soft mountains on the cliff's side I clung to.

More sounds. More mewls. More words I didn't understand.

I might not comprehend, but I did recognise the voice.

The woman I loved.

The girl I wanted more than anything.

The soul I would never let go.

"I don't know where you are or what's happened, El, but rest now." Tears echoed. "Please be okay."

My brain rearranged nonsensical into something I

remembered.
Language.
Why was this goddess sad?
I wanted to ask her, but my tongue wouldn't work.
My heart slowed.
My mind blanketed.
I inhaled the rich scent of the woman I'd killed for and then...nothing.

Pimlico

A NEW DAY.

A new morning.

And I'd hoped a new Elder as well.

I'd envisioned him waking up, fully healed and ready to triumph.

But he didn't.

The sun shone over his strewn body, dappling his bandages, soaking into his strained face. He looked at peace rather than in agony.

His fever had broken sometime in the night, and whatever had happened during sex meant he'd somehow forgotten his pain.

However, even slumbering and peaceful, his face never stopped being severe. His dark eyebrows and thick eyelashes were permanent domination on his tanned skin.

He'd slept curled around me all night, and I'd remained cocooned in his arms. I hadn't dared move. If I did, he groaned, his body seizing from his wounds. As dawn broke, he'd rolled away, hugging a pillow and slipping into a deeper rest.

And now as I stood over him, I did my best to figure out what the hell happened last night.

I wished I had an answer. I hadn't slept while tucked in his arms—that question on a never-ending loop.

What made him switch from coherent to unintelligible?

How had he ignored every pain and seemed so happy? So complete? So *sated*?

Rubbing my arms, I worried he'd done too much. That he'd hurt himself even more by giving in to whatever games his brain played.

I'd wanted to stay here to protect him, but perhaps I'd been wrong.

Maybe he needs to be back on the sea to heal properly.

We'd been here almost three days, and he was no better than before—if anything, I'd made him worse.

Stupid, Pim. So stupid.

What was I *thinking* sucking him after washing him? I'd been greedy and selfish, and now look what I'd done.

He's broken.

If we left today on the Phantom, Elder might rally round faster, but it was only a matter of time until the Chinmoku found us, and then what? Would Selix fight on Elder's behalf? Would Elder stay out of it?

I rolled my eyes.

As if.

Elder would be at the front of the cavalry despite dislocation, fractures, and bullet holes.

My heart bruised to think he'd been living with violence for so long that he no longer knew how to truly find peace. He'd forgotten how to be happy.

But despite all that, I couldn't keep him prisoner here. I'd been in that situation, and I would never do that to him. I would let him choose. I'd been wrong to make that decision without his input—thinking I was saving him just like he'd saved me.

Because he *did* need saving. Absolutely.

But love might not be enough. Perhaps only his own forgiveness could do that, and there was no quick way to make self-loathing switch to self-acceptance.

Either way—setting sail or spending another day here—he wasn't in a state to move yet. When he woke, we'd discuss, but for now, my stomach was empty and my mind a mess.

Food and a walk would clear my head.

My shoulders straightened. I was glad I had a plan instead of standing here fretting while he slept.

Tiptoeing toward the door, I tossed my still-damp hair over my shoulder. I'd had a shower and dressed in simple jeans and dusky pink hoodie. It made me feel my age. Made me remember in numerical value I was still so young, but in life value, I was ancient.

Elder never woke as I looked back one last time and headed down the corridor.

Treading down the stairs, my mind flittered once again to his oddness last night. How he'd vanished on me. How his body had switched from pain-brittle to sensual-smooth. How his words made no sense. How his eyes held no focus.

He'd been high as a damn kite and hadn't had any weed.

How?

I'd never seen someone so mellow and woozy, so utterly focused on sex before.

Reaching the bottom of the stairs, female voices floated from the lounge followed by a baby cooing.

Damn.

My stomach turned to lead. As much as I wanted to talk to Tess again, it hurt too much to be around baby Lino.

She was right before—when Elder was only seconds from arriving and bringing disaster—right about her chosen profession saving slaves from cruel masters and having a baby around. Either the women were too fragile to see such innocence or they only saw evil in the infant from their own past. It had the potential to pour salt into festering wounds and make them worse.

Like me.

Torn apart by a bastard never to conceive.

Fading back against the doorway, I held my breath, eyeing another way to leave the house. The front door beckoned as Suzette's French accent reached my ears. "Another bruise worn with pride, huh, *mon amie*?"

Tess's soft laugh echoed. "Another for the collection, I guess."

They giggled together, whispering something that, even soft and murmured, vibrated dirty with sex.

Tess spoke louder as they laughed again. "I know, I know. I should play harder to get. But my God, Suzette. He really knows how to make me lose myself." Her feminine lilt teased with something sinful. "I should be used to the man by now. But nope...he still manages to surprise me."

"You think I didn't see what happened between you two before you managed to make it up the stairs?" Suzette snorted. "He has you so well programmed you sink into subspace the moment he gives you that look."

I really shouldn't be eavesdropping on this.

I wasn't exactly comfortable being around those who were in a sexually explicit power play. I'd never judge those who enjoyed domination but with a past like mine...it made me wary.

My feet itched to leave, but my body swayed forward to listen. Naughty, disgusting habit to spy on others' conversations, but I'd heard that word before.

Subspace.

It prickled my skin, making old memories come back. It made me wonder...

"What look?" A baby rattle sounded while Tess couldn't hide the smirk in her voice. "There's no look."

"You know *exactly* what look." Suzette added a flirt to her tone. "The look that ought to terrify a normal person. He'd just had a fight. He was covered in blood. That look he gave you said he wanted *you* to be the one covered in blood. And what do you do?" She sighed dramatically. "Fall into subspace like a good little *esclave* instead of run for your life."

Tess lamented theatrically. "Ah...yes, *that* look."

The two women dissolved in a fit of laughter.

Tess lowered her voice. "But it's so addictive, Suzette. It's scary at how quick it happens. He just alters my mind until I can barely see and definitely can't talk. All I want is him."

"You're hopeless." Suzette snickered.

A baby's chatter interrupted the very adult conversation and the topic switched to if it was too soon for Lino to learn how to build skyscrapers with the Legos Franco bought last week.

I stayed where I was, lurking in the foyer, thinking over what Tess had mentioned.

Subspace.

Did she engage in sexual pain to capture such a thing?

I'd heard of it before I was kidnapped. Stumbled on a blog or two that broke down the physiological and psychological pros and cons of being in a Dominant/submissive relationship.

My mother was fascinated with the idea that a human's brain could have the power to switch off sensory reflexes if it reached an oversaturation of pleasure.

She had a wild theory that hypnosis worked on the same principles as subspace. That triggering such a mind state was similar, if not entirely related to the cataclysm of sexual depth.

I slammed to a stop.

Elder...

Did he reach subspace last night?

Was that what happened to him? He hadn't made any sense. His eyes didn't focus on mine. His lips couldn't form words. All he could do was fuck me then snuggle close as he passed out.

In one of the studies my mother made me read, it mentioned entering subspace for the first time required a careful balance of prolonged pain and heightened erotic pleasure.

Well, he had copious amounts of pain running in his system. Couple that with his OCD on needing to reach three orgasms, it could be possible he'd slipped. He could've entered a singular focus and forgot to care about anything else.

And if he *had* been in subspace...could he enter it again? What was it like?

Could he teach me to do it?

I wouldn't deny the thought of giving up all motor and cognitive control terrified me. But to have someone I trusted with utmost certainty take care of me while I gave in....

To have someone show me nothing but mind-stealing bliss?

The idea was intoxicating.

I looked over my shoulder, debating if I should run to him and climb back into bed. But the front door opened and in walked the older woman Q had kissed in the kitchen carrying grocery bags with a fresh baguette sticking out the top of one and celery sticks from the other.

She looked me up and down as if she fully expected me to be lingering, uninvited in the lobby. "Ah, you must be Pimlico."

Conversation in the lounge ceased immediately as I eyed the woman, stomping on the residual fight or flight whenever I encountered new people. Forcing myself to smile instead of snarl, I nodded. "I am."

"Great, lovely to meet you. I've heard a lot about you already." She gave me a kind grin and passed over a bag of groceries, somehow making me feel part of the family.

Her white hair matched her blouse while her navy skirt clung tight to generous curves. "I'm Mrs Sucre. Mr. Mercer's chef and kitchen minion."

"Minion? Where on earth did you learn a word like that, Mrs S?" Tess appeared, bouncing Lino on her hip, giving me a sweet smile. "Morning, Pimlico." Her smile carried another element too—something that hinted she knew I'd overhead more than I should and didn't care in the slightest. Her blasé comfortableness when it came to sex made me tense and relax at the same time.

"Morning." I returned her smile, looking at her son then back to her. I didn't know why, but Tess made me strong and weak within the same breath.

I wanted her as my friend, not because I was starved of female interaction, but because she came across so self-assured and happy.

I wanted to learn how to be like that. *I* wanted to be self-assured and happy.

I'd had flashes of self-assurance and definitely tasted happiness, but my past still cast shadows no matter how bright the sun. I still needed to learn, once and for all, how to walk away from that darkness and lock the door forever.

Mrs Sucre answered her, shuffling past and into the lounge with her bag of baguettes. "I learned that delightful word from *Despicable Me* that *maître* bought for Lino." She tutted under her breath. "That child is too young for international thieves and terrorist plots, even if it is wrapped up in a kid's movie with yellow sausages with glasses."

Tess chuckled. "I'll keep that in mind and tell Q to buy more baby appropriate films."

Mrs Sucre shook her head as if she couldn't believe the youth pretending to be parents these days. "You two will be the death of me. Mark my words...the world is in peril." Her eyes glowed with love, though. So much love and family joy.

I stood awkwardly with my bag of food, honoured to be a part of such a simple moment but unsure if I was truly invited.

Tess laughed, slinging her free arm around Mrs Sucre's considerable bulk and ambling with her to the kitchen. "You love us really."

Mrs Sucre sniffed, fighting a smirk.

Suzette giggled at the two women then came closer toward me, holding out her hand for the remaining grocery bag.

I didn't want to part with it—almost as if it were a passcode into this wonderful simple world—but I handed it over.

"Thanks." Suzette made to follow the others, but at the

last second, she stepped closer and leaned in.

All the blood in my veins turned to red ice, so unused to nor ready for someone to invade my personal space who wasn't Elder.

Her eyes narrowed as I stepped back, inhaling quick.

Instinct was what moved my legs, not choice.

Instantly, I chagrined, wishing I hadn't revealed yet another weakness.

She didn't let my running away phase her though, acting as if she'd seen it all before—which I guessed she had living in a halfway house for recovering women.

Pretending nothing had happened, she rested one hand on my tense shoulder then kissed each of my cheeks in French hello. "*Bonjour*, Pim." With a quick squeeze, she let me go then flounced toward the kitchen, beckoning me to join them. "Come on."

Brushing past Tess, she whispered something that made Tess laugh and blush at the same time. Something Parisian and most likely dirty just like their last conversation.

Whatever inside joke they'd shared, I wasn't privy, but Tess looked back at me, laughter still on her face and welcome in her eyes. "Come on, Pimlico. You must be starving. While the men aren't around, let us women enjoy some naughty conversation over equally naughty cupcakes."

* * * * *

The morning passed faster than I could've imagined.

Instead of being wracked with nerves and fraught with the need to return to Elder, I enjoyed one of the most normal, simplistic times of my life.

Hanging in a kitchen, sitting on a barstool with my legs swinging, I watched Mrs Sucre prepare culinary magic all while Tess and Suzette ribbed her. I laughed with the other women as the cook delivered dry one-liners straight back.

Sometimes, conversation slipped into French, adding a sprinkle of exoticness to the English dominated jokes and enquiries, but most of the time, I could follow the thread, chuckling with them at silly antidotes of life in the countryside and the joys of housing a pack of rescue dogs—dogs who apparently Q hadn't wanted but now was besotted with.

Brunch was served at the breakfast bar. Suzette and I sat while Tess stood next to Lino strapped into a baby chair clamped to the bench, feeding him morsels from her own plate.

On the menu turned out to be scrambled eggs cooked with copious amounts of Colby cheese and fresh baguette double grilled in the oven with lashings of butter. Such a simple meal but with the French flair and Mrs Sucre's talent, it was the best I'd ever tasted.

Once we'd finished, the chef—who'd joined us for her own portion—bustled around making more. I'd thought Q and the rest of the men were away somewhere, but I was wrong. Apparently, according to the trays Mrs Sucre made up with fresh coffee, eggs and baguette, and an iced cupcake on the side, Q and the others were hidden around the estate.

Once the meals were ready, Mrs Sucre waved us into the kitchen to collect. Tess took one to wherever Q was lurking, Suzette took one to Franco, and I carried one to Elder.

Three women. Three men. All taking mutual care of each other.

I'd never known something could feel so right.

Climbing the stairs with the comfortable weight of brunch and the smell of heavenly butter, my mind ran away with of visions of stepping into the bedroom, rousing Elder with a sweet kiss, and finding him healthy and happy. He'd be strong and healed and scold me for leaving him only to demand I make it up to him.

Reaching the landing and padding down to the bedroom, I smiled, hopeful and eager.

Nudging the bedroom door open with a toe, I already lived the fantasy I'd imagined.

I'll feed him, dote on him, make him feel—
"Oh, Selix."

My little scenario popped like a cork from a wine bottle,

smelling faintly of ruined opportunity.

Selix looked up from where he stood over Elder. His eyes fell on my tray as he gave me a half-smile, pointing at the side table. "Put that over there. He's out cold still." He frowned. "I'd expected him to be awake by now, but I guess he needs more rest than I thought."

My fingers clutched around the tray handles, guilt cloaking me. A confession sat salty and heavy on my tongue, but I daren't admit that Elder *had* been talking and awake before I'd let lust get the better of me and drained him of what little he'd gained.

Once again, lust had been the enemy. Only this time, it hadn't been a man's destroying my life but mine destroying a man's.

When I didn't move, Selix rubbed his face, raking his fingers through his three-day old stubble. "He needs sleep more than he needs food at the moment."

I agreed and disagreed.

Elder had slept most of the night after we'd had sex. He'd be hungry and dehydrated by now, seeing as he'd removed the drip from his hand.

Moving across the room, I deposited the food where the scents would hopefully waft over him and encourage his stomach to overpower his dreams. "Shouldn't we wake him to get him to drink, at least? He's been out for hours."

"He'll be okay now." Selix nodded at the new drip inserted into Elder's vein, stuck down with a white strip. "I noticed he'd ripped it out in his sleep. Michaels gave me strict instructions to keep this stuff flowing—even showed me how to administer. He thought Elder might remove it prematurely, so he made sure I came equipped to handle his stubborn ass."

His lips curled in an odd smirk. "He'll sleep comfortably while that goo works. However, in another hour or so, someone will have to help him to the bathroom. I'm not averse to injecting him with needles but inserting a catheter? Yeah, that's beyond my friendship loyalties I'm afraid."

I smiled, despite myself. Selix no longer scared me after the depth of affection he'd shown for his comrade over the past few days. We had a lot to discuss as far as where he'd been the night the Chinmoku arrived, but I trusted he was one hundred percent committed to Elder and therefore safe.

"I don't mind helping him." I was about to add that I'd done it during the night, but if Selix knew Elder had been awake and coordinated enough to shuffle to the bathroom, he might ask other questions that would reveal just how badly I'd screwed things up by being unable to say no to sex.

Selix shook his head, a snicker falling from his lips. "I think he'd rather you remember his cock is used for other purposes rather than pissing." He cleared his throat. "I'll tell you what. I'll stay for a bit. I have a few things to catch up on and can do that while keeping an eye on him. You can have the night shift before we get the hell out of this place."

"Oh, okay." My eyes flickered to the tray of unwanted food. I didn't want to leave, but I also didn't want to overstep. Selix was his friend. I wouldn't barge my way into Elder's life and displace him. I'd had my time playing nurse. I wouldn't be greedy. "If you're sure."

"I'm sure." He moved toward a chair by the window and pulled out his phone. "Have some business to take care of—repairs on the Phantom, plans going forward, etcetera. Need the peace and quiet."

I understood the dismissal. "Thanks for being there for him. I know he appreciates it."

Selix's head snapped up, his eyes locking with mine. His lips parted to say something, but he waved a hand as if to say it was no big deal even though his tension said it was a very big deal. "Don't need to thank me. He'd do the same."

"I have no doubt he would." With a grateful smile, knowing Elder wasn't alone, I headed downstairs to spend the rest of the day with women instead of men.

* * * * *

"You can hold him if you want." Tess looked up as I

gawked at the effortless way she dealt with a squirmy baby.

She'd just finished changing his diaper on a blanket in the lounge, redressing him in a yellow onesie with a giraffe on the front. A messy, thankless job and one that, for once, didn't make me crave to be in her shoes with a bouncy baby boy.

He might be small but oh my God, the mess he made…*eww*.

For a moment, her invitation didn't register.

I continued to stare as she managed to hold him even as he turned into an octopus, doing his best to slither out of her embrace to grab the dog's tail.

Twilight had arrived, signalling a foreshadowing end to this strange, simple day. Not an hour had passed when I didn't look at the ceiling and wish I could go to Elder. But no matter how much I missed him and became desperate to know how he was, I didn't climb the stairs out of respect for Selix.

Elder was in his capable care. I shouldn't worry. I should enjoy the chaos of domestic bliss and hang with two women who juggled family, real estate empires, and charities as easily as if they were an army of staff and not just two people.

We'd retired to the lounge where multiple dogs played, taunting Lino to crawl after them. He'd squeal in joy if one bowled straight into his tiny body while playing tug of war with a litter mate, then burst into tears if they stole his afternoon biscuit snack, caking his chubby fingers in canine slobber.

His range of tiny emotions varied from one extreme to the other in a matter of seconds, yet it didn't faze Tess and Suzette. Lino's noises were just life sounds and not distractions as they achieved tasks in a way I'd never seen. They did paperwork with one hand, discussed a charity dinner party and fundraiser next week, then switched to investment topics on properties in Southeast Asia.

At the same time, Tess would grab her son's hand and wipe away dog germs, prepare new menus with Mrs Sucre, and still find a way to talk to me in the mayhem.

We'd discussed everything normal women would: what I'd

done for work and school before I was taken. What my parents were like—and offered sympathies when I mentioned my father's death. They enquired after my favourite food and drink. Favourite season. Favourite thing about Elder.

And once we'd stumbled onto the subject of men, we stayed on it for a while.

I'd learned snippets about Q and Franco from sources that knew them better than anyone. I'd giggled at things most men would be horrified to know their significant other's had shared and became enlightened on more than one sex act that I might or might not have the guts to ever try with Elder.

So by the time Q stalked into the lounge and gave Tess a broodingly heated look, I no longer cursed him for what he'd done to Elder or feared him for his personal tendencies but saw him in a gentler light. His gruffness and clenched jaw didn't scare me because I knew he flat out adored his wife and baby and nothing made someone more human than that.

"Piiiim? Earth to Pim. Did you hear me?" Tess waggled Lino my way. "Did you want to hold him? You've been watching him all day."

Watching, yes.

Cataloguing, yes.

Learning how every day exposure to different stimuli helped evolve humans from wriggling carpet larvae to walking, talking, capable species.

But touch him?

Hold him?

Feel his heavy baby weight and smell whatever shampoo Tess washed him with?

No.

I can't.

Right now, I could study him the way my mother would. The way any student of psychology would—as a separate entity, granting fascinating boundless entertainment. An exhibit, for lack of better a word.

If I held him, he'd cease to be a study in human

development and become *real*.

Far, *far* too real.

Shaking my head, I laughed to hide the horrid secrets of why I would never hold her baby. "No, I'm fine. I'm happier just watching. Thanks, though."

"Not a fan of children, huh?" Tess winked. "I get that. They require a special kind of tolerance. Sometimes holding them is a feat in power with how they squirm and get into mischief." Lino pulled her hair and growled a baby growl, proving her point. "But if you change your mind, the offer is always open. Just grab him."

I didn't want to come across cold-hearted and untouched by her generosity to share her son, but I also couldn't endure the pain of correcting her.

Instead, I laughed softly, letting her believe her reasons were mine, looking away to fixate on something less painful.

Unfortunately, I caught Q's eye as he bypassed the couch with a black folder tucked under his arm.

With a knowing stare, he leaned down and scooped Lino from his wife's embrace.

Tess rose on her knees to claim a kiss before Q gave me a narrowed look and murmured to his wife as if I wasn't there. "She won't change her mind, *esclave*."

Tess shot me a look, then glanced back to her husband. "She might. I know people who say they don't want children sometimes change their minds."

Q shook his head, piercing me with a green glower. "I apologise, Pimlico. My wife is far too optimistic and doesn't see what is staring her in the face." He shot her a disapproving, adoring look. "She's too resilient, I'm afraid. Forgets sometimes."

I shifted on the couch, uncomfortable. "I'm not sure I understand—"

His nostrils flared as Lino tugged on his lapels. He shut down as if he didn't want to admit what he meant.

I should've just let it go. I should've read between the

lines. I should've saved myself a world of hurt.

But I didn't. I was an idiot. "Tell me."

He sighed heavily as if it cost him deeply to be honest. "What Tess doesn't see is that it isn't because you don't want children, it's because you can't. That's why you won't hold my son." He inhaled hard, his eyes apologising even as his voice remained cold, stripping me to pieces. "You're not the first to come into my care who can no longer have children from what was done to them. Under no circumstances should you feel less than or broken."

My shoulders curled. I gasped as a fresh wash of agony crashed.

His tone softened as Lino cooed. "This is a private matter, but I myself believed I was infertile for a time, so I understand the pain of wanting something but never knowing if it's possible."

I hugged myself, rolling over my knees.

"Q…stop." Tess turned white, clambering from the floor and moving to his side as if to prevent him from saying any more.

I was glad she tried to shut him up. I wouldn't be able to tell him to quit butchering me with his cold compassion. I had no breath in my lungs to breathe, let alone waste any on arguments trying to convince him he was wrong.

I so desperately wished I could laugh coyly and throw him off the scent of my tragedy. To convince them and me that children weren't living, breathing ghosts in my blood, never to become real.

But Q didn't listen to his wife, determined on lashing me to nothing, even as he tried to be kind. "I understand infertility and the loss you must feel but don't think you will forever be without. There are other ways."

"Q," Tess hissed, reaching for Lino. "Let it go."

He ignored her. "We donate and run many charities who save orphaned children and animals from around the world. In fact, one of the orphanages I helped set up is right here in

Blois. It's one of the few left. People don't believe in orphanages anymore, but I do. I've seen how living in a safe community can help heal trauma because my own home is an orphanage for abused slaves. Children need the same network—"

"Q!" Tess snapped, her cheeks red and lips thin. "I said, *enough*."

Bleak darkness entered his gaze as if he couldn't quite believe he'd spilled such truths and forced himself into my problems. "*Merde*, forgive me, Pimlico." He muttered something in French, something self-derisive and sharp followed by strained English. "Just like my wife didn't think, it seems I have the same flaw."

I can't do this.

I can't be here anymore.

Stumbling upright, I swayed as my lungs stayed tight, restricting air. "It-it's okay." Gulping oxygen, suffering the familiar pressure of panic seeping like glue into my chest, I fought against the tunnelling of my vision, the clawing of my throat.

I needed to find a place where I could be alone.

I needed to be free to gasp and gulp and rid myself of the pictures Q and Tess had put inside my mind.

"I-I'll be right back."

Tripping in my haste, I didn't look where I was going.

I didn't care I lied and had no intention of coming back.

I didn't care I just proved everything they'd said was true.

I just flew.

ELDER

INFERTILE.
Broken.
You're not the first who can no longer have children from what was done to them.

Mercer's words flew sickly inside my skull.

Screw him.

Curse him.

What in the ever-loving fuck was he *thinking*?

I stood swaying in the foyer, frozen to the spot, scalding hot with fury.

Some might say my timing was perfectly orchestrated to hear the horror Pim had kept from me. Others would say it was cruel to listen and not give her the chance to tell me herself. I would say the only one at fault was that French fucking bastard who once again hurt the one creature I loved more than anything.

It wasn't as if I'd planned this terrible circumstance.

It wasn't as if I'd hobbled down the stairs, still faint from injury and woozy with weakness, just in time to see Pim break apart.

"Shit," Selix muttered, crossing his arms beside me. "Want me to kill him?"

I bared my teeth. "If anyone is killing him, it's me." I

didn't care another fight would most likely put me in a coffin instead of a hospital.

He'd overstepped the line.

Again.

The past hour, I'd enlisted Selix's help in climbing from a stale bed, removing boots and bandages, and showering away the filth Pim had missed in my sponge bath. I'd eaten the cold meal left on the bedside table, submitted to oral antibiotics in return for having the drip removed from my hand, and then grimaced my way through dressing in loose trousers and black t-shirt.

My temper hadn't been the best when I'd woken and found Selix as my nurse instead of Pim. And it'd only grown worse the more pain and frustration I suffered as I prepared to leave this hellhole.

Hopping down the steps like a cripple had not been easy.

Seeing the foyer where I'd wanted to kill Q and failed wasn't good on my self-control.

But *this*?

Hearing the very man I wanted to murder tell the love of my life that she couldn't have children in such an arrogant, heartless way…yep, I wanted to fucking behead him.

Gritting my teeth, I took a pained step toward the lounge, ready to deliver another round of carnage. But a Pim-shaped bullet flew from the double doors, careened over the foyer tiles, and slammed directly into my chest.

"Fuck." I grunted, cursing as my ankle bent in a way it shouldn't, and her trajectory pounded my fractured ribs. Despite fresh agony, my arms instantly claimed her, wrapping tight, ruined shoulder and elbow clutching her close.

Her face tilted up, her lips slightly blue, her eyes totally wild, and I understood exactly where she was.

In the heart of panic. In the eye of an attack.

Fear for her overrode any discomfort I felt. "Come with me." I wrapped my arm around her waist as she buried her face into my chest, gasping as her lungs made a desperate attempt for breath.

Shit.

"It's okay, Pim. I've got you." Half-hopping, half-stalking into the library opposite the lounge, I focused on getting her away from that asshole and breathing again.

Selix remained where he was, a buffer between me and Mercer.

Pim didn't try to fight me, and the minute we were alone in the library, she darted from my embrace while I struggled to close the double doors with one hand.

As privacy and quietness fell around us, I spun to face her only to find her on the carpet by the cold fireplace. Her arms wrapped tight around her ribs, her mouth open, her gaze latched onto something I couldn't see.

She rocked gently on her knees, her hair swinging around her shoulders. No noise, no tears, nothing to hint at the destruction of panic inside.

Goddammit, she'd been so brave and beautiful—tending to me, doing everything she could to ensure I was comfortable and cared for—and now, when she'd needed me, I hadn't been there for her.

Shit, the guilt.

"I'm so sorry, Pim."

She didn't register, still locked in icy panic. Her vacancy to outer world things reminded me of me and what'd happened last night. I'd descended into an odd place during sex—a place I'd never visited and wasn't sure if I loved or loathed. It'd robbed me of a few memories but given greater clarity to others. It'd twisted something I already enjoyed into something I was desperate to attempt again. I'd never been so present in one task. Never been so consumed by a single factor—even with my OCD.

It had been magic. But no matter the individualism of what'd happened, it didn't stop me recalling just how incredible she'd been and just how much it broke me now to see her like this.

She hung her head, her lips still wide for breath.

I didn't speak again. Words couldn't reach her, but touch could.

Moving toward her, I lowered myself painfully into a leather buttoned chair close by, then leaned forward and ran my fingers through her hair.

The instant I touched her, she shattered like fine crystal.

Tears sprang from nowhere, and she scrambled across the carpet to wedge between my legs. Her strong, slim arms wrapped around me as her face pressed into my thigh.

Having her seek comfort and help—seeing her this way on her knees before me, knowing she was hurting far more than I could ever understand—ruined the final pieces of my already ruined heart.

"Ah, Pim." I bent over her, stroking her back, kissing her hair, holding her as she sat on the carpet and clung to me. "Breathe. Just breathe."

I cupped her head as she half-strangled, half-sobbed. She trembled so much, she made my body quake to match hers.

Her pain might not be physical, but she hurt, and I wished I could take it all away. I'd chop it into tiny fragments and burn them one by one. I'd burn everything until there was nothing left to torment her.

Including that bastard.

"It's okay, Pim. It's okay." I kissed her forehead, brushing aside sweaty strands, rubbing away the clammy fear on her skin. "Don't listen to that fucking Frenchman. He doesn't know what he's saying."

How dare he upset her with hearsay and incorrect assumptions? She was young. She was healthy. There was no earthly reason why she—*we*—couldn't have children if she wanted—

We.

Me…a father.

The thought struck me dead.

How funny that I'd spent my entire life pining for a family

who didn't want me, purchasing toys for cousins, creating safe havens for relations, only to never dare contemplate making my *own* family.

So what I'd been banished from one? I could create another. One with Pim who I loved more than anyone. A son or daughter who would love me for me and not hate me for my past.

Holy fu—

"No." Pim interrupted my coal-chugging thoughts. She shook her head, another sharp sob falling from her lips. "He's right."

"No one that egotistical is ever right."

She blanched. "But…in this matter, he is."

"What…what are you saying?" It was my turn to suffocate beneath the heaviness of horror. "Pim, what do you mean?"

She buried her face in my lap, crying harder.

As much as I wanted answers, as much as I snarled to know if I should cull such concepts of children, I let her hide. After all, I needed the time to piece together my own torture.

I couldn't pretend, sitting in this library, that this was the first time I'd thought about having a kid. I had. Of *course*, I had—no matter what bullshit I fed myself. A man like me who lived for family would look at every avenue to replace what was lost.

However, I could never bring something I loved so implicitly that they had the power to kill me if anything bad happened into this bad, bad world. Too many dangers. Too many criminals and thieves.

I should know.

I am one.

Having a kid would surely put me in an early grave with worry and concern, and besides, my life was about vengeance not procreation. Not until I'd cleansed the world of the Chinmoku could I, or any loved one, be safe again.

You're lying again.

Even before coming face to face with Q's son after our

fight the other night, I'd known he had a child. I'd seen the baby toys the moment I entered his home. It was hard not to with an overanalysing brain like mine. He lived a dangerous existence, just like I did, yet he'd found a way to protect his loved ones.

I wouldn't say it was easy being around children after being denied any involvement with my younger cousins, but I'd long since stopped tearing myself up, wishing for things I could never have.

Lying again.

I balled my hands, admitting to myself what I hadn't wanted to face.

Eventually, once all the shit I'd caused was righted, I *might've* broached the subject of pregnancy with Pimlico. *Only* if she reached a happier place. *Only* if she married me. And only if we were in a much safer existence.

Only then would we have sat down and discussed expanding our love to others we co-created. But whatever children we might or might not have had, it didn't change how I felt about her. Having a son or daughter wasn't a requirement to be happy.

That echoing emptiness inside me had filled the moment I found Pim. It'd remained filled having her in my world. I didn't need anyone or anything ever again. Just her.

Only, now...that emptiness returned, recognising the same emptiness in her, hating that she hadn't trusted me enough to tell me what burdened her.

Using the gentlest tone I could, I stroked her with soft fingertips. "You're not capable of having—"

"No!" She burrowed deeper between my legs. "I'm sorry. So sorry."

"Why are you apologising?"

"Because I can never give you a family!" Her tears grew louder, her breathing fast and chopped, instead of laboured and stubborn. "Because I can't give you what you need."

"What *I* need?"

"A family of your own, El. A son or daughter to replace—" Her sadness interrupted her. "I-I never thought I wanted that. I never believed—" She gulped harder. "I want it. So much." Her face scrunched as yet more anguish found her. "I want it so, *so* much, and I can never have it."

Fuck me.
Fuck.
Fuck.
Fuck.

Bending completely over her, I didn't care if she was smothered. I had to hold her. Had to show her she didn't need to hide her pain from me. I'd known she could see past my walls and read me better than anyone, but I hadn't been prepared for her to totally understand me.

To know that family was what drove me.

Not money.

Not power.

Not revenge.

I was a simple man with simple goals and she saw me far, far too clearly.

And she wants that just as much as I do.

As fast as I'd gone from refusing a scenario where Pim would bear my child, now I couldn't erase the image of her pregnant and beaming.

As I held her crying form, I finally understood what ate away at her. What she'd been harbouring, festering, hiding deep, deep down so I wouldn't share her agony.

That fucking bastard, Alrik, had taken her past *and* her future. She'd walked away from his corpse, but she'd never truly walk away from his ghost—forever reminded of him thanks to her barrenness.

I clutched her harder, hugging far too tight but needing her to understand I got it. I knew exactly where her mind was and, although I didn't have answers or fixes, I would be there for her no matter what.

"Pimlico…you need to talk to me." Leaning up, I pried

her face away from my lap with sturdy fingers. Holding her jaw so she had no choice but to look up, I murmured, "When did you find out?"

How long have you been lying to me, little mouse?
The hospital? The police? The check-ups?

That hurt worse than the terrible news of her infertility. The fact that she hadn't trusted me. That she'd willingly withheld.

What else had she kept from me, believing it was for my own good?

"You lied to me," I whispered. "You said the tests all came back fine."

Her skin cast pale cream; her eyes red-rimmed and puffy. Her gaze darted away before she found the courage to make eye contact and hold it. "I *am* healthy, so in a way, the tests *were* fine." She inhaled hard, waiting for me to explode or berate her.

I merely grazed my thumb over her cheekbone and didn't push her to continue. She had to find the best way to tell me, and I had to allow her time to do it.

Finally, she slouched, defeated and drained in my hold, spilling everything in a rush. "They said my insides are messed up from what was used on me. That the incorrect lubrications and unsanitary items have ruined any chance of conceiving. The scarring both physical and chemical...it's too extensive."

My analytical brain immediately chose disbelief as a rational argument. Pim was mine and she was perfect—therefore, there couldn't possibly be anything wrong with her. She wasn't flawed or broken. She'd *never* been flawed or broken—no matter what sort of things she'd lived through.

Clutching her hand, I squeezed, partly for her benefit and partly for mine. "That's one person's conclusion. Doctors sometimes get it wrong. We'll look for another opinion."

She squeezed back, guilt and shame and apology all over her face. "The doctor in charge said the same thing. That was why she had someone else look at the results."

"Fine, we'll get a third." I smirked, playing to my flaws, hoping to cheer her up. "You know my love of such a number."

She smiled faintly, her panic attack finally fading from her gaze. "There was a third. Followed by yet another examination. They all said the same thing. I didn't want to tell you this way. I'm sorry for keeping it from you, but I had no idea how to bring it up. How to destroy any hopes of having children in the future. How to hide the fact I went from a silly slave to a desperate mother all in one moment."

Her head fell forward as if praying to the false idol that was me. "I've never felt anything like it before. When people say you know if you want children and you know if you don't, I understand that now. I know one hundred percent I want them—only, my body no longer has that option so…I'll come to terms with it. I'll be fine." She looked up through chocolate bangs. "I'm sorry for scaring you, Elder. I'm okay now. It's not a big deal."

"Don't sell yourself short, Pim. Don't sugar-coat how gutted you are. It's a huge fucking deal." I cupped her chin, leaning close. "And you're not the only one it affects. I won't lie and say it doesn't tear me up inside. Knowing how much you're hurting and finally seeing just how perfect you truly are—it *kills* me. You want a family as much as I do. You want kids as much as….I never dreamed—"

I kissed her.

I couldn't stop myself. I couldn't prevent my tongue from lapping up her salty sadness and doing my damnedest to steal her grief.

She flinched into our kiss, her mouth hesitant to dance with mine. She spoke against my lips. "I'm sorry I can't give you the family you deserve, El."

"Bullshit." Grabbing her from the floor, I tugged her onto my lap. I didn't care about aches and pinches and pain. She came unwillingly, not because she needed the space but because she eyed up my injuries and bandages and tried to keep from adding more pressure to damaged parts of me with her weight.

Too bad I didn't give her an option.

I needed her close.

I needed her to truly hear this and believe me because it was the God's honest truth and would never fucking change.

"Stop fighting me. Sit down."

Wincing a little as if sharing the agony I lived with, she sank the final way, giving me the privilege of holding her.

Sighing heavily, she whispered, "I didn't want you to know. I'm sorry for that."

"First, you need to stop apologising. None of this is your fault." I kept my feelings about her hiding things locked away. She'd guessed her lies were part of what I struggled with—I didn't need to enforce her fear that I would flip out or blame her for any part of this.

I never would.

Fucking ever.

Holding her close, I breathed in the sweet scent of her skin. "Second, why didn't you want me to know?"

"Because I know how highly you hold family and you've fallen in love with a girl who can't give you one."

Chuckling under my breath, doing my best to scatter the sudden heartbreak she'd caused, I brushed hair behind her ear. "Pimlico…you *have* given me a family."

Her eyes widened. "How?"

"You've given me you."

She sucked in a breath. "But—"

"No buts." Pressing my nose to hers, I whispered, "No one else can give me everything I've been missing in one perfect package. You're it for me. Regardless if we can have children together or not. I don't need them. Not anymore. Not while I have you."

This time, she let me kiss her.

She kissed me back.

She let me heal a small part of her while I buried my own pain that we'd always remain a duet instead of a trilogy.

But as she moaned and melted in my arms, something insanely grateful washed through me. Something hot and thick and overwhelming in love and thankfulness for falling head over heels for this girl.

Any problems could be overcome. Any injury could be healed. Any bad news could be solved. But true love—real soul-deep connection…that could never be faked or forged.

Everything else was just white noise compared to that gift.

Pim kissed me harder, looping her arms carefully around my sore shoulders. "I missed you."

"I missed you, too." I kissed her back, our tongues tangling.

This moment would've been perfect but for one thing. One tiny thing such as privacy and personal comfort. I'd had more than I could stand living in someone else's house.

"We need to go home, little mouse." I nipped at her bottom lip. "I miss the sea."

"Home." She fluttered kisses on my lips. "Yes, let's go home."

I needed the ocean.

I needed open spaces.

I needed Pim all to myself to heal these new heartbreak wounds she'd given me.

Pimlico

"WE'RE LEAVING," ELDER snapped as he guided me (slowly and doing his best not to limp) into the lounge. "Right now."

Tess and Suzette looked up from the couch with Lino squished between them.

Selix and Franco mimicked each other with crossed arms and spread legs, glowering from their chosen corners of the room. The animosity from the two seconds-in-command ran rife and pungent, thickening the air with violence even as Lino giggled and blew saliva bubbles.

Elder tensed, taking in Selix's wariness and Franco's temper at having to share his domain.

I held my breath as I focused more on the two silently fuming males rather than little Lino. The panic attack that'd struck with diabolical persistency left me weak, wobbly, and woefully unprepared to face yet another happy baby cooing moment.

The one blessing in the powder-keg of a room was Q had disappeared.

I hope he stays away until we're gone.

Tess cleared her throat, standing from the couch. Ignoring Elder's comment about leaving, she came toward me with shoulders down and hand out-stretched as if coaxing me not to run again.

I swallowed hard as her warm blue eyes hurt for me, apology bright on her face. "Pim, I need to say how sorry I am for—"

"Don't." Elder pulled me tighter against him. "I think you and your husband have done enough. Don't you?"

She flinched, dropping her hand. "You're right—"

"Don't you dare talk to my mistress that way." Franco stepped forward, his body bristling in his immaculate suit. "Disrespect her and you disrespect this house." He balled his fists. "On second thought. Go right ahead. Insult her. Give me another reason to kick your ass."

Selix growled, moving toward Elder and me, his breathing harsh and tight. "If anyone is kicking anyone's ass, it's me kicking yours."

"Like fuck it—"

"Boys!" Suzette shouted. Leaping upright with Lino in her arms, she joined Tess in front of me. "No more fighting. There's been enough of that nonsense already."

Tess gave her a grateful look then glanced back at me. "I truly am sorry for overstepping. I know Q is, too."

"It's okay." I nodded, hoping I could ease some of her concern. Like Elder, I was ready to leave. The sooner, the better. We'd overstayed our welcome, and we didn't belong here. Nothing could have proven that better than babies and buildings rather than seagulls and sea.

Despite my need to leave, I didn't want to be unkind. Tess had gone out of her way to befriend me. The least I could do was ease her mind that it wasn't her fault I ran away like a freak. "You didn't cause the panic attack. I've had them for a while. A by-product of Al—" I cut myself off. Never again would I utter that bastard's name. Neither in my head nor out loud. He was dead to me. I was done invoking his hold over me every time I uttered it. "You understand."

Tess clasped her hands together, fully aware what I meant

and what I wouldn't say. "I do understand, and it's the truth when I say you're incredibly strong and I'm in awe of everything you've overcome." Leaning closer, doing her best to whisper so as to avoid Elder's glare, she added, "If you ever want to talk about anything…the weather, movies, babies or anything else, please feel free to email or call. Don't be a stranger, okay?"

"I will. And thank you."

We smiled again as Elder shifted angrily by my side. He held her accountable for my attack, but I didn't. It wasn't her fault. It wasn't Q's fault. It wasn't even my fault. My mind had done such a great job at protecting and shielding me from topics I couldn't bear to face that it still relied on such crutches. It would take time to slowly trust—to believe I was strong enough. I wouldn't berate myself for not being perfect just yet.

I'd been drugged and kidnapped and originally hated this place and the people in it, but somehow, in a few short days, I'd come to truly care for them and found comfort I might not have found elsewhere. I still wanted to know Tess's tale of captivity, but I would happily trade it to be back on the open ocean with Elder.

I was ready to be on our own again and hope to God that the Chinmoku didn't find us for months or even years. By then, Elder would be in fighting form and his artillery on the Phantom would kill them before they even stepped foot on board.

What are the chances of that coming true? I had a terrible feeling it wouldn't work that way.

But dreams…they were free, and I'd indulge for now. It was the cost of them becoming real that were sometimes too high.

A maid appeared behind us, hugging my torn red and blue ballgown. "Here. Better not forget this."

Elder took it from her, tucking it under his arm, blanching a little as another dose of pain administered. "Thank you."

I repeated his thanks, grateful to have it returned. I

plucked the hoodie I wore, looking at Tess. "I can change. Give you these back before we leave."

She shook her head. "Don't be silly. They're yours. Take them."

"If you're sure."

"I'm sure."

I'd never been good with goodbyes—not that I'd had many experiences with them—but social niceties had been completed. Therefore, we were free to leave.

Aren't we?

Elder stood brooding and itching to go beside me, Selix had already inched toward the exit, and there was nothing left to do but step out of their lives.

I sighed in relief and anxiety at what would become of us.

"You'll say goodbye to Q for me?" I asked. "Tell him I'm sorry for running. It wasn't him. It's just a tender topic so soon after—"

"He'll understand, Pim. He doesn't deserve your apology." Elder tucked me close, hugging me equally as hard as the ballgown under his other arm. "Thank you, Mrs Mercer, for allowing me to rest in safety." He bowed a little, ever the gentleman even as his blood boiled. "I hope to never see you or your husband again."

"Safe travels," Tess said softly.

"Let's go, Pimlico." Elder turned toward the foyer, guiding me through the double doors and toward Selix who held open the front door. "Helicopter primed and ready to fly?"

Selix nodded, his black hair shiny under the warm lights above. "Mercer refuelled us from his own supply. It's ready to go."

"Shit." Elder scowled. "That fool truly knows how to put his nose in places it's not wanted." He exhaled, full of annoyance. "Now I can't fucking leave without paying him for the gas."

Tess and Suzette followed us into the foyer. Tess peered upstairs as if she could see Q through the floors and found him doing something that pinked her cheeks with love. An adoring smile appeared then settled into a more professional one. "That's okay. He doesn't need your thanks. I'm sure I can say on his behalf that he's sorry things went so far between you, and he promises he'll listen more closely to the girl he's rescuing next time." She laughed. "No more shooting first and asking questions later."

Elder nodded curtly. "Fine. I'll send reimbursements online." Limping forward, he sped up at the sight of open grass with its invitation to leave.

Stepping over the threshold, he cursed under his breath as his muscles rippled against mine.

I frowned, looking up to see if he'd strained himself or needed help getting to the helicopter, but he turned around, facing Tess once again.

Clearing his throat, he gruffed, "Even though I still want to kill him; even though I would happily wring his ugly French neck, I'm not vain enough not to recognise he did me a favour that night."

I froze, gobsmacked that Elder could be so pragmatic even while he trembled with violence.

He bit out, "He shot me and took my woman, and for that I will never forgive him, but for killing my enemies and giving me another opportunity to protect Pimlico when I failed to do so, he will forever have my gratitude." Spitting the last word as if it tasted horrendous, he faced the exit again. "Tell him that—"

"Tell me what?" A slightly cruel, slightly inquisitive French accent drifted down from the top of the stairs.

Elder spun me in a circle, facing Q as he climbed down the stairs smooth as water and polished as glass.

"Nothing." Elder bared his teeth. "It was easier leaving the message with your wife than admitting it to your face."

"Ah." Q ran a hand over his jaw, yet another file tucked under his arm. "I'll ask my beautiful wife to relay your message when we are alone then. Perhaps, I can give her my reply in a language she understands all too well."

Tess blushed an elegant pink, moving to his side as he reached the bottom of the stairs.

Almost unconsciously, Q's entire body gravitated to her—not just his arm as it settled possessively around her waist but his every limb. All magnetized to the woman he'd chosen.

Elder huffed under his breath, bowing stiffly. "Goodbye, Mr. Mercer. I hope we never cross paths again."

Q shook his head, waving the file in the air. "Your goodbye is premature, Mr. Prest. I am afraid you have nowhere to go. Not yet, at least."

"What the fuck are you talking about?"

Ignoring Elder's question, Q let Tess go and closed the final distance between us, standing on the exact spot where the two men had tried to kill each other only a couple of days before.

Raising the file, he tapped it with his forefinger. "I'm talking about this." Pulling out the first sheaf of pages, he passed them to me with a look that made my knees water and breath mist. Not from sexual potency—even though he swam in that—but in vicious violence I'd grown accustomed to seeing in Elder.

I blinked, glancing between the two men, understanding the animosity on a different level.

Q and Elder hated each other—no one could deny that. But it wasn't purely about what'd happened on the Phantom or here. It was more than that. It was primal and probably not even noticed.

They're too alike.

Two alpha wolves used to being top dog and not happy with a rival in their kingdom. Both prickly and hard to love. Both loyal and affectionate until the bitter end.

"Here." Q urged me to take the papers, ignoring the warning glare from Elder. "This is for you."

Hesitantly, I took the thick file, skim reading the header page: *Dossier on Dismantling the Quarterly Market of Beauties.*

My head shot up. "What is this?"

Q narrowed his eyes at Elder as if assessing him for a threat before talking to me.

His shoulders never relaxed, but he must've deemed it safe to continue when Elder didn't throttle him. "I've been doing what I do for many years. In that time, I've been lucky enough to earn the trust and resources from local and international law enforcement. Thanks to them, I've been able to track down any mention of the QMB and the names of girls sold in recent years and bring each cocksucker who bought them to justice."

His voice thickened with passion. "I told you the other night that you were the last one. I meant it. I've had a flag on the QMB in every police database around Europe, with a few other enforcers in Asia and South Pacific. I'd almost given up on you—especially when we came across a very gruesome scene at the home of the man who purchased you. Along with that discovery, we linked another man, Monty Nilsson, to a past sale through the QMB. I believe, thanks to evidence we found, that you knew him."

Elder stiffened beside me, seething with fury.

My heart hid behind its ribs, flinching as sordid memories of just how well I knew Monty swelled. The fact that he wasn't there to kill him when Elder exterminated Alrik, Tony, and Darryl was a sore that never healed.

Q wasn't fazed by Elder's rage or my stunned silence, carrying on in his cool, crisp voice. "He's dead now, just like the rotting carcasses in that house. I doubt you'll grieve, knowing he died a rather painful death for what he'd done to other women."

He's dead.

The one loose end from the bloodbath when Elder claimed me.

Lightness filled my chest. A freedom from things that still haunted me.

"I hope you made him pay." Elder breathed hard.

"Oh, he paid." Q smiled coldly. "Just like the others who

bought slaves through the QMB. The in-house code to protect the identity of their buyers was useless, but it did take longer than normal to find you, Pim, due to your cut-off location. When we found the decaying bodies, I worried someone had killed them and taken you for themselves."

He gave Elder a pointed look. "Their deaths didn't stop me from hunting the potential new owner, though, even with no forwarding clues."

"Did you report the deaths?" Elder growled. "Did you leave any evidence behind at that bastard's place?"

Q scowled. "Who do you think I am? Some fucking amateur? We set it alight, corpses included. It's secluded enough to burn to the ground. Your secrets are safe." He smiled, teeth sharp. "Who killed them?" His face softened. "There was a lot of blood that didn't belong to the dead. Was it yours?"

Elder couldn't control his snarl. "He tried to sever her tongue. Another second and I would've been too late." He squeezed me so hard it hurt. "He wanted to turn her mute."

Q's face matched the darkness on Elder's. "In that case, I hope you made him suffer, not just for the things he'd done, but for all the things he was."

Somehow, a comradery struck up between the men talking about death and vendettas. "He died along with his maggot friend, but it wasn't a death they deserved." Elder looked at me, his eyes black and twisted with memory. "Pim fainted from lack of blood. She was my first priority. My *only* priority."

Q clenched his jaw, his eyes drifting to Tess with his own black memories. "I understand."

Selix came forward, cutting into the graphic conversation. "This is all fascinating, but why exactly can't we go home? What do you know that we don't?"

Elder snapped back to the present. "True. Stop wasting time and spit it out."

"When has information ever been a waste of time?" Q passed a single piece of paper to Elder but not before I caught a glimpse of the black and white image it depicted. "Information is power, as you well know. While you've been my guest, I've had someone watching your boat. He just sent me this."

My stomach bottomed out, splattering to my toes.

Oh, no.

"Fuck," Selix hissed.

"Shit." Elder's hand shook, holding the photo of his beloved Phantom with three Chinmoku scaling the sides and shadows of four more on the deck. His fingers dug into the glossy paper, entirely focused on his home. "How did they find us?"

Q licked his lips. "You obviously haven't taken note of the pleasure spotters online."

"The what?" Elder shot back. "What the hell do they have to do with me?"

"Everything." Q pulled another piece of paper from his file—a website print-out called *Spot the Special Elitist*. "This is just one of the many recreational groups online that spend their days tracking the rich, famous, and their toys. Helicopters, private jets, holiday homes. And in your case, yachts."

"What?" Elder speed-read the article where an unauthorised photo of the Phantom sat moored in a port I hadn't been to before. "Holy fuck, that's Calais." He squinted at the time on the blog post. "This was three days ago when we docked."

"They're rampant little leeches who think they're having harmless fun—tracking the itineraries of boats and schooners, but in reality, they're a massive security problem." Q took the page back, granting the information we needed to know in bullet form. "From what I can gather, they've been tracking the Phantom for years—just like they track every other super yacht around the world. They have check-ins and checkouts. They post when you have shipments of supplies and state how many days at sea you were before reaching a new port. It's a game to them. A stupid, silly game that has spoon-fed your enemies your every move."

Elder turned a furious red. "For fucking Christ."

I didn't want to be untrusting but just because Q had a photo showing the Chinmoku on board the Phantom didn't mean they were still there. They could've investigated, found no one, and left. We could still be free to return and set sail immediately—disappear into open waters where none of these weekend boat watchers could track us.

Nudging Elder with my shoulder, I whispered, "We've been here for days. They might have left. We could still go—"

Q shook his head, tapping the corner of the page Elder still held. The one with Chinmoku infesting his pride and joy. "This was sent to me twenty minutes ago."

"Twenty minutes? Fuck, my crew." Elder spun to face Selix, uncaring of injuries. "No one has called. Do you think—"

As if Jolfer himself had been waiting for this exact time to ring—determined to cause the most dramatic entry as possible—Selix's cell phone jumped into a jingle, demanding to be answered.

ELDER

I SHARED A look with Selix as his phone vibrated with urgency.

Two options.

Either the Chinmoku had slaughtered my crew and were calling to brag or Jolfer had somehow managed to get everyone to safety and was calling with a status update.

Either way, I had to answer.

Selix passed me the phone while I shoved Pim's dress at him. He tossed it onto the side table, completely forgotten.

My stomach knotted as I barked, "Yes?"

An eon of silence where my ears throbbed for good news but convinced they'd only receive bad.

"Prest, it's Jolfer."

Thank Christ.

Anxiety washed over me as my shoulders slouched and tensed at the same time. "Are you safe? What's going on?"

"Yes. We were hostilely boarded about thirty minutes ago. Luckily, the motion sensors picked up their arrival, giving everyone plenty of time to get to the safe room."

"That's good news." I paced away from Q's watchful eye, heading toward the library. "Where are you calling from? There's no reception in that bunker."

"I—eh, I got stuck. I tried to bypass your office. You left

your laptop out. I didn't want them having access to whatever important documents you might have on there. But I was cut off."

"Fuck, man. Who cares about the laptop? Every business account is encrypted. They can't steal shit." I didn't tell him they weren't there to rob the place but to kill anyone they could to teach me a lesson. "Get to the safe room. *Now.*"

"No can do." His voice dropped to a whisper. "They're searching each level. I can't understand them as they're speaking Japanese, but I did overhear the word Mercer and Blois. That's why I had to call you. Isn't that where you are?"

I wanted to hurl the phone across the room and punch every book in this godforsaken library. "For fuck's sake, they hacked my browser history."

I groaned at the ceiling. Christ, I'd been so careless.

When Jolfer passed on the radio call after we'd searched tirelessly for where Pim might've been taken, I'd looked up Mercer, learned enough to know I hated him, then rushed out of there too fast to shut down the web history.

I hadn't erased the search.
I hadn't used a ghost mode to hide my online movements.
They had Mercer's name.
They had his location.
Motherfucking hell.

Rushing from the library, I hobbled on my sprained ankle, breathing far too heavy for my broken ribs enjoyment.

My shoulder had a hole in it; my elbow didn't work probably. I still had bumps and bruises and stitches. But none of that mattered now. Q didn't matter. What he'd done didn't matter.

The only thing that did was Pim was once again in danger. *Because of me.*

And not only had I put her life at risk but I'd also put the entire Mercer household in the Chinmoku's crosshairs. Once again, I'd put a family in the path of death.

I'd been selfish and idiotic and sloppy.

My body had better heal itself in the next ten minutes because if I couldn't fight—if I fought as bad as I had when I'd tried to murder Mercer—then we were in huge fucking trouble.

If the Chinmoku came here, then only one outcome was possible. No opportunity of losing. No attempt at a truce. I'd have to win. I'd have to kill all of them.

And I'll fail.

My heart filled with sharp rocks as I glanced at Pim. Her face tight, her fingers looped together as if granting false comfort that everything would be all right.

Goddammit, I can't fail.

I couldn't because if I did…she'd die.

They'll all die.

And it would be my fucking fault just like my brother and father.

I can't…I can't go through that again.

A plan unfurled in my head, bright as lightning and deafening as thunder. All this time, I thought I had a choice on how this fight would end. I thought I would be the victor, when really, I'd condemned myself the moment I fell in love.

There was only one outcome, and I couldn't outrun it anymore.

My mother was right.

Jolfer whispered, cutting through my destroying conclusion. "Prest, they're leaving. Someone is shouting. I'm hidden in a laundry chute, and there's some sort of chant. They're getting amped up."

I knew that chant.

I knew the incantation before battle.

"Laugh at our prey's pleas, feast on our defeated cries, no one survives while the Chinmoku thrives."

That part of my life had been brief, but fuck, it'd imprinted itself onto my soul in more ways than one.

"Thanks for the warning, Jolfer." I pinched the bridge of my nose. "Stay safe."

Hanging up, I cast my eyes over the people standing in the

foyer. The Mercers who I didn't know, didn't trust, didn't like, but were now my priority. My responsibility. My burden.

I couldn't look at Pim.

I couldn't let her see the resolution in my eyes or the goodbye I was about to utter.

Clenching my fists, I braced for yet another war, already knowing how it would end. "They're coming."

Pimlico

"THEY'RE COMING?" MY eyes popped wide as instant terror iced my veins. "What do you mean *they're coming?*"

Elder tossed the unwanted cell phone at Selix and marched/hopped directly toward me. The torment swirling in his gaze shuttered, blocking me from reading him. His jaw tight and unyielding, a master of the situation with all the answers and no uncertainty. "I mean, I need to get you out of here. Right now."

"But—"

A black blur charged, bowling into Elder, wrapping furious fingers around his throat and slamming him against the wall. Elder groaned as his body suffered yet another attack.

Q panted in rage, his hand white from squeezing as he repeated my question with venom. "What the fuck do you mean they're coming?"

He lost all hint of being generous and friendly, showing just how nightmarish he could be. The blackness on his face reminded me all too well of the men I'd been sold to and the life I'd once led.

I wanted to save Elder, but I couldn't stop the self-preservation in my blood. Falling backward, I bumped into Tess who grabbed my hand. "It's okay. He'll calm down in a—

"

Q roared, shaking Elder who chopped both his hands on the grip Q had around his throat. With a twist and skill gained from years of fighting, he dislodged Q and stood braced like a predator about to attack. "They looked up my browser history. The last thing I searched was you, asshole."

"And you didn't fucking wipe it? You didn't encrypt it?" Q dragged hands through his hair. "For fuck's sake!" He launched into a tirade of French, growing louder and harsher with every syllable.

Tess stayed beside me, knowing not to interrupt anything—human or beast—when their temper was this unravelled.

"I can't believe this!" Q snarled, switching back to thick English. "I can't *believe* you've brought danger to my family. To my wife. To my *son*! How the fuck could you?" His eyes turned wild, nostrils wide, skin white with fury. "I failed my *esclave* once. I let her be taken because I was a goddamn idiot and didn't cover my tracks. And now you've gone and done the same fucking thing!"

He whirled on Elder, slamming his arm against Elder's collarbone, pinning him once again to the wall. "This is your fault. This is your mess. Get the fuck out." Grabbing Elder by the scruff of his t-shirt, he yanked him toward the door. "Get out. Now!"

Elder tripped and whatever decorum he clung to shattered as his ankle bent and pain drenched. He matched Q's anger lash for lash.

Tearing Q's hold off him, he shoved the Frenchman and stalked him. "Don't lay another fucking finger on me." He pointed at me. "*She* is the only thing I care about, and believe me, we're leaving. I'm not staying here for those assassins to take her from me."

"So you'd let those assassins take my family instead?" Q laughed bitterly. "What a fucking cunt." Another stream of French fell from his lips as Tess stepped toward him and laid a gentle hand on his heaving chest.

He breathed hard as Tess murmured things I couldn't hear. Her gaze fixed on her husband, imploring him to calm down and listen.

Slowly, breath by breath, Q blinked away his bloodlust and focused on whatever his wife said.

Elder spied his opportunity. "Come on, Pim. We're leaving."

I froze to the spot.

I'd only ever known Elder to be selfless and hold family—any family—in the highest regard. The fact he wanted to leave Q and Tess alone to face the Chinmoku, knowing how deadly and ruthless there were with no support——wasn't right.

It went against everything I knew about Elder.

It made me wonder if he wasn't as pure hearted as I thought.

Shaking my head, I crossed my arms, rubbing at a sudden awful chill. "We can't go."

Elder hobbled toward me and grabbed my bicep. "We can, and we are." Dragging me toward the front door, he muttered, "The sooner we leave, the sooner we can intercept the Chinmoku."

My heart kick-started again with a flash of understanding. He wanted to leave, not to avoid whatever battle was about to happen, but do his damnedest to prevent it from happening here—where innocent babies and a marriage that had no right to be caught up in Elder's ancient war existed.

I fell into even deeper love with him, willingly moving toward the exit.

Selix pulled his gun from his waistband, clicking open the chamber and counting whatever bullets he'd stocked it with. "If we're going to do this, we need more ammo, Prest. I'm with you one hundred percent, but we don't know how many there will be and—" He looked Elder up and down. "You're not exactly a weapon yourself right now."

Elder brushed past him, jumping on one leg down the

steps to the driveway. "I know how many there will be. Thirteen."

"How do you know that?" Selix trailed after us.

"I know because that's how many the leader takes with him to exterminate those he's lost patience with." Elder smiled tightly. "Men like me." His fingers bit into my arm as he guided me across the lawn to the awaiting helicopter.

Selix's eyebrow rose. "If we're intercepting them, why are we going in the helicopter? It will be too hard to spot them. We won't be able to land. We'll be stuck shooting the ten measly bullets I have from the air."

Elder huffed as his body dared remind him it wasn't up for a trek so soon after being injured. "You're going in the helicopter with Pim. You're going to take her somewhere safe."

"Oh, hell fucking no." Selix slammed to a stop. "I suppose you think you're going to fight them on your own, right?"

Elder didn't answer, but the set of his body and steely glint in his ebony eyes said that was exactly his plan.

What?

No, no, no...

Selix laughed coldly, arguing before I could. "Be realistic, Prest. They'll kill you the moment you find them."

"Exactly," I managed to puff. "It would be suicide—"

Elder's fingers dug deeper into my arm, silencing me. "I know."

"Then you can't be serious—" Selix and I asked together with matching threads of horrified disbelief.

"I'm deadly serious." Looking at me, Elder's face melted with utmost love. "I'm so sorry, Pim."

Tears instantly sprang to my eyes. Tears fashioned from understanding that he carried far too much responsibility and guilt and shame and knowledge that he'd caused this and it was time he finished it—even if it meant ending it in the way he'd tried to avoid all these years.

By dying.

"No, El." I couldn't stop my wet sob. "You can't."

"I can if it means you stay safe." He stopped, dragging me close and cupping my cheek. "I love you, Pimlico, but I'm not being fair to you by dragging you around the world hoping to stay away from these men. These men I used to work for." He bent his head and kissed me ever so softly. "These men I invited into my life and haven't been brave enough to face ever since. This is my cross. Not yours."

I cried out at the blistering, excruciating pain that this might be the last time I ever kissed him, the last time I ever saw him.

No!

He can't do this.

Clinging to him, I cried, "This can't happen. I won't let it happen. We'll come with you. We'll help you fight." Even as I promised such things, I knew I would never be able to keep them. I was utterly useless when it came to war. I would be nothing more than a hindrance, a shackle.

If only he was healed. If only he was capable of taking on thirteen highly-skilled fighters and winning.

"Please, Elder." I clutched his t-shirt, not caring if I prodded bruises or poked stitches. "You can't do this. You can't. Let us come with you."

If only to let us die together.

Dying beside him was better than dying decades from now after a lifetime without him.

He chuckled sadly, kissing my forehead. "I have no doubt you would fight any manner of evil for me, Pim, but I can't let you do that. I love you too much." Kissing my mouth, he pushed me toward Selix. "Go. Before it's too late."

Selix crossed his arms, neither grabbing me nor fighting Elder's stupidity on martyrdom. "Don't do this, Prest. Like Pim said, it's suicide."

Elder's eyes flashed. "If my death means they'll leave the people I love the fuck alone, then is it really suicide?" He breathed hard with dreadful passion. "I've been living a lie, telling myself I would do anything to avenge Kade and Otōsan, when really, I've been running this entire time. All I need to do is let them kill me. Then this—this horrible, shitty mess—is over. I should've done it fucking years ago. I see that now."

I bent over, hugging myself as another crash of sorrow and frustration battered.

How *could* he?

How could he talk about dying as if it was his choice whether to extinguish his life?

Don't I have a say?

Don't I have a right to disagree?

He shouldn't have to die. None of this was normal or acceptable. There *had* to be another way.

Anger devoured my panic, snapping my back straight and balling my hands. "I won't let you do this." I wanted to jump on him and tell him what an idiot he was being. I wanted to waste every breath and pay every tear if it meant I could somehow change his mind. "You can't."

Even as I shouted in his face, I knew it was pointless.

I knew Elder.

I knew he was stubborn.

And I knew he was proud and loyal and old fashioned in his role as protector. My and Selix's arguments would fall on already decided ears. Elder wouldn't listen. He'd stay steadfast to the plan he believed benefited everyone.

"Elder...please, please don't do this," I begged quietly, relinquishing my anger as quickly as it'd arrived.

He flinched, swaying toward me as if every molecule and heartbeat demanded he obey and grab me. His fingers fluttered in my direction, his eyes turned glossy with bone-deep need, and he bit his lip so hard he drew blood, fighting the connection, the link, the emotional rope binding us together.

"I...I'm sorry." With balled hands and stiff joints, he backed away from me instead of succumbing to the blistering bond between us. He back-stepped toward the black Town Car Q had pulled up in when I'd first seen him holding Lino. "I'm so sorry, little mouse."

"No!" I dug my toes into the grass to run after him, to glue myself to his side if need be, but a booming French voice silenced the night-time chorus of cicadas, freezing all of us. "*Arrêtez*. Stop. For fuck's sake."

Leaping down the front steps, Q kept his hands balled as Tess trailed after him, her blonde hair the only thing light in the black night.

Stalking to Elder, he growled. "I hate you for this. I hate that you've brought death and decay straight to my door."

Elder vibrated with hostility. "I know."

"What will happen to my family?" Q paced in front of him. "What will happen if they come and you're not here?"

"I'll cut them off before they arrive. They won't—"

"But if you don't." Q slipped into dangerous darkness. "If you're not here? If you don't find them in time?"

Elder stood taller, accepting blame but unwilling to buckle beneath his enemy. "They will kill everyone. As a message…" He pinched the bridge of his nose, visualising the carnage. "Fuck."

"Exactly." Q dragged fingers through his hair as if trying to keep his hands busy so they didn't punch Elder in the face. "You're not going anywhere."

Elder's head snapped up. "I don't bow to you, asshole. This isn't your fight. It's mine." Stalking toward Q, he shoved him back. Rage cloaked him, overflowing from the well of emotional pain he always carried. "I ought to have killed them fucking years ago. I know that. I blame myself every goddamn day that I still haven't faced what I should've faced the day they made me into what I am."

His features turned brittle and black. "They took from me and I still haven't taken from them. Don't you know the fucking guilt I carry? Don't you get the depth of shame that I haven't fucking fixed this? That I continue to put those I love in danger? That I haven't delivered the revenge I swore I would deliver?"

He pointed at me with a shaking hand. "Don't you think

I'd rather stand and slaughter every bastard in order to deserve her? I've failed her time and time again and it fucking rips me to shreds that even now—even now, on the eve of finally ending a lifetime of regret and misery, I can't do anything to save her."

Silence fell as Elder stormed away, masking his limp with sheer temper. Whirling around, he snarled, "You might not get honour, Mercer, but I've lived a lifetime being cast from it. Dishonour is the only thing I know anymore and if it means I have to leave the one thing I love most in the world to finally earn a smidgen of self-fucking-respect. Then, I'll do it. I'll do whatever it goddamn takes to fix this. To *end* this."

Q didn't speak.

No one did.

Elder's outburst faded from shout to soul.

Breathing hard, Elder shrugged as if he had nothing left—no other way to prove his dedication to this disaster. "I'll find them before they come here. I'll stop them before they kill anymore—"

"You'll die so others might live." Q backed down, his fury beaten into submission by Elder's.

Elder stiffened with loathing. "Exactly. It's the only thing I can give and I'm willing to give it. I'm willing to die...for her."

"Fuck." Q looked at the ground, laughing sickly as if he couldn't quite believe the offer he was about to extend. "I hate you, Prest, and I'll never fucking forgive you for putting my family in danger but...*merde*, I can't let you die for your stupidity."

He looked up, eyes on fire and reluctance in every vowel. "I made my own mistakes by shooting you and bringing you here. My wife kindly reminded me that I played a role in this catastrophe, and you just reminded me that honour separates man from monster. I can't kick you out when you most need my help."

"I don't need your help, Mercer," Elder snapped. "This was never about you. This is about me protecting what I love."

"Yes, and this is me protecting those *I* love. You leave, you die. You stay, you might live. We *all* might live." Glancing at Selix then back at Elder, Q grunted, "Hatred can blind us, but for now, I can see. And the only scenario I can see is the one where you stay."

"If I stay, they'll—"

"They'll come." Q shoved his hands in his pockets. "You'll stay. They'll come. But that's the last thing they'll ever do. We'll fucking kill them and be done with this." He smirked coldly. "At least then I can go back to hating you with a clear conscience."

There *had* been another way.

Elder didn't have to die, but the stubborn ass didn't move or accept the truce. He studied Q as if he hadn't spoken English—as if his offer was riddled with booby-traps.

And perhaps it was, but for now...*Elder doesn't have to die.*

Q sniffed and muttered a French slur.

Yanking his hand from his pocket, he held it out spear-straight, poised for Elder to accept. "What are you waiting for, Prest? We have a fucking war to win."

ELDER

WHAT COULD I say that wasn't ungrateful, suicidal, or plain melodramatic?

Thanks, your help isn't wanted?
Your offer to save me from dying isn't needed?
I don't require your meddling so just fuck off?

I hated him but I couldn't deny I was blown away by his olive branch.

What sort of bastard did that?

I hadn't meant to blow apart every truth festering inside me. I hadn't meant to explode or reveal every condemnation and self-disgust I carried.

But he'd pushed and fucking pushed and now...everyone knew.

I didn't know why he'd chosen to extend his hospitality to include shared warfare, but whatever the reason, he'd fucked me because Pim barrelled into my arms, kissed my cheek, and winced in sympathy as I groaned in pain from my stupid wound-filled body.

She wriggled closer as if she wanted to climb inside and erase the darkness I lived with. As if the purity of her love could save me.

I loved her.

But she couldn't save me.

Only facing my past could do that.

I wanted to clutch her hard and heal, so I could be the man she expected me to be. I wanted to be immortal and invincible so she would never be alone or unprotected.

But I was just a man.

A man who'd fucked up too many times.

A man who had to make a decision.

Mercer never took his eyes off me; his hand outstretched unwavering, waiting.

We stood toe to toe, glaring at each other. I'd fought this man—I'd shed his blood like he'd shed mine, and now, as he waited to strike a bargain with death, I looked past the aloof arrogance and saw something I didn't want to see.

He was me.

We were two men who'd fucked up a lot, but when it came to protecting those we cared about, nothing and no one would get in our way.

In this instance, *I* was the one in the way. I was the reason Pim and the Mercer family were in danger. And instead of casting me out and allowing me to die so no one else had to, he offered me a life-line of resources.

How could I refuse?

How could I trade living over death?

The answer…*I can't.*

Barely breathing and still drowning in thoughts of pain and carnage, I slotted my hand into his.

Touching him made every instinct want to strike him down before he could strike me. There was an undercurrent in him that fed the undercurrent in me. Something that said the man before me wasn't truly who he portrayed. He was something society would never appreciate or accept.

I related because I had that same dirt, that same need to control and slaughter. That same bone-cracking drive to be better than I was and failing at every turn.

We clasped strongly.

We squeezed with intention.

We sealed the bargain with seriousness bound from mutual hate.

The moment we relinquished our bond, Q turned to his wife. "Take Suzette, Lino, Pimlico, and the on-site staff and lock yourself in our bedroom."

Pointing at Franco, he commanded, "Round up the security team. Let's get ready to hunt."

* * * * *

Three hours.

Three interminable hours when time stretched on, torturing us.

I couldn't tell if I wanted yet more of the same torturous waiting or for the clock to strike D-day and get it over with.

Depending on how the Chinmoku arrived, they could appear at any second. The drive from the port only took four or so hours—at approved speed limits—and I didn't have a clue if they'd have other methods of transportation.

We were literally sitting fucking ducks, waiting for the hillbilly with his shotgun to arrive and blow us into feathers and pâté.

It'd almost been as hard to watch Pim leave with Tess and the maid, heading to safety, as it had been to say goodbye. The next time I saw her—*if* I saw her—this would all be over and who knew what sort of world would be left.

The disabilities I suffered ached deeper as I did my best to pump ruined muscles with adrenaline, preparing for yet another battle. I couldn't focus on the way breathing killed me or walking was a debilitating chore. I had to be functioning. I had to be invincible.

For three hours, we'd reconvened in the games room hidden beneath the stairs. Neither the library nor the lounge would work as headquarters with the number of windows and visibility from the outside.

Instead, we'd spread out floor plans of Mercer's chateau on top of his large pool table. Used whiskey glasses acted as markers for where we would try to direct the Chinmoku for better target practice. A strategy contrived by all of us, including help from Mercer's in-house security team.

Twelve men.

Twelve well-trained, ruthless men who all had kills under their belt in one way or another, according to Mercer.

In an ordinary fight, I'd say our odds were better than good. Mercer's men had automatic guns, wicked sharp blades, and honed instincts on how best to slaughter.

However, this wasn't an ordinary fight.

This was the Chinmoku, and they wore red gloves for a reason. Their hands were as sharp as blades, their kicks as merciless as bullets. If Mercer's security had never come face to face with a trained martial arts master, they were as useless as I was in my current condition.

I rolled my shoulder, contemplating making a brace out of a tea towel hanging on the bar in the corner of the room. The ache in the gunshot wound had increased since we'd started talking military action.

I wanted to numb the throb but couldn't have alcohol, and I refused any more painkillers that Selix kept in his back pocket.

I needed my brain clear. I needed to become one of them again if I had any chance of outsmarting my old master.

Q interrupted my thoughts, his hands splayed on a schematic of his home, his lips damp from a sip of whatever amber liquor he'd poured. "Anything to say to the men, Prest? You know these bastards. How would you defeat them?" He cocked his head, obviously remembering his part in mowing down the men who'd infiltrated the Phantom the other night. He'd already killed a few, and his cocky smirk showed it. "I went to your boat trigger happy. I didn't give them a chance to get near me. Is that what you suggest?"

I nodded, balling my hands, ignoring my stiff broken finger that refused to bend. "That is the best advice. These men have been honed since birth to kill with nothing. If they underwent the same initiation I did, they'll have had their senses robbed—making them fight blind then deaf then crippled—teaching how each malady is nothing that they can't overcome. As each skill is mastered, they become better and better at being unseen, unheard, unknown until it's too late."

I narrowed my eyes at the men around the room. "Let them come close and they will find a way to destroy your gun, break your bones, and steal your life before you even look into their eyes."

The dark-suited army shifted and cleared their throats. One by one, they nodded. "We'll shoot the moment we confirm they're Japanese and not one of ours."

"Good." I inhaled hard; the room swam a little as more pain made itself known. I wished to fucking God I wasn't the weakest link. I wished I could meet the leader on Mercer's lawn, rip off my shirt, don my old pair of crimson gloves, and challenge him.

That would be the surest way to end this with no further bloodshed of others. The only people bleeding would be me and the leader of the Chinmoku.

They were assassins and traffickers and drug dealers, but they were also the most honourable men I'd ever known.

They had a code.

That code was stricter than law—it was their heartbeat and absolute.

Law number one: run from your mistakes and they'd kill everyone associated with you until you were dead.

Law number two: once a Chinmoku always a Chinmoku.

If you broke law number two, you could die at your hand or theirs—honourable or dishonourable. Or…challenge and win.

If I had the ability to challenge, this would all be over because it didn't matter if I won or lost, the moment my life was claimed, every scrap of history between us would vanish and they would bow and walk away, leaving Pim, Selix and Mercer's family alone.

Their karma scales balanced and bound by their code.

But if I won....

If I was strong and well enough to kill Daishin—the current emperor of the Chinmoku—then I would become God and have the power to tell them to stop. Fuck, I could command them to fall upon their samurai swords and they'd have no choice but to obey.

Daishin.

Ha!

I rolled my eyes as old memories filled me. Of lethal commands and a heartless ruler. What a laughable name. In Japanese, it meant *Great Truth*. A Buddhist name—a temple—yet he was one of the most feared, secretive men in the world.

Mercer continued talking to his team, pointing out weaknesses in his front line, sipping his drink while listening to fresh strategy. His right-hand man, Franco, stood by his side, glowering at Selix and me, blaming us not so subtly for everything.

I didn't even have the energy to hate him or Mercer anymore.

After three hours of waiting, the only thing I felt was guilt. Guilt and shame for being stupid enough to put yet more innocent people in peril because of my screw-ups. Guilt that Pim wasn't safe. Guilt that she'd fallen in love with a man who lacked in so many ways.

Pim.

Fuck, I missed her.

My eyes trailed for the thousandth time to the ceiling where I assumed Pim was locked away and untouchable with the others. I had no clue where Mercer's bedroom was, but I hoped to hell it was well fortified.

Because even with the men we have, we might not have enough.

Mercer clapped his hands, ending the current discussion. Abandoning his station and schematics, the glint in his eye said he was satisfied his men knew their part to play.

Carrying his crystal goblet half-full of liquor, he stopped beside me, eyeing up my bandaged shoulder and curling his lip at the brace around my ankle. "Perhaps, you should go with the women."

I wanted to wring his fucking French neck. "I may not be running at full capacity, but I can still kill a Chinmoku or two. And that's more than I can say for you."

He sipped his drink, smiling slyly. "If they're anything like you when you fight, then I won't have a problem winning."

"You'd shot me, asshole. It wasn't a fair fight."

"I've been shot before and still killed my enemy. Been stabbed a few times, too." His eyes darkened. "Don't give excuses for failure…especially when failure is not an option." His attention flickered to the ceiling, no doubt thinking of his wife just like I thought about Pim.

I narrowed my gaze. "Who?"

"Who what?"

"Who shot you?"

He shrugged, swallowing his secrets with his liquor. "No one still alive."

We stood in silence for a while, listening to the murmuring of men and occasionally studying the security feeds showing every vulnerable part of the house.

When would they arrive? The tension in the room multiplied until the very air hissed with pent-up aggression and need to attack.

Franco marched up to us followed swiftly by Selix, who treated Franco as a dirty shadow, constantly trying to erase his presence by turning on a proverbial light.

Ignoring me, Franco spoke to Q. "I wish to fuck we hadn't dismantled those snares and traps in the gardens. What if the motion sensors fail at the perimeter?"

Q shot back the rest of his drink. "We had no choice. I couldn't let my son crawl around or Tess run with the dogs knowing any wrong step could mean their remains became fertilizer on the flowers."

Franco grumbled something that didn't sound like he totally agreed. Returning to his post, Selix rolled his eyes as if to say he was over the dramatics of Mercer's second and followed.

Mercer twirled his empty glass, his own gaze drifting to the ceiling again.

I spoke before I could censor and stop myself. "You love her very much."

His green eyes latched onto mine, a dare lurking in their depths, just waiting for me to say something bad about her so he could attack. Slowly, the rage simmered. "Yes."

I looked at where he was staring, imagining Pim and Tess above, laughing and safe—exactly how they'd stay as long as we did our job correctly. I'd done unspeakable things and some in the name of protecting Pimlico. Had Mercer done the same? "Have you killed for her before?"

His sharp chuckle ran nails down my back. "I've ripped out hearts for her before."

"Interesting analogy."

"Interesting fact." He smiled with sharp teeth.

"How?"

He cocked his head. "Strange question."

"I mean how did you rip out a man's heart?"

He rolled his shoulders, working out a kink in his neck as if this conversation was locker room talk and something to be humble about rather than hidden far, far from society and never mentioned. He said he had cops on his payroll. Online media called him France's golden boy. How had he kept his feral side a secret for all these years?

He truly was a monster living in plain sight.

"Tess was given to me as a bribe." His voice thickened. "Normally, I would've sent her straight home. But…" He shrugged. "This time, I couldn't. I turned into something I'd promised myself I never would, and then I went and did the worst thing I could ever fucking do."

I shifted, trying to find a more comfortable position for my throbbing ankle. "Falling in love with her."

His nostrils flared as if he wasn't quite prepared for me to read him so well. But it wasn't a matter of reading him—it was a matter of knowing myself and the fact that falling for Pim was both the best and worst thing I'd ever done.

Q stared into his empty glass, pensive. "I fell for her, and my natural instincts were blinded. She had a tracker in her neck. They knew what I was by then…so they took her from me." His fingers tightened on the glass, his knuckles turning white. "I couldn't stop what happened to her, but I could stop the men who did it."

He pinned me with a glare. "When I found him, I slit open his chest, cracked his ribs with my bare hands, and I ripped out that motherfucker's heart while he breathed."

A chill worked over my skin. A chill of disgust but also of utmost awe. He loved to the depths that I did. A love that wasn't encouraged because it made men do terrible things and somehow honour became wrapped up in sin.

I opened my mouth to tell him I understood or empathised—something to show him he needn't hide with me—but a shrill tune cut through the air, silencing the room and everyone in it.

Franco hissed under his breath. "The sensors never went off."

Everyone scrambled to the staircase, avoiding travelling up them until Mercer and myself charged to the base and listened once again to a doorbell melody as the Chinmoku boldly announced their arrival.

* * * * *

This was Mercer's house; therefore, it was his door to open.

But as we strode across the foyer, shoulder to shoulder, guns holstered in our waistbands and our army trailing behind us, he fell back, giving me permission to be the one to begin this.

I still hated the bastard, but I couldn't deny I had newfound respect for him.

I picked up my speed as best I could, unlocked the multiple high-tech locks, and opened the impressive front door.

And there was Daishin.

The man who'd lent my father money to buy my dust-broken cello.

The man who'd whispered to me late at night that I had so many gifts if only I had somewhere I could use them.

The man who'd hugged me and told me I was like a son to him, only to smear my lounge's walls with the blood of my father and brother when I'd disappointed him.

Our eyes locked.

Black to black.

To the Western world, it was obvious I had exotic blood mixed in my veins. My jet black hair, lean build, almond eyes, and tanned skin hinted that I wasn't quite like them. But to the Eastern world, it was evidently clear I was an imposter.

Daishin was quintessential Japanese with salt and pepper hair, pockmarked cheeks from terrible childhood acne, and eyes that would put any cat to shame. Despite his age and imperfections, he was willowy with Asian grace, long fingers encased in bright red gloves, lips well-formed but not full, a nose visible but not overpowering, and an effortless way of moving that made everyone around him seem clumsy and untrained.

He smiled, tight lipped and cold. His voice so familiar, slipping into a language I hadn't used in a very long time. "Well, if it isn't my favourite pupil, Miki-san."

I mimicked his welcoming grin, replying in Japanese. "I haven't been Miki in a very long time, Daishin-san. And I've long since stopped being your pupil."

He clasped his hands in front of his crisp black suit. The stitching looked tight and unforgiving, the buttons and tailoring as impeccable as any Western designer, but I knew from experience the material he chose was stretchy, giving his clothing incomparable agility when it came to war.

"If you had remained my pupil, you wouldn't be about to die, Miki-san."

"And if you hadn't kept hunting me, you wouldn't be

about to see your entire faction stolen from you, Daishin-san."

We laughed together, merciless and chilling. Once again, my stupid brain fixated on the differences a smile could be. Smiling at Pim, I was full of sincerity and softness. Smiling at Mercer, I was full of mistrust and malevolence.

Smiling at Daishin?

I was full of heartbreak for my family, disgust for myself, and utmost reverence for the man I'd bowed before.

Not because he was a good person but because he was the worst I'd ever come across, and that sort of brutal power deserved recognition.

Mercer appeared on my left, eyeing up my old master with disdain. Franco appeared beside him, equal partners in defending this estate while Selix arrived on my right, his presence known through a sixth sense brought from years of friendship and fighting.

Selix deserved all my thanks and more, and after tonight, I wouldn't wait any longer to give him what he was owed. Screw it if I hadn't paid back my debt in full. He'd been by my side for too long not to claim what was rightfully his.

Looking past Daishin, the courage in my veins to fight despite my current condition faltered as I counted more men than I should.

The rules of the Chinmoku had been simple: betray them and die.

Death came in stages: first a one-on-one fight. If you survived, then more men joined the siege until you fell at their feet. If you ran, they'd never stop hunting. First with three men, then seven, then thirteen.

They'd sent seven last time.

This time should be thirteen.

Yet as I quickly tallied up the Japanese men all in matching uniforms behind their chosen leader, I counted more.

Seventeen to be exact.

My heart turned to stone.

Chinmoku used tradition to enforce their laws, but it could

also be used to monitor their flaws. Before us were seventeen men.

But that isn't all of them.

I supposed I should be honoured, awed even that Daishin judged me as his ultimate rival. He didn't just see me as his student anymore but as his successor.

There was no other reason he'd brought the full amount of men one could bring to extermination.

Turning my head to Mercer, I whispered harshly, "Wherever the women are, send men to guard them. Now."

Mercer's face blackened as he glowered at Daishin on his doorstep. With a French slur and finger snap, he ordered a couple of black suited guards to charge up the staircase behind us.

He hadn't asked questions. He hadn't challenged me.

In this, he'd trusted me, and I couldn't be more fucking grateful. Because we were in a shitload of trouble. A fuck-load of trouble.

I'm going to die tonight, after all.

I just had to hope like hell that Daishin would stand by his law the moment I did and walk away.

Crossing my arms, even though it hurt like hell with my elbow and shoulder, I drawled in Japanese, "Where's the rest of your entourage, Daishin-san?"

He smiled just as relaxed and pompous, knowing exactly what conclusion I'd just fallen into. "Forgive me; I don't know what you mean."

I stepped forward, reducing the distance between us to merely a metre. I didn't care I looked like shit or the brace on my ankle gave away my injury. He would know I wouldn't be in top form after losing previous warriors trying to put me down.

"The other three men. Where are they?"

"You think we stuck to the same archaic rules we had when you wore our colours, Miki-san?" He laughed long and slow, building in mirth as if I was the village idiot. "You poor fool. Haven't grown any wiser, I see, even though you have aged rather poorly."

I vibrated with loathing, barely reining my temper and forcing myself not to attack prematurely. "One, three, seven, thirteen, and twenty. That's how honour is delivered to trespassers."

Daishin adjusted his cufflinks, flashing the katakana character of long life in my face. "I thought I'd break a little from tradition if you don't mind, Miki-san. I guess you'll find out how many helpers I brought soon enough." His teeth flashed in the night. "But then again, maybe you won't. Depending on how long you live, of course."

I'd had enough of this small talk.

I'd had enough of restraining both the violent call to murder and the petrified question that demanded to know what would happen if I died.

I wanted to know if Pim would be safe if I let him gut me here and now, but I was terrified of the answer and what it would ultimately make me do.

Uncrossing my arms, I sank into the same crouch he'd drilled into me through endless lessons and raised my hands. My posture wasn't that of yoga or spiritual gain—it was slipping from the scabbard that turned me into a sword.

Fingers bent but loose, wrists straight but uncocked, joints ready but fluid.

I wiped my mind of Pim and broken futures. I pushed aside failing and conquering.

All that mattered was here and now.

All that existed was this.

Pimlico

"HERE, TAKE THIS."

I looked up from watching Suzette bounce Lino on her lap while female staff milled around the rotund tower of Q and Tess's bedroom. Eight women or so mingled and whispered, looking out the tall window to the gardens below, probably wondering why they'd been dragged out of bed at this time in the morning to hang out in their master's bedroom.

Tess urged something into my hands. "Here. It's old but still works."

I curled my hands around the ancient dagger, wincing against the ice-cold hilt and running my thumbs over a giant emerald inlaid in the end. "Where on earth did this come from?"

Tess shrugged as she headed toward Suzette and passed her a similar blade; however, hers was shorter with a wicked hooked barb on the blade tip. "Who knows? Q has a collection on his mantel." She pointed at the large fireplace with deer and who knew what else carved into the surround. Above was a rack of swords and old-style muskets. "I love the sexist view Q has of protecting the weaker sex—that weaker sex being me." She laughed softly. "But we all know women aren't damsels in distress. I have a son to protect. I'll rip out the entrails from anyone trying to harm him."

Her ferocity scattered goosebumps down my arms. I loved her confidence that women were just as capable as men in defending their property.

Stroking my new friend the dagger, I eyed up the rest of the bedroom. It might seem odd to have medieval weaponry overlooking the bed but it fitted perfectly.

A tower.

The only tower on the estate and the only room inside it. The floor area ensured the master suite impressed with its massive space, hidden enclaves behind hand-painted screens, and apparatus tucked behind thick velvet curtains.

Suzette had eyed up the items as we'd entered, knowledge dancing over her sweet features as to what lurked behind their wrappings.

Unfortunately, I only had my imagination to guide me. If what Tess had hinted at about her and Q's sex life, I dreaded to think what sort of 'toys' or more like torture equipment existed hidden away.

Settling back on the bed with her own knife of choice—a simple dagger with blue scroll painted on the hilt—Tess smiled at Suzette as she jiggled Lino in her arms.

Luckily, the baby had his thumb in his mouth and clutched a piece of Suzette's hair, fast asleep with chubby pink cheeks and dusky delicate eyelashes.

He was the only one unfazed by what was coming.

Everyone else in the room shifted nervously, never staying in one spot for long, legs jiggling and fingers twirling.

I was no exception. Although, thanks to my recent captivity and the common occurrence of living in high-doss circumstances of stress and silence, I did the opposite to fidgeting.

I locked down.

I barely breathed.

I found it hard to look around the room rather than fixate on a spot that wouldn't get me into trouble. I didn't care if my joints started to ache from being in one position for too long. I didn't mind I grew lightheaded from scarcely breathing.

I merely sat and waited for the worst to come.

Tess turned to face a girl on the opposite side of the massive bed. "How are you doing, Caroline?"

The brunette flashed her a weak, feather of a smile, shaking her head once. "I'm fine." Her voice hinted she was anything but fine.

Her obvious discomfort didn't faze Tess who nodded sympathetically. "Despite what might happen downstairs, we're safe up here. Okay? No one is going to hurt you again."

She bit her lip. Her eyes searched Tess's as if desperate to believe her but not quite able to. I didn't need anyone to tell me that Caroline was a recent addition to the Mercer household and someone who'd walked in my shoes.

The moment she'd entered the bedroom, our eyes had locked, and we'd known.

She had the same bruises.

The same shackle marks.

The same cuts and chain imprints.

I'd given her a sad smile but also a happy one because no matter what she'd lived through, she was free. She'd been found, and I had no doubt time would repair her mind just as it had mine.

If the Chinmoku are defeated, of course.

My heart drummed an alarm button as I looked at Lino again. We had no choice but to win, because if we didn't, it wasn't just us who would die tonight but everyone—no matter age, race, or sex. Even baby Lino.

I stood, running my fingers along my newly acquired blade, allowing rebellion to fill me instead of previous slave training.

I slashed the empty air, getting a feel for the weight and precision of my new weapon just in case I would have to use it.

I wouldn't shy from drawing blood. I wouldn't qualm over taking a life.

I'd pulled the trigger in the white mansion.

I would stab someone here if it came down to it.

As I fileted empty air, a fist pounded loud and heavy on the massive wooden door.

I jumped, almost cutting myself with the knife. My heart wheezed with anticipation and preservation.

Tess sprang to her feet as Lino woke and grizzled. Suzette clutched him close, murmuring into his tiny ear while glancing at Tess with terror in her eyes.

We hadn't heard any fighting. No gunshots. No war cries. The house had been silent apart from the chirp of a doorbell a few minutes ago.

We'd all looked at each other at the oddity of the bell going off at this time but decided it might be the police who Q had on his payroll according to Tess.

Three hours had been long and boring, but I would happily wait three years if it meant tonight had a happier ending.

The knock hammered again.

Being the one closest to the door, I gave Tess a look then inched closer toward it. "Who's there?"

The absurdity of asking while in the prelude to battle made me flush with complex nerves.

What if I spoke to the enemy?

What if they'd silently murdered Elder and the others and come to finish their culling with us?

Should I be less polite? Should I growl and curse and demand to know their names so I knew who I would be slaughtering?

Before I could rephrase my question, the pounding fist was replaced with a gruff voice. "Phillip, ma'am. We were sent by Mr. Mercer."

I looked over my shoulder at Tess, verifying she knew these men and it wasn't a lie.

She came closer, crossing her arms as if she couldn't quite recognise.

Phillip added through the door, "The enemy has arrived in greater force than planned. We were tasked to protect you."

I looked at Tess. Were they here to protect us, or was it a lie? And if they *were*, was that a compliment from her husband or confirmation that he believed we were less than capable at survival?

Oh, my God, Pim. Why choose now to compare the pros and cons of different sexes?

That was my mother's genes choosing to focus on human nature rather than focus on the task at hand.

Blinking my attention back to important matters, I asked, "Do you know him?"

Tess lowered her arms, marching to the door. "I know him." Throwing open the deadlock, she ushered the two guards inside and locked it again just as fast. "What's happening down there?"

"Nothing, Mrs Mercer." One of them clutched his gun higher. "That Prest fellow and another Japanese bloke are talking."

"Talking?"

He nodded. "That's it as far as I'm aware—"

A loud crack silenced him, vibrating around the countryside, bouncing off the sleeping trees, echoing off napping clouds.

"Oh, no." I slapped a hand over my mouth knowing exactly what that noise was.

A gun.

A pistol.

Something with the power to steal a life with one trigger.

"It's begun." Tess sprinted to the window, barging past staff members to investigate. She slapped the window sill in frustration. "Shit, I can't see anything."

"Ma'am, step away from the window. You're a target." The guards ran after Tess and I ran after the guards. All of us huddled at the glass, peering into the night for clues on what'd happened.

The turret faced away from the front door toward the garages and other buildings. It didn't stop Tess from unlocking the window and bending her body as far as she could outside to catch a glimpse.

"Ma'am." A guard clutched the back of Tess's top, trying to stop her but still governed by her authority.

Tess stood straight, obeying the command. The moment she was back in the room, the guard locked the window and stood beside us with his legs braced and gun drawn as his colleague went to fortify the door.

Two areas of weakness.

Two men for protection.

I placed my fingers on the glass, glaring through the hazy gloom as my heart got on its knees and begged to know Elder was okay. I wished I could fly from this tower and go to his side.

He'd agreed to stay.

But he hadn't agreed not to stick to his original plan of dying to protect us—the one move I couldn't do equally. The one strategy that was entirely his decision with no input from me.

Frustrated tears glossed my eyes.

Don't be a hero, Elder. Be safe and come back to me.

Another boom sounded as a bullet flew from gun to target—not knowing if it was our men or theirs who fired.

Sweat slicked my spine as I dropped my gaze from the sprawling gardens to directly below us, searching for a drainpipe or vines—something I could use to escape and find Elder.

But my attention locked onto yet another nightmare.

A flash of three shadows blended from grass to brick, darting through dead spots left by the security lights, streaking toward the tower like night crawlers.

"Look." I elbowed Tess.

She latched onto the evil coming for us, understanding like I had the danger we were in.

Two guards wouldn't be enough if they reached us. She swore as colourfully as her husband, dragging hands through blonde hair. "They're going to climb."

"No. Surely, they won't—they don't know where we are." Suzette squeezed between us, staring at the same calamity we did. Far, far below our turret, the three shadows emerged at the base and looked up.

The distance and gloom hid their faces, but their intention flew up the round ancient walls, infiltrating us with their purpose.

I clutched my dagger as the security guard cocked his gun, his face determined to do whatever was necessary.

Tess trembled, the first sign of fear she'd shown. Her eyes flickered to a barcode with a sparrow flying in the centre and the number fifty-eight etched on her wrist. "I can't be taken again."

Suzette placed a hand on her mistress's shoulder, clutching baby Lino close. "I won't let them."

I placed my hand on her other shoulder. "Me, either."

We stood bound by the promise and understanding of what we meant. The horror of being captured again, sold again, raped again…it turned us from women to warriors.

Our oaths to prevent such a future were as binding as blood. A mutual understanding that plaited us together and made us responsible for each other.

We wouldn't let them take us alive.

Not this time.

Not anytime.

Another gunshot.

Followed by another and another.

Masculine shouts came short and snatched from inside the mansion.

As one, we all turned to the door, searching for answers but finding none.

The walls were too thick, the distance too great to hear who cried in pain and who yelled in triumph.

All we could do was forget what happened out there and focus on our battleground in here. The window was our weakest spot.

Ignoring the door, we looked back through the glass as three shadows left green grass and melted into the stonework of our tower.

Their fingers sure, their toes nimble, their bodies hauling them heavenward.

Climbing.

Coming.

Hunting.

We had our knives.

The guards had their guns.

No unwelcome visitors would enter this tower tonight.

With a fierce look, Tess opened the window and the guard prepared to fire.

ELDER

HAD THERE EVER been a moment in my life when I didn't live with pain?

Had there ever been a time when I wasn't fighting to stay alive?

It seemed the answer to those questions was no.

No.

No.

For the past fuck-knew-how-long, I'd been fighting. Figuratively and literally. Fighting my past, my future, my mistakes, my accomplishments.

I'd fought until I forgot *why* I fought.

At some point in this war, I'd entered with thoughts of defending a man's home, of battling beside that same man who was more stranger than friend, who'd stolen my woman and ruined my life, and instead of doing my best to kill him, I did my best to keep him alive.

Time stopped ticking.

I didn't know if we'd been in this purgatory for ten minutes or ten hours, but for once, my OCD helped keep me sane.

The agony in my wounds was worse than any drug or obsessive chant. It coiled in my brain, it decorated my bones, it hissed hotter and louder with every swing, duck, and punch.

It grew so loud, it distracted me enough that I almost missed an obvious attack, leaving Mercer to pick up the slack. That was when my OCD decided to latch onto something else—something less debilitating and useless.

I swallowed my pain deep, deep down, and fought with brighter purpose. Clarity came from counting the cadavers we left behind. A tally of death that encouraged me to add to it again and again.

Hand-to-hand combat.

A shot to the chest with gunpowder and buckshot.

A serrated slice to the jugular with steel.

As the minutes bled into hours, my counting switched to incorporate another tally. This one just as handy and granting even better precision. I had an over analytic brain that loved rhythm and symmetry and numerical harmony. It relished in counting uppercuts and finger snaps. It begged to count screams and gurgles from the men I wrenched from living to dead.

I tried to keep count of how many deaths we caused while tucking away vital spread sheets of delivered punches versus the probability of who had the highest chance of success.

I lived for figures.

I craved odds and evens, hoping the final sum would equal our victory.

From the moment the doorbell rang till now, I'd counted, growing more and more frenzied the deeper into chaos I fell.

The first two to die were Chinmoku—just as I'd hoped but feared wouldn't happen.

Mercer's men had listened, and my man didn't need to be told.

Bang.

Bang.

Two Chinmoku shot between the eyes, courtesy of Selix and Franco.

Q's man and mine.

A joint effort and an equal commitment to this overthrowing of power.

Selix had been the first to shoot, knowing full well what the Chinmoku were capable of, thanks to me teaching him their ways every morning on board the Phantom. He'd overstepped and decided my conversation with Daishin had reached a mutually conclusive end—that there was only one place to go from there and that was most likely my death by sacrifice.

He hadn't waited for me to make that vital mistake or confirmation from me that I wouldn't.

He didn't need to.

In this matter, and in all matters, he was my equal, my brother—just like the bastard Franco was Mercer's brother. He was true to his word, shooting a fraction of a second after Selix.

I'd prepared for Daishin to attack me in the midst of two of his warriors' untimely ends, but he'd surprised me by falling back with his remaining men, leaving the bodies of his fallen to become gruesome garden ornaments, spreading out like cockroaches too fast to be plucked off with bullets.

It fucked me off, but I couldn't blame them. They were men, after all. They could equip themselves with every skill imaginable. They could become the best in the world and kill with their bare hands, but unless they could turn their flesh into Kevlar they were still vermin who bled.

As they'd melted into the night, Mercer yelled, "Shoot on sight."

I'd leapt off the stoop, buckling under the avalanche of agony in my ankle, tearing/hopping in pursuit of the bastards who'd run. I expected us to separate, but Mercer stayed beside me, sprinting with agility and hardly out of breath as we rounded the first corner of his home and slammed into a Chinmoku.

I delivered an uppercut on instinct, whipping the man's head up and cracking his teeth together. I waited for him to plummet to his knees, ready to chop the nerve in his neck and suffocate him.

But Mercer had other ideas.

The moment I incapacitated the fighter, he yanked out his pistol and shot him point blank in the face.

For the longest second, we stared at each other, the scent of sulphur still strong in the air. I hated him for taking my first kill but was grateful, because the world swam with sickness and pain, and I needed to conserve every ounce of strength I had left to survive the night.

The strangest thing wasn't the fact we'd worked as a team or the fact that we'd fought side by side when only hours ago we'd fought tooth for tooth—the strangest thing was how fucking easy it had been.

How smooth.

How rehearsed.

How *right*.

We grinned in the dark, shedding our human skin and letting pain and lust for death drive us. Not my ankle, shoulder, elbow, nor any malady could stop me as we jogged through his gardens, peering into shadows, steadily listening to the popping of guns from his security team as they found their own Chinmoku to eliminate.

Racing into a large conservatory with palm trees as high as the Phantom and the coos and trills of exotic birds, we ducked as a Chinmoku launched from behind an aviary, going for my jugular in an artery pinch I knew well.

One touch and my nervous system would stop talking to my brain and *boom*, unconscious and easy prey. Instead, I whirled and performed the same trick on him.

He collapsed into a bag of bones, and Mercer finished him off with a single trigger squeeze. The crack of his gun ricocheted around the glass conservatory, startling roosting birds and making them soar around their gilded cage.

He murmured something in French, linking his fingers through the wire as his gaze darted between the feathered bodies of different jewelled colours.

Outside, more shots fired.

I counted.

One, two, three, four.

I didn't like that it wasn't a perfect trio but I loved the noise and visualised my enemies falling.

So far, I estimated eleven Chinmoku had been dealt with. Unfortunately, that probably meant at least one from our side would've been killed in retribution for not shooting fast enough or believing he could take on an expert fighter barehanded.

In this fight, we were nothing more than cardboard cut-outs of villains and heroes. I didn't care about the Chinmoku's motive to kill me. I didn't care what it would mean if I lost or won.

All we focused on was that elusive finish line.

Bang.

Bang.

Two more down.

Did that make thirteen Chinmoku in an untimely grave or more of ours as worm food?

Mercer gave me a pointed look, standing over the fresh corpse. There was no time to wait and no safe places to dawdle.

Thirteen down did not make this war won. If Daishin had brought twenty of his men—despite his attempt at throwing me off age-old tradition—then we were closer to winning than we'd been at the start.

Keep going.

Keep living.

We faded into the foliage, letting shadows do our camouflaging for us.

I couldn't allow thoughts of Pim to consume me. I couldn't permit worries over Selix to distract me.

I had enough distractions with my injuries.

As we crawled through the night, my ankle turned weak, burning with agony, forcing me to hop more than run. My elbow screamed at being used as a balancing rod while my shoulder singed hot around the pinpoint of stitches.

I'd probably have to spend another week in bed after

this—*if I survive*—but I refused to think about that now. The only thing that mattered was extermination.

Mercer guided me through the aviary and down a long corridor with black and white images of real estate and high rises. We bypassed a pool and found another Chinmoku slinking up a back staircase.

Instantly, I lurched forward and grabbed his ankle. Yanking him down the stairs, I smashed his face into the steps and stomped on his spine, snapping something vital.

Mercer cleaned up my mess with yet another bullet to the back of the guy's head. We weren't here to drag out a defeat or let them see who we were before they died. If we could slaughter each one without them noticing us, that would be the best outcome.

Clean. Ruthless. Efficient.

Fourteen dead?

Or maybe the Chinmoku had brought guns of their own, even though it went against their code, and Mercer and I were the only ones standing.

We wouldn't know until we came face to face with either victory or defeat.

Stumbling forward, I chased him as he melted back into darkness, stalking through his own home, looking for infiltrators.

My hands throbbed for throats to squeeze and lives to steal.

We'd been killing for hours or was it days? No matter the tick in my brain, I couldn't seem to keep time straight anymore.

Another few gunshots, more men shouting in French and Japanese.

Bang.

Bang.

Fifteen, sixteen?

Are we close?

Are we winning?

Mathematical equations and probability calculations

whirred in my brain as we skidded around another corridor and into the foyer again.

Two Chinmoku this time.

Bright red gloves and black uniforms with matching brutality on their face.

I took one.

Mercer took the other.

My method was hands-on and swift.

Mercer's was coldblooded and sharp.

Both achieved the same result with glazed eyes and soul-dead carcasses.

Tripping back into a run, I gasped and swiped at fever-sweat stinging my eyes. My vision had once again gone hazy, my ears ringing, my body begging for rest. But I kept pushing, kept killing.

Soon.

Soon this will all be over.

Falling through the front door again, I spotted Selix fighting a young Chinmoku. He couldn't have been more than late teens. A spitting image of me when I'd stupidly sold my soul into their custody.

The two men grappled on the grass. Selix's gun just out of reach; most likely kicked out of his hand for hesitating before firing. The Chinmoku was just a kid—a kid intent on spilling blood. With a quick move, he yanked Selix into a throat lock.

A death lock.

No way in hell would I watch my friend be murdered.

Throwing myself toward the battle, Mercer fell back as if understanding Selix was my responsibility just as Franco was his. Not giving me a second glance, he veered to the left, his attention on his friend who also fought a Chinmoku, holding his own but not for much longer.

I stopped paying any attention to anyone but Selix and bowled straight into the bastard doing his best to kill my friend.

We tumbled to the ground, limbs flying, wounds bleeding. I kneed him in the balls as he tried to pin me on my back.

Unsportsmanlike behaviour but I didn't give a fuck as I wrapped my fingers around his throat and squeezed. Even with my broken digit and no strength in my elbow, I slowly siphoned the life out of him as Selix picked up his gun and held it to the man's temple.

He didn't fire, watching coldly, letting me steal the world of yet another Chinmoku while providing backup if my hands failed in their task.

Slowly, the life drained from him. He faded into nothing and I let go, hating the touch of flesh that was no longer possessed by a soul.

As the dead man fell into a pile of limbs, a slurry of shame filled me. The Chinmoku might've been a good kid. He might've got wrapped up in this terrible faction the same way I did. He didn't deserve to die just so me and mine could live.

"Prest." Selix bent down, holding out his hand.

His voice, still filled with rocks from being strangled, snapped me from my haze. That Chinmoku would've killed my only friend—he didn't deserve my mourning.

I clasped Selix's palm gratefully, creaking upright, and for the first time, I truly felt my age. My injuries fucking crippled me and I honestly had no clue how I was still awake, let alone murdering men.

A terrible thought struck that I might not get through tonight, after all.

If my maths were correct there should only be two or three Chinmoku left, give or take. My calculations were as fuzzy as my stupid eyesight.

Selix pulled his hand away as we broke into a tired amble.

I tripped, almost face planting into the manicured grass.

He grabbed my shirt, providing leverage to keep me upright. "Stay alive for me, Prest."

I nodded and tried to speak, but my tongue was as useless as the rest of me now. I shook my head, doing my best to see as we picked up our pace. I tripped again, this time crying out as my ankle turned into the Grim Reaper's sickle.

"Fuck's sake," Selix muttered, wrapping his arm around my waist as we hobble-jogged back to the large house.

I wanted to curse him for thinking I was weak. I wanted to push his bulk away and prove I didn't need his support.

But this time? This time, I had no energy left to waste on lies.

I knew how I felt, and if I looked half as bad on the outside as I did on the inside, well, I must look like death nuked in a microwave.

Blood trickled from my nose and not from an injury but overuse, overtiredness, and a body slowly shutting down from lack of care.

I blinked and squinted into the darkness, doing my best to distinguish glimpses of black security from Mercer's team and black Chinmoku from the enemy's side.

Only the red gloves helped differentiate the two.

Climbing the steps to enter Mercer's home, ready to find the Frenchman and rally our killing unit one more time, I slammed to a stop as Daishin appeared.

From the library.

With Pimlico's hair wrapped around his fist.

A smug smile on his lips and victory in his heart.

Fuck.

I slammed to a stop. Every method of slaughter and principal of carnage vanished from my mind. Selix froze. The battle was over.

All that mattered was Pim.

And Daishin had her.

A cut marred her pretty cheek. Blood puddled around the collar of her hoodie. And the metal thimble with a wicked sharp fingernail that Daishin favoured as his killing method nicked her jugular.

He believed killing with a simple slice was far more elegant than wielding something larger and cumbersome. He'd been affectionately known as the Wasp while I trained under his strict command.

His sting was just as poisonous and cruel.

I couldn't take my eyes off Pim.

She stood deathly still, one twitch from death, one scratch from murder.

Apologies and promises danced on my tongue. My wounds faded under a greater, deeper agony.

The agony of having my heart suffocated by the one person who knew how to hurt me the most.

Pimlico was family.

And Daishin was well versed in taking family away from me.

I sighed heavily, almost relieved to have it over.

I wouldn't have to fight anymore.

I wouldn't have to hurt.

Looking into the eyes of the woman I loved more than anything, I gave up.

I did what I should've done all those years ago.

I put my fate in the hands of honour.

I kneeled before my greatest enemy.

Pimlico

THERE'D BEEN A few times—probably more than normal—when I'd wished I wasn't a girl.

I'd wished I was a boy the night Mr. Kewet asked me to dance and strangled me.

I'd wished I was a boy the evening I was auctioned and men laughed in my face when I offered to buy myself.

I'd wished I was a boy every day of my life that I belonged to that bastard who I would never name again.

But that wish had ended with Elder.

I'd finally come to enjoy being a girl—a woman. Every time Elder looked at me, every hour his feelings evolved from wariness to interest to love, I was beyond grateful I'd been born a girl.

I was happy to be who I was and stopped wishing to be something I wasn't.

Especially now.

Especially the moment the guards miscalculated our visitors and didn't follow instructions. Especially now that I'd witnessed the fall of men and rise of women.

The guard beside us by the window fired too late and with no aim. With my ears ringing, I watched in horror as a rain of bullets left his gun empty, us vulnerable, and only two out of three Chinmoku shot.

Two plummeted back to the grass.

But one...he kept climbing.

Tess and I raised our knives, ready to slice at the climber's hands as he reached the window sill but the guard pushed us away, thinking he knew better, believing he was doing us a favour by taking on the Chinmoku on his own.

The only help he accepted was his colleague who gave up his post by the entrance and came to his side with a fully loaded gun. He switched off the safety and angled himself to shoot. They were so focused on picking off the remaining climber, they forgot about the door.

We all had.

We'd all been stupid.

We missed the tell-tale scratching of someone picking the lock. We were deaf to the sound of the door swinging open and two more death deliverers walking into our safety chamber.

Until it was too late.

The moment violence found us, the guards leapt to attention.

The one with remaining bullets had good aim and shot true, killing one interloper right on the threshold. The other guard who'd wasted his ammunition and had nothing but bare hands and useless coordination couldn't prevent mayhem as the other Chinmoku ran directly toward us and grabbed a hostage from the Mercer staff.

Using a maid as a shield, he was unkillable.

Seeing his hands on her. Hearing her screams.

It'd done something to me.

Something not quite human.

I forgot that the guards were the first line of defence. I forgot men versus female and who normally won in a fight with brawn.

The blade in my hands spoke to me; it whispered how easy it would be to stop him from touching her. How quickly I could prevent him from taking her and delivering her to the same sort of fate so many other girls had suffered.

Like I had suffered.

Like I never would again.

I didn't think.

I just acted.

Instinct took over, and I leapt on him.

My weight shoved him to the side, dislodging his hold on the staff member and delivering a precious moment of surprise. Left unarmed and undefended, I didn't hesitate as I sank my blade into his soft abdomen. He buckled over, blood seeping, turning his black clothes an inky maroon.

Fighting through the pain, he cursed in Japanese and wrapped fingers around my throat. His nails dug into my windpipe in a move so fast, every cell in my body forgot how to operate.

My knife was useless.

My confidence shattered.

But Tess had done what I had and let a lifetime of being hurt by men overflow, snapping with pissed off power.

She mimicked my attack, lodging her dagger into my assailant's throat, ripping through it like chewy steak, exposing the very same thing in him that he tried to squeeze in me.

As the Chinmoku's hand's lost strength, I tripped backward and landed on my ass, bruised and neck-swollen, unable to talk once again. My blade scattered on the carpet covered in blood.

Tess gave me her hand, helping me from the floor, only for the window to smash fully open and women to scatter as another Chinmoku landed in the room.

The two guards fell on him but it was too late.

In a flash of red gloves, the guard holding the gun had a broken neck and the guard with nothing was shot between the eyes with the stolen weapon.

Killed with no fanfare or salutation.

Women had taken down one Chinmoku while men had failed. In that moment, I was proud of my sex. Proud at how

I'd attacked even if I'd fallen prey. Tess had had my back and together, we'd won.

The two Chinmoku cornered us, stepping over the bodies of the guards and their fallen comrade. Women banded together, standing as one against our enemies.

The ultimate standoff.

We outnumbered them and I no longer doubted my power just because I was a girl. But it didn't help that we had very few weapons and they were weapons in every breath.

Looking into the eyes of the black-shrouded mercenaries, we made a collective agreement to be smart not reckless. We might win in a fight thanks to sheer numbers, but the cost of winning would be too high.

They had the gun.

We had three knives.

No one else would die tonight.

Instead of sacrificing ourselves in combat, we all rallied together, placing Suzette with Lino in the middle, acting as a living wall between innocent and evil.

The Chinmoku merely laughed at our display of defiance, crossing their arms, in no hurry to reprimand or disband our fortress.

"We're not going to hurt you," one said in accented English. "We've got much better plans than that."

I wanted to laugh at how predictable they were—regardless of race or age, a man who believed they were untouchable treated everyone else as disposable.

My heart raced, tasting a plan half-cooked and unproven. The only chance we'd have at stopping this would be to run. And the only one who had a direct line to the open door and freedom was me.

As a collective group of women—compete strangers but entirely on the same wavelength when faced with monsters in black—I reached backward into the throng and waited for a hand to grasp mine.

Tess.

I didn't need to look to know it was her, and I didn't need to speak to know she understood I was about to bolt.

Goosebumps sprang down my arms, filling me with nerves and fear.

If I ran, I had to commit.

If I ran, I would suffer whatever consequences came with it.

But I couldn't stay.

We needed help.

I will bring that help.

With a squeeze of my fingers, I promised I would come back.

I sucked in a breath, ordered my legs not to fail me, and took one last look at the men, both alive and dead. I snapshotted the entire scene, a tintype reminder never to fade or discolour no matter how many years I might live.

I was a woman.

And I would never wish that away again.

I squeezed Tess's hand one last time.

Then…I flew.

A shout signalled one man gave chase, but I didn't look back.

I forgot everything but the rhythm of how to gallop.

I leapt from the room and scurried down the spiral stone staircase as fast as I could. Around bends and tripping down uneven steps, I focused only on finding someone. Finding Elder. Finding a weapon better than a knife.

My breathing came noisy.

My throat throbbing from strangulation.

I ran so, so fast.

And I would've reached the landing if something hard and agonising hadn't flown from behind and wrapped around my ankles.

I tumbled headfirst down the final three steps, coming to a smashed heap at the bottom, unable to breathe, move, or speak.

My lungs stuck together as the force knocked the wind out of me. I blinked back silver stars as a middle-aged Chinmoku with a long goatee plaited with a red ribbon unwound whatever lasso he'd used to ensnare me. His hands on my legs made me shudder.

The moment I was free, he yanked me to my feet and wrapped his hand around my hair.

My list of ailments increased from unable to speak from bruising to unable to breathe from falling. I didn't care about my voice, but I did care about getting oxygen into my frazzled, frightened body.

A trickle of blood seeped from my hairline—a headache forming from impact.

Without a word, he dragged me through the house, following the labyrinth as if he'd been born here. How he knew where he was going astounded me, but slowly, parts of the house I recognised appeared, and I inhaled my first deep inhale as he prowled across the foyer, dragging me beside him, and handed me to the oldest man of the Chinmoku.

A man reeking of refinement and dripping with cold-heartedness.

A man I knew instantly to be the one in charge and Elder's greatest foe.

I was traded from one to another as the leader squirrelled me away into the library. There, he relished in the quiet normality as he regaled me with tales of the upcoming auction they'd arranged to replace the destroyed QMB. He laughed low and smooth as gunfire and curse words were fired and cut short.

Sitting down with me trapped on his lap, he stroked my hair as anarchy rained outside and spilled every business proposition he'd been working on.

How his new auction house would never have a name or permanent location so it could never be found. How he was so much smarter in this game than his old competitors.

He kissed my cheek as men thundered past and murmured

that whatever price I earned would go into a fund and ensure Elder's family was all exterminated because this was personal now and above honour.

And when he pulled me close, wrapped his fist in my hair, and wedged the sharpest, tiniest blade hooked on his finger to my throat, I'd wanted to tear his heart from his chest.

Not because I didn't want to be sold again.

Not because I believed anything this man said would come true.

But because if I'd failed in my quest to bring help to Tess and the others.

I didn't know where Elder was. I didn't know if he was alive or dead, but for the first time in my life, I felt whole.

Whole and healed and *furious*.

I didn't need Elder to complete me.

I didn't need time to cure me.

I only needed to trust myself and I'd finally remembered how to do that.

There were no more holes in my heart, no more bruises in my soul, no more breaks in my bones. I was a girl and I was better than all the men who'd dared lay an unwanted finger on me.

I'll ruin you.

Commotion sounded outside and the Chinmoku holding me smiled a knowing smile. "Ah, it's time."

Despite my loathing and newfound commitment to destroy every man, boy, and bastard involved in hurting innocence, I flinched as the leader smiled and brushed back my hair with a condescending look. "Know what time it is, little girl?"

Even if my throat wasn't closed from his servant trying to kill me, I wouldn't have spoken to him. I would never stoop so low.

He chuckled as if my angry silence was a well of entertainment. Touching my nose with his tiny blade, he grinned. "It's time to crush the heart of my pupil."

Words vanished as knowledge slammed into me.

Elder…

Pushing me from his lap, he manhandled me until he shoved me out of the library, just in time to see Elder.

Elder stumbling over the threshold, bruised and bleeding, worn and weary but still giving everything he had to give.

Elder barely alive and about to die…because of me.

And then, I knew.

I knew I'd singlehandedly caused this. I'd run from the tower when I'd been told to stay. I'd taken the leverage of my existence and used it against the one I loved the most.

I'd stripped him down to nothing.

And it's all my fault.

I couldn't stop what was about to happen.

Because there was Elder.

Staring at me.

Loving me.

Forgiving me even as he prepared to die.

He collapsed to his knees with a heavy sigh, bowing his head as if ready for an axe to come swinging from hell to end him. He gave up his life for me because I was once again a stupid, *stupid* girl and I'd fulfilled my purpose.

While I finally embraced my power, I'd overlooked the one terrible truth.

I might be powerful in my own right but that power also ensured I made him weak.

I stripped him of everything because he put me above himself.

He made me his master and I'd killed him with stupidity.

I tried to speak, but my throat was still too bruised. I tried to warn him not to trade his life for mine. That I preferred to be dead over what was in store for me. That I would give anything—including my own life—not to witness his be taken from him.

I can't.

I can't watch him die.

If he was ready to end this, then at least kill me first.

Please, El…

But I couldn't utter a sound, not a peep. And Elder didn't look up; he just focused on his ex-leader's shoes and waited.

His voice came heavy and strained but etched with a snarl that said he might be kneeling, but he wasn't cowering. Not yet. "Leave her alone, Daishin-san."

It didn't make me feel any better to have a name for the man holding my life in the tiny blade pressed against my throat.

He waggled the thimble, a gentle reminder for me to behave as he cooed, "I'm glad you remember your manners, even in unhappy circumstance, Miki-san." Twisting my hair, he made me wince with a fresh flash of pain. "Perhaps all my lessons weren't in vain, after all."

Dragging me over to the double doors we'd just came through, he pulled a piece of black rope from his pocket and wrapped it around my hands before tying it to the door handle.

Focusing on Elder, he blatantly ignored me; happy knowing I was bait and would ensure Elder would obey as long as I remained his.

Leaving me captive, he linked his fingers together and stood over his defeated. "Let's see what else you remember, shall we?"

I tugged at my bindings, desperate to get free so Elder's honour-bound handcuffs could be removed. He needed to kill his ex-leader, not submit. He needed to live, not die.

With another hard jerk, the door merely swung toward me then yanked me back, willing to move a little but not letting me go.

I cursed my stupidity with every passion I had left. After years of being mute, I hated having the choice of speech stolen when I had the most to say.

The most to swear.

The most filthy of responses to distract Daishin from his fascination with Elder.

Elder's gaze flickered to mine before settling back on

Daishin. "Stop this. We both know who you truly want." Elder slowly levered himself back to his feet, swaying a little, not putting weight on his braced ankle. Even now—nose bleeding and body broken—he was still just as handsome, still just as majestic and heroic as when I first met him.

My heart pounded with love even while I drowned in fear.

"Let her go and I won't fight when you kill me." Elder bowed his head, but his eyes blazed black flames. "Do it. I'm tired of this."

Daishin laughed, circling Elder as if seeking just how true his offer was. "You've given up on trying to kill me already?" He rubbed his chin. "I'm disappointed."

Elder cringed; once again, his eyes skittered over me with so much hurt and affection my knees buckled before he looked at Daishin and turned void of emotion. "You know why I won't attempt it now. You broke the rules of combat. You have something that belongs to me."

Daishin laughed. "I taught you to be above human affection and personal possession, did I not?"

"You did."

"Yet you fell in love."

"I did."

Daishin circled again. "In that case, I would say goodbye if I were you. It will be the last time you see her. I'll be generous and give you the opportunity to say farewell. Call it a gift after you didn't get to share final words with your father and brother."

I opened my mouth to scream, to beg, to cry but only a distorted moan came out.

Elder's eyes widened in horror as he searched my lips for signs of blood; his white skin hinting that the memories of carrying me with my tongue half-severed hadn't left his mind.

I hated for him to worry.

I loathed I was the reason he worried, even now.

Arching my chin, I revealed the heavy bruising I could already feel forming on my throat.

He clenched his jaw, his hands balling as fury filled him with a final injection of energy.

Turning to face Daishin, Elder's posture didn't change. He didn't crouch or antagonise. He merely stood ready and supple, a snake in the grass waiting to strike.

Only I knew something had changed. Only I saw the steely glint that maybe he wasn't ready to die, after all.

A resilience.

A promise.

A final attempt.

I held my breath as he drawled, "You know, I always looked up to you, Daishin-san. I believed you when you said you wanted to help me with my habits and idiosyncrasies. I was too naïve to hear the lies behind the promises."

Daishin inspected his fingernails. "You weren't naïve. You knew what you were and what you were doing. You ignored the truth because of one fact, Miki-san." He speared Elder with a harsh glare. "You were too self-absorbed. So focused on what others could do to fix you that you forgot about fixing yourself." He tutted. "Don't blame others for your downfalls. Take ownership and defeat them."

"Defeat them like I'll defeat you?"

Daishin froze, assessing Elder in the split second before peace switched to chaos.

Elder charged.

The two men clashed together bone to bone, body to body. A rumble of determination. A quick explosion of intention.

I jerked hard against my imprisonment, bashing the door in its hinges, wriggling like a fish caught on a line.

Let him win.

Please, let him win.

My attention danced between Elder and Daishin as I wriggled and snapped, doing my best to untether myself.

He grunted as Daishin kicked him in a flurry of high-powered dances. Healthy against wounded. Master against pupil.

Tears ran down my cheeks. I wished I could help. I didn't want to see this. I didn't want to be destined to witness the worst thing in my life.

I winced every time Elder was struck.

I rejoiced every time he hit Daishin.

I grew sick with worry as Elder lost ground, piece by piece.

This was worse than him being beaten on the Phantom. Worse than watching him be shot by Q. Worse because I couldn't see any way he could defeat this man, and he was already dying.

I cried silently as the fight wore on.

Fists swinging.

Legs arching.

Bodies dancing left and right.

They would've been evenly matched if Elder hadn't been plagued with stitches and fever. Unfair, unright, the outcome was already decided.

My tears ran hotter as Elder's spine curled beneath the weight of trying to stay alive. His energy deserted him swing by swing until he was hunched over and breathless with exhaustion.

Any second now, Daishin would deliver the killing blow.

Any moment now, Elder would cease to exist, and I would never smile, live, or breathe again.

A fast-moving shape caught my attention, plummeting down the stairs. For a heartbeat, I didn't understand what'd happened. I couldn't marry why baby Lino was screaming in a black-dressed Chinmoku's arms.

Blood and claw marks smeared the warrior's face—the same warrior who'd climbed through the window—speaking of a fierce battle to remove babe from mother.

Tess.

What happened to her?

What happened to the women upstairs who I'd selfishly

left and hadn't returned to?

Lino wailed at the top of his lungs as the Chinmoku clutched him tighter, marching toward the door.

No!

I fought harder against my tethers, jerking and jiving, desperate not to let the Chinmoku disappear outside. If he did, I doubted we'd ever see Lino again.

"Stop…" My voice came out whisper-thin.

The Chinmoku put one foot over the threshold, smelling freedom.

A thundering roar sounded, a streak of violence echoing in the darkness.

Q appeared from outside, bolting into his home and snatching the Chinmoku around the throat. His speed and fury barrelled the Japanese back inside, both of them tripping and stumbling.

In sheer strength, Q righted him and ploughed his enemy backward. He didn't look at Elder and Daishin as they continued to duel. He didn't notice me tied to his library door. All he focused on was the man who'd dare touch his son.

It only took a few seconds to turn alive into dead.

Q held his throat with one hand and sucker-punched him in the temple with the other. The blow knocked the man out in a single delivery. Q back-stepped as the Chinmoku toppled, ripping Lino from his clutches and snarling.

The moment the Chinmoku hit the floor, Q crunched his shoe into the man's throat and pressed down with the blackest, cruellest look on his face. Spools of French spilled from his lips as he slowly suffocated him.

Bored of the game, Q hoisted Lino to his hip, pulled out his gun and *bang, bang, bang,* emptied three bullets into him without flinching.

Lino bleated and squealed. His chubby cheeks blotchy with terror, but Q was past offering commiseration and sweet nothings to the child.

He was in murder frenzy, and three bullets weren't

enough.

He shot again.

And again.

But then another blur appeared; this one in a blue jumper and jeans, doused red with blood and tangled blonde hair. She didn't stop.

Racing down the stairs, Tess skidded beside her husband, grabbed his gun, and unloaded the rest of the clip into the corpse of the man who'd stolen her baby.

I had no idea what'd happened upstairs. How the Chinmoku had stolen Lino or how Tess had gotten free. Whatever war had taken place, I knew who'd won, and it wasn't the men.

My heart vibrated with murder as a final bullet found a new home in the Chinmoku's skull.

Only once the air was laced with gun smoke did she throw the pistol into the face of their dead baby-snatcher and turn to Q.

She reached for her son, but Q held him away.

I gasped in horror as he wrapped his fingers around her throat and marched her backward, stepping over the body as if it was a new rug.

His eyes shot black, lust tainting the air as vicious as violence.

The moment Tess's back slammed against the foyer wall, he fell on her.

Kissing her. Mauling her. Totally savage.

Lino continued to scream, clutching at air and kicking in Q's arms as he continued to maul his blood-soaked wife. He devoured her, thrusting into her, grabbing her leg and hoisting it over his hip.

Only once Lino's screams reached ear piercing did Q struggle to pull away—reluctantly crashing back to humanity.

And then a noise ripped my attention from them, sucking me back to the awful fight before me.

My heart iced over as I looked at Elder.

As I looked at a man who'd given up everything.
A man who'd embraced every demon he'd run from.
A man who'd finally had enough.

ELDER

I WAS A man born of honour.

I was a son made of regret.

I was a lover forged from protection.

I'd entered this fight willingly, but even with my training at the hands of my old master, I was losing.

I'd studied and practiced for a moment such as this, and I'd failed. I'd accepted my grave without truly, truly trying.

Pim would soon be without me.

I would soon be without her.

And life would continue without any say or sway from me.

That couldn't happen.

I'd been stupid and feeble and wrong.

I'd believed I was ready to kill my past, but I wasn't.

Not really.

Until now.

Until this very moment where Pim looked away because she couldn't stomach to see me defeated and Daishin laughed, knowing he'd won.

My destiny was already written, my burial already planned.

But I finally reached that edge.

That jagged, dangerous edge ringing the well of feral blackness inside me.

I'd run from it my entire life. I'd feared it. I'd hid it.

I cursed it because it twisted everything good that I'd tried to be.

But now, I had nothing left. I had limited heartbeats and rationed existence…so I sank.

I sank and sank and breathed deep, deep, deep, admitting that I wasn't just a man born of honour and regret and protection. I was a Chinmoku bred for pride and service and heartless, ruthless extermination.

I was a killer.

And I'm ready.

The parts of my body I could no longer feel blazed with raw power. My forsaken limbs and broken bones knitted together for one purpose and one purpose only.

To win.

To murder.

To save.

I saw red.

Lots and *lots* of red.

Blood of my brotherhood, blood of my brother, blood of the woman I'd taken as mine.

I'd spilled waterfalls of blood, but I'd yet to spill the most important one—that of my leader. His needed to rain if I ever had a chance at being free.

I'd wasted enough time.

He'd taunted me, enjoying my weakness, my humanity, my hesitation.

No more.

I didn't pause to think. I didn't second-guess. I no longer believed the story my body whispered—telling me to lay down my fists, to stop this useless attempt at winning, to honourably accept defeat.

The instincts I'd let loose when I'd found Pim with her tongue partially severed unravelled into something I could no longer control.

I'd been getting in my own way, believing I could win without killing. That I was better than the Chinmoku when I'd forgotten the most important thing.

I *was* them.

I was better than them.

I had the power to end this.

I backed away from Daishin, breathing hard, streaming with sweat and sickness. Our eyes met as I stopped breathing and bowed my head.

That was the only warning I gave.

A simple bow in ode to everything he'd made me become.

Goodbyes weren't required and respect wasn't given. I centred myself, reached deep for everything I'd chained inside, and gave myself over to the method I knew best.

The method he himself had taught me.

The method that didn't require anything but sheer, brutal talent.

Rushing at Daishin, he stumbled backward, sensing everything had changed and unable to prevent my descent. His hands struck, doing their best to subdue me. His body parried, doing its best to avoid me.

But it was too late.

I wouldn't kill him by gun or blade.

That would be too easy.

And this was personal.

Grabbing his neck, I willed every strength I had left into my fingers and dug my nails into his throat.

He dropped to a knee, scrambling at my hold, eyes bugging, lips gasping as I dedicated myself to no more.

No more fighting.

No more running.

No more losing.

I'm done.

With a savage twist of my hand, I broke his spine, crushed his windpipe, and turned living into corpse.

And then, I fell with him.

I'd done what I feared I never would.

I became him just as he'd promised.

I smiled as everything went black.

Pimlico

MY SCREAMS WERE silent as Elder ripped out Daishin's throat then collapsed beside him. My tears were dry as blood gushed from his old leader's throat, cascading over both of them.

I didn't move or blink as someone untied me from the door.

I didn't breathe or speak as I stumbled to Elder and kneeled beside him.

Gathering his head, I pulled him toward me, hugging him, stroking his drenched black hair.

I didn't know how long he stayed unconscious.

I didn't know how long blood seeped into my skin where I kneeled and I didn't care conversations and life went on around us.

All I cared about was the man who'd just become a weapon.

A man who took a life with a single touch.

Elder had given himself over to something dark, and he'd won.

He'd become more dangerous than any man who'd tried to buy me. More terrifying than any moment I'd endured so far.

He was everything I was afraid of and everything I'd

grown to adore.

I was confused.

I was afraid.

I was in awe and shock and thankfulness.

He'd defeated his past, conquered his enemies, and proven once and for all he was unstoppable.

But at what cost?

What sort of man would he be when he woke up?

And what could I do to make the monster I fell in love with return to me?

ELDER

I WOKE LIGHTHEADED and nauseous.

My eyes opened to let in blinding light, followed quickly by the most beautiful thing I'd ever seen.

Pim stared down at me, her nose almost on mine, tears dangling on her lashes like jewels. "You're awake."

I swallowed back the rank stench of death and jerked in her arms as every injury and illness I suffered returned in full force.

The pressure almost knocked me out again.

Fading, promising, whispering.

I was so close to succumbing—to letting the sanctity of sleep prevent more buckling pain.

All it would take was one breath and slip.

But I couldn't.

I clung tight to life even though it hurt like fucking hell.

For any normal person, passing out would be met in equal amounts of relief and exhaustion. They'd accept that they'd done enough…for now…and to rest—to be able to admit that they'd reached the point where nothing else was possible and to finally, *finally* relax after decades of running and revenge.

But I never claimed to be normal.

The blackness I'd embraced still coated my insides and thoughts. An inky slime that whispered of power and destruction as deadly as gunpowder.

I didn't want to give up its power, but at the same time, I didn't want to touch Pim with such filth residing in my heart.

If I passed out now, who knew what I'd be when I woke. Who knew if Daishin's soul would hitch a ride on mine. If reincarnation would switch my life for his and I'd forever end up in purgatory for what I'd done.

No.

The only thing I could do—the only thing possible, even in my current state of brokenness, was to stand and breathe and *live*.

Looking up, I winced at the terror on Pim's face. She studied me as if afraid of the same thing I was—searching my eyes, hoping to see the man she knew but horrified she'd find something different.

Flinching beneath every agony, I reached up and cupped her cheek. "I'm okay, little mouse."

She crumpled over me, her hair curtaining around us as she kissed me everywhere. I permitted her love, stroking her back, willing her to understand I hadn't forgotten who I was or what I'd promised.

I wanted to snap my fingers to a time where we were alone and safe and the aftermath of this carnage was behind us so we could rest, but it wasn't over yet.

I had other tasks I needed to complete.

"Help me stand," I whispered, grateful when she obeyed, scurrying off me and lending me her strength.

In an impossible move, I managed to trade the floor for air and stood swaying as vertigo twisted my world upside down.

I stumbled forward—barely cohesive—holding onto the woman I needed more than anything.

My ankle had put in its sick notice and stopped working days ago. My elbow was a close second to pulling a worker's strike, and my shoulder felt as if the bullet hole had increased until my entire joint was open to the elements.

In short, I needed to rest after some serious medical

attention.

But I couldn't.

Not yet.

Tonight wasn't finished even though dawn had arrived.

I grunted as Pim kissed me again, dragging my thoughts from things to do to people I needed to care for. Her lips were rampant and passionate, more forceful than she'd ever been.

Latching her arms around me, she pressed kisses to my sweaty, bloody face and breathed strangled whispers into my ear. "I'm so glad you're okay."

I pulled her away, narrowing my eyes at the finger lacerations swelling purple around her neck.

Goddammit.

I'd done my best to keep her safe, yet again, I'd failed.

I shook my head, cursing the unstable room and the steady creep of my condition tiptoeing into my tiredness.

The mess.

Fuck, the mess all around us.

The stench of death. The reek of blood. The sight of utter mayhem. My condition normally meant I was tormented by numbers and patterns. As long as I could avoid repetitive songs or thoughts, I could get by.

But not today.

Today, my OCD latched onto the vile ruin of Mercer's home, and I couldn't focus on anything else.

Brain. Gore.

Mess, mess, mess.

Pushing Pim away, I regretted the hurt I put on her face but couldn't ignore the hated voices inside my head. They were a demanding lot—a cruel task master with the never-ending chant of clean, clean, *clean*.

But they were better than the blackness I'd sampled—the blackness I would never taste again. I accepted the punishment and hiccup in my thoughts, bowing beneath the pressure to obey.

I dragged my good hand through my hair, finding more

bruises on my scalp than yesterday. "It's too much. I need to clean."

I had no products, no bleach, but I'd fallen down the slippery slope to the pit where I'd always hoped Pim would never see me. I wouldn't be able to stop the compulsion until the mess was gone and everything righted the way it was before.

Throwing her a look of utter dismay and self-condemnation, I dragged my weary form back to Daishin and pulled at his ankles.

I'd done this.

I'd fix it.

Pim drifted closer as I commanded my depleted body to haul the dead man's weight. The determination to toss him outside and stop him from marring this perfect family home was too loud to ignore.

Soft hands landed on my shoulder blades. "El." Pim's voice remained battered and bruised, stilted and stiff. "El, stop."

"Can't. Need to get it clean."

"You need to rest. We all need to rest."

I shook my head, tugging Daishin's ankles once again, sliding his corpse through disgusting body fluids. "I'll rest once it's clean."

Voices sounded behind me as someone guided Pim away from my angry jerks that weren't quite strong enough to lug a body. Female voices murmured as a black shadow fell over Daishin, hinting I had company.

He didn't touch me, but his French voice lowered with understanding rather than judgment. "It seems the men most bound by their passions are the worst to pay." A hand wrapped around one of Daishin's ankles, bumping me away until we each held one leg.

I didn't like sharing tasks. This mess was because of me. I would be the one to clear it, but Mercer appeared in my vision, distorting my drive, my endless craving to disinfect.

I blinked, focusing just long enough to understand Mercer tried to offer me a lifeline before I drowned in compulsive complication.

He carried his own wounds and injuries from a night of fighting, but instead of condemning me or ridiculing me for a chemical unbalance I couldn't change, he nodded as if my need to eradicate tonight wasn't a stupid idea at all.

He didn't smile, deadly serious and just as intense as he had been while killing trespassers in his home. "I have migraines. Had one ever since you entered my house. I get it, Prest. I'll help you clean. And then...fuck, then I'm taking my *esclave* to bed and not coming out for days."

Knowing he'd help me fix this slaughterhouse ought to have taken pressure off my rampaging need to clean, clean, clean, but just like I didn't want help removing Daishin's body, I didn't want him taking away my other jobs.

I didn't want help cleaning. I needed the sole responsibility—the gluttony of hard work. The utmost satisfaction of putting something right that I'd damaged.

Having his help ruined that.

Snatching my hands off Daishin's ankle, I skipped to another chore I could do without his interference.

It was suddenly very, very important to my analytic brain. "I need to count them."

Twenty plus Daishin.

There had better be twenty-one dead Chinmoku. Otherwise, my tired and agony-riddled brain might very well have a stroke and finish me off for them.

"Okay. Go count. I'll ask my staff to help fix this catastrophe." Mercer clapped me on the back, smiled at Pim, then wrapped his arm around his wife and vanished into the house.

I should be grateful.
I should thank him.
But I wasn't grateful.
I was furious he'd stolen any hope at redemption.

Good riddance.

If I had the energy, I'd tear around cleaning before he had time to rally his help. But that was the point in all of this. I didn't have the energy to do anything, and that made my brain even worse.

Franco and Selix stood by, no longer enemies but soldiers in the same war. I nodded at Selix, thanking him without words for what he'd done.

He nodded back, a quick salute to his temple before following Franco to find more cleaning gear.

Alone in the foyer with the dead leader of the faction I'd been terrified of with the woman I was now petrified of scaring away with my stupid fixating brain, I slowly turned to face her.

"Pim, I…"

What could I say? How could I explain the bone-deep need to clean this place from top to bottom? How could I admit that sleep would be impossible, rest, healing, sailing away—all of it utterly banned to me until I'd done this.

She pressed herself close, threading her arms around me and tucking her head into the crook of my neck. She didn't care blood covered us or that I stunk to high heaven; she merely held me and didn't need to say anything else.

Accepting what she gave me, finally trusting her when she said she loved me enough to overlook my flaws and accept me unconditionally—just as I'd accepted her with her scars and panic attacks and any other issues that might haunt her for the rest of her life—we turned together and headed outside to complete the grisly tally of death.

* * * * *

It took hours.

Between my hobbling and stiffness and the scattered locations of the Chinmoku's resting places, dawn turned to morning long before we'd finished counting.

With each body we found, I ticked it off on a mental checklist, and my brain settled a little more.

Pim held my hand the entire journey, never complaining

or suggesting someone else finished counting for me.

I didn't know if it was because her throat was still too sore to talk or if she'd reverted to her favouritism of silence—but I was grateful.

We'd won but we'd lost a fair few of Mercers men. Four lives to be exact. Four lives that had died yet again for me.

Guilt sat heavy. Triumph over winning not an option.

Tallying the deaths took us all over Mercer's estate, and by the time we counted the final bodies and trailed down the spiral staircase from Mercer's bedroom, the foyer had already been removed of carcasses and stank of fresh bleach.

Maids and security guards alike donned rubber gloves, mopping, scrubbing, removing any evidence of what had happened.

The crime scene was erased.

Once again, I wished I was normal and could breathe a sigh of relief and be done with it. But my idiotic brain couldn't let me rest.

Even though my eyes barely functioned, my eyelids drooped heavily, and I now leaned on Pim instead of walked beside her, I kept patrolling the house until I found Mercer speaking to Franco in hushed French in the kitchen.

They both looked up as Pim and I interrupted, their faces just as ashen and drawn.

At least one good thing about tonight had come true. Daishin had lied when he hinted he'd brought more than law stated to fight me. He'd stuck to the twenty men permitted.

And we'd found twenty-one with him included.

All of them dealt with and no longer a threat to Pim or my family.

Some had fatal stab wounds. Others had bullet holes. But all of them were deceased.

Thank God.

Mercer raised an eyebrow, knowing full well I wasn't here for a social call. "Need something?"

"Yes. A truck."

"A truck?"

I nodded. "Something large with lockable doors and opaque panels. And I need to buy it off you because I won't be returning it."

"Quoi?" He shook his head at his slip, morphing effortlessly back into English. "Why?"

"Because I'm going to load up the Chinmoku and drive them to Calais."

"What?" Pim piped up, the first word she'd said in hours. "You can't be serious. It's almost lunchtime. What the hell are you going to do with twenty-one bodies at the port?"

I smiled, revealing a pastime I was well versed in. "I'm going to make them disappear."

Mercer understood straight away. He prattled something off to Franco. I caught the words van, keys, and hurry.

Turning back to me, he added, "I have my own way of disposing of them. You don't need to—"

"Yes, I do." I allowed my temper to show. "This is my mess. It's mine to clean up. You stole any chance I had at physically cleaning. The least you can do is let me take them out to sea and drop them into the deepest part of the ocean I can."

Tess walked into the kitchen, her eyes widening as she towel-dried freshly washed hair. In grey track pants and black hoodie, she looked as if she'd just come back from the gym and not a shower to wash away an evening of murder. "Are you sure? All of them? Will your boat hold the weight?"

"The Phantom can carry hundreds, if need be. So yes. I'm sure."

"In that case." Mercer clapped his hands as Franco reappeared and handed him a key. "I guess we'll help you load your cargo."

* * * * *

I'd never driven a delivery van before.

Not that I would be driving today with my arm and leg buggered as they were.

Almost three p.m. and each Chinmoku was tucked up

tight in plastic bags to prevent leakage and strapped into a massive sandwich of bodies.

The only thing hiding them from the public eye was a thin piece of metal siding and an old logo of a food delivery service.

Mercer returned after taking a phone call as we placed the last corpse inside.

He tucked his phone away then glanced at the van and back to me. "That was the chief of police. I've cleared a path for you. You shouldn't encounter any road blocks or drunk driving barricades at this time of day. However, if you do, no one will ask questions. My reach doesn't include border security or port officials, so you're on your own there." His eyes narrowed, evidence of his migraine paling his skin. "Please tell me you're not going to drive onto the pier and unload bodies in plain sight—night or day?"

I smirked, fighting the heaviness of exhaustion. "No. They're going to stay in the van. That's their coffin."

Mercer didn't ask any more questions—either he didn't want to know or he understood more than he should. "In that case goodbye, Prest. I'll store your helicopter until you're ready to retrieve it and you have my email if you need anything." He stuck out his hand. "I'd say it was a pleasure. But it wasn't."

I shook his grip, wincing as my body cursed me for yet another painful action. "Likewise. I would prefer to forget this entire incident, but unfortunately, I have a token to remember you by with the gunshot to my shoulder."

He grinned. "I have been told I'm unforgettable."

"Yes, well." I broke our handshake.

I should say thank you. I should promise to pay him back if he ever needed help, but I just wanted to get the fuck away as soon as possible.

I backed toward the van, and Mercer backed toward his home. We'd said all the farewells we were interested in, but our respective women drifted past us and met in the middle of the driveway. They smiled awkwardly then leaned in for a hug.

Suzette, the maid, also hugged Pim, offering Mercer's son

for Pim to cuddle in one last attempt.

With a laugh but a very visible wince, Pim denied the chance to hold the sleeping baby and slotted herself into my side. "We'll stay in touch, I'm sure."

Tess nodded. "I'd like that."

More awkwardness settled, signalling our time to leave.

With nothing else to do and a van full of rotting Japanese samurais, we waved one last time and climbed into the vehicle.

Selix took the driver's seat, I took the passenger, and Pim sat in the middle.

All of us silent.

All of us ready to go home.

Pimlico

FOUR AND A half hours was a long time to be trapped in a van's front seat with the stench of decay in every breath.

I couldn't sleep.

I couldn't relax.

I couldn't stop thinking about the men all jiggling and discarded behind us.

Elder didn't sleep either, even though his nose steadily trickled blood and he groaned with every bump or pothole.

Selix had already called the Phantom to ensure the crew were safe, that no more infiltrators lurked on board, and to prepare to sail the moment we arrived.

Elder spoke to Jolfer and planned the departure route but only after he'd advised Michaels of the long shopping lists of maladies he now needed his on board surgeon to repair.

I had no doubt Michaels was cursing him already.

Once calls were made and the Phantom ready to leave the moment we drove into her belly, we all settled into companionable silence.

We had no energy to talk and no desire to rehash what we'd seen and done in the past few days.

The only thing we were interested in was bouncing along cobblestone roads and staring at black and white cows as we drove our makeshift hearse through French countryside.

As rural life gave way to town life and we switched lanes for main arterial highways, we merged with evening rush hour—as men and women, hungry and blurry-eyed from working all day, sped home to loved ones.

Unbeknownst to them, they sat in traffic with twenty-one dead Chinmoku, one saved slave, one friend who kept secrets, and one thief who'd stolen enough money to make himself an almost billionaire.

We were an odd bunch with odd morals and compasses, but Elder and Selix were two of the best human beings I knew.

Even if blood stained their hands.

That didn't matter.

It never would.

Because I was in love with Elder.

And blood stained my hands, too.

ELDER

CLIMBING ON BOARD the Phantom, I expected the same homecoming and safety net I always did. Admittedly, that comfort had been missing when I'd left Pim in Monte Carlo, but she was beside me now. I should step onto the Phantom with relief and contentedness.

Especially now the Chinmoku were dead, we'd made a new ally through battle, and I was finally free from vengeance and being hunted by my enemies.

Nothing was wrong.

For the first time in forever, things were finally *right*.

Yet, the Phantom felt unfriendly. As if she didn't agree with the cargo she was about to carry.

Jolfer had already arranged for staff to re-jig the garage to make space for us. The Town Car was pushed into a further berth and expensive toys juggled closer together.

It'd been a simple matter of driving the van straight on, applying the chocks and straps, and clambering out onto Phantom territory.

Moving after almost five hours in a cramped car with injuries that had been overused and abused meant my inner thoughts were full of filthy curses as I inched stiffly toward the cab door and dropped down.

I tried to hide the level of my pain but feared Pim knew

how close I was to shutting down and not having the power to restart again.

I'd never felt this wretched. This torn and shattered and exhausted.

All I wanted was a shower and bed and not to wake until I was back to full health. But that would have to wait because my evening wasn't finished yet.

I'd removed the Chinmoku from Mercer's house.

I had yet to remove them from mine.

Jolfer met us as the three of us took the elevator from garage to top deck. His face was sombre; his eyes serious. We needed to debrief and talk about the Chinmoku stealing on board a second time. We needed to have staff meetings on what protocols worked and what didn't. We needed to make sure everyone was on the same page going forward.

But right now...we had more pressing things to attend to.

Grabbing Pim's hand, I pulled her to face me and tucked a loose, messy strand behind her ear. For a woman who'd already endured her fair share of evil, she'd been bathed in it since meeting me.

I wanted to take her into my room and wash her gently. I wanted to hold her as she fell asleep and beg her to tell me what she was thinking. We hadn't talked since this started. I had no idea if she was okay or freaking out or shutting down.

But again, our reconnection would have to wait.

My brain had fixated on finishing this. And I had no choice but to carry that out.

"Go to bed, little mouse." I kissed her forehead, inhaling the faint smell of Pim under the sickly stench of death. "There's something I need to finish."

She knew what sort of gruesome work I spoke of, and her days in the darkness had provided her with enough apathy to deal with the dead—especially the dead who'd dabbled in slavery and dwelled on the wrong side of the law.

However, I didn't want her taking part in the next stage. Even if my yacht judged me—whispering that my past might've been dealt with, but I still had other bridges to cross and repair. Even if I hobbled and hurt and hadn't slept in days, my task was not yet over.

My task.

Not hers.

She looked up, her fingers landing on my chest like tiny butterflies. I barely registered she touched me, yet my body burned beneath her fingertips. "I want to help."

I shook my head, kissing her again and pushing her gently toward my quarters. "You've done more than enough."

"But—"

"No buts. I need to do this on my own."

Our eyes locked; arguments rose and fell on her face. I understood her desire to stay by my side and be equal in each task, but I didn't want to layer yet more insanity onto her. She knew what I was about to do, and I rather she stayed away.

I'd leaned on her too much as it was. I'd failed her too many times to count. In this, I wouldn't be swayed.

"Go." I pointed at my room. "I'll come to you soon."

Her lips pursed, but finally, she nodded. Flicking a glance at Jolfer and Selix beside me, she gave me a sweet, sad smile. "Don't be too long." With weary steps, she turned and disappeared in the direction of my quarters.

The moment she was gone, I snapped my gaze to Jolfer. "Sail now. When you hit deep water where the shelf falls away and there are kilometres between us and the bottom, let me know."

The unusual request was met with a raised eyebrow but utter obedience. "It will take a few hours, at least."

"I'll wait."

I'd wait all night if I had to, but I would wait far away from Pimlico.

I wouldn't relax. I wouldn't move into a fresh future—not with the bodies of twenty-one Chinmoku rotting in a van beneath my feet.

Jolfer stepped toward the bridge. "Oh, what's the itinerary

this time around? Do you have a destination in mind? Or is this a 'see where the tide takes us' kind of journey?"

I closed my eyes, hating how they stung from lack of rest. I'd sleep for a century once this was finished.

The right answer would be to just sail. To see where the currents took us with no pressure or deadline.

Pim deserved that.

I deserved that.

Shit, everyone deserved a holiday after the past few months.

But just like the Phantom was no longer entirely my confidant and friend, my own heart wasn't satisfied with ending this way.

I'd cleaned up my mess.

It was time to tell those who mattered that they were no longer hunted for my mistakes.

"Set course for America. It's time I paid my family a visit."

* * * * *

Seven hours.

That was how long it took to clear boat traffic and reach an area where the sonar showed a cliff far below us. The world fallen away beneath our feet—a shelf turning solid into nothingness.

The void was over two kilometres deep.

A perfect grave for men I never wanted to be found.

For seven hours, I'd permitted Michaels to try to put me back together. I rested at his instruction, I ate what he ordered, and swallowed medicine he concocted. I even submitted to the braces and slings he dressed me in to start the lengthy recovery to full mobility for the parts of my body I could no longer feel.

While he tended to me, I sent Selix off to tend to his own superficial wounds and to sleep. Staff kept me updated on what Pim ate, when she'd fallen asleep, and if her rest was peaceful or full of nightmares.

I hated that I wasn't up there with her, but I preferred the black tomb of the garage. It was fitting for the undertaking job

I was about to perform.

The main engines stopped whirring as Jolfer held us stationary and Selix appeared from my wake-up call.

I'd given Jolfer extra instructions tonight: *turn off all lights. Disable the radar.* I wanted to be as incognito as possible.

We truly were a phantom, a ghost, a death ship that needed to stay hidden. Two kilometres was a long way down, but I wanted to be sure no one would investigate the coordinates or concern themselves with why we'd hovered over the abyss for longer than normal.

I hobbled over to the van, tossing Selix the keys. Night once again blanketed the horizon. Yet another evening spent dealing with Chinmoku, and the last one I ever wanted to waste. "Ready?"

He yawned. "Yep."

"Good. Let's get these bastards off my ship." Moving toward the back of the garage where a wall with fortified seals and waterproofing hid yet another submersible entrance like that with the Viper submarine, I entered the code and waited for the lengthy process of hydraulic bolts and locks to unfasten.

Once the seal broke and door opened, Selix hopped into the van and drove it into the specially designed cube. He parked the heavy van full of Chinmoku on the correct fulcrum point for ease of tipping.

Killing the engine, he tossed the keys back inside and slammed the door. Together, we opened the double doors of the vehicle and braced ourselves against the reek.

Disgusting body excretions and rigor mortis by-products had been contained thanks to the plastic bags. At least, my ship would remain sanitary from their decay. The plastic would also act as a sarcophagus and prevent any lightweight items such as credit cards and driver's licenses from floating free. Identities and mementoes would remain in their pockets, never seeing the light of the surface or shore again.

We had deliberated, in the seven long hours it took to sail here, if we should cut off their fingers and remove their teeth to ensure they forever remained John Does, but neither Selix nor I had the stomach for more gore, especially seeing as our enemy had already fallen.

We'd won.

We didn't need to dismember the dead to confirm such a grisly conclusion.

Besides, by burying them all together, we removed any need to attach heavy weights or other methods to keep them submerged. All we'd need to do was crack a couple of the cab's windows and punch perforations into the panels of the van to ensure seawater filled up the vehicle and it sank like a boulder.

Funny to think, as I stared at the ragdoll pile of useless limbs, that somewhere in there was Daishin. He didn't have prime real estate rotting on top of his men. He could be on the very bottom or face down in someone's asshole.

He'd been the leader for decades.

And now he was nothing more than fish food.

I didn't smile, knowing he was dead. I didn't celebrate or dance on his grave. I only felt empty and tired...so, so tired.

"Let's get this over with." Slamming the doors, I ensured they were latched and locked before winding down the windows for the upcoming seawater. Once completed, I looked back at Selix.

Without waiting for instruction, he disappeared into the garage and the well-stocked tool kit we kept for our mechanics. He came back with a sledge hammer, a chisel, and a sharp knife.

Handing me the knife, he headed to the old delivery logo on the van and held the chisel against the metal. With a hard whack, he hit it with the hammer and broke through the thin metal in one strike.

The noise boomed around us, joining more and more, louder and louder as he made his way around the truck, hitting holes that were too small for evidence to float out of but big enough for small fish and seawater to dissolve the contents inside.

While Selix tweaked the vehicle, I took the knife and slashed all four tyres.

No point in having anything that had air while sinking to the bottom of the sea. We wanted this bitch to plummet not dawdle.

My back fucking killed from bending over, but it didn't take long for the loud hissing of escaping air to deplete, leaving us with suspenseful silence.

"Ready?" I jammed the knife into my waistband and headed toward the exit.

Selix followed, returning his tools to the chest from where he'd taken them. We reconvened at the control panel where I pressed a switch and closed the door to protect the dry dock and everything inside it—including us.

We waited while every lock and seal slid back into position and the sensors announced that it was safe to proceed.

I always got nervous flooding my ship, but I had to trust in the fail-safes I'd built into this convenient trap door. I'd tested the locker multiple times in the design and construction phase. And I'd used it once to discard evidence of another crime I'd committed all in the name of building my reputation.

I knew how it would work.

And the waterproof cameras inside the room would film in full colour, letting us witness the final farewell.

I hit the second button and large pumps whirred into action.

Gushing seawater splashed around the slashed tires, rapidly turning the area from dry to drenched.

Selix and I waited the entire time it took for the cameras in the top of the room to drown in icy blue. Once the water hit the roof, the pumps stopped and a green light appeared on the control panel before me.

Ready to Evacuate Contents.

Selix glanced at me as I pressed the button and began the final step. The siding of the Phantom parted from the mothership, opening wider and wider until only ocean blackness was visible instead of metal reinforced shell.

The cameras in the room showed the van already rocking back and forth, gravity stolen and ready to swim.

Unlike the floating garage that housed the submarine, this one tilted to discard unwanted items rather than waiting for it to propel itself out with motors.

The hydraulics were silent as, inch by inch, the van's roof tilted in the camera angle, following the trajectory of the floor as it quickly turned into a slippery slope to the yawing mouth of Davy Jones' locker.

It didn't take much.

A simple recline and the van started to move.

Slip, slip, slip.

Reaching the lip of the Phantom, it paused for a second then tilted end up, flashing the entrails of brakes and axels before floating out of sight with no bubbles, no noise, no hint that it had ever existed.

I expected a pause.

I waited for some part of me to curse the Chinmoku or say goodbye in some way.

I needed to prove to myself that this was real and not a dream I'd had countless times before.

This was *real*.

He was dead.

But in that moment, all I needed was the knowledge he was off my boat and out of my life because I had much better things to do than say goodbye to a past that'd shaped and defined me but also ruined and destroyed me.

I'm free.

We didn't speak as I pushed the button again and waited as the floor switched from slope to horizontal, then reversed the pumps to evacuate the thousands of litres it'd pumped into the chamber.

Only once the room was empty of ocean did I roll my shoulders and breathe properly for the first time since I'd been cast out of my family and turned to revenge as a coping mechanism.

"It's over," I murmured. "I can't believe it's fucking over."

I didn't care there were more Chinmoku out there.

They didn't matter.

I'd killed the leader. I *was* their leader. But because I never had any intention of claiming that seat, they would forever be leaderless until a takeover happened, the faction broke up, or good old politics instated a new commander.

Either way, I would be forgotten or revered and no one would dare come after me again.

Not now.

In a twisted code of honour, it would prevent them from hunting me down. I'd proven my worth, and the worthy were permitted to live.

Pim was safe.

My family was safe.

And my enemies were beneath me in the deep, deep sea.

Pimlico

ELDER CAME TO bed at sunrise.

His silhouette showed a sling and brace, hinting he'd submitted to medical attention. He might have antibiotics in his system and outer tools to heal him, but no amount of painkillers or doctors could prevent the seizing of stiff muscles that'd been well and truly overworked.

Our eyes met in the warming light as he crawled under the covers and scooped me close. He didn't undress. He didn't speak. He just clutched me hard and exhaled deeper than I'd ever heard.

His hips twitched to get closer, spooning me tight. But there was no sexual connotations—just comfort.

I was in his bed for the first time.

I'd slept fitfully by myself, looking around his room without his magnetic presence distracting me. And now he was here, and there was no mention of rules and restrictions. No hints at managing his OCD or for me to find my own sleeping quarters.

After what we'd lived through, our connection had reached an almost reverent level that didn't need to be discussed or analysed. All that mattered was we'd ceased to be two people with two separate pasts and futures and blended into one.

And because of that, his exhaustion was my exhaustion. Weights dangled on my eyelids as sleep finally wriggled into my brain. I calmed with his arms around me. I snuggled ever closer.

He moaned under his breath as dreams found him, claiming the man who was utterly invincible, beyond intelligent, and almost super human in his drive to survive.

He was unconscious before I'd fully wriggled into comfort. His belly expanding. His lungs breathing. His body heavy and hot around mine.

Whatever he'd done was over.

The Chinmoku were gone.

We'd well and truly earned our tomorrows.

* * * * *

The moon rose, chasing away the clouds that'd plagued most of the day at sea.

Large swells and rocking yachts meant I'd been happy to stay in bed while Elder slumbered beside me, never waking— even when I stole away to the bathroom and winced at the circlet of bruises around my throat. Not when I went to grab lunch from the kitchen and filled my empty belly with sustenance. Not when I sat in his office chair and scribbled notes to No One about wars and chains and things I never wanted to live through again.

Transcribing my thoughts to paper helped organise my scattered ideals and conclusions and find the ability to once and for all put it behind me. Just like I'd learned to speak without fear, I was ready to live every day without looking over my shoulder, without second-guessing myself, without doubting those I'd slowly learned to trust.

I was whole now thanks to whatever had clicked inside me while Daishin held me captive. I was no longer lost or afraid.

By the time day turned to evening and I'd napped beside Elder for the third time, his eyes finally opened just as stars twinkled above.

He'd kissed me and gingerly climbed from the bed. After a bathroom visit, he captured my hand and escorted me into the shower.

There, we washed each other silently. Both content not to talk, healing in silence and warm water.

Afterward, once he'd winced his way into a new t-shirt and track pants, Elder summoned Michaels who arrived with his black bag of medicine and checked him over, doling out new antibiotics and painkillers, before ordering him back to bed.

Elder tried to fight his lethargy. He called the kitchen for dinner and strong coffee, but the moment he'd eaten, his body shut down and he tumbled back into sleep.

* * * * *

For two days, Elder couldn't stay awake for long.

He'd rouse, talk, eat, shower, then fall asleep for long stretches.

Every time he woke, Michaels was there to administer drugs and painkillers, ensuring Elder's healing kept progressing while his body demanded as much rest as it could get.

On the third day, when Elder once again summoned coffee from the kitchens in a bid to stay awake, he sat up in bed with the doors open for fresh air, and tolerated Michaels's daily visit.

His eyes locked on mine where I sat across the room in a comfy silver suede chair.

Selix had kindly rustled up a laptop for me to use, and for the first time in forever, I had access to the internet and the news of the world that I'd been hidden from for so long.

As Michaels ensured Elder would live another day, I tried to log into old email and Facebook accounts, forgetting passwords and having to jump through hoops, confirming I was who I said I was.

Luckily, I'd never been issued a death certificate, and none of my profiles had been taken down—not that there was anything newsworthy when I finally did log in.

My email account had been suspended with a bounce back

saying it was no longer active. My Facebook feed looked like a stranger's with girls and boys from school now men and women embarking on careers, marriage, and adventures.

My lonely page was a scrapbook of my past life. A photo snippet of a party I went to but hated. A tag from someone in class making fun of the teacher. A mention in a lip-sync contest held at our sister-school.

Things that would've meant something then but now meant absolutely nothing.

I looked up, meeting Elder's gaze again, and smiled.

The only thing that meant something was him.

Michaels finished assessing his patient, giving me a wave as he packed up and left.

Ever since we'd embarked on the Phantom, there'd been no stupid discussions of me returning to my suite below; no attempts at pretending we needed space from each other.

Elder and I were a couple in every sense of the word.

In fact, couple was too lacking a phrase.

I was his, through and through. No other terminology would suffice.

"Come here." He patted the bed where he sat propped by pillows, a faint sheen of discomfort on his forehead.

The remnants of a Caesar salad for lunch sat on the bedside dresser.

My heart fluttered.

Closing the laptop, I carried it with me and curled up close to him. "How are you feeling?"

He chuckled, wincing a little as he shifted. "Like I've been at war for the past few decades."

I moved to sit cross-legged, placing the closed laptop on my thighs. My shorts kept my legs bare in the warmth of the suite, my yellow t-shirt draping off one shoulder thanks to being a size too big. "Well, you kind of have, so it's understandable."

He looked at the ceiling for a moment, thoughts racing in his eyes. "Is it strange that I feel almost lost?" His gaze flickered to me. "Now that I've achieved everything I set out to, I'm left wondering what other purpose I have?"

I shook my head, reaching over to wrap my hand around his bandaged one. "Not at all. You deserve to rest and just enjoy the moment for a bit."

"I've done enough resting. I'm *bored* of resting."

"Your body seems to think differently."

"My body can just get over it. I need to do something."

"You need to just relax."

He snorted. "Relax? Have you met me, Pimlico-san?"

My eyes widened at the Japanese address.

He sucked in a breath, licking his lips. "Sorry. After talking to Daishin, the other part of my culture is a little more alive in my brain at present."

"Would you tell me something in Japanese?"

His eyebrow rose. "Like what?"

I shrugged. "Anything. I'd just like to hear you."

I didn't say how sexy I found it or how his lips were born to speak in different languages.

He paused, clenching his teeth as if weighing up the pros and cons of embracing a little of his culture that he'd always run from. "You know...my father encouraged me to speak Japanese to make my mother happy." He sighed. "I always preferred English, though. Probably because I preferred my father over my mother. She was hard to love—mainly because earning her love wasn't easy and I always failed. Kade, on the other hand..." He drifted off, laughing softly. "He had that witch wrapped around his little finger."

I let him speak, glad he could finally discuss his family with me.

"Kade loved to speak Japanese." His voice turned gentle, wistful. "He'd scribble Hiragana and Katakana characters all over the house—sometimes on the walls in our mother's lipstick. If I'd ever done that, I would've been smacked. But Kade...he got away with a lot."

He glanced at me, full of ghosts. "He was my mother's

favourite. I knew that and was content with it. I had my father's friendship and my cello, which was enough for me. I suppose that's why she blamed me so much." His eyes darkened. "Because I killed her favourite son and survived."

I rested my head on his shoulder, earning a slight hiss from him. "Oops, sorry." I pulled away from his stitched wound, but he pulled me back. "No, stay."

I relaxed as he kissed the top of my head, breathing, *"Aishiteru."*

My belly tightened at his husky, sensual tone. Something about Elder speaking a different language pulled a cord deep inside me.

I shivered as he nuzzled my hair. "It means, I love you. But not many people in Japan say it that way."

"They don't?"

He shook his head, his nose still buried in my hair. "No."

"How do they say they love each other then?"

"They show them."

I twisted a little so I could look at him. Our noses brushed. Pressing upward, I kissed him on the lips.

He froze as I pressed gently but firm. I didn't deepen the kiss. I didn't pressure for more. I just kissed him because I was in love with him and we were alive despite overwhelming odds trying otherwise.

He kissed me back, his lips softening beneath mine but not deepening the chaste romance. The last remaining tension in my spine finally, *finally* siphoned away.

Nothing else mattered but this.

Him.

Me.

Us.

Pulling away, he murmured, "Was that your way of showing me you love me?"

I nodded. "I have many other ways to show you, too."

"You do?"

I smiled. "I can be inventive when I put my mind to

things."

He chuckled. "In that case, I look forward to finding out just how much you love me." He kissed me swift and hot. "I have so many ways to show you. The minute this fucking body of mine is back to working order, you'll find out."

We laughed together as I slotted against him.

I stroked the laptop lid, wondering if any of my school friends had found someone as incredible. I pitied them if they hadn't even though they probably pitied me for what I'd lived through to find Elder.

Silence fell between us, and I guessed he'd fallen asleep again, bound to his body's healing whether he wanted to or not.

But a faint whisper fell onto the covers around us. "Will you go somewhere with me, Pim?"

"I'd go anywhere with you," I answered immediately, looking up and locking onto his brilliant black eyes.

"You don't need to know where?"

"If you're there, I don't care."

He smiled nervously, his gaze alternating between my lips and my gaze. "It probably won't be fun."

"If it's important, then you don't need to ask or tell me. I'll go wherever you need."

"You're far too good to me." He kissed my mouth again, murmuring against my lips, "I've asked Jolfer to sail to America. There's one more thing I need to do before I can put my past behind me."

Understanding burst inside as he pulled away, searching my features for my reaction.

Anger filled me at facing the woman who'd been so cruel to him. Then forgiveness followed, remembering everything she'd lived through with losing her husband and son. The complex recipe made me nervous, but it must be nothing to what Elder must live with.

He'd done everything he could to earn their forgiveness: the deck full of toys and suites for guests who didn't want to visit. The house in Monte Carlo open to family who spat on its existence all because it was Elder's.

He might've slayed the Chinmoku's hold on him, but he'd yet to do that with his family.

I cupped his cheek. "You're going to see your mother?"

"Only if you'll come with me."

"I'd be honoured."

* * * * *

Another couple of days passed.

A pilot Selix hired flew the Phantom's resident helicopter to us from France and accepted a lift back to the closest port, thanks to Selix acting as taxi driver.

Life chores were completed and hours crept steadily onward.

Unfortunately, Elder ended up with cabin fever, demanding to be let out of bed. Michaels gave him strict instructions to obey doctor's orders and remain put. After the abuse he'd put himself through, his body needed time to knit together properly. Michaels was adamant, and after a screaming match which Elder didn't win, he reluctantly agreed—pissed off and bored but staying in bed…for now.

The next day, while Elder worked on his laptop and spoke to his factory in Monte Carlo about new orders and existing clients, I went online again and read up on what had happened while I'd been captive. It'd been rather eye-opening to read news reports and see just how much life had passed me by.

I read about my mother and her court appearances. I read about myself and my disappearance. And once I was bored with history, I turned to the future and opened a new email before entering in the address Tess had given me.

I hadn't meant to write to her.

I had nothing much to say.

But with nothing much to do and endless horizons over the next couple of weeks, I found myself opening a new message.

From: Pimlico
To: T Mercer

Subject: Thank you
Hi Tess,
I just wanted to say thanks again for all your help.
I'll never forget you and your family and what you do saving girls like me.
I hope Lino is okay after what happened and pass my hello to Suzette.
Thanks again,
Pim.

I didn't expect a reply.

To be honest, I wasn't sure I wanted one. For all my ideas of earning a female friend, now I was back on the Phantom with Elder by my side, I had no cravings for anything else. I was exactly where I wanted to be with the exact person I wanted to be with.

So when she replied a few hours later, I suffered a small case of nerves, especially as Elder read over my shoulder.

From: T Mercer
To: Pimlico
Subject: Re: Thank you
Hi Pim,
Lovely to hear from you.

I'm assuming, since I haven't heard otherwise from news channels, that you got away safe and are sailing far away by now. It was our pleasure to help, and I hope you'll stay in touch.

Don't forget, Q and I sponsor an orphanage and many other child charities here and around the world. I know this is completely overstepping, but I still feel awful about what happened that day when I tried to make you hold Lino.

My heart breaks that you can't have children—and I know I'm once again overstepping—but I wanted to reiterate that it's not the end of the dream.

If you ever decide to rescue another as Elder rescued you, then our doors are always open.

Tess.

"Orphanage?" Elder asked, a strained rasp in his voice.

"Fucking hell. That woman really doesn't know when to stop, does she?" Elder reached over and slammed the laptop closed. "I'm so sorry, Pim."

I let him take the computer, shell-shock making me mute and frozen.

It wasn't the fact she'd reminded me all over again that having children naturally would never happen for us. It was the fact she offered a family so readily, so easily, so *soon*.

I'm not ready.
I don't know if I'll ever be ready.
Adoption?
I…

Shaking off new fears and questions, I smiled reassuringly—more worried that Elder would stress out than about my own shortcomings. "She's fine. She only means well." Kissing his cheek, I bounced off the bed. "I'll go rustle up some snacks. We'll watch the sunset."

Elder grabbed my wrist before I could leave, pulling me back and cupping my jaw. With blazing black eyes, he ran his thumb over my bottom lip, staring way too intense and way too knowingly into my soul. "I love you, Tasmin Blythe." He kissed me sharp and deep. "Don't ever forget that."

Whatever worries or heartaches I'd had at being incomplete vanished.

I was his.
He was mine.
We were a family already.

* * * * *

Another few days passed while Elder recuperated.

Slowly, he left his bedroom and ventured onto the deck where warmer airs and gentle currents meant sunlight and dinners alfresco injected health back into his body.

Jolfer gave us daily sailing reports, and on the ninth day at sea, when we finally neared America, he asked if Elder was ready to dock or would prefer to sail a little more to allow final healing.

Elder gave me a look and a grin so innocent and pure, it took my breath away. "What do you want to do, Pim?"

"It's not what I want, but you."

"Wrong. It's about both of us." He limped toward me, his body tall and tight even with his sling and ankle brace. "I want to keep you all to myself, for a little longer."

I smiled. "What did you have in mind?"

He turned to face his captain. "Jolfer, I think we'll take the scenic route."

Jolfer broke into a grin. "Right you are, sir. Good choice." With a quick salute, he made his way back to the bridge.

I waited until he was out of ear-shot before I followed Elder to where staff had set up a platter of smoked salmon, cheese, and homemade lemonade beside very comfortable looking red and white deck chairs. "Scenic way?"

Elder smirked, easing his way into one of the recliners with a wince. Even with his stiffness and fading bruises, he looked more like the man who'd demanded a penny for my thoughts rather than the one who'd limped to bed in pieces.

My penny bracelet jingled on my wrist as I sat down, agreeing with me.

Being bed bound Elder hadn't had another episode like the one he'd had after the battle with the Chinmoku. His tendencies had given him some breathing room and it showed in how light-hearted he was—untormented for a change.

Taking a sip of lemonade, he said, "The Bahamas."

I froze, cheese and cracker halfway to my mouth. "We're going to the Bahamas?"

He shrugged. "Why not? It's technically on the way. Kind of." He laughed. "I think we deserve a vacation, don't you?"

I shivered with absolute joy. Why not indeed? "I don't know what to say."

"Say you'll come to the Bahamas with me." He chewed a cracker, sunshine dappling his blue black hair.

How insanely incredible had my life become, and what did I ever do to deserve it?

Unable to contain a laugh full of bubbling happiness, I nodded. "I'll come to the Bahamas with you. Since you asked so nicely."

* * * * *

I'd seen a lot of things in my short life.

I'd lived a lot of things.

But this? This azure blue paradise? It was the first time I'd been dumbstruck by natural beauty and near tears at how grateful I was to witness it.

The Phantom sailed around the inlets of the many islands in the Bahamas. I didn't know the names of each different atoll or land mass, but each was as stunning as the last.

The sun set before we laid anchor, and I fell asleep in Elder's arms trembling with anticipation of tomorrow.

The next day was spent admiring the view from the deck. Relaxing under the hot sun, we grew browner by the hour. Elder looked longingly at the water and even opened the railing to assess what the jump from the deck to tide would do to his freshly knitted-together ankle.

Michaels came running just as Elder stripped off his t-shirt and tossed away his sling with a disgusted look. All ideas of swimming were curtailed thanks to strict doctor's orders.

The following day we did the same—minus the attempt at swimming—relaxing and sailing around various parts of the islands, taking our time to find the perfect spot. The beauty of the tropical wilderness beckoned us to explore, and we both grew antsy to trade water for land.

The third day, we docked at an island called Eleuthera. The warm breeze carried scents of sand, coconuts, and palm trees. The need to feel the icing sugar sand between my toes and search for waterfalls had me pacing the polished decks of the Phantom as if I were in captivity once again.

Finally, Elder had had enough of being an invalid and summoned Michaels to perform a final check-up. His stitches were removed, his ribs checked, his finger splint discarded, and his sling retired. His bruises and cuts had healed faster than mine ever had, leaving no trace of violence on his skin.

The constellation of injuries had shrunk to just one—his ankle.

Michaels wasn't happy with Elder's slow recuperation on the joint and refused to take the brace off just yet. Elder had to obey to avoid worsening the already irreversible damage to his tendons and ligaments.

Once Michaels had delivered the stern instructions, Elder shooed him away and did the exact opposite by storming to the bridge to talk to Jolfer.

I had no idea what they discussed, but he came back looking less pissed off and promised a surprise tomorrow.

That night, as I stood on the deck watching the stars curl with smoke from Elder's medicinal use of marijuana, Selix appeared with a satellite phone and passed it to me.

I raised my eyebrow. "What is it?"

He smiled. "Someone wants to talk to you."

I shrank back, staring at the phone as if my past was trying to make contact and drag me back. My new present seemed too good to be true. I was so in awe of the effortless way Elder had introduced me to travel and luxury; even now, I pinched myself regularly to make sure I hadn't fallen into a coma back at the white mansion and might wake up at any moment in horror.

It seemed without the threat of death or mortal injury casting a shadow over us, I couldn't accept that life could be this…uncomplicated…this *wonderful*.

Selix chuckled. "It's not going to bite you, Pim."

"I don't know anyone who knows this number. *I* don't even know this number."

He grabbed my hand and slapped the heavier-than-normal cell phone into it. "You know one person. I suggest you speak to her."

Leaving me speechless, he wandered off, cocking his chin at Elder for him to follow.

Elder inhaled the last puff and tossed the discarded joint into the waves below. "Talk to your mother, Pim. I have things to discuss with Selix."

I didn't have a choice as he left me alone with the galaxies above.

My hand shook as I raised the phone to my ear. Elder and Selix laughed at something in the distance, strolling to the other side of the yacht.

"Hello?" My voice remained quiet and hesitant, still distrustful no matter what I'd been told.

"Are you Tasmin Blythe?" a curt female asked.

Thanks to Elder occasionally using my true name, it no longer sounded as foreign as it once did. "I-I am."

"And do you accept a toll charge from Sonya Blythe, prisoner 890776E?"

My fingers clutched the phone tighter. "I do."

"Connecting you now."

A crackle and hiss and then my mother's anxious voice. "Min?"

I fought the need to sit suddenly. "Hi, Mum."

She exhaled heavily. "I've been trying to call you for weeks. Is everything okay? I feared that you'd been taken again. That something awful had happened."

"Why would you think that?"

"Because you said you'd call and you didn't."

"Oh." Shame filled me. "I'm so sorry." I'd been on my own and blocked from all communication for so long, I'd forgotten the simple requirement and expectations from others to check in now and again. "I didn't think. I'm so sorry. I'm fine. Just had a couple of interesting weeks but everything is better now."

"Define interesting." Her voice turned sharp.

"Oh...nothing really." I waved my hand in the air, struggling to omit rather than lie. "It's over now, so it's in the past."

"Well, that's good to hear." Her sharp tone switched to a smile. "It's so nice to talk to you. Almost as incredible as it was to see you that day."

I padded barefoot over to a lounger and sat. Knowing my mother was in jail for killing my murderer still wasn't easy to comprehend—especially when speaking to her like any normal conversation on the phone.

"It was amazing seeing you, too. How are they treating you in there?"

She chuckled. "Fine."

"Are you okay?"

"I'm okay, Tasmin. But that isn't why I called. I'm far more interested to know how *you* are."

I smiled, looking around at the starry skies and warmth of the Caribbean. "I'm doing wonderfully."

"Oh, do tell."

I laughed, unable to link the woman asking for details and genuinely caring about my answers to the cold-hearted mother from my childhood.

It was as if she'd followed my thoughts, interrupting before I could reply. "You know, I'm not that person anymore, Min. I've given up being so suspicious and judgmental. Living in this place…it teaches you to be wary and keep your guard up, but it also shows the depth of human connection and compassion. I want to know about your life. I need to know you're happy."

Tears filled my eyes as I struggled with things to say. Assurances that I'd never hold back again, fully willing to have this relationship with her.

Once again, she jumped into the silence, not as comfortable nor as friendly with it as I was. "Oh, I almost forgot. I arranged my lawyer to release the funds I was holding in a trust fund for you. Your Mickey Mouse watch from your father is also in the trust. Whenever you're back in town, you can collect it from their offices."

I snapped back to reality. "Wait, what?"

"I told you I took your watch back from that bastard."

I sat tall. "Yes, I remember and I'm ever so grateful, but about the other stuff you just said—"

"What? About the money from selling the apartment? It doesn't equate to much, thanks to the large mortgage I had, but at least you'll have a couple hundred grand to buy your own place or pay for your adventures rather than rely on Mr. Prest."

Wow.

"I-I don't know what to say."

"You don't need to say anything. That money is yours. It's been waiting for you while gathering a piddly amount of interest over the years. It's yours and ready to spend on whatever you want." Her voice softened. "I'm happy you've found love, Minnie Mouse, but I also don't want you to trade one captivity for another."

"What do you mean?"

"I mean being with him because you love him is one thing. Being with him because you have no means to get away is another." She sighed as if this topic taxed her. "I want you to be happy, but I also want you to be free. I gave away my freedom, hoping to give you yours. I failed, but Mr. Prest didn't. I will forever be grateful to him, but if there's ever a day when you need to leave, then you now have the ability to do so. You deserve love and freedom, Tasmin. Don't ever confuse the two or believe they go hand in hand."

I blinked in the darkness, staring at the majesty of the Phantom and the shapes of Elder and Selix as they shared a drink. I couldn't imagine ever not being happy with him, but if it meant so much to my mother, how could I not accept? "I don't know how to thank you."

"You can thank me by sending some photos of where you are and what you're doing."

I laughed, chest tight with amazement at how generous she was. "That I can do."

I didn't know why but guilt sat heavier with every breath. Guilt that I was here in paradise on a yacht worth more than ten of our apartments in London and she lived in an eight by eight cell.

Swallowing, I admitted, "We're sailing to America."

I'd save the Bahamas for another day—a day when I could deliver such incredible news without coming across as bragging or spoilt. I feared the awe inside me for this wondrous place would come across as rude if I gushed.

"Are you going via the Caribbean? If you left from England, that would be an easy detour."

I rubbed my arms as a cloud ghosted over the moon, drenching us in darkness.

Damn.

I paused before saying quietly, "We're moored off the island of Eleuthera right now. I didn't know how to tell you."

She laughed. "You didn't know how to tell me you're in one of the most beautiful places on earth with a man who I hope is taking care of you? Tasmin, that's *exactly* what I want to hear. It makes my existence so much easier in here knowing you're out there living the life I'd always hoped for you."

"I can...tell you more if you'd like."

"I'd love that."

I reclined against the lounger, shy all of a sudden. What did daughters tell their mothers? Were all avenues of life permitted or was it more selective and private? "Where would you like me to start?"

She sighed, giggling gently. "How about from the moment you left me when you came back from the dead and I found out I still have a daughter?"

"Okay, well..." I stretched out, testing the waters on this new dynamic. "First, there was a beautiful dress that Elder bought for me and then a ball at the most spectacular manor."

"Sounds incredible."

"And then there was the bracelet Elder gave me and..."

And for thirty magical minutes, I spoke to my mother like I'd never spoken to her before.

I told her about Hawksridge Hall, my penny bracelet, the way my heart soared and pattered whenever I was around Elder. I told her about Monte Carlo and finding out what she'd done for me. I told her about Morocco and how Elder stood beside me in a storm and waited for me to decide not to die.

I told her all the good stuff and withheld the bad.

I didn't tell her about the Chinmoku, or Q shooting Elder, or the battle in France.

I didn't tell her about my tongue and how long it took me to speak.

We'd both had enough death in our lives to permit it power over our conversation.

By the time an officer kicked her off the phone, we'd lived in a world of laughter and friendship, learning once and for all how to be family.

ELDER

THREE WEEKS FLEW past.

Three incredible, normal, so relaxing they were almost boring weeks, where Pim and I holidayed in the Bahamas.

We cruised the islands and chose our anchoring spots based on weather, location, and what adventure we wanted to enjoy that day.

The first week was spent sunbathing on sugar soft sand, enjoying the facilities of five-star hotels, and drinking fruity cocktails.

The second week was spent wandering local townships—me walking as normal as I could with my booted ankle, and Pim evolving from brave girl to beautiful woman.

I only had to look at her to grow hard.

Keeping my distance grew more and more difficult, but with my body still suffering, I didn't want to add sex to my list of complications just yet.

By the third week, I grew tired of the brace and against Michaels's instruction, removed it completely.

The joint was weak.

It rolled at the slightest misstep and pounded enough to give me a headache from gritting my teeth. But I got on with it because no way in hell did I want to miss out on showing

Pimlico the hidden jungles and waterfalls of the Caribbean.

By day, we explored untouched islands and used a jet ski to skim around the different atolls, choosing a spot for a picnic and walk.

By night, we ate a dinner on board—sometimes in the dining room and others informal on the deck.

For three weeks, we learned how to be together without panic attacks or revenge plots. We got to know each other all over again, and every day as we woke side by side and explored side by side and ate side by side and went to bed side by side, I fell all the more in love with her.

Every hour.

Every day.

All the goddamn time.

A simple smile, *boom* my heart exploded.

A barely there touch, *crash* my body crumpled.

A kiss beneath the stars, *bang* my soul was no longer mine but hers, through and through.

I wanted to stay here forever and forget about stressful reunions or obligations to a family who hated me, but I also wanted to right everything I'd done wrong so I no longer had to worry or condemn any future happiness.

Once I'd apologised and set my consciousness to rights, Pim and I could return here and never leave.

On our twenty-third night in paradise, I arranged the kitchen to prepare a local delicacy and sat down with Pim as if it were any other night.

But it wasn't any other night.

I'd deliberately kept my distance from her sexually for the past month—letting my body heal until I could hold my own in stamina and ensure my stupid brain wouldn't over focus.

I didn't want to act like I had when Pim gave me the bath.

I'd taken from her that night.

Tonight, I wanted to give her everything.

We fell into companionable conversation about the journey to New York in the next few days. We chatted about tourist attractions and things she'd like to visit and experience.

My skin sizzled beside her. My heart raced inside me. I barely registered what I ate because all I could think about was her.

Dessert was a blur as Pim finally noticed my strange behaviour and instead of asking what was wrong, she understood wholeheartedly what I needed.

The chemistry that'd simmered for weeks while swimming naked at night or exploring local towns in skimpy vacation clothes ignited into an all-out blaze.

Electricity sparked and spat, reaching an entirely new level.

A level that crackled in my lungs and hissed in my fingertips.

I died to touch her.

I begged to kiss her.

And she knew.

How could she not?

I couldn't stop touching her, feeding her, running my finger along her lip as she accepted vanilla ice cream from my spoon.

She knew what I wanted, and from the way she squirmed on her chair, she wanted me, too.

Halfway through dessert, I dropped the spoon to clatter against the plate and stood.

Her eyes widened as I held out my hand. "Please, Pim."

She bit her lip, inserted her hand into mine, and followed me silently to my—*our*—quarters.

* * * * *

I loved Pim.

I knew I wanted to spend the rest of my life with her.

Yet, for some stupid reason, until the moment we stood on the carpet beside my bed and Pim slowly undid the buttons of her loose-fitting shirt and shimmied from her shorts, I hadn't ventured any further into the future than the next day or next week.

I was so used to living in the *now*—never having the luxury to believe I would be granted another tomorrow—let alone another year or decade.

But Pim…she made me believe I could have those things and if I could have them—if I'd *earned* them—then I had to do something to tie her to me for the rest of my life. Through any means necessary that wasn't illegal or morally corrupt such as buying her and never letting her off the Phantom.

Marriage.

The idea whispered as she moved toward me, her eyes liquid heat, her body welcoming invitation.

I let her tug my t-shirt over my head then groaned as she fell to her knees, and unbuckled my belt with deft fingers.

She didn't give me time to think as she pulled my shorts and boxer-briefs down. Releasing my pounding erection, she seamlessly inserted me into her hot mouth.

I bowed over her, my sense of balance stolen at the first lash of her delicious tongue.

Sinking fingers into her hair, I swayed on my feet, my eyes snapping closed, my muscles locking in delirium. "Fuck, Pim."

She sank deeper, taking my length, somehow scrambling every thought I had left. Shouldn't I be doing this to her? Wasn't tonight about her, not me?

Somewhere deep inside, I had the strength to pull away and scoop her into my arms. "Tonight isn't about me, Pim."

She shivered, breaking out in goosebumps as I placed her on the bed and kicked away the rest of my clothing. "I want to do such bad things to you, but I'm going to settle for torturing you first."

She gasped as I copied her and fell to my knees. Ignoring flares of residual pain and forcing my cock to behave, I grabbed her thighs, sank my fingers deep into her skin, and pulled her toward the edge of the mattress.

The moment she was close enough, I locked my mouth around her pussy.

She cried out, her hands fisting the covers, her head lashing to the side. I placed a heavy hand on her belly to keep her down as she wriggled away from the intensity.

I growled a warning as I inserted my tongue into her. She was the one who'd directed how tonight would go. She'd jumped straight into forceful foreplay. No sly looks or shy touches.

I'd been willing to drag out tonight—to take my time adoring her.

But no…she'd sucked me as if she'd wanted me rock hard and ready to enter her that very fucking moment.

It's my turn.

If she wanted me ready to break, then I wanted her ready to shatter.

I licked and nuzzled her, forcing her to switch from wet to drenched, from needy to downright dirty with begging.

"Elder…damn it, El." Her back arched as I pierced her with two fingers, nipping at her clit.

I wanted to bite her everywhere.

I wanted to consume and mark and eat her in a way that turned her into a meal rather than a woman to worship. My lust became tainted with something powerful and violent, annihilating my self-control.

I loved her.

But right now, I wanted to punish her for making me love her so much. For making me worry about her leaving me. About making me want her with every fucking part of me.

I wanted to marry her.

But before I did that, I wanted to destroy her.

But no matter how I tried to punish her with pleasure, no matter how deep I drove my tongue or fought for the cries of her climax, I loved her.

I burned with it.

I suffocated with it.

I couldn't stop myself from launching upright and yanking her off the bed.

The thick carpet cradled her as I pressed her onto the floor.

Her fingers latched around my hips as I spread her legs and squeezed her perfect breasts.

My eyes hazed red with lust. "I-I can't be gentle."

It fucked me off that that was true.

I'd avoided her for a month so I *could* be gentle. So I could give her kindness and softness and romance.

But here we were, her bucking beneath me, mouth wide, eyes wild, and her body begging me to fuck her.

Her fingers latched around my cock, jerking me forward until I fell over her, only millimetres away from being inside her.

My stomach flipped as the first slick of hot wetness hit my crown.

"Do it. I've wanted you to do it for weeks."

I crashed over her, capturing her dirty mouth and thrusting into her as hard as I could.

She screamed. I groaned. We both swore equally into the wicked hot kiss.

Our tongues fought as we kissed wider, deeper. My cock did its best to climb inside her with every thrust.

Her nipples pressed tight against my chest as I thrust again, belly to belly, not caring my weight pinned her to the carpet or her legs tangled over my ass, ankles locking to grant leverage to drive herself up while I rocked down.

We clashed together, again and again. Her eyes dark and gleaming; her lips wet and glistening.

The soft light from my desk painted her skin in a golden patina, showing every silver lash of every scar she'd earned before I'd found her.

Something primal tore through me as I bit her throat and licked at every scar. I wanted to erase them so I could brand her with new ones. I wanted to delete any hardship so I could be the reason she bruised—bruised from being loved so damn much.

I surged harder into her, already feeling the hot tearing warning of an orgasm.

Pim screamed as I shifted upward, rubbing myself against her clit as I drove harder, faster.

Her pussy clenched around me, fist-like and ripple-strong, ripping the rest of my self-control into nothing.

I roared.

I came.

We rode each other with single-minded determination.

And once our bodies had reached the pinnacle and plummeted back to sanity, I crawled off, grabbed her arm, and pulled her upright.

Barely able to breathe with sweat drenching my flesh, I guided her until I sat on the chair where I used to play my cello.

I no longer had a cello but I had Pim, and fuck, I wanted to play her.

She shivered as I spun her to face me then waited for her to straddle my lap. We groaned in unison as she sank down my length. I couldn't tear my eyes away as my cock vanished into her body.

Once connected and inseparable, her arms looped around my shoulders, her gaze going to my gnarly scar from being shot. It no longer hurt as much, which I was grateful for as I ran my hands down her back and found the beads of her spine.

Pretending they were notes and she was my instrument, I thrust up while pushing her down.

"God, Ell!" She bit her lip as her eyes shot closed, giving herself entirely to me, trusting me, loving me, flushed and lusted and absolutely fucking beautiful.

She hypnotised me as I brought her closer and bit her neck, moving her hair out of the way as I played different chords and songs on her spine.

She wriggled as I rocked harder, searching the second blistering release already living in my blood.

I didn't let her get away, holding her tighter, breathing harder, faster.

My fingers flew quicker, my music turning into death metal: crude and loud and untamed.

I grappled her writhing hips, forcing her to take this strange melody instead of orchestrating it with me.

Her skin was so soft. Her breasts heavy and nipples crimson pink.

My orgasm switched from burning to exploding, and I tumbled down the cliff a second time.

I fisted her hair, holding the chocolate silk until her head fell back and the vulnerability of her stretched throat begged me to lick and bite.

I cursed as my teeth sank into her skin and I spurted inside her.

She rocked on my lap as I froze, overloaded with sensitivity. Having her fuck me instead of me fuck her screwed up my already screwed-up brain, and I struggled not to come again.

"Christ, you know how to destroy me," I breathed into her shoulder as my head toppled, heavy and spent.

"You're not destroyed...not yet, at least." Her fingers landed in my hair, brushing back damp strands and digging into the back of my skull. "One more, El. And I know just how I want it."

Before I could argue that I was the one in charge tonight, she stood, her body trembling as my cock slipped from her pussy.

I couldn't say a word as she spun around, looked at me over her shoulder, then sank to all fours with her ass in the air, waiting, taunting, inviting.

Fuck me.

She was swollen and slick, nothing like the terrified, abused girl I'd rescued. She was the temptress I'd always seen in her, and I couldn't fucking breathe without her permission.

Slipping off my chair, I crawled to her like the beast she made me, not stopping until my hands covered her fingers and the front of my thighs kissed the back of her legs.

My cock found her entrance, desperate to return home.

But I waited, I tormented. I let her rock backward seeking

what I could give her and crying out when I did.

One deep impale.

One swift fuck.

Her back hollowed as I curled my fingers around hers and held her still.

She was small beneath me, small and soft and utterly submissive as I took her from behind.

I forced myself deeper, savage and stabbing, my skin pricking with need as she gasped and matched me violence for violence.

"You want this?"

"Yes."

"You want me to fuck you, little mouse?"

"Hell, yes."

"Tell me how much."

She bucked beneath me, spearing herself onto my cock as far as she could go. My entire length lived inside her.

I hissed, my eyes shooting black and my third orgasm spiralling into existence.

"That much," she groaned. "I want you to fuck me that much."

"Christ, you're going to make me come."

Her fingernails dug into the carpet as I gave up on making this last. This was the finish line. Pimlico was as wild and unhinged as I was.

The least I could do was give her another soul-searing release so we could collapse and try to breathe again.

Unlocking one hand from hers, I squeezed her swinging breasts then palmed her ass before following the contours of her hip to her belly and finally between her legs.

"You're going to come for me."

Her legs snapped together as I rubbed the bundle of nerves guaranteed to make her shatter. I expected a fight. She'd already come. She was overly sensitive. But as I pinched her clit and growled with self-restraint on my own climax, she shattered.

Wave after wave of bliss rippled right down my cock,

sucking me deeper until I forgot I was a man and not a monster.

I rutted into her senselessly, mercilessly, yanking her back with my hand on her clit, holding her firm as I fucked harder.

The tip of my cock buried so deep inside her, she cried out.

But instead of moving away, she swayed back, allowing me to hurt her, permitting me to do exactly what I needed and bruise, mark, and own her.

Every nerve ending incinerated into fire, singing the music from my cello, spinning into a place I couldn't survive unless I came.

A masochistic place where the blazing, blistering pleasure was pain personified even as it sliced through my veins and granted the highest of highs and sharpest of sensations.

Climaxes were cruel.

They were cruel at how single-mindedly they could consume a person. Cruel because it took a joint act with our two bodies locked and joined into a singular purpose of release.

One, two, three times.

The perfect trio of bliss.

The ricochet of pleasure faded as I slowly returned to sanity. My brain finally accepted an ending, cutting the ties to my limbs and letting me tumble to the side, bringing Pim down with me.

Climaxes were cruel.

But sharing the aftermath with someone I loved more than anything?

Absolute fucking heaven.

Pimlico

WAKING UP NEVER failed to jolt me into awareness. Not because of the obviousness of switching sleep to consciousness but because my body and mind sometimes believed I was still in the white mansion in Crete.

Before, opening my eyes was never a favourite pastime. I'd wished I could sleep forever to avoid what my days entailed. But now…now I opened my eyes and my heart suffocated from pure, unfiltered joy.

It was Christmas and birthdays and every hallelujah moment when I woke and found I no longer lived in hell.

I lived with Elder.

Elder.

Asleep beside me, a slight frown marred his forehead, his lips pressed sternly as if he battled sleep demons even though the ones in real life had been vanquished.

I rubbed my chest where my heart swelled to ten times its normal size.

Love.

I'm in love.

I'm safe.

I'm happy.

I stopped breathing.

I'm…happy.

Such simple words—a sentence normally said flippantly or taken for granted.

But for me? To be able to say I understood what that string of letters meant and to fully grasp the depth of contentedness and gratefulness in just being alive?

Wow.

Rolling onto my back, I looked around Elder's room and the carpet and chair where we'd had sex last night.

We'd gone from hardly touching and living with strict rules to attacking each other.

I had carpet burn on my spine, internal bruises that ached, and a bitten lip from kissing too hard.

But I wouldn't trade them for the world. I loved every scratch and scrape.

There was no stopwatch counting down to another war. No shadows waiting on the fringes to steal our newfound happiness. All we had to do was visit his mother and then decide where we wanted to explore next.

More islands or mainland? Hot or cold? Uncivilized or city?

Once again, my body heated with utmost gratefulness and love for the man who'd made this possible.

Turning my head, I focused on the open cupboard where his cello used to rest. The straps and padding to protect the instrument looked strangely lonely with nothing to hold.

For so long, I'd hated whenever he played. I'd cringe the moment any thread of music infiltrated the silence of the Phantom.

But last night, I'd become his cello, and it'd reminded me just how much he missed his outlet. I hadn't heard his songs since we'd returned from France. I hadn't even noticed his favourite possession was missing.

I *hated* that I hadn't noticed.

I regretted that I hadn't asked him why he ceased playing.

Elder hadn't told me what happened, but as I slid out of bed and padded naked to the empty cupboard, the sole of my foot hit something sharp tucked in the soft carpet.

Bending down, I plucked it from the strands.

A tiny shard with a few small pieces of horse hair still attached.

My heart sank.

Oh, no.

Was this part of his bow?

I'd seen how hard he was on those things, tearing the strings with music, turning it from neat to straggly and broken.

Running my fingers over the strange pockmarks in the cupboard, I pieced together what'd happened.

Bullets.

My shoulders fell.

Elder had lost his cello the night he'd lost me.

And unlike fighting for my return...he couldn't do anything for his cello and had to bury his treasured instrument.

Glancing at Elder still sleeping behind me, I wished I could find a way to—

"...at least you'll have a couple hundred grand to buy your own place or pay for yourself on your adventures rather than rely on Mr. Prest."

I had money now.

My mother had trusted me with her life savings. I had my own pennies and dollars that I could use to gift back what was lost.

The instant the idea arrived I sped into the bathroom and stole a terrycloth robe from the back of the door. Covering my nakedness, I looked at Elder one last time before vanishing from the bedroom and stepping onto the bright sunny deck.

Unlike the muggy heat of the Caribbean, we'd sailed overnight and entered the slightly crisper air of America. New York glittered on the horizon with the Statue of Liberty barring entry to the harbour to anyone who didn't deserve passage.

I didn't have much time before I had to dress and prepare for the day. I wasn't looking forward to it, but I'd do it a hundred times over if it made it easier for Elder.

Keeping my thoughts on cellos and music instead of what

today entailed, I scurried along the polished deck, smiling at staff and waving at Jolfer in the bridge. I found who I was looking for as I rounded the stern and skipped to a stop. "Selix."

He looked up from where he wrote in a manifest, ticking off some maintenance check. The Phantom was a living, breathing thing, and I'd come to respect the toil and time it took to ensure her rigging, instruments, and every-day upkeep was impeccable.

Lowering his clipboard, he scanned my hastily tied robe, arching his eyebrow. "You're up early this morning."

I blushed a little as the neckline gaped. I'd become used to clothes, and no longer hated them, but I still wasn't as modest as I probably should be. Skin was skin. But I clutched the robe tighter, re-cinching the belt. "I was wondering if you could help me with something."

"Help? With what?" He cocked his head. "Shouldn't you be asking Elder?"

"I can't."

"Why?"

"Because it's for him, and I want it to be a surprise."

Selix stilled, looking over my head toward Elder's quarters. His loyalty sometimes meant he didn't sway from the status quo.

I rushed, "I know his cello is gone. And I can't believe I'm saying this, but I miss his music."

"What's that got to do with me?" He crossed his arms, the clipboard slotting against his chest.

"I want to replace it." I brushed back whipping hair from the ocean breeze. "I have money given to me by my mother. I received notification last week that the account was available and in my name. I-I want my first purchase to be for Elder." I shrugged. "After everything he's given me...it's nothing in comparison. But I want to do something nice. Something that he wouldn't expect."

"So you want to buy him a cello?"

"I do."

"It's not a simple matter, Pim. Things like that are personal. He'd want to test them."

"But I want it to be a surprise."

Selix sighed. "You know what today is, right?"

I nodded. "Yes. That's why I want to do this...so at least he has something nice when we get back home. Just in case..."

He rubbed his face. "Yeah, okay." He shot me a smile. "You're annoying, but you treat him well. I like that."

I blushed again. "So...you'll do it?" I had no idea how much cellos cost or where he'd have to travel to get one. I hadn't exactly been in the market for one before, but I trusted Selix to achieve the impossible.

"I'll do it." He placed the clipboard on a giant spool of rope. "I'll go now so I'm back for when you guys are ready to leave." He came closer. "What's your budget? Those things aren't cheap."

I stood taller. I wanted to say he could have every penny in the account, but that would be unfair to my mother. That money was essentially to make her feel better. For her to know I would never again be trapped by anyone. But it would also be hers when she was released. And no way in hell would I blow through it like some ungrateful brat. "Buy two of the best ones you can find."

"Two?" His eyebrow quirked. "Why two?"

I moved away, aware time was short and Elder would be waking any second. "So he can choose which he prefers, of course."

"You're as crazy as he is."

"I'll take that as a compliment."

He chuckled, brushing past me. "I'll send the bill to you if I find something decent."

"You're the best." I blew him a kiss as he headed off to arrange a speed boat or submarine or whatever method of transportation he needed to race ahead of us, dock, and shop before Elder and I were ready for today's appointment.

Today wouldn't be fun.

His mother's forgiveness wouldn't be as easy as buying a cello, but at least if everything went to crap, I'd be able to give him a tiny piece of something he'd lost.

Then it was up to other people to give the rest.

I just had to hope that one day, they would.

* * * * *

I swear time wasn't uniform.

I was almost positive an allotment of minutes could change, depending on how enjoyable or unwanted a situation was.

Years as a slave...an eternity.

Months at sea...a single second.

And now, as Elder clutched my hand while we stood on the stoop of a nondescript, cookie-cutter house in Brooklyn, I swore time had systematically sped up to deliver us to this moment, then slowed to decades now we were here.

I didn't speak—it wasn't my place.

My place was holding his hand and supporting him.

Selix slouched with his arms crossed behind us, guarding the black car. He'd given me a nod when we'd docked as he returned from my errand.

He'd bought what I'd asked—not that I'd seen them—and, hopefully, Elder would appreciate my gifts rather than hate them.

"Christ, why is this so hard?" Elder muttered under his breath as he reached up and knocked on the black-painted front door.

I squeezed his fingers, staying silent. His question didn't need an answer.

He knew.

This was hard because his family had shunned him for years, and he was a sucker for punishment. Any other person would've walked away by now. Anyone else wouldn't have put up with the cold shoulder for so long.

But Elder...he never stopped blaming himself and living

in their disgust. This was his past, and it had so many unfinished threads.

Footsteps sounded inside the dwelling, responding to his knock.

I froze as Elder's fingers vised around mine.

The front door swung open.

A man I didn't recognise blinked, glanced at me and Elder, then scrunched his nose in confusion. "Can I help—" He did a double take, his forehead wrinkling as shock took hold. "Holy hell. Mik? Is that really you?"

Elder swallowed, jutting his hand out to shake. "Hello, Uncle Raymond. Nice to see you again."

Instead of taking his hand and accepting Elder's hello, he pushed forward, forcing us back off his stoop and closing the door behind him with a worried glance inside. "What are you doing here? You know she doesn't want to see you."

Elder sighed painfully. "I know, but I have news. I need to tell her in person."

Raymond rubbed the back of his neck. "I'm not so sure about—"

The door swung open behind him. "Ray, what the hell are you doing lurking— "

Elder sucked in a breath, his full attention locked on his mother. "*Okaasan*."

"No." She growled, moving to slam the door. "Go away."

Unlike before in Monte Carlo when Elder stood by and let his mother dictate his replies and stayed subservient to her pain, he slapped a palm against the door, keeping it open. "They're dead."

His eyes blazed, not wasting breath on apologies or requests for her to listen.

His mother turned white, her hand still on the door, flimsy and loose. "What?"

"The Chinmoku who killed Kade and Otōsan. They're dead. Finally."

His mother stumbled backward, landing in a cane chair

with shoes neatly placed on a rack beside it. "You killed them?" Her tone was accusing and grateful all at the same time.

Elder moved into the foyer and fell to one knee in front of her. He didn't dare touch her, but he murmured, "I swore to you that I'd avenge them. It took longer than I hoped, but it's done. You're safe now, and I'll respect your decision not to see me again but I had to let you know I kept my promise even if I was the reason they're dead in the first place."

His mother stilled, her eyes filling with tears.

Elder shifted closer, bowing his head and whispering things in Japanese.

I wasn't privy to what he said, but his mother's face shattered from hatred to sorrow. She bent over, wrapping her arms around her waist as tears fell swift and fat, plopping onto the dark red dress she wore with white cranes on the front panels. Immaculately dressed with greying black hair tied into a bun—a woman coming apart before her son.

Her tears looked healing as well as agonising, but even in the depth of her grief, she didn't reach for Elder, didn't embrace him, didn't apologise in turn for all the harsh cruelty she'd thrown in his face throughout the years.

But Elder didn't need any of that.

Whispering a little longer in his native tongue, he stood and pressed a kiss against her hair then backed away. Crossing the threshold, he jumped as Raymond, with equally greying hair and smart corduroys, rested his hand on Elder's shoulder. "Thank you."

Elder gritted his teeth. "I understand she'll never forgive me, but at least, our family is safe now. I had to tell you in person. I'm sorry for the years of uncertainty and the pain I brought upon us."

Raymond shook his head. "Time is a healer, Miki-san. You were young. We all make mistakes. It's not the mistakes that should be held against us or define who we are but how we deal with them."

Dropping his hand, he smiled. "You went above and

beyond to repair what was broken. Your mother might not be able to move past her grief right now, but eventually, she'll learn to see that you are her only remaining son and you fought for her safety every day of your life. She does love you. Probably too much and that's why she has kept her distance."

Elder nodded, unconvinced. "Regardless, I can accept her need never to see me again now I know she's safe." He bowed. "Goodbye, *Ojisan*. Thank you for giving her the family I stole from her."

Elder took my hand and pulled me away from the house.

I didn't ask questions or pause to see if his mother only needed time to cry before running out with arms outstretched and love scripted on her heart.

We reached the gate, trading quaint garden path for street curb. I looked back, expecting to see the front door closed and no grieving widower watching her son disappear.

Instead, I gasped as Elder's mother clutched the frame with a hand balled over her heart. She never took her eyes off Elder and he froze to the spot as he met her gaze.

They stared for an eternity.

They stared for a lifetime.

And then, finally, after so much bitterness and heartbreak, she nodded.

A single nod, a simple bow. A motion that spoke of heaviness and pain and years of bottling up emotional tragedy.

A thank you. An apology. An acknowledgment that she no longer needed to live with ghosts.

Elder nodded back.

And then we left as if that soul-tearing moment hadn't been years of struggle to reach. As if there was nothing to celebrate now the ice had cracked and a thaw had finally begun.

It'd happened so fast.

We'd sailed all this way for a ten-minute visit.

I wanted to do something to encourage love to sprout and laughter to fall, but I didn't know how. This wasn't my place, and I didn't want to make it worse by interfering.

Elder seemed satisfied with what his mother had granted. I had to be, too.

As we climbed into the car and Selix jumped into the driver's seat, I snuggled close to Elder who hadn't relaxed at all.

He sat stiff and poised as if shell-shocked that his mother had finally shown a different side to her cruelty.

Wrapping my arms around his middle, I pressed a kiss to his throat. "I know she loves you."

My voice broke his spell.

Gathering me close, he returned my kiss, placing a delicate one on my hair just as he'd done for his mother. "Thanks to you, Pim, I no longer need her forgiveness to be happy. We've spent so long apart now that I can live the rest of my life without her in it as long as you are with me. At least I can die knowing she's safe and I've done my best to fix what I broke."

Family were fragile creatures, and I didn't know if his mother would reach out again or be satisfied with this ending.

All I could do was be his new family for as long as he wanted me.

* * * * *

We didn't return to the Phantom that night, or the next, or the next.

We spent a week exploring New York, eating in a variety of restaurants, staying in different hotels to sample all styles of architecture and lifestyle in the city.

The first two days exploring, Elder was quiet, his mind still on his mother. I'd dreamed of a happier reunion—of her leaping into her oldest son's arms and promising never to be distant again. I still flinched in hope whenever Elder's phone rang—hoping it was a belated apologises or invitations to talk and share.

But no call came, and we continued living as two. Well, three technically.

Selix was always by our sides, exploring and delivering sarcastic quips on locals and tourists alike.

The week flew by and New York showed us her best, but

as much as I loved the bustling, vibrant metropolis, I was ready for the rock and sway of the ocean.

On our last night in the city, we went to dinner in an exclusive club reserved for Wall Street officials.

Elder was invited by a client who'd ordered a yacht earlier last year and wanted to introduce him to some cashed up friends who wished to order something similar.

Just like with the meeting with the prince in Morocco, I listened proudly beside Elder as he took control of the meeting with his effortless charisma and skill, scribbling amendments on blueprints before scanning them back to his workers at the warehouse.

Unlike Morocco, this time I talked if a question was asked. This time, I was confident to converse with men in four-thousand-dollar suits and wives in fifty-thousand-dollar diamonds.

I was no longer afraid of this world—they were just people, and I was with Elder. And he wouldn't let anything bad happen to me.

His new clients were courteous and kind and ensured I was included in conversation while Elder was asked about delivery time-frames, budgets, and recommendations on what he believed would best suit their needs.

Elder might've stolen a colossal amount of wealth, but he'd made his own through hard work, great vision, and determination.

By the time desserts were finished and after-dinner coffees sipped, Elder had secured three new commissions with a price tag of a hundred million dollars each.

As we left the restaurant, he slapped Selix on the back. "It's official, Selix. A few more instalments to my debt and all of this is ours."

"Yours, not ours," Selix immediately responded.

Elder chuckled, stalking forward to open the car door for me. "*Ours.* I've already had the necessary paperwork drawn up. The moment that final instalment is paid, I'm signing over fifty percent of my company to you."

Selix slammed to a stop. "Is this your way of telling me to fuck off? That you don't want me sailing with you anymore?" His eyes flickered to mine, mirroring my uncertainty.

Elder laughed again. "Hell no, you're family as much as Pim is. I never want you to leave, but I also don't want you to keep up this employee act." Elder waved at the car. "I can drive myself, you know. I have staff capable."

Selix huffed. "You know why I do what I do, Prest." Pain shadowed his features, sending messages and stories that I didn't understand. All I knew was Selix had suffered heartbreak in his past, and perhaps looking after Elder was his way of soothing those wounds.

"I know, and you can continue doing so if you wish." Elder lowered his voice. "But the company wouldn't exist without you. *I* wouldn't exist without you. It's time you had your own piece of what we created together."

"We'll see about that." Selix huffed again and slid into the driver's seat. "Let's go home."

"On second thought." Grabbing my hand, Elder pulled me from the car then laughed at his old friend as he growled in annoyance. "We'll take a walk in Central Park before we leave. Consider this your night off, Selix. Go be reckless."

Before Selix could argue, Elder slammed the door and strode off with me in his grip.

I trotted beside him, looking back as Selix gripped the steering wheel looking entirely pissed off.

"Was that wise?" I asked, wincing as Selix flipped us the bird as we crossed the road to the park.

Elder chuckled. "It's time he learns."

The farther we moved away from streetlights and Selix, the more nerves filled me at walking on our own. After being hunted by the Chinmoku and being kidnapped, my wariness wasn't exactly on the lowest setting.

Considering Elder had come to New York to find closure with his mother, the week here had been good for him. He'd shared tales of his life living on the streets. He'd pointed out stores where he pilfered a hot dog after not eating for two days. He regaled me with stories of snatching wallets from prams as new mothers strolled past.

He wasn't proud, but he was honest, and New York was more than just a city to visit but a ghost town full of past choices.

Stepping into the night-shrouded park, I tensed even as pretty path lights shooed away the darkness and the occasional dog walker or jogger made it a welcoming place.

Elder noticed my nervousness, raising my hand to kiss my knuckles. "Don't worry, Pim. I'll take care of you."

"It's not just that," I whispered. "It's just…it's hard to believe it's all over."

"I know. I'm struggling to believe it, too." He looked over his shoulder. "Even now, I feel like we're being watched even though I know it's just paranoia."

I copied him, glancing into the shadows and the manicured paths and hedges. My skin prickled as if eyes were on us.

Someone is watching.

A twig snapped, sending me closer to Elder's comforting bulk. "Are you sure we're safe?"

He narrowed his gaze into the gloom. "It's just the park."

"The park?"

He strode forward. His body relaxed, but his eyes never lost their sniper glare on everything around us. "The trees have a way of making you feel like you're being watched." He flashed me a half-smile. "Living on the streets, you constantly feel like you're being stalked. Central Park is no different." He laughed under his breath. "In fact, I met a guy here on my second year living rough. A guy called Penn Everett. I was good at stealing things, but he was great at staying hidden even in plain sight."

Moving under the moon with skeleton trees and tiny leaves creating stencils on the pavement, I asked, "What happened to him?"

"No idea. He vanished one night and never came back."

Ideas that he'd been murdered or arrested filled my mind. I hated to think so many people had it rough and not all of them ended with happy endings like mine.

Another twig crunched, whipping me to a standstill as I looked over my shoulder. "I swear someone is following us."

Elder turned, his hand still around mine while his other tightened into a fist. He called into the night, "Who's there?"

No reply.

He marched forward into the black spots untouched by streetlights. He didn't pause as he reached a bush where a faint rustling noise came from. Shooting his arm into the undergrowth, he shook the branch of a sapling. "Who—"

Something tiny shot from the foliage, bashing into my legs and squeaking in fear.

"Oh, my God." I jumped to the side as Elder bolted forward and scooped the racing body from the ground.

He held the wriggling, terrified puppy aloft. "I think we've found our stalker."

The puppy yipped as Elder cuddled it close, uncaring about the dirty fur or the tiny teeth.

I looked into the bush, searching for a pissed-off mother or more litter mates but found nothing. Only bracken and forgotten rubbish swept into hiding by the wind.

Moving toward Elder, who'd calmed the puppy with a gentle hand on its head, I asked, "Where do you suppose he's come from?"

"Probably abandoned. I've come across lots of pets in this place. All unwanted…kind of like the humans who inhabit this place illegally."

I shivered. "That's terrible."

"That's life." Elder held the puppy aloft, looking at the dangling, gangly legs and hesitantly wagging tail. "He's just a mutt. He'll either survive or not." Placing the pooch back down, he came toward me. "Circle of life even if it is cruel."

I couldn't take my eyes off the little dog. Sensing freedom, I expected it to charge off and vanish, but it sniffed around our legs, bright black eyes inquisitive if not a little wary. Bending down, I let it sniff my hand. "Hi, little one."

It licked me.

And that was it for my stupid heart.

Tess had mentioned adoption—that a baby could come from other ways than just my broken body. She'd hinted that sometimes adoption was the better choice as you were saving a life rather than creating one.

Here, I had the chance to save a life.

A little canine life who wriggled his way into my heart in an instant. If that was the way it would be with adoption, then...perhaps, just perhaps, it wouldn't be as terrifying as I'd thought.

Beckoning the puppy closer, I rubbed his little face before looping my hands beneath his belly and hoisting him into my arms. He didn't yip this time; he snuggled close as if we'd earned his trust in such a short time. As if he knew what I was about to say.

Turning to Elder, I opened my mouth to argue for the little one's life.

Elder crossed his arms and laughed. "Oh, Christ. That fast, huh?"

I laughed, shrugging, loving the way the pup licked my chin. "Do I need to put forth a debate?"

"A debate would be interesting, but I already know what you're going to say."

"In that case..." I grinned. "Can we?"

He rubbed his jaw, shaking his head with mirth. "The Phantom isn't equipped for a dog, Pim."

"Does it matter?" I giggled as the puppy squirmed closer, burrowing into my neck.

"Fuck, hearing you laugh makes me hard and hurt all at the same time." He stepped closer. "If I'd known a simple mutt would make you this happy, I would've stolen one for you the moment I stowed you on board."

I looked up, accepting his gentle kiss and shivering at the utmost adoration in his gaze. He didn't look at the dog, only at me.

My tummy clenched. My heart whirled. I fell all over again. "So, we can keep him?"

Elder tickled the pup under its jaw, pressing a kiss to my cheek at the same time. "How can I say no?"

"By being honest and saying no." I held my breath, my heart already bleeding at the thought of letting this little creature fend for itself in the cruel, cruel world.

Elder's face softened as he cupped my cheek. "I'm always honest when it comes to you, Pimlico."

"So you don't want him?" I did my best to hide my pain, clutching the stray harder rather than preparing to let him go. I would obey Elder's wishes, but it would hurt like hell.

"If he's going to be a sea dog, he'll need a proper name. Nothing stupid like Snoopy or Spot."

"Truly?!" I leapt into his arms, squishing the puppy and raining Elder's face with kisses. "We can call him anything you want."

"Why am I already sensing this was a bad decision?"

I shut him up with a kiss.

That night, we sailed from New York with a new addition to our family.

One with four legs and a tail.

One who would most likely be called Spot.

ELDER

RETURNING HOME TO the Phantom, I had an odd sense of closure and relief from seeing my mother, followed by uncertainty about bringing a land-dwelling animal onto an ocean-faring vessel.

It hadn't exactly been the closure I needed, but my mother's acknowledgment that I'd tried to fix my mistakes was enough....

For now.

Besides, I meant what I said about never needing anyone else as long as I had Pim. She was everything and now I had to share her with a mutt.

The moon stayed hidden behind clouds threatening drizzle as Pim carried the pup into our bedroom and set him on the floor. Rigging creaked and engines hummed, waking from their seven-day nap as Jolfer prepared to set sail for a midnight cruise.

I hadn't asked where we were going—this time, the itinerary was his choice. The only instruction I'd given was to follow the summer and to hold a poll with the staff to find any destinations they'd like to visit.

I'd been sailing with vengeance for too long.

This time, I wanted to have fun—for everyone on board.

Pim dashed into the bathroom, returning a few seconds

later with her arms full of clean towels.

I sat on the bed with a smirk, rolling my eyes as she fashioned a bed for the newest member who was far more interested in exploring the bedroom and sniffing scents of blood and fighting even though the room had been cleaned since.

Pim giggled as the mutt raced back and leapt all over her. I'd never heard a sound like it fall from her lips. Something so pure and simple. I'd always hoped I'd be lucky enough to hear her laugh so freely but didn't think it would ever happen.

Whatever I thought about owning a dog, I now loved that damn fleabag as it gave Pim yet another avenue of healing.

She fucking glowed, and it took all my willpower to just sit back and watch instead of scoop her up and make love to her.

If I didn't know her past horrors, I would've thought she was innocent and confident—someone far too unsullied for the likes of me.

Sometimes, I looked at her and felt ancient in comparison—as if she was too young to withstand my bullshit brain and the emotional baggage that came with it. But then I'd see a flash of a silver scar or see her wince on sore bones, and I'd remember she'd withstood things far worse than anything I could ever do.

Her body had been in a battle, her soul had lived far more than it should, and it'd transformed her into someone so much wiser and better than I was.

I could spend hours watching Pim bathe and settle in the cute rascal, but my desire for her kept escalating.

My obsessive brain sticking on one thought.

Her.

It was her fault.

She shouldn't be so fucking sexy when she was happy.

I needed to tell her how much I loved her. How watching her be so sweet and gentle with the dog raised caveman urges to protect and care for her, too.

But I also didn't want to interrupt her joy at settling in the mutt who leaped and chased, tumbling beside her to get his belly scratched. Its short fur and random collection of sherry and amber spots meant he wasn't the prettiest thing, but he sure looked fucking happy.

His concave little belly also looked empty.

How long since the poor thing ate?

Using my cell phone, I called the kitchen and requested food suitable for a puppy and fresh water to be brought up.

I'd give Pim and her four-legged beasty a little longer to get acquainted, but once the mutt's midnight snack arrived, Pim was all mine.

I don't particularly like sharing.

We didn't have to wait long. The gentle knock on the door shot me upright.

I strode to open it, smiling at Greta holding a tray full of shredded chicken and gravy with a jug of water and an extra porcelain bowl.

Handing it to me, she grinned. "New pet, I see."

"Something like that." I smirked. "Have a good night."

"You, too."

Closing the door, I set up dinner and water by the towel bed Pim had designed and made a mental note to take her dog bed shopping the next time we reached a port. For now though, the mutt was safe, fed, and had somewhere to call his own.

That means Pim is all mine.

Taking her wrist, I pulled her from the floor, intending to push her onto the mattress and do whatever I damn well pleased with her.

However, she rolled her arm and dislodged my hold. "Not yet."

"Not yet?" Frustration bubbled. "What do you mean, not yet?"

"I mean, I have something for you." She smiled down at the dog as he woofed and shoved as much chicken into his tiny mouth as he could. "I want to give it to you."

I chuckled under my breath. "And I have something for you, so let's get into bed."

She laughed. "Mine is real not just sex."

"Not just sex, huh? Are you already over sleeping with me, Pim?"

She narrowed her gaze. "You know that's not possible."

"Then...what is it you have to give me?" Glancing at the bed, I cursed the heavy ache between my legs. "Can't it wait until morning?"

She backed away nervously, shaking her head. "No. I asked Selix to buy it for me. We've been away a week and then we found Spot and he's distracted me and now you're trying to distract me and I know if I don't give it to you now, I'll worry I did the right thing. I'm *already* worrying I did the right thing."

Nerves flickered like fireflies in her eyes. "I've been dying to show you, El. I want to do it now...before we go to bed. Before anything *else* distracts me."

My heart squeezed at how much this meant to her. I'd never seen her flustered before and, fuck, it made me want to do terrible things to her.

Christ, I love her.

As much as her skittishness appealed to the possessive part of my brain, I missed the carefree girl from before. She needed to find that light-hearted place. I needed to see her giggle again.

Stalking forward, I pretended sternness and towered over her in dominion. "Hold up. *Spot?*"

She barked a laughed. "I say all that and all you focus on is what the dog is called?" Her worry spiralled away as quickly as it'd cloaked her.

I crossed my arms, ignoring how my heart beat faster whenever she was happy. "I thought we agreed no stupid names for the dog."

"Your fault for picking one that suits his spotty coat."

"Who cares about his spots? He looks like he has a bad case of measles."

"We can call him Measles, if you'd prefer?" She bit the inside of her cheek. "Measles has a cute ring to it."

I groaned. "If you want something literal for him, how about Slobber or Fleabag?"

Her face glittered with happiness. "Slobber could work."

It was my turn to laugh. "We're not calling the damn dog Slobber."

"Fine, you name him."

"Me?"

Looking at the happily munching puppy, she nodded. "He's a little jumpy right now, but his curiosity makes him brave. Spot suits him, but if you want to call him Nemo or Neptune or something to do with the ocean, then by all means." She spun toward the doors, giving me a look over her shoulder. Her delicious glossy hair caught the starlight. "Meanwhile, I'll focus on getting your gift."

Marching toward her, I ran my fingers through the chocolate strands while wrapping my arm around her. "You complain of distraction but you're the one who's a master at it."

Pressing my lips to hers, I murmured into her mouth. "However, I can be just as good." Deepening the kiss, I groaned as her tongue feathered mine. "Come to bed, little mouse. Let me show you my gift before you show me yours."

She melted into my embrace, shuddering as I pulled her hair, arching her neck back to kiss her harder. My cock thickened. I lost rational thought. All I wanted was her in my bed.

Backing toward the mattress, I pulled her with me. Breathless, she kissed me back. I might not have won on naming the damn dog Spot, but I had won in making her forget about giving me something.

I didn't know why but accepting a gift from her made me awkward and full of guilt. She had no need to buy me things.

She'd given me herself.

There was nothing else I'd ever need.

The bed hit the back of my legs. I sat heavily, dragging her between my thighs while keeping her mouth on mine. I grabbed her hips, intending to ease her on top of me, but she resisted, somehow slipping from my hold and blinking with bright, desire-filled eyes. "You almost made me forget again."

Wiping red-kissed lips, she pouted. "I want to show you, El. Please…let me."

Sighing heavily and rearranging my throbbing erection, I stopped being an asshole. "Okay. You win. What is it?"

Her cheeks flushed pink, a blush filled with worry. "I-I hope I've done the right thing."

I could already tell her she hadn't.

She was about to give me more than I deserved.

Before I could speak, she dashed to the sliding doors to the deck and vanished outside. A loud clunking noise filtered in, followed by a feminine curse.

"What the hell?"

The puppy lost interest in his chicken and chased after her. Following them, I slammed to a stop as Pim tried to navigate a box almost as big as her.

My heart pounded.

The box wasn't an ordinary box.

It was a shaped case I knew well.

Fuck.

How?

"What did you do, Pim?" Striding forward, I grabbed the neck of the cello container, taking the weight before it crushed her.

She ducked her eyes shyly. "I wanted to give you something after you've given me…everything."

"Where did you even get this?" I forced myself not to run my fingers over the satin case or crack open the latches to see what was inside.

"I asked Selix to buy two of the best they had. It's your choice which you prefer—"

"Wait." My fingers latched around the case's neck. *"Two?"*

She nodded, pointing at a shadow tucked by one of the lifeboats. "Yes. I didn't know how or what to look for." Her voice dropped, threading a little with panic. "I know I can never replace your old one. And it's not my intention to overshadow it in any way. I just…I know how you feel about music, and I hate that it was stolen from you the same night as I was."

She looked up, her eyes blazing with love. "You found me and fought for me. The least I could do was give you back your music. I hated it for so long. I cursed every note and song every minute of my life with him, but with you…you healed that part of me, and I actually miss hearing you play."

I couldn't speak as I rested the box against the wall and cupped her cheek. My hand shook with awe that she'd overcome one of her worst fears just for me and then somehow found a way to give me something I would never have been able to buy for myself.

"Thank you, Tasmin."

She gasped as I bent to kiss her.

I kissed her with gratefulness and worship and every other little emotion falling in love with her had made me suffer.

She pulled away, resting her hand on my forearm. "Will you open them? I want to see what they look like."

I laughed softly. "You haven't looked?"

"No. It didn't feel right. They're yours. You should be the first to see."

"How the hell did you become this creature?" Clutching her close again, I tucked breeze-teased strands behind her ear. "You're the best person I've ever met, and I can't believe you're mine."

This time, I kissed her with passion and frustration and a thread of anger that she'd bought me two very expensive gifts when all I'd ever done was give her origami figurines or make her steal a dictionary and hotel spoon.

Pulling away, I kissed the tip of her nose. "I don't deserve you. I'll never fucking deserve you."

I wanted to ask where she'd got the money from. I needed to know how she'd done this, but at the same time, I didn't want to be rude and delve into secrets she hadn't told me. I'd tried stripping her of her secrets at the start and look how that'd turned out. I'd hurt her instead of healed her.

I promised I wouldn't do that again.

"Please." She pushed me toward the awaiting cellos. "Open them."

It physically hurt to look away from her, but I did as she asked and ran my hands along the case reclining against the wall. Holding my breath, I cracked open the latches and lifted the lid.

Inside was a stunning black-lacquered cello with bronze scroll, pegs, bridge, and tail spike. The strings had never been played; the bronze bow nestled in cream velvet begged me to be the first.

Pim stood beside me as I gawked at such a gorgeous instrument.

I'd never think anything but fondly for the beaten up second-hand cello my father had bought me, but the craftsmanship of this machine promised whatever I played would be almost magical.

Pim drifted away, ducking to the other case and manhandling it upright. Spot tried to help, licking her hands and sniffing everything.

Striding toward her, I helped her put it upright. Once in position, I opened the lid.

I stopped breathing.

The polar opposite of the black one I'd just fallen in love with winked beneath the stars. White lacquer gleamed with silver scroll and accents, its bow sleek as a sword and just as lethal.

Night and day. Land and sea.

Both were stunning. Both would've cost a fortune.

"Why did you spend so much on me?" I turned to face her, my heart pounding like a drum.

She pressed herself against me, her body heat intoxicating and adding more flames to the fire inside. "Because you never understood what sort of gift you gave me with every origami you folded, every kiss you gave, every safety you wrapped me in. I can only buy you something tangible, but you gave me so many things that can't be seen or touched. You gave me my freedom, Elder Prest, and that is worth so much more than what money can buy."

I turned weak. My knees shook for everything she was. "But don't you see? You've repaid me ten times, no, a thousand times over. I'm already well in your debt, little mouse."

Slotting herself into me, she kissed my chest. "I'll never be able to repay you, and there are no debts between us. Please, just accept the cellos, accept me, accept my gratitude. Let me say thank you...for everything."

EPILOGUE

ELDER

** FOUR MONTHS LATER **

HOURS OF HEAVEN.
Days of happiness.
Months of paradise.
Four months of sailing wherever we pleased, exploring whatever we fancied, and enjoying everything I could ever want while fearing it would all be taken away.

I had everything.

I was so fucking happy, but something niggled my mind, slowly growing more and more persistent.

I'd never been one for trusting in good things. It didn't matter I'd paid my final sum for the lottery ticket I'd stolen or that Oliver Gold had received the exact amount he'd won. It didn't matter I'd signed over fifty percent of my company to Selix and he'd grudgingly accepted what he deserved. And it didn't matter I woke every morning to Pim and Spot, safe and happy beside me.

I was too used to everything being ruined whenever I let down my guard.

Yet it never happened.

My habits were kept at bay with the occasional joint, and Pim kept me centred with her affection. Ever since she'd given me the two cellos, my OCD had once again become manageable.

Some days, I played the black cello, pouring the last of my grief into my music. Its strings lived for death metal, dark punk, or a brutal blend of the two. Some days, I played the white cello, strumming with newfound happiness and love, creating classical and pop and pieces my father would've been proud of. And some days, Pim sat between my legs and I taught her anything she wanted to know, slowly taking back, note by note, the past that was stolen from her.

A couple of weeks ago, after chasing the summer, we'd sailed into the Fijian archipelago. Surrounded by beautiful islands, I spent my mornings working, afternoons swimming with Pim, and evenings in tropical hotels.

Pim had taken to caring after little Spot as if he was more than just a dog but a child. I couldn't deny I'd done the same thing, both of us doting on the little critter.

I'd never had a pet growing up, but Pim taught me to let go and live voraciously through the eyes of a canine. Simplistic joy and wholehearted connection in everything he did from napping to playing to hanging out with us while we watched a movie in bed.

Pim laughed louder, smiled wider, and had so much life compared to a year ago when I'd carried her bleeding and unconscious from that bastard's house.

I had to admit, having another little soul on board—a soul that was so grateful for every scratch and ball throw, a soul that thrived under our nurturing love—helped my untrusting heart believe that maybe, just maybe, I finally deserved to find some happiness.

My fear at losing Pim might never go away, but I slowly stopped searching the skies for chasing ships or new enemies.

The niggle in the back of my mind would hopefully quieten in time, and the greed for more perfection, more happiness, more everything would hopefully be satisfied with everything we already had.

That was what I hoped.

However, that was before the niggle turned into a craving.

It happened suddenly.

It happened sharply.

It happened while overlooking an island called the Seven Turtles where four helicopter-crash victims had struggled to survive.

I looked up from amending a blueprint while Pim read beside me. She absentmindedly threw Spot's favourite ball for him to fetch, and an overwhelming punch of emotion crippled me.

It sank in claws and made me beg for this.

All of *this*.

Pim and me and Spot and freedom.

Forever.

I couldn't breathe.

I couldn't move.

I couldn't imagine another day of my life without this woman beside me.

All I could do was suffocate at how perfect she was—how perfect she made *me*.

I'd earned something I never thought possible but in some horrible, awful twist, it wasn't enough.

With the setting sun tangling in Pim's chocolate hair, I couldn't ignore the pain of never being able to bring a son or daughter into this world. I couldn't stop picturing *more*. Of a precious child who would never know the meaning of hate.

What good was my wealth if I couldn't use it to make others happy?

I'd already given a few million to each of my family members. I'd already paid my debts and ensured Selix would be set for life. I'd called my lawyer and updated my will to ensure Pim had my fortune if I passed far too early. I'd taken care of everything I could think of, yet sitting there in that idyllic simple moment…something fundamental was missing.

Something I couldn't buy or steal.

Something I couldn't bribe or manufacture.

Something that could only be saved…as I'd saved Pim and she'd saved Spot.

I supposed it was karma's way of completing a full three sixty—the circle of life and all that bullshit.

Adoption.

Pim hadn't uttered the word since we'd left France, but I'd read the email from Tess a couple of times, wanting to bring up the subject but never knowing how.

At the time, I only wanted to know if Pim was okay with her body's limitations. I didn't care if she'd never need more than a dog to fill that need to tend and care.

But now, as I stared at the woman I loved more than anything, *fuck*, it hurt.

It hurt to think we had so much to give and no one to give it to.

It killed me to think others were out there who needed saving, just like her.

I was suddenly hungry, greedy, downright starving for the chance to do something beyond myself. Yes, it was selfish too, but my reasons were born from the desire to rescue those who'd been forgotten.

I couldn't shake the idea, no matter how preposterous it was.

But is it preposterous?

Mercer had mentioned they were ambassadors and benefactors for multiple charities. They were in the business of saving lives.

I hadn't saved Pim out of the goodness of my heart. I'd saved her because something about her affected me right down to my core. I'd recognised her for being a part of me even as a stranger. I'd felt the shift inside, knowing I'd met my other half—even before I understood.

I was selfish because I'd only saved Pim.

I hadn't had a drive to save another as I no longer had any room in my heart to love someone as much as I loved her.

But now...now my heart had swollen, grown, morphed into an empty cavern ready to love again.

Ready to love a child.

The fact Pim hadn't spoken to me about the possibility made me think she wasn't ready. That she still held onto the hope she would one day be able to conceive.

And I hoped that, too.

I would keep hoping that one day she'd become pregnant with our baby. But I wouldn't pin my happiness on something that might never happen.

There were other ways.

Just as happy ways.

My heart grew impossibly bigger, larger, wiser sitting in this perfect domestic moment.

We had everything we could ever need. Therefore, we could offer someone who needed saving everything *they* could ever need.

Three questions popped into my head.

Three loud, obnoxious, unable-to-be-denied-any-longer questions that needed answers immediately.

Shit.

My hands shook with urgency. My body jumpy with need.

I hadn't had an over focus episode since needing to clean Mercer's place after the Chinmoku, but in that moment, all I could focus on was those three questions.

Bang.

Bang.

Bang.

Answers needed.

Now.

Rolling up the blueprint, I weighed it down with an empty beer glass and stood. Standing over Pim, casting her in my shadow, I held out my hand for her to take. "Come to bed with me."

Her eyebrow rose as she threw Spot's rubber chicken that we'd picked up at some local market in Viti Levu and placed her hand in mine. "I love it when you're bossy."

I smirked, pulling her upright. "You'll love me even more with the mood I'm in then."

"Mood? What mood?" Her gaze danced over my face as I strode toward our suite. "Everything okay?"

My hand shook harder. How could I ask what I needed and what sort of answers would I receive?

I knew Pim better than I knew myself most days. I knew she loved her coffee not too hot, she loved the smell of coconuts but didn't like the milk, she was a morning lark rather than a night owl, and she watched me while I slept because her eyes touched me just as potently as the rest of her.

But I didn't fucking know the answers to my questions.

I have to know.

"Everything's fine. I just…have a few things to ask you."

She paused as we crossed the threshold. "What things?"

I yanked her inside. "Things you're about to find out."

Pimlico

BEING IN BED with Elder Prest was like going to war.

He was my saviour and enemy all in one. My comrade and opponent with his wicked tongue, talented fingers, and dirty mouth.

I hadn't stopped thinking about that time at Tess and Q's where he'd drifted away from a complex cocktail of pain and pleasure.

Tess had called it subspace, and I wanted to try it. I was ready to experiment and embrace anything to do with playing together.

But tonight wasn't about fun or light-hearted connection. A heaviness existed in his every touch—a fatefulness that made my skin prickle and tummy clench.

He was delicious every moment I spent with him, but when he was this intense? He was mesmerising.

As he stripped me bare and laid me down, I didn't know if this would be all-out war with three merciless battles or more of a hostile takeover with three well-placed attacks.

I wasn't prepared as he climbed on top of me and filled me completely with a determination that sent my heart racing. The glint in his gaze and seriousness on his brow worried me. His ruthless thrusts and vicious kisses concerned me.

But even worried and concerned, I couldn't stop my body from reacting to his touch—inside, outside, his kisses and penetration.

My only choice was to dig my nails into his shoulders as he brought me with him, up and up, building my body for a toe-curling orgasm.

We chased each other onto the battlefield, neither of us soft and both of us violent, feeding into one another a certain kind of anger that I didn't understand. A thread of fear I couldn't unravel and a whisper of uncertainty that made my legs quake and voice vanish.

We clashed on that battlefield, riding each other, driving each other, and when we came, we did it together with a tattered groan from him and a breathless moan from me, rippling and falling for long, blistering moments.

Only once we remembered how to breathe and blink did he push onto his elbows, cup my cheeks with strong fingers, and ask his first question: "Do you like living on the sea in the Phantom or would you like to live on land in the house on the hill in Monte Carlo?"

I hadn't expected such a thing.

I had no reply.

I loved living on the Phantom, but I also wouldn't be adverse to spending time in the house on the hill. I still remembered how homely it made me feel. How calm and curious I'd been to step inside. The memories were somewhat tainted thanks to his mother, but I could visualise us living there far too easily.

I squirmed beneath him as he quickly hardened once again inside me, his body preparing for another round thanks to certain chemicals in his brain.

"Answer me, Pimlico. It's important that you answer me."

He didn't need to explain why it was important.

His OCD appeared in the most unlikely of places, and sometimes, vanished altogether.

After his cleaning malfunction at the Mercer's, he couldn't

care less about a little clutter or mess caused by Spot. Some nights, he would play his cello for a few minutes, and others, he'd play for hours. And some nights, he would hold me close and never need a smoke from the marijuana he kept in his bedside drawer while others he'd stand outside smoking for hours.

He truly was an anomaly and totally unpredictable.

Running my fingers through the sweaty hair at his temples, I answered as honestly as I could. "I could live in both. What's to say we can't spend a few months on the Phantom and a few months there? Do I truly have to decide?"

He smiled, kissing me. "That's good enough. I'm of the same opinion."

Then, as if the conversation hadn't existed, he thrust up, catching me unaware, making me clench around him.

He didn't speak anymore—his body did that for him.

He flipped me onto my stomach and climbed inside again, driving me into the mattress with every stroke. His teeth latched onto the back of my neck as his hips arched harder, faster.

I bowed beneath him, my clit pressed against the sheets, finding delicious friction to heat and spindle a second time.

It wasn't often I came with him for his second release—my body wasn't nearly as potent as his. But this time, driven upward by his intensity and burning up with questions of my own, I cried out as he bit me harder and spilled inside me.

My pussy clutched his cock, over and over, turning me boneless as well as sweat-misted.

As if he didn't want to drag out each question, his lips landed on my ear, his chest sticking to my back as I lay on my belly pinned beneath him.

"My second question demands a direct answer, Pim."

"Okay," I breathed as he put more weight on me. The heaviness of his body seemed to add heaviness to his question, electrifying the air with anticipation.

Running the tip of his tongue around my lobe, he

murmured, "Will you marry me?"

My eyes snapped open. All languidness gone.

I was awake and vibrating and more alive than I'd ever been.

"What?" If I wasn't pinned beneath him, I would've jolted and spun to face him. I needed to see his features, to dive into his gaze, to see if this was truly, truly real. But all I could do was tremble as tears shot into existence. "What did you just say?"

"I said..." He kissed the back of my neck, nuzzling. "Will you marry me?"

"Are-are you serious?"

His teeth latched into my skin, biting sharp in warning. "Deadly. And I need an answer immediately. Don't make me ask again."

The commitment in his voice. The utmost pledge in his tone.

It's real.

I wouldn't deny I'd been living in a dream and enjoying all my fantasies in one incredible adventure for months. That was more than enough, but some evenings, when lip locked in bed or skinny-dipping in the sea, I did wonder if he'd ever ask me.

If he'd ever feel the need to bind us together officially even though it'd happened organically without the need for a piece of paper or name change.

I'd already sewed my life to his in every way I could. My soul was his whether he wanted it or not. I didn't need this question but it was also the only thing I'd ever wanted.

I melted into the mattress as his hips thrust once, his cock waking up, hardening under his body's need for a perfect trio of releases.

"Will you marry me?" he asked again, his body swelling with every heartbeat. "Answer me. I *need* you to answer me."

"Yes," I whispered into the pillow, shock and amazement sending lightning bolts inside me.

"I didn't hear you." He thrust again, his fingers digging into the same pillow I'd whispered into.

Turning my head, I looked at him over my shoulder. I fell in love with the black fire in his eyes—the need for me to become his and the overwhelming lust and affection he always carried.

If I married Elder Prest, I would never want for anything. I would never be unwanted. I would never be hurt. It was him I wanted—not his money, his assets, his business.

Just him.

"Yes. Yes, I'll marry you."

He swooped down and captured my mouth, kissing me deep and arching my neck to accept his lashing tongue. "Thank fuck for that." His hips worked faster, digging into me in all the right ways. "Now I can finish this and ask my final question."

I had no control over what he wanted. After his proposal, I existed in the highest of heavens, and I had no way to float back down.

I let him ride me, consumed with the prickly heat rapidly building in my core.

Rolling onto his back, Elder brought me with him until I lay on his front. His large hands clasped my hips, keeping us joined while my breasts jiggled with every rock. We moved to the same beat, our breathing wild, our skin damp, and when that third orgasm found us, Elder wrapped his arms around me and squeezed so tight; pulling me into his chest, he hugged me as if he could never let me go.

When the shockwaves stopped battering us, he once again nuzzled my ear and asked his third question softly, gently, fearfully. "We've adopted an animal. What do you say about adopting a child?"

ELDER

PIM WENT DEATHLY still.

I scrambled upright, disengaging with a wince and spinning her to sit on my lap and face me. Naked and sticky, joined together in the most intimate of ways, Pim cupped my face with shaking fingers. "What?"

I didn't know if I was right to ask. It was probably a stupid, stupid idea. But I needed her to know I was on board with the idea. That we had more than we could ever need. That we had help and trusted staff and a lifestyle that could be offered to countless others with no effect to us if we didn't want it.

The more I thought about an unknown baby or child being abused or lost and unwanted, the more my OCD latched onto the injustice and grief.

Tess Mercer was right.

Sometimes, saving a life was better than creating one. And we had the ability to save multiple—if Pim could open her heart to the idea of sharing the colossal amount of love and fierce protection I knew existed within her.

Cupping her nape, I brought her forehead to touch mine. "You can say no, little mouse. You can say—"

"Yes." She wound her arms around my neck, holding me

close. Tears cascaded from her stunning green hazel eyes, drowning my heart and making me swallow thickly. "My answer is yes."

I fractured at the sob hiding in her voice. I kissed her, licking away her tears. "Truly?"

She pulled back, more moisture tracking down her cheeks. "I'll never give up hope that one day I might have a miracle and fall pregnant, but I've been thinking about it, too. We're young, we haven't been together all that long, but I just know in my heart it's the right thing to do."

I nodded, swallowing again as her entire being lit up with the purest kind of love. "I'll get in touch with Mercer. See if we qualify."

She smiled. "I think we'll qualify." Pim climbed off me, pulling my hand as she scrambled off the bed. "Come shower with me. Then we can write the email together."

I couldn't deny this woman anything and slid to the floor, narrowly missing Spot as he shot from beneath the bed and attacked my ankle with a fake growl.

Showering together calmed my rapid heartbeat and soothed the sudden nerves in my belly.

As we dried off, grabbed the laptop, and climbed into bed naked, my fingers shook as we opened a new document.

In one instant, Pim had agreed to marry me, irrevocably agreed to take my last name, share in everything I owned, and become family on paper as well as in heart. Not only had she given herself to me, but she'd also agreed to become mother to someone who needed a second chance.

Someone who had been saved just like her.

I already thought of her as my wife.

Therefore, as we typed the email ready to change our world and someone else's, I signed the message the only way I could:

We're ready to save a life.
Any life.
Elder and Tasmin Prest.

EXTENDED EPILOGUE

Pimlico

** TWO MONTHS LATER **

MONTE CARLO.

The city where I'd fallen in love, walked away from love, and been arrested.

The city where my life had truly begun again all thanks to Elder Prest, my fiancé, the love of my life, the man I was tying myself to in sickness and in health until death did us part.

Elder held my hand as we stared at each other. His black eyes on my green hazel.

We'd arrived a few days ago and moved into the stunning house with the Asian accents and Mediterranean relaxation, perched on a hill overlooking the ocean Elder loved so much.

Selix had helped us arrange a marriage license and we'd gone shopping the day before for a simple suit for Elder and a basic white sundress for me.

Elder had sent invites to his family with no expectation of their acceptance, but for once, it didn't gnaw at him or steal any of his happiness. He'd come to terms with what he'd lost but also with what he'd gained.

If I dared break eye contact and look to the side where our

witnesses stood, I'd see Selix as Elder's best man and Louise, a sweet maid from the Phantom, as my maid of honour.

Two witnesses to sign the marriage certificate once we said the magic words.

That was all we wanted.

Just us.

The under-decorated magistrate office held a flag of Monaco and some official looking banners. No flowers. No garlands.

It didn't matter.

It could've been the most beautiful place on earth and I wouldn't have noticed.

All I cared about was him.

My husband to be.

Elder squeezed my fingers as the justice of the peace asked, "And do you, Elder Miki Prest, take Tasmin Pimlico Blythe as your lawfully wedded wife? To cherish, protect, and worship for as long as you both shall live?"

Goosebumps ghosted over my arms as Elder smiled. "I do." Twisting a little, he held out his hand to Selix who placed a ring I'd never seen onto his awaiting palm. Splaying my fingers of my left hand, he slipped it onto my digit along with a simple gold wedding band. My wedding and engagement rings given in one go.

Tears immediately glassed the sparkling diamonds, conjuring rainbows in my vision. The brilliant cut was simple, the diamond big and beyond flawless. It sat on my finger as if it had always belonged.

Elder leaned in, whispering, "I had Jethro Hawk give up another one of his diamonds. I think they suit you." He ran his thumb over my penny bracelet as he cleared his throat and looked once more to the gentleman marrying us.

The justice of the peace turned to me, asking me the same slightly amended question. "And do you, Tasmin Pimlico Blythe, take Elder Miki Prest as your lawfully wedded husband? To adore, cherish, and love as long as you both shall live?"

I nodded, my heart dressed up in pretty flowers and nodding with all its ventricular might. "I do."

Louise bent forward, passing me a ring I'd only just had commissioned in Monte Carlo. I'd had to judge Elder's finger size from watching him sketch yacht drawings the week before. Once armed with measurements, I sent Selix on yet another errand to tell the jeweller who I'd bought from online to make the correct size.

The thick gold glinted as I pushed it onto his finger and read the engraved inscription aloud. "You did more than love me. You saved me."

Elder clutched my hand so tight it hurt.

The justice of the peace closed his folder, clasping it in front of him. "I now pronounce you husband and wife. You may kiss the bride."

I expected Elder to peck me sweetly—to avoid the compulsion of his needs. We couldn't jump into bed after this. We had another appointment to attend to.

Just as important.

Just as vital.

However, he launched himself at me, scooping me up and kissing me fierce.

Applause came from Selix and Louise as I kissed my husband back, just as fierce, just as violent for the very first time.

* * * * *

"Are you ready?"

I clutched Elder's hand as we climbed from the black Town Car and made our way to the hotel where we'd agreed to meet.

"Not at all." I laughed, doing my best to hide my nerves.

We'd just got married.

The timeline for a baby would normally be another few years, not a few minutes.

It'd been two months since we'd messaged Tess and Q about saving a life, and in that time, I'd flip-flopped between utmost elation and absolute terror. The responsibility of this decision had woken me up in the night in a full-blown panic attack only for Elder to calm me down and give me a chance to pull out only to induce another panic attack at the thought of not having what we'd already become so attached to.

Poor Spot didn't understand why my emotions leapt from one extreme to the other. Only Elder knew because he felt the same way. We'd spent many a night talking in the dark, wondering if we were doing the right thing, discussing every outcome, testing every scenario.

But all it came down to was the love we had for each other. The blessed situation we were in and the family we were desperate to create.

Elder gathered me close, wrapping his arm around me. His gold wedding band winked in the bright sunshine, binding him to me for eternity just like the flawless diamond on my finger bound me to him.

We can do this.

We are *doing this.*

"I can always keep the engine running if the brat's ugly and you change your mind." Selix nudged Elder with his shoulder, taking an extremely heavy situation and turning it light.

"Ha ha," Elder said dryly.

All of us still wore our wedding clothes—more dressed than we'd been in months while living in Fiji and other Pacific islands.

I'd watched Selix whenever we'd discuss the soon-to-arrive stowaway. His face had shut down at any mention of children, hinting that the pain he carried was in some way related.

I hadn't enough courage yet or enough nosiness to ask him outright what'd happened but I hoped by saving one child's life, it would somehow save him in return.

This adoption might have my and Elder's name's on the document, but the child would earn so much more than just us.

They'd step into an already tight-knit, wonderful family with captains for uncles and skippers for playmates.

Entering the hotel lobby, we followed the directions Tess had sent in her email and took the elevator to the thirty-sixth floor.

Selix stayed behind us, giving us silent support but letting us bear the brunt of this life-changing decision.

Finding the right room number, Elder took a deep breath, gathered me close, then knocked.

Footsteps sounded inside before the handle unlocked and the door swung open.

"Pim. Elder. How wonderful to see you again." Tess smiled, opening her arms for me to step into her embrace.

I hadn't seen her since walking away after the bloodbath with the Chinmoku, but it felt as if it was only yesterday.

Giving Elder a quick glance, I traded his arms for hers, still shaken and amazed, unable to believe I'd become a wife and soon-to-be a mother all in one day. "Hello, Tess."

"I'm so glad you made it." She kissed me on both cheeks before stepping aside. "Please, come in."

Elder accepted her welcome, looking past her into the room where Q appeared with his hands in his pockets. *"Bonjour."*

"Hello." Elder nodded in return.

We hadn't told them we'd got married today. Not because we didn't want them at our wedding, but because we'd wanted one last thing just for the two of us.

We were parents now. But our marriage was ours.

"Come," Tess said, moving toward Q and holding out her hand for a tiny silhouette hiding behind him. "Let me introduce you to Aria."

My heart wrapped itself in wire, bleeding with a mixture of fear and elation as a little girl stepped out from Q's legs and watched us warily. She didn't speak, but Tess had warned us of that.

This little girl had been saved from a trafficking house that held auctions for pregnant women to sadistic creeps. The women not sold in time had their babies in overcrowded bedrooms with other pregnant women, doing their best to shelter and keep their infant's minds from twisting with evil from their environment.

Q had dismantled the organisation and managed to rehome most of the children and their mother's—either together or separate, depending on the mother's wish. Aria was the hardest one because she had yet to talk. Her mother had been killed in front of her, and families wanted a bubbly happy child and couldn't understand the psychological depth of what muteness could offer as protection.

But I did.

Elder did.

We were prepared to either live with a silent child or nurture her until one day, just like me, she trusted her voice, herself, her surroundings, to give up that safety net and live.

"Hello, Aria." I ducked to her level, studying her white blond hair and pink cheeks. Her ice blue eyes seemed eerily so much older than her four-year-old body. Too skinny for her age and preferring oversize boy clothes to nice fitting dresses, she was an enigma I couldn't wait to get to know.

Elder came to join me, balancing on his haunches with his fingertips digging into the carpet for balance. "Hello, little one."

Aria shied backward, eyeing us with suspicion.

We didn't take it personally.

Tess had done a good job preparing us for the initial period, and we'd checked into the same hotel for the next few days to get to know Aria slowly, so she didn't feel like yet another world had been snatched from her.

I'd like to say she leapt into our arms and overcame her fear that afternoon.

I'd like to say the next breakfast, when we all met in our suite for room service, she understood how much we wanted to care for her and no longer stayed too far away to be hugged.

I'd like to say our forage into parenthood was as easy as saying the binding words in our marriage ceremony.

But it wasn't.

She made us work.

She made us try.

She made us realise we already loved her more than words could describe.

And that was what made it so much more precious when on the second to last day, while Elder and I sat on the couch in Tess and Q's suite sharing a cocktail and discussing Elder's business, that Aria finally came toward me on her own accord.

She abandoned the Legos blocks we'd bought her and willingly came closer. Her eyes latched onto my throat as I waved but didn't speak. She cocked her head as if confused why my lips didn't move.

I knew what it was like to be so focused on sound. And I knew what it was like to be comfortable with silence. Now, I recalled what it was like to prefer muteness because it was the only power I had left, and for the first time in a very long time, I pilfered the hotel stationery and turned to writing instead of voice.

I motioned her closer.

Inching toward the chair where I sat, she didn't take her eyes off the paper as I drew a circle with a stick-man, stick-woman, and stick-girl all in the circle.

She traced the picture with her tiny finger as I slowly drew more stick-men on the outside, men with pitchforks and badly drawn guns. Things that no four-year-old should recognise but she did.

Shying back, she shook her head, staring at me accusingly.

I held up my hand, asking her to come closer again as I drew more and more lines around the circle protecting the stick family from the bad men outside, then pointed at Elder and myself and then her.

It took a few seconds, her face scrunched up until it smoothed out in understanding.

She might not be ready to write to No One, but she could understand drawings (no matter how bad) and she understood my message.

That we would protect her.

That we were hers.

That all she had to do was trust us and we would never, ever break that trust again.

ELDER

WE ENDED UP staying in the hotel an extra week after Tess and Q returned to France.

We didn't want to upset Aria by moving her so soon—not until she was ready.

Somehow, Pim had achieved the impossible and earned the little girl's trust.

They regularly sat for hours drawing nonsensical pictures which would make Pim nod and grab something Aria had asked for or for Aria to smile hesitantly.

She allowed me to come closer and sat beside me without flinching one night at dinner, and by the end of the second week, she eagerly sought out hugs from Pim and didn't shy away when I hugged Pim in return.

When we finally took the plunge to take her back to our house in Monte Carlo, she blossomed.

The gardens became her favourite place to be, and Pim proved me right when I'd guessed she'd be an incredible mother. My heart somehow continued falling in love with both these girls, and for the first time in my life, my OCD faded in favour of just sitting and watching my new family.

A few months passed while we lived on the hill, and I grew itchy to be back on the ocean.

One night, after Pim had put Aria to bed and we'd had a breakthrough with earning a full-fledged laugh from our rescued daughter, she snuggled close in bed. "Let's return to the Phantom, El. I'm missing the ocean. I want to show Aria how perfect it is chasing the summer on the waves."

The fact she'd embraced what I loved and made it as important to her as it was to me made me clutch her hard and kiss her.

The idea of being able to show Aria the life beneath the sea thanks to a silly submarine and watch her tear into toys that'd been unopened for years just waiting for someone to play with them filled me with joy.

We spent most of the night making love rather than sleeping, but I embraced my tiredness the next day as I told Jolfer to prepare the Phantom for her next voyage.

Last month, the ship Alrik had commissioned me to build had been completed, and I'd presented the keys to Pim with a mixture of relief and disgust. The Hammerhead was the final thing tying her to her past. She could afford to run it now thanks to having half of everything I had, but instead of accepting the yacht, she requested a courier bag and my mother's address in New York.

That night, she wrote a letter to the woman who'd forgiven me but still maintained her distance, sealed the keys and photos of the immaculate yacht, then posted them.

She never let me read what she said, but the morning we left the house on the hill and took Aria shopping for some last-minute necessities in Monte Carlo shops, I received a phone call that I never expected to receive.

My mother accepted the gift Pim had given her.

She accepted me.

She enquired after her new granddaughter and asked if we could meet somewhere for a holiday where we could all finally learn to live in this new future rather than the tainted past.

I couldn't believe Pim had once again given me something so priceless, and fear filled my veins that something would go wrong. I feared Aria would hate the sea, or she'd miss her garden, or she'd never talk to me or give me her trust.

But as we stood as a family on the deck and Jolfer blew the horn and the Phantom disembarked from her long slumber, Aria lit up in a way I hadn't seen on land.

I almost died with absolute joy as my daughter, the girl of my dreams and keeper of my heart, took my hand and pulled me down to her level.

I stopped breathing as she pressed a kiss on my cheek before dashing off to stand at the railings and watch Monte Carlo fade into the distance.

Pim found me speechless, rubbing my cheek in shock.

"Did she speak to you?" she asked softly, taking my hand and kissing my knuckles.

Surveying my home, my wife, my family, I spun her around and kissed her lips. "She speaks as loudly as you did when you were silent, little mouse. One day, she might use her voice, but if that day never comes, we can understand her just fine."

Pim returned my kiss, adding a layer of heat that ensured thoughts of watching the city disappear and enjoying a drink in the setting sun faded in favour of a private bedroom.

Aria must've heard my intention and didn't approve of me stealing her mother away. Dashing over with Spot chasing her with his little pink tongue hanging out, she took both our hands and dragged us to the railing to wave goodbye to our house on the hill.

We were free.

We were safe.

We were a family, and no amount of pennies and dollars were needed because I had two of the most priceless things on earth.

I was officially the richest bastard alive.

* * * * *

That night, as Pim showered after putting Aria to sleep, I checked my emails quickly to find one from Mercer.

One that made my heart whir and future unspool.
From: Q Mercer
To: E Prest
Subject: How Is The Little Life You Saved?
Bonsoir, Prest,
Are you ready to save another?

As Pim opened the bathroom door and walked toward me with steam curling behind her and her stunning chocolate hair wet against scared skin, I closed the laptop and dragged my wife into my arms.

Mercer had another child needing a family, and I had a boat with hundreds of spare rooms.

I grew hard and hot and pressed kisses to her eyelashes and lips before unwrapping her towel and cupping her breasts.

She moaned, hugging me close.

"I love you, Tasmin."

"I love you, El."

I kissed her deep, dragging her down and rolling her onto her back. With our tongues tangled, I grabbing her wrists and placed them above her head.

She smiled, sultry and dark, believing she knew where my intentions lay.

But I had something else on my mind first.

Something extremely pressing.

Dragging my lips along her throat, I whispered, "I have another question to ask you, wife. A very, very important question."

FINAL EPILOGUE

Pimlico

DEAR NO ONE,
It's been a while since I wrote to you. I hope you don't mind.
I suppose I have no need to write when I live with you, love you, and get to see you every day. I get to see you become the most incredible dad. I get to witness you become the most selfless, amazing man. And I get to love you every day as my super-star husband.
You gave me everything I was missing.
You gave me everything I didn't know I could have.
You don't know this, but when I speak to my mother on the phone, I tell her every little thing you've done for me. I regale her with tales of how incredible you play the cello, and how you're teaching Aria to master the same songs that once haunted me. I inform her of how patient you are with Rosie, our little black-haired daughter, and her quirks of hiding food around the yacht, unable to be convinced she'll never be hungry again. And I can't stop gushing about what an amazing role model you are to James, our newest son.
It's funny that Aria chose the day James arrived to finally shed her silence and welcome her new brother to the Phantom. It's funny how effortless our family works, sailing the seas, exploring, teaching our children life lessons, and being there for them through every torment from their previous worlds.
You are the glue that makes all of this work. You are the best-friend

Selix needed to finally shed his grief, fill up his emptiness, and start to live again. You are the reason I am alive and living in this perfect fantasy.

I don't really have anything else to confess. I have no panic attacks to admit to. No nightmares to succumb to and that's all because of you.

For years now, you've been more than just my husband and father to our children but also my protector and best friend. I owe you more than I could ever give and if I could go back to that first meeting when you pushed a penny toward me for my thoughts, I would claim it and look into your eyes and speak boldly.

I would say my thoughts are priceless because they are all of you.

I would say my life is blessed because I share it with you.

Our children might've been born to different people and learned first-hand what it is like to be hurt, but now they are ours. Their blood is ours. Their future is ours. And in return, we are theirs.

I love you, No One.

I will always love you.

Thank you for accepting my very first letters and for waiting for my first word.

Thank you for marrying me and giving me a dream come true.

Thank you for finding me, for saving me, for fixing me.

Thank you...for everything.

Yours forever and ever,

Tasmin Prest

-THE END-

Teaser for The Body Painter

Coming 2018

Déjà vu pounded me from both sides.

Justin still hadn't let go of me and it had passed the point of discomfort to annoyance. Politely, I laughed and slid sideways to get away from his embrace.

Gilbert's gaze flicked to mine then back out the window.

The other two men kept silent, letting Justin have the stage. How odd that so many years had passed, yet in this room it seemed like only moments.

Justin.

My ex.

Gilbert.

My nemesis.

Release Date To Be Announced

Cover and Blurb Reveal Soon

ACKNOWLEDGEMENTS

First, I'd like to thank the beta readers who helped give insight on this book. To my veteran readers: Tamicka, Melissa, Melissa, Yaya, and Vickie THANK YOU. I will never be able to repay your time and kindness in being honest and helpful.

I will admit that this book was not easy to write. I don't enjoy endings, which is strange to admit. I find them harder to write than the darker elements I'm known for. I never know if I'm doing the story justice. I panic that I haven't tied up loose ends or the ending doesn't live up to the expectation of the reader. I hope I've given a conclusion that is at least acceptable and want to thank four new beta readers who helped make this book stronger: Julia, Heather, Smruti, and Kelsey. Thank you for pushing me and for your kind, wonderful critique.

Thank you to Nina for running Social Butterfly and helping with blog tours and marketing.

Thank you to Selena for running my groups and being a such a staunch supporter.

Thank you to my hubby for letting me ignore him for long hours while deep in the Dollar Series world.

And thank you to you, the reader, for once again coming on a journey with me. I can promise you that I have something pretty big coming next and I'm BEYOND excited to announce it.

Thank you for all the friends I've met online and in the horse world and thank you to all the authors who I'm lucky enough to look up to and admire.

Finally, thank you to Sonny (my horse) for giving me another element to life and ensuring I stay fit and active after sitting on my butt writing all day. He reminded me to never forget about living and it's a privilege to look after him.

xx

PLAYLIST

Indebted by Blue Boy Jack
Rag'N'Bone Man - Human
Rag'N'Bone Man - Skin
Clean Bandit - Symphony feat. Zara Larsson
Sia - To be human
Ed sheeran - Shape of you
Alessia Cara - Stay
Martin Garrix, Troye Sivan - There For You
Shawn Mendes - Mercy
Scars to your beautiful - Alessia Cara
Don't Let Me Down- The Chainsmokers ft. Daya
Rag'N'Bone Man - Life In Her Yet

ABOUT THE AUTHOR

After chasing her dreams to become a full-time writer, Pepper has earned recognition with awards for best Dark Romance, best BDSM Series, and best Hero. She's an multiple #1 iBooks bestseller, along with #1 in Erotic Romance, Romantic Suspense, Contemporary, and Erotica Thriller. With 20 books currently published, she has hit the bestseller charts twenty-eight times in three years.

Pepper is a Hybrid Author of both Traditional and Self-published work. Her Pure Corruption Series was released by Grand Central, Hachette. She signed with Trident Media and her books have sold in multiple languages and audio around the world.

On a personal note, Pepper has recently returned to horse riding after a sixteen year break and now owns a magnificent black gelding called Sonny. He's an ex-pacer standardbred who has been retrained into a happy hacking, dressage, and show jumping pony. If she's not writing, she's riding.

The other man in her life is her best-friend and hubby who she fell in love with at first sight. He never proposed and they ended up married as part of a bet, but after eleven years and countless adventures and fun, she's a sucker for romance as she lives the fairy-tale herself.

For more information on Pepper and her work please follow:

Facebook: Peppers Books
Instagram: @Pepperwinters

Facebook Group: Peppers Playgound
Website: www.pepperwinters.com

OTHER WORK BY PEPPER WINTERS

Pepper Winters is a multiple New York Times, Wall Street Journal, and USA Today International Bestseller.

Her Dark Romance books include:

New York Times Bestseller 'Monsters in the Dark' Trilogy
"Voted Best Dark Romance, Best Dark Hero, #1 Erotic Romance"

Multiple New York Times Bestseller 'Indebted' Series
"Voted Vintagely Dark & Delicious. A true twist on Romeo & Juliet"

Grey Romance books include:
USA Today Bestseller
"Voted Best Tear-Jerker, #1 Romantic Suspense"

Survival Contemporary Romance include:
USA Today Bestseller Unseen Messages
"Voted Best Epic Survival Romance 2016, Castaway meets The Notebook"

Multiple USA Today Bestseller 'Motorcycle Duology'
"Sinful & Suspenseful, an Amnesia Tale full of Alphas and Heart"

ROMANTIC COMEDY written as TESS HUNTER
#1 Romantic Comedy Bestseller 'Can't Touch This'
"Voted Best Rom Com of 2016. Pets, love, and chemistry

EROTIC ROMANCE DUET
Truth & Lies Duet
5 weeks on the USA Today Bestseller lists

THANK YOU FOR READING!

Printed in Great Britain
by Amazon